I0797110

TORONTO
TERROR

65

IF YOU *Love* ME

NEW YORK TIMES BESTSELLING AUTHOR

HELENA HUNTING

65

IF YOU *Love* ME CAST

ROMAN HAMMERSTEIN

TERROR GOALIE
BEST FRIEND TO HOLLIS

CHILDREN

PEGGY HAMMERSTEIN

PARENTS

CYNTHIA HAMMERSTEIN

TEAMMATES

HOLLIS HENDRIX
BEST FRIEND TO ROMAN
BOYFRIEND TO AURORA

DALLAS BRIGHT
BEST FRIEND TO ASH
ENGAGED TO HEMI

ASHISH PALANIAPPA
HUSBAND TO SHILPA (TEAM LAWYER)
BEST FRIEND TO DALLAS

FLIP MADDEN
BROTHER TO RIX
BEST FRIEND TO TRISTAN & DRED

CONNOR GRACE
TERROR ENFORCER

KELLAN RYKER
TERROR BACK UP GOALIE

TRISTAN STILES
BOYFRIEND TO RIX
BEST FRIEND TO FLIP
SIBLINGS: NATE AND BRODY

NATE STILES
BROTHER TO TRISTAN
FLIP'S ROOMMATE

ALEXANDRIA FORRESTER

(LEXI, ANGEL)
TERROR ASSISTANT COACH

SIBLINGS

OPHELIA &
CALLIOPE

PARENTS

KRISTOFF
FORRESTER

BADASS BABE BRIGADE

MILDRED REFORMER
(DRED)
NEIGHBOR TO FLIP
PLATONIC FRIEND OF FLIP'S

PEGGY AURORA HAMMERSTEIN
(PEGGY, AURORA, HAMMER, PRINCESS)
DAUGHTER TO ROMAN HAMMERSTEIN,
GIRLFRIEND TO HOLLIS HENDRIX

HEMI REDDI-GRINST
(HEMI, WILLS, HONEY)
BEST FRIEND TO SHILPA
ENGAGED TO DALLAS BRIGHT

TALLULAH VANDER ZEE
(TALLY/TALLS)
DAUGHTER OF TERROR COACH
IN FIRST YEAR OF UNIVERSITY

SHILPA PALANIAPPA
(SHILPS)
BEST FRIEND TO HEMI
MARRIED TO ASHISH PALANIAPPA

BEATRIX MADDEN
(RIX, BEAT, BEA)
SISTER TO FLIP MADDEN
ENGAGED TO TRISTAN STILES

ESSIE LOVELOCK
RIX'S BEST FRIEND

Published by Helena Hunting
Cover Design by Hang Le
Cover Image by @rosiesfables
Developmental Edit by Becca Mysoor Fairy Plotmother
Editing by Jessica Royer Ocken
And
Erica Russikoff of Erica Edits
Proofing by Julia Griffis
Amanda of Drafthouse Editorial Services
Sarah at All Encompassing Books

ACKNOWLEDGMENTS

Husband and kidlet, I adore you. You inspire me every day and I'm so grateful for your love.

Deb, thank you for being such an amazing friend.

Becca, this one was a beast, but we tamed it. Thank you for coming on this journey with me.

Kimberly, thank you for always being in my corner.

Sarah, you are amazing and I'm so lucky to have you and your magical organizational skills.

Victoria, thank you for handling all of the things I can't with such grace, you are a blessing and I adore you.

Alpha-Betas your eagle eyes are amazing, and I appreciate your input and support.

BBB, it's an honour to have you on my team, you are so appreciated.

Shaye and Lindsey, you are amazing and I'm so thankful for you and Good Girls.

Catherine, Jessica F and Tricia, your kindness and wonderful energy are such a source of inspiration, thank you for your friendship.

Jessica, Erica, Amanda, Julia, and Sarah, thank you so much for working on this project with me. I couldn't do this without you.

Kate and Rae, thank you for being graphic gurus. Your incredible talent never ceases to amaze me.

Beavers, thank you for giving me a safe place to land, and for always being excited about what's next.

Kat, Marnie, Krystin, thank you for being such incredible women. I'm so thankful for your friendship.

Readers, bloggers, bookstagrammers and booktokers, thank you for sharing your love of romance and happily ever afters.

For the ones with the biggest hearts, who love the hardest and fall the deepest.

CHAPTER 1

ROMAN

"No fuckin' way."

Standing at the front of the room, looking like a damn vision, is the woman of my dreams. Quite literally, she's been the star of them for the past three-plus years. At least once a month I wake up with a massive hard-on, the wisps of yet another dream featuring her slow to fade. I love those nights as much as I loathe them. They're a reminder of what I had, briefly, and lost.

"Alexandria Forrester comes to us from the Ontario League..."

Coach Vander Zee keeps talking, but I don't hear any of it, because I'm too busy staring at the siren of a woman next to him and the GM, trying to figure out what the hell is going on.

And now I have a last name to go with the one I groaned and whispered like a prayer.

Alexandria Forrester.

Lexi.

It was hands down the best forty-eight hours of my life. Most of it was spent naked.

And now here she is. In three dimensions. Real and tangible and more beautiful than she was the last time I saw her.

I tune back in as Vander Zee says, "She'll be joining the Terror as our new assistant coach."

My entire world inverts. Because the woman of my dreams—the one who disappeared without so much as a goodbye note—just became my fucking boss.

CHAPTER 2

LEXI

I did not accurately account for the level of anxiety that would come with seeing Roman again in person. The best goalie the league has ever seen.

I've never met Roman *The Player* before—only Roman *The Man*. There's no way he would remember me the way I remember him. And I remember every last detail of my time with Roman Hammerstein.

Owner of my fucking body. Provider of magical orgasms. Biggest dick I've ever had the pleasure of trying (and failing) to deep throat. But my effort was applauded, appreciated, and rewarded with more multiple orgasms than I've ever received in a weekend.

Roman was an incredible, intelligent, filthy sex machine. But maybe all the ladies he spends time with feel that way. Maybe he's just that good. And where does that leave me?

Except now, I'm left standing in front of my new team, staring at the man who rocked my entire world and made everyone I've tried to date after him seem like elevator music.

My stomach is a roiling mess. Starting a new job is never easy, but being a woman under thirty on the coaching staff of a pro hockey team? If they smell my fear, I'm finished before my skates even touch the ice.

"Let me introduce you to some of our key players," Coach Vander Zee says after the guys have been given the go-ahead to grab a plate and get in line for the buffet.

The other two assistant coaches, Ralph Boxer and Arnold Thomas, and the equipment manager, Donnie Richards, have joined the line and are chatting with the players. Ralph seems nice, a little quirky, but he's the goalie coach, so that tracks. Arnold and Donnie have been a touch remote, but maybe they were tight with the previous assistant coach. Both of them are quite a bit older than me, so that could be a factor as well.

Vander Zee scans the room, and of course the closest person happens to be Roman. I can barely breathe as Coach calls him over. This could go one of two ways. Neither is awesome.

Roman's expression remains impassive. He's grown even more attractive in the years since I last saw him. Gray flirts at his temples. He's broad and thick and stupidly gorgeous, and while I convinced myself there's no way he'd remember me, I'm suddenly worried I could be wrong. But I can't rewind time and fix it.

"Alexandria, I'm sure you recognize Roman, the most outstanding goalie in the league," Vander Zee says with genuine pride. "Roman, this is Alexandria. She coached the men's team in Windsor and the women's team in Niagara before coming to us." Vander Zee claps Roman on the shoulder. "Roman will be a great resource for you as you learn the ropes here."

Roman smiles and extends his hand. "It's nice to meet you, Alexandria."

My knees nearly buckle at the sound of my full name in his exquisite, rich voice. Several other things I've heard that voice say crowd my mind.

You're going to be my good girl and let me feed you my cock, Lexi.

Such a pretty pussy. I'm going to make it weep for me.

Show me what you like, Lexi. I'm going to make this gorgeous body sing.

And then reality hits. His face is entirely neutral as we shake hands. *He really doesn't remember me.*

No doubt I'm one of many faceless women who've been on the receiving end of his exceptional off-ice skill set. *The things we did.* The way he took control and brought out a side of myself I hadn't experienced before him. And haven't experienced since.

I didn't want him to find out I was hockey obsessed and think I'd slept with him so I could use him for his contacts. So instead of letting him take me out for one last coffee like I'd promised, I'd snuck out of the hotel room on Sunday morning and flown back to Niagara without saying goodbye.

I meet his eyes and slip my hand into his waiting palm. Goose bumps rise along my arm, and the hairs on the back of my neck stand on end.

"It's such an honor." It sounds like I swallowed a frog.

I drop his hand after a moment and clasp mine in front of me so I don't hand talk. I can't read his expression.

"It's a big move from the Ontario to the National League," he notes.

"Alexandria has a great resume." Vander Zee seems like he's reassuring his star goalie.

"I'm sure you do. How long did you coach in Windsor and Niagara?" Roman acts like this is the first time we've ever spoken. Like he didn't wrap my braid around his fist and whisper dirty things in my ear while he fucked me from behind.

Get your head out of the gutter, Lexi.

"I was in Windsor for two years and Niagara for a year." I took the position with the women's team because my mom and stepdad were killed in a boating accident and my half-sisters were suddenly parentless. They lived in Niagara. Moving them to Windsor with me would have taken them away from their friends and everything familiar.

Not that me taking this job didn't do the same exact thing.

But it's been a year since the accident took their mom and dad, and this is my dream job. I hope the move won't be too hard for them to overcome.

"The women's team in Niagara dominated in the finals last year, didn't they?" Roman asks.

"They did." I poured my heart and soul into that job. I needed the distraction from all the loss and grief. "Our team went from being in the bottom third of the league to second overall."

"They must have been sad to see you go," Roman says.

"It was a difficult decision, but I couldn't pass up this opportunity."

"No, I imagine you couldn't."

"Roman, buddy, they have the salted-caramel dip and green apple slices you like." Phillip "Flip" Madden, one of the players, slaps him on the back. "You should grab some before they're gone."

My eyes flare. We had salted-caramel-dipped fruit the first night we spent together. A lot more than fruit was dipped in the sauce.

"I don't want to miss out on those," Roman agrees. "Welcome to the Terror, Coach Forrester." He gives me a curt nod.

"Thank you."

He heads for the buffet, and I can finally breathe.

Flip Madden wipes his hand on his pants and extends it. "I'm Phillip. Most people call me Flip. It's great to have you on board. Very excited to have a shot of estrogen on the ice with us." He cringes. "That did not come out right. I just mean it's great to have a fresh, new perspective on the team."

I smile and shake his hand. "I'm looking forward to working with you." I'm not naive enough to believe there won't be growing pains as the first female assistant coach in the league, but the Terror has a good balance in management, so I'm hopeful.

Vander Zee introduces me to a few more of the guys, but my

mouth feels like it's full of cotton. I grossly underestimated how challenging working with Roman would be. But he doesn't remember me. And it's better if it stays that way. Besides, he's in the last year of his contract. I can handle anything for a year.

There's a lull in the introductions, leaving Vander Zee and me alone for a moment. He tucks his thumbs into his pockets, expression serious, which I'm learning is typical. "I know this is all pretty new for you, and I get that you might be a little starstruck with some of the players who have had long, legendary careers, but never let them see that, Alexandria."

"I understand, sir." It's better that he thinks I'm starstruck than find out the truth.

"Professionalism is imperative. If you can't handle them, you're no longer an asset to the organization. Do you understand?"

"Absolutely, sir." I worry about how transparent I seem to be. I can't afford to show weakness, not with Vander Zee, the other coaching staff, and especially not with any of the players.

"You should grab something to eat. I know you still have unpacking and settling in to do."

"Okay. Thanks." I'm grateful for the dismissal as I move toward the beverage station. Food sounds like more poor decisions and I've already made enough of those.

"Don't let Vander Zee scare you," Ralph says, somewhat reassuringly, as I reach for a glass. "His bark is mostly worse than his bite."

"Thanks." I smile.

Arnold Thomas, the assistant coach who works primarily with the offensive players, is talking to Donnie over at one of the tables. His eyes slide my way for a moment.

"And don't worry about Donnie," Ralph adds quietly as he loads up a plate with fresh fruit. "He's just sore he didn't qualify for the position."

"My position?" I ask.

He nods.

That explains the lack of warmth coming from him and Arnold.

Another player calls Ralph's name. "Join us after you've grabbed something." He leaves me alone with the beverages.

My nerves were shot after the introduction to Roman, and now I find out I was given the job over an internal hire? It's as much an ego boost as it is another thing to worry about. The pressure of this job is a weight in my stomach.

I scan the juices, finally trying to focus on the reason I've been standing here. Choosing a drink should not be overwhelming. As I reach for the freshly pressed carrot-apple-ginger, a shiver runs down my spine.

"I suggest watermelon lemonade over that one," Roman says quietly. "It's a little sweeter, more to your taste."

Panic shoots down my spine, and for a moment I forget how to breathe. Everything I've just finished convincing myself is true has reset.

He remembers me.

But any potential warm and fuzzy feeling dies as I turn toward his intense, displeased expression. His gaze roves over my face, and I feel it everywhere. "I'd say it's nice to see you again, but..." The next words out of his mouth destroy me. "I don't lie."

CHAPTER 3

LEXI

After Roman drops his bomb, I turn my attention to the juices again, unable to hold his gaze. I need to speak with him privately. What if he tells management about our history? Or worse, what if he tells his teammates? I could lose their respect before I've even had a chance to earn it.

This job means everything to me. Working in pro hockey is the pinnacle. That it could end before it's even begun because of something I did years ago would hurt worse than slipping on ice a thousand times.

But before I can find the words, he heads in the direction of a young woman and leads her out of the room.

I guess that private conversation will have to wait. Maybe it's better that I have time to prepare for it. When I took the coaching job, I was focused on how amazing it would be for my career. Not how fucking awkward it would be to work with my former two-night stand.

After I finally select a juice—the watermelon lemonade, because of course I follow Roman's advice—I spend another twenty minutes chatting with Ralph and Kellan Ryker, the goalie who will be stepping in for Roman at the end of the year. Eventually I'm able to escape to my office. But I can't even appreciate my nameplate fixed to the door. Or the fact that I have a freaking office with a window. Or that I've scored my dream job. I don't know how to deal with this. And I don't have anyone to talk to.

In three years, I haven't told a soul about my weekend with Roman. For forty-eight hours, he was all mine. And I was wholly, undeniably his. I wanted to keep it that way. For so many reasons. But mostly because our time together felt special and sacred, and it wasn't something I wanted cheapened because of who he was to everyone outside that hotel room.

My phone buzzes in my pocket. My stomach flips. *What if he's calling me*?

I'm instantly relieved and then concerned when my younger sister's name flashes across the screen. There's a big gap between the three of us. Ophelia is in her final year of high school, making her twelve years my junior, and Calliope is eight and in third grade. This move hasn't been easy, and Fee has had to take on a lot of responsibility with Callie. I relate. I went from sister to mom from one blink to the next.

"Is everything okay?" I ask as I answer the phone.

"Everything is fine," she assures me. "Callie wanted me to call you about dinner." The way she says *dinner* tells me this has very little to do with food.

I grin. "She did, huh?" Callie is very excited about me working for the Terror. Ironically, she loves Roman Hammerstein and all things hockey, just like me. She's the goalie for her team.

"She asked for chicken fingers and fries, but homemade, and I wasn't sure how late you'd be tonight since it's your first day and all," Fee explains. "She also wants to talk to you, if you have time."

"Put her on."

"Did you meet Roman Hammerstein?" Callie asks.

I can feel her excitement. "I did." *And he was not happy about meeting me again.*

"What about Dallas Bright? And Flip Madden and Tristan

Stiles? Did you meet them, too?" Every word comes out in a sliding rush.

"Yup. The whole team was there."

"What about Connor Grace? I saw that he got traded there."

"How did you see that?" The team just found out, and the announcement only went public this afternoon.

"I checked sites when I had computer time after school. Is it true?" Her voice rises with anticipation. She adores Roman, but Grace is her favorite player of all time.

"It's true. And I met him." Getting the team to accept him won't be easy. He's an excellent defensive player, but it's no secret he and Madden don't get along. The question is why…

"Oh my gosh! This is so cool! Both of my favorite players are on the same team! Will I get to meet them?"

"Of course. You can come to a game and meet the whole team," I assure her.

"I can't wait! Fee wants to talk to you again. See you when you get home!"

"Sorry. She would not stop asking to call you," Fee says quietly. "I can go out and get groceries to make dinner easier."

"Don't worry about it. It's your first day, too. How was school? Did you make any friends?"

"I said hi to some people, but I like the friends I have."

"Online friends are good too. Maybe, you'll find someone close to commiserate with about The *Way We Weren't* and *Lord of the Rings* fanfic. I'll stop for dinner on the way home. Don't let Callie eat too much sugar."

"I'll do my best."

"Also, maybe try to unpack a few boxes." The past week has been a whirlwind. We moved three days ago from a house with a backyard to a three-bedroom condo on the twentieth floor. The bedrooms and the kitchen were the priority. Now it's a matter of unpacking everything else.

"Already tackled four boxes of books and put them on the living room shelf."

"You're the best."

"I know. I gotta go. Callie's playing hockey in the living room again."

"Give her the stress puck!"

"Already did."

"Love you, Fee."

"Love you, too, Lexi."

I end the call and drop into my executive chair. I love my sisters, and I wouldn't change my relationship with them for the world. But me becoming their legal guardian has been hard for all of us. It wasn't just the overwhelming grief and changes after my mom and stepdad died. Between taking a lower paying position to keep stability for the girls and trying to manage a household on a single income while we waited for the estate to be settled, last year was a financial struggle. But we did it, and we can do this too. I can handle working with Roman for a year. As long as he doesn't blow this chance up for me.

A knock on my office door has me bracing for more of the worst. I fully expect a confrontation with Roman, and the sooner it happens, the sooner we can both move on. But it's not Roman standing in my doorway, it's Wilhelmina Reddi-Grinst, the team's key PR liaison. There was enough attention on her public engagement to Dallas Bright that her name would be hard to forget. You need thick skin to deal with the backlash from that.

"Hemi, right?" I push my chair back and stand.

"That's right." She smiles. "I had a meeting right after they introduced you, but I wanted to pop in and welcome you to the team. Looks like you're settling in." She glances at the pile of boxes in the corner and then at the art I hung on the wall. It's a watercolor of the lake we used to vacation at when our mom was still alive. Ophelia drew it in her grade ten art class, and I had it framed. She hates it—although that extends to a lot of things—and said I couldn't hang it in the condo, so I brought it here.

"I am," I reply. "Everyone has been welcoming so far."

Except for Roman and Donnie, but at least I know why on both counts.

"The team is fantastic, and the head office is super supportive," Hemi assures me.

"I've heard great things, and I'm looking forward to working with you and Shilpa. I love what you're doing with the women's team." The attention they've garnered over the past year has been fantastic, and there are so many gains being made for women in the sport.

"That's been such a passion project for me."

"Well, it's incredible. And last year's gala was out of this world with the money you raised for all those charities. Plus, I can't believe there's a horse named after Dallas Bright." The way the team always comes together is impressive and one of the reasons I couldn't pass up this job.

"I couldn't have managed the gala without Hammer's help. She's my right hand."

"Hammer?"

"As in Peggy Aurora Hammerstein. The team calls her Hammer. She works with me in PR."

"Right. Yes." That's another thing I didn't consider. Working with Roman is one thing, but his daughter, too…The layers of complication keep multiplying.

"She was in the meeting this morning, but you were probably overwhelmed with all the people. She's out at a promo op with her dad, but she'll be in tomorrow. I'll introduce you."

"I would love that." That my words don't come out laced with anxiety is a miracle.

"I know you probably have a lot to do, but some of us are heading to the pub after work, if you want to join. We're all very excited to have you on board. It's nice to have another woman on staff. The other coaches don't usually join us—they have young kids and a lot going on—but we'd love to have you. If you can make it, you'll meet Hammer and Shilpa, plus a few players. It's a nice way to get to know them in a more relaxed environment."

While I'd love to make friends in the office, if Hammer is there, the potential for awkwardness is real. And if Roman shows up… A conversation is imperative, but not with all our colleagues and his teammates around. "Thanks so much for thinking of me. Can I take a rain check? I still have some unpacking to do." I motion to the boxes.

"Absolutely." She nods. "Maybe next week would be better."

"That would be great."

I've dodged that bullet for now, but I can't avoid my office colleagues indefinitely. I'm pretty sure this will all get harder before it gets easier. Who knew having your dreams come true could feel like a nightmare?

CHAPTER 4

ROMAN

"You okay, man? You seem…really tense." Hollis Hendrix glances pointedly at my fingers tapping on his center console.

I grab my coffee to keep my hands occupied. "Yeah. I'm just up in my head." *Not a lie.*

I slept like crap last night. I kept waking up from X-rated dreams featuring our new assistant coach. In one, I was on the ice, dressed in full goalie gear, and she was spread out on top of the net, naked and beautiful and begging for a tongue fuck. My brain is an asshole.

"The reality of this final season setting in?" he asks, tone shifting to empathy.

My stomach twists as I lie to my best friend. "Pretty much."

Before yesterday, that's exactly what I would have been worried about. But this new development is taking all my bandwidth. How the hell am I supposed to concentrate with Lexi around—excuse me, that's Alexandria, or Coach Forrester? It's my last damn season, and I don't need distractions.

I can't get her shocked expression out of my head when I let her know I remembered her. Did she think I would forget that weekend we spent together? Never.

"I know there's a lot of change now with the team and management, but let's go out on top, right?"

I must be in a fucking mood if Hollis is being all Positive Pete with me.

"Yeah, you're absolutely right," I say. "And Ryker will be a great goalie. I'm just worried about Grace and Madden on the ice together." Especially since Grace will be mine to deal with because he's defense. "Plus a new assistant coach." Whose body I explored every inch of for an entire weekend. "It makes for a bumpy start to the season."

"Forrester has a solid background, though," Hollis replies.

"She does."

I looked her up last night.

She's been a few hours away all these years. And she knew who I was when we met in New York. That's what's messing me up the most. Yet I never felt like Roman Hammerstein the goalie. I was just a regular guy who liked baseball and wanted to travel for reasons other than work. The fact that she knew changes how I view that weekend.

"Might not be the worst that things are shaking up, you know?" Hollis says, maybe interpreting my silence as skepticism.

"I'm sure management has a plan in place." I'm more concerned with how I'll deal with watching Lexi in action. She's a lethal combination of gorgeous and competent. Some of the younger guys on the team are all hormones. I cannot handle one of those horny little shits eyeing her like the fucking treat she is.

Our phones light up with an influx of new messages in our group chat. Hollis and I are tight with several of the guys on the team.

"I'll check that," I offer. The first message feels like a bad fucking omen.

DALLAS

Anyone else curious about the impact of estrogen on practice?

TRISTAN

I'm more concerned about Flip and Connor knocking each other out.

ASH

This ^^^

FLIP

Fuck you guys.

The chat devolves into hockey fight gifs.

"What are the guys saying?" Hollis asks as he pulls into the parking lot.

"They're pushing Flip's buttons over Connor."

"I seriously wish we knew what the deal was there," Hollis grumbles.

"Don't we all," I reply.

He pulls into his parking spot at the arena, and his phone pings. It's my daughter. I can tell by the ringtone. His eyebrow pops as he reads the message.

"Everything okay with Peggy?" For a while she wanted me to call her by her middle name, Aurora, which is how Hollis often addresses her. But since they started dating, she's backed off. I'm the only one who calls her Peggy now, and she doesn't seem to mind the way she once did.

"Yeah. The girls are going to the Watering Hole after work."

"Again?"

"Dred can make it this time, I guess." He types a quick response as we exit the car. "Hopefully drinks with the girls doesn't turn into a girls-only night. Especially since we're about to start traveling."

I rub my bottom lip as we enter the arena. "Peggy's sublet is up in November."

"I know. I'm ready for her to move in full-time now," he says.

"One step at a time, right?" I bite back all the fatherly responses. Like, she's only twenty-one. She's still young and has a lot of growing to do. Hollis knows this, and he loves the hell out of my daughter. Also, by the time I was her age, I had a three-year-old.

It doesn't make it any easier to walk this line, though. Sometimes it feels a lot like I've lost my little girl and my best friend. Hollis and I are still close, but he's my daughter's boyfriend now, and soon they'll be officially living together. My life looked completely different a year ago: strong career, raising my daughter, working with my best friend. Now, I'm trying not to feel unmoored.

"Hey, my dudes. How's it going?" Dallas Bright calls as he and Ashish Palaniappa fall into step with us.

"Not bad. How about you two?" Hollis asks.

"Ready to hit the ice," Ash says.

"Wills is stressed." Dallas is the only one who calls his fiancée, Hemi, this.

"Please tell me Flip isn't causing her PR problems already," I grouse.

Dallas shakes his head. "Nah, he's been on the straight and narrow. Mostly she slept like crap. Lots of changes inside the organization this season—hopefully most of them for the better, but I think we're all a little rattled, you know?"

"Yeah. I absolutely do." In more ways than they realize.

There's a tense edge in the locker room as we enter. My mental shift is immediate. Sure, we're all still friends, but as soon as we cross the threshold, I'm in game mode.

Grace's cubby is on the opposite side of the room from Madden's. At least management got that right.

Madden and Stiles sit beside each other on the bench, already suited up except for their jerseys. They talk quietly as they lace their skates.

"Quite the somber mood this morning," Hendrix mutters.

I grunt my agreement, but don't respond otherwise. When

I'm suiting up, everyone knows to give me space to do my thing. I check over my equipment, set my green apple for after practice in the top right corner of my cubby, and begin to prepare, removing my clothes one item at a time, folding them and putting them away before I suit up.

"Bro, cover that shit," Stiles says.

"The fuck, man?" Hendrix gripes.

"Your back, Hollis." Stiles gives him a meaningful look.

"What about it?" Hendrix runs his hand over his shoulder, drawing attention to the crescent-shaped marks dotting his skin.

"For fuck's sake." Like I need this today.

Stiles sighs and shakes his head. "Don't you look in the mirror before you leave the house?"

"Yeah, but I'm not looking at my back."

"The girls need to go for manis apparently." Bright is probably trying to diffuse the tension.

"Fuck all of you guys," I snap. I don't want to be thinking about the marks my daughter left on his back—ever.

Everyone startles. I'm usually silent until we take the ice.

"At least you're taking care of your girl," Madden says unfucking-helpfully. I swear, if he tries to high five anyone about my daughter's orgasms, I'm going to lay him out.

"Pretty sure you were singing a different tune when your bestie and your sister started up," I fire back and raise my hands. "This whole conversation ends now. Rookies and newbies, word to the wise, dating inside this family is fucking complicated, so avoid it, or you get to deal with this." I motion to my teammates, who are also my closest friends.

"He's not wrong," Madden agrees somberly.

Vander Zee pokes his head into the locker room, expression intense. "All right, guys, enough chatter. Let's hit the ice."

I finish suiting up and follow my teammates out of the locker room.

But my shit mood takes a further nosedive when we reach the rink.

Lexi—Coach Forrester—is already out there, wearing her coach's jacket and looking every bit the part. Don't get me started on the way her track pants highlight her curves. Which I should not be admiring.

Her long, thick hair is pulled back in a french braid. Another inconvenient and highly stimulating memory from our weekend together floats to the surface. She was braiding her hair before we got in the hot tub, and I stepped in and took over. She'd been putty in my hands after that. So pliant, so eager to do whatever I asked. The control she gave me was a heady drug. I couldn't get enough of it. Of her.

I've spent the past three years obsessing over her, and suddenly she's here, in my world. I don't know how to handle this, and it's all coming out as anger. But it's a mask for the disappointment that followed waking up alone in that hotel bed with no explanation as to *why*. And seeing her here like this? It's the mindfuck of all mindfucks. No one ends up coaching the pros if they're not fully obsessed with hockey, but the woman I spent the weekend with didn't so much as mention the sport.

"Get a grip." I skate to the net, where Ryker is waiting for me.

He tips his head. "Sorry, what was that?"

I force a smile. Ryker doesn't deserve to be on the receiving end of my bad mood. "You feeling good today?"

"A little tense in the locker room, but hoping the energy shifts now that we're on the ice."

"I'm sure it will." Although I'm not convinced. Everything feels off.

Ryker and I warm up with stretches while coaches Vander Zee, Boxer, Thomas, and Forrester refer to their clipboards. Forrester will work with Ralph on defense. And me. And Ryker. It's all too close for comfort.

Grace is warming up next to a rookie player. Madden and Stiles are across from them, and Bright and Palaniappa are to my right.

The coaches break and Lexi—Coach Forrester—glides across the ice, her braid swinging as she heads for Grace.

Everyone's eyes seem to follow her. I sure as hell can't look away as she comes to a stop a few feet away from the newest, not entirely welcome member of our team, Grace.

Madden and Stiles move closer, bringing them within earshot of Grace and Coach Forrester. Grace is in the middle of an inner-thigh stretch, which, granted, makes it look like he's humping the ice. That's how everyone looks doing that stretch. The number of viral videos featuring warm-up stretches is unreal. His gaze lifts slowly, taking in Coach Forrester's long, athletic thighs—which I've had wrapped around my waist and my head. I shake off another memory because hard-ons in a cup are uncomfortable.

"Hey, Coach, you wanna give me a hand with my stretches?" Grace smirks as he hops to his feet.

The rookie beside him looks shocked as hell.

Unfamiliar rage shoots heat down my spine. I don't think, just act as I move in their direction, but Palaniappa grabs my jersey.

"Get your fucking hands off me," I growl in a tone I don't recognize.

Palaniappa releases me immediately and raises his hands. "Whoa, buddy. Where's your head?"

Before I can tell him to mind his own business and back off, Madden slams into Grace, knocking him off his skates as he shouts, "That's our fucking coach, dickbag!"

Grace grabs the front of Madden's jersey and says something none of us can hear. But whatever it is, it sends Madden off the deep end. His fist connects with Grace's jaw before Stiles, Bright, and Palaniappa pull him off.

"Enough!" Coach Forrester blows her whistle.

"You can't let Grace get away with that shit," I snap.

Coach Forrester turns my way. She arches one sexy brow and

levels me with a glare. "Are you the coach now, Goalie? You want me in your net?"

The answer is actually yes. I poke my cheek with my tongue.

She turns back to Grace and Madden. "This. Whatever it is, it stops now."

"You heard what he said," Madden grumbles irritably.

"That's enough, Madden." Forrester waits.

Madden drops his head.

"Grace, if I hear a comment like that come out of your mouth again, you will be facing a suspension. Do you think that's funny? Do you think it's appropriate to talk to Vander Zee or any other coach like that? Absolutely not. Worse, would you talk to your grandmother like that?"

"No, Coach." Grace hangs his head like a scolded child, face red with embarrassment as he skates away from Madden, moving closer to Vander Zee and Forrester.

"I am here to be part of this team. If you're not looking to treat this staff or your teammates with respect, get off my ice." She turns to Madden. "Don't pretend your chivalry is on my behalf. You're looking for any reason to go off on Grace. It's unprofessional and childish."

"That's not…" He stops talking when she tilts her head and his cheeks flush.

This woman is something else. I experienced some of her sass and her fire in New York, but this is different. She's stepping into her role, showing these boys who's the boss. And it's sexy as hell.

"The two of you clearly need a place to channel your aggression, and ice sprints are a good way to give you time to think about your choices and how they impact the rest of your team. And because this is a team, and we're supposed to function as a unit, all your teammates will join you." She holds up a hand when the grumbling starts. "Don't add to your problems. Ten ice sprints each."

Ryker sighs. It's one thing to do ice sprints in regular gear, but we're carrying more weight than everyone else.

"I'll take one from each player," Grace offers.

"No, you and Madden will do ten extra regardless. We won't tolerate your personal bullshit here at work. You're too late for winning favors."

Vander Zee nods his approval. "You heard her, boys."

We line up and wait for her whistle.

Ice sprints are as expected: hellish. Two of the rookie players vomit. Grace does his ten and then keeps going, side by side with Madden.

But even after that, practice is a mess. Ryker and I take turns in net, and we let in four goals apiece. I feel bad for him. I know why I'm off my game, but he has the new-guy pressure to perform.

We're all exhausted when we leave the ice, the usually buoyant mood dampened by the obvious tension among the team. We need to figure out a way to manage these boys or we're in for a shitty season. Everyone in the league knows about Madden and Grace's mutual disdain. It shines a light on our weaknesses and makes us vulnerable for the next exhibition game.

I can't escape the locker room fast enough after I shower. But before I get far, Vander Zee calls me into his office.

"Sorry about my performance in net today," I say as I step inside.

"Everyone was off." Vander Zee closes the door behind me.

I smell Lexi's perfume before I register her presence in the room. She sits in one of the conference chairs, still wearing her coach's tracksuit, braid hanging over her shoulder, clipboard in front of her. Composed. Poised. Like this is where she belongs.

I shut down my invasive, frankly infuriating thoughts about her in much more recreational situations and take a seat at the conference table. I cross and uncross my legs and try to keep my gaze from drifting to her.

"Roman?" Vander Zee looks concerned.

"I know Ryker is taking his lead from me, and I'll do better," I say.

Vander Zee and Fielding exchange a look. Lexi seems very interested in her clipboard.

"We have a whole season to get Ryker ready. This is about Madden and Grace," Jamie Fielding, the GM, explains.

"You're tight with Madden," Vander Zee says.

I sigh. "You want to know why they can't stand each other." I'm the team dad. I've been playing professional hockey longer than anyone. The boys come to me for advice, and management looks to me to help settle the ones who come in with dicks blazing.

"We don't want to put you in a difficult position, but any insight would be helpful," Fielding says.

I lean back in my chair. "Honestly, any time Grace's name comes up in conversation, Madden shuts it right down." I look to Thomas. "It might help if someone less involved personally talked to him."

"Maybe," Thomas says noncommittally.

"Have you asked Stiles or Bright?" I ask. "They all went to the Hockey Academy together. And Stiles and Madden have known each other their whole lives. They might have some sway with him."

"You mind sticking around while we call them in?" Vander Zee asks.

"Sure." What else can I possibly say? I don't want to appear as though I'm not interested in helping the team succeed. But the sooner I'm out of this office and away from Lexi, the better.

CHAPTER 5

LEXI

Roman looks like this is the last place on Earth he wants to be.

Can I blame him? After three years, I show up with no warning. And he clearly remembers not only what we did together, but also that I left with no explanation. Hindsight is a jerk. If I could have a do-over on how I handled my introduction as the new assistant coach, I would play it so differently. I should have swallowed my pride and reached out privately to let him know I was joining the team. It would have been awkward, but this is worse. I'd rather that than his anger. I thought my anxiety yesterday was bad. It has nothing on how I feel now. And I can't believe I called him out on the ice, especially since he could still blow this all up for me.

But I couldn't have him or anyone else come to my rescue. The only way to earn the team's respect is to show them I don't need saving. Especially not by their beloved goalie. This isn't just a job, it's where my heart is.

Roman taps agitatedly on the conference table. I try and fail not to notice the way the muscles in his forearm jump every time his long, thick fingers hit the wood. I know exactly how skilled those fingers are.

Stop thinking about sex with one of your players, Lexi.

That's a sobering thought.

There's a knock on the door, and Roman gets up to open it. Tristan Stiles and Dallas Bright glance around the room, assessing, before they take the seats across from us.

Dallas looks the part of the small-town, Ontario-raised player he is, complete with dark jeans and a short-sleeved, plaid button-down layered over a Tragically Hip T-shirt. Tristan is massive. Probably close to six and a half feet, broad shoulders, and dark blond hair that swoops in the front like it wants to do its own thing, which is basically his vibe.

"Where's Madden?" I was under the impression he'd be joining us.

Tristan looks around the table. "He had a thing."

I tap my pen agitatedly against my clipboard. "What kind of thing?"

"An appointment he couldn't miss," Tristan explains.

I hope that's not a convenient excuse, but while we have them here we might as well see what we can learn. "Can either of you explain why Madden hates Grace so much?"

Dallas and Tristan exchange a look.

Roman rubs his bottom lip. He needs to stop drawing attention to himself and all the parts of his body that have made contact with the most sensitive parts of mine.

"What is that about?" I motion between Dallas and Tristan. "You obviously know something. Don't you think it would be helpful for us to understand why these two can't be in the same room without Madden trying to rip Grace's head off?"

Vander Zee tips his chin in approval. Tristan runs his fingers through his hair. Dallas scrubs a hand over his mouth.

"I appreciate your loyalty to each other, but it's not helping us manage the team." Of the two, Dallas looks most likely to crack. "Bright, come on. Help us out."

Tristan shakes his head. Dallas sighs.

"May I say something?" Roman asks.

I meet his gaze. Which is a bad idea. In an instant, my entire body is ready to go up in flames. When we were together, it was me asking for permission, not the other way around. I clear my throat, channel confidence I don't feel, and am beyond thankful that my voice doesn't crack. "Of course."

He turns to Dallas and Tristan. "This is affecting the entire team. Everyone already knows Grace and Madden aren't the best of friends. How will that impact the season if we can't get them to play nice?"

"If we say something, he'll know it was us." Tristan laces his fingers. His hands are as massive as the rest of him.

"Well, that's his fault for not dealing with his shit," Roman says.

"He's working on it. The guy's in therapy. Like literally, right now, he's with his therapist. Give him a break," Tristan argues.

At least we know he's not willfully skipping out on a meeting.

Dallas grips the arm of his chair.

These guys are tight. I've worked with teams where there's dissension and posturing. They usually struggle as a unit. But the Terror really stand up for each other.

"So…" Dallas shakes his head. Looks at the ceiling. Sighs. "There was a rumor at the Hockey Academy. I can't confirm it. I don't know if anyone can, except maybe Grace. But good luck there."

I sit up straighter. I've heard the rumors about Madden. Everyone has. He's spent the past few years splashing his sexual exploits across the internet, apparently not caring how it reflects on him as a person or on his team. But that has changed over the past year, possibly because his sister is now dating Tristan, who from all reports is his best friend. Maybe therapy is part of it. "What kind of rumor?"

"There was a sandwich incident." Dallas' ears turn red.

"Dude." Tristan shakes his head.

"This is over a sandwich?" Vander Zee's disbelief is written all over his face.

"Look, I understand that you want to get to the bottom of this. But none of you thought to have a conversation with Flip or the rest of the team before you brought Grace on. And you did that knowing he and Flip don't get along, and that Connor has a history of being a team problem. He and Bowman are good friends. He had an ally in New York, and he *still* couldn't be a team player. Now you bring him here and expect us to solve the issue for you?" Tristan says.

"The plan was to speak to Madden directly, but he's not here and you are," I explain.

And Thomas doesn't seem all that interested in approaching Madden. I'm the new girl, still trying to figure out my role and not step on toes in the process.

"We're asking for some clarity," Vander Zee replies.

"And we're telling you there were rumors at the Hockey Academy. So now you know this rivalry goes back a long way. I don't mean to be unhelpful, but if it comes from us, the divide only gets bigger. And I won't be disloyal to my teammate over a decision I didn't have a hand in making." Tristan crosses his arms. "We can talk to Madden, but what you're asking here is a line I can't step over."

"What he said," Dallas agrees.

"I understand the importance of team loyalty and the difficult position you're in," I reassure them. "And we appreciate the insight."

"I don't like it, but I get where you boys are coming from," Vander Zee agrees. "Hopefully we can get to the bottom of things before the official season starts." He glances at his watch. "My youngest has a cello performance tonight, so we can reconvene tomorrow morning before practice and decide how to proceed." He pushes his chair back, and we all stand.

"Sorry we couldn't be more helpful," Dallas says as we exit the conference room.

"We appreciate your candor," Vander Zee replies. "Forrester, we'll see you in the morning. Good work today."

I don't know how deserved that compliment is, but I'll take it. "Thanks, Coach."

As I skirt around the players, Roman opens his mouth to say something, but Tristan interjects. "We're grabbing a bite to eat at the Watering Hole. It's a local pub a couple of blocks down. It might be a good way to get to know some of the team. Flip will be there. And all the girls. You can meet my fiancée, Bea, and Hemi and Hammer are coming."

"I heard my name." Hemi pokes her head out of the door across the hall.

"And I heard mine." Hammer appears behind her. "Hi, Dado." She crosses over and wraps her arms around Roman's waist.

All his tension seems to melt away with the affection. He squeezes her back. "Hey, kiddo."

"What's going on?" Hemi asks as Dallas moves toward her.

"Hi, honey." He kisses her on the cheek. "Tristan was inviting Coach Forrester to the Watering Hole."

"Oh yes! You have to come! They have the best nachos," Hammer says.

Hemi arches a brow. "Time to cash in that rain check?"

I glance at Vander Zee. I don't know what protocol is here. I want to connect with the team, but I don't want to do anything that might not reflect well with upper management. He nods.

Which is good because it means I don't have to say no to Hemi again. And Tristan is right. Getting to know the guys off the ice could help us get to the bottom of the Grace-Madden issue. And maybe I'll be able to pull Roman aside and have the awkward discussion that's hanging over our heads.

"Sure." I force myself to smile. "I can come for nachos."

CHAPTER 6

LEXI

The players head out to grab a table, and Hemi, Hammer, and Shilpa wait while I stop in my office to pick up my purse and shut my computer down. We pass Coach Thomas and Richards on the way out. They say hello, but seem deep in conversation. Gray clouds blanket the sky, the air is heavy with the promise of thunderstorms, as we walk down the street.

"You said the other coaches don't usually come out, right?" Vander Zee gave me approval, but maybe it was more about getting to the bottom of the Grace-Madden situation. It would be nice to make some friends in the office, though.

"Arnold has three kids under five. He and Donnie are tight since their four-year-olds play hockey on the same team. Boxer has a forty-five-minute commute because he lives outside the city," Hemi explains. "So we usually just see them at games and in the office."

"That makes sense." And also makes me feel a little better. I'm younger than the other coaches by a good decade. And obviously Donnie and Arnold are friends outside of the office.

"Dallas said you schooled Grace and Madden at practice."

"Just setting expectations for behavior," I reply, trying to be diplomatic.

I don't know these women well, and all three of them are in relationships with players. I've done my research. Shilpa was married to Ash before she became the team lawyer, Hammer was also involved with Hollis prior to being hired, and Hemi's on-ice proposal was pretty damn public. I don't know where their allegiances lie, and I'm the outsider here.

"I'm not surprised Madden and Grace got into it already," Hemi muses.

Shilpa hums. "Those two are always a problem when they're on the ice together. It would be good if they could settle whatever it is between them."

"I wonder if Rix will have any insight," Hammer says.

"Who's Rix again?" The name is familiar, but I've learned so many recently.

"Tristan Stiles's fiancée," Hemi says. "She's also Flip Madden's sister. Tristan calls her Bea because her name is Beatrix, but the rest of us call her Rix. There are a lot of nicknames in this group, so don't feel bad if you need us to create a spreadsheet."

I can't tell if she's kidding. I might need one.

"The team calls me Hammer, my dad calls me Peggy, and Hollis calls me Aurora," Hammer adds.

"Or Princess," Hemi adds.

"That's sweet," I say.

"You'd think, wouldn't you?" Hammer's grin turns sly.

I'm trying to keep track of the dynamics of this group, but I feel weird about cozying up to Roman's daughter. I'm keeping this secret from her, and everyone else.

We arrive at the Watering Hole as the first drops of rain fall. The second I step inside I fall in love. One wall consists of massive TV screens, all playing sports. The floors are wide hardwood planks. Booths with plush cushions line the walls, and in the center are long, wide tables with bar chairs. The bar is dotted with businesspeople and casually dressed locals.

Four women wave at us. Three look to be in their mid-twenties, and the other looks closer to Ophelia's age. One I recognize from Tristan's social media.

"Come on." Hemi touches my arm. "Let me introduce you."

"Sure. Yeah. That would be great."

"Ladies, this is Alexandria Forrester, the Terror's new assistant coach and a hundred percent badass," Hemi announces.

"Outside of work, I usually go by Lexi." I lift my hand in a wave. I'm so out of practice with socializing off the ice.

"Tristan told me about the Connor-Flip debacle. Impressive metaphorical balls you've got." She extends her hand. "I'm Rix, Tristan's fiancée and Flip's sister."

"You're in school for nutrition, right?" I overheard Tristan talking about it to Dallas during warm-up before all hell broke loose.

"That's right. I just went back." She touches the shoulder of the girl beside her. "And this is Essie, my childhood best friend and our resident makeup artist."

Essie smiles and waves. She looks runway ready with her long black hair and perfect makeup.

"And next to Essie is Tally," Rix says.

"Hi." Tally gives me a wry smile. "Vander Zee is my dad."

Is it weird to be hanging out with my boss's daughter? Why is navigating a new workplace so treacherous? "It's nice to meet you, Tally."

"And I'm Dred," the woman to my left says. "Short for Mildred. I'm related to none of these wonderful women by blood or boyfriend, but Flip is my neighbor, and these ladies took it upon themselves to fold me into their crew."

"We have no regrets about that, and we hope you don't either." Hemi smiles fondly at her.

"Having a hockey player as a friend has turned out to be the best thing that's ever happened to me," Dred replies. "Have a seat and join the party." She pats the spot beside her.

I slide onto the chair, envious of their tight bonds and easy conversation. For the last year I've been trying to keep my head above water as I managed two grieving kids, my own grief, learned how to parent my siblings, and oh yeah, did my job. At the end of the day, I was too exhausted to entertain going out with friends.

Dallas sets a pitcher of margaritas on the table and another of water, Flip following with glasses. The rest of the guys from the team line one side of the bar. Roman's gaze shifts toward me for a second, so I quickly look away. Pulling him aside to talk won't be easy in this intimate environment.

"Sorry about today, Coach," Flip says. He doesn't look like the fuck boy without a care in the world. This is the man who cares about his team.

"Lesson learned, I think." Part of me want to pull him aside and see what I can learn so we can fix the issue with Connor. But I need to earn his trust first, and being social is one way to show him and everyone else this is more than just a job for me.

"My legs will remind me to keep my fists to myself in the future," he says wryly. "Talls, you need a refill on your soda?"

She shakes her half-full glass. "I'm good, thanks."

Flip and Dallas join the other players at the bar, leaving me with the girls. They pour margaritas and pass them out, but I opt for water.

"How's your university experience so far?" Dred directs the question at Tally.

She glances over her shoulder, then drops her voice. "Classes are fine. But I went to an off-campus party with a couple of girls in my program, and it was just a lot of stupid drunkenness and boys peeing wherever they felt like."

"That sounds accurate, and like parts of my job," Dred says dryly.

"Where do you work?" I ask.

"The public library. Sometimes people suffering with addiction issues use the space to stay dry and warm. Especially in the winter," she explains.

"Oh wow. That must be hard." My library experiences were limited to the local one in my smallish town growing up. I imagine it's different in a big city.

"Everyone needs a safe place to go. We also get a lot of teens from the local group homes because we have a few special programs," Dred continues, her smile soft. "Those kids are my favorite. I grew up in the foster system, so I commiserate. Big chips on their shoulders until you offer them cookies and a juice box."

"I still love a juice box and a cookie," I reply.

"Same."

My phone pings with a message from Ophelia. "I need a second. This is my sister."

BIG PHEELS

Today's baking adventure courtesy of mini croissants.

Callie wants hot dogs for dinner. Please tell her that's not food.

LEXI

I'm at a restaurant. I can bring something yummy home!

"What's your favorite thing on the menu?" I ask Dred. "I want to bring my sisters dinner."

"Everything is good here. You can never go wrong with their loaded potato skins though."

"Perfect. Thanks." I relay that message and send a link to the menu.

BIG PHEELS

Will look and report back.

"That's cool that you and your sisters live together." Dred sips her drink. "You must be so close."

"I'm actually their legal guardian."

Her eyes flare. "Oh. Wow. That's…Can I ask how old they are?"

"Yeah. Sure." This is always such a hard conversation. "Ophelia is seventeen, and Calliope is eight. They're my half-sisters. We have different dads, and the same mom. Had." I shake my head. "My mom and stepdad passed away last year in a boating accident."

"I'm so sorry." Dred touches my shoulder. "That must be so hard for all of you."

I nod, not wanting to talk about my own feelings. I've learned how to compartmentalize them. It's the only way I've made it this far. "But they're great girls, and I love them. We're all learning as we go."

"You're the real deal, aren't you? You really have your shit together," Dred says.

I laugh. "Is that how it looks? Sometimes I feel like I have no idea what I'm doing." Should I have said that out loud? Usually I have a decent handle on things. I live for hockey. Getting what I want out of a player, what the team needs out of a player, feels damn good. But right now...everything seems unsteady.

"I think we all feel like that at some point." She props her cheek on her fist. "This might sound super woo-woo, but we're drawn to places and people for a reason, right?"

"That doesn't sound woo-woo."

She motions to the table and drops her voice. "I think you belong here, Lexi. These women, this team? They're the most amazing family, and I get to be part of it. If you want it, you can be, too."

I'm suddenly overwhelmed with emotion. Family feels like a pretty bedtime story. What she's describing is nothing I've had before. For the past year it's been me and my sisters, and before then, I still didn't truly feel like I quite fit anywhere. I loved my mom, but she and I had our struggles. And my dad loves me, but he's married to his job. I know what it is to feel alone. To belong? I crave it, but it seems impossible.

"Shit. I'm making you emotional." Dred gives me a side hug. "Subject change. What's your favorite board game?"

I laugh. "What?"

"Favorite board game. Everyone needs to have one. What's yours?"

"Mastermind."

"Hell yes." She cups her hands and shouts. "Flip, I have a new board-game bestie. Lexi and I are Mastermind soul mates."

"Finally, you can beat someone else at that fucking game!" he calls back.

The server delivers platters of nachos and appetizers. We eat and laugh and talk, and I find myself yearning for more of this easy friendship.

When Ophelia messages with dinner requests, I excuse myself to place a to-go order.

"You're a new face." A businessman nursing a lowball glass of amber liquid flashes a dimpled smile my way. "You with the team?" He inclines his head across the bar to where Roman and the guys are chatting and watching sports highlights.

"I am, yeah."

Roman's shrewd gaze meets mine for a moment before it shifts to the guy beside me. As soon as I avert my eyes, I feel Roman looking at me. I'm suddenly hot, and anxious, as if I'm doing something wrong. Which is ridiculous. I'm just making polite conversation with another man. Roman and I can't be anything to each other. I can't ever be his perfect, naughty angel again. I'm his coach, and he's a player. That's where it starts and ends.

Thankfully, the server comes over. I place my order and return to the table. I swear I still feel Roman's eyes on me, the weight of them pinning me in place. And sure enough, when I glance in his direction, he's looking. Unease slithers down my spine. These tentative friendships are on shaky ground until Roman and I discuss our past. I'm the outsider, he's not.

He and I have unfinished business and ignoring it won't help. I didn't get where I am in life by avoiding conflict.

It's closing in on six by the time my takeout is ready. And it's pouring rain now. Me and my to-go order will be soaked in seconds.

Roman approaches our table as I'm being hugged goodbye by the girls. He waits until they're done before he inclines his head toward the door. "I can drive you home." It's not a question.

The desire to do whatever he wants is immediate and inconvenient. So of course I do the opposite. "The subway is only two blocks."

His eyes are as stormy as the sky outside. "My car is parked around the corner. The closest station is at least a five-minute walk, unless you want to catch your death."

My snarky response shocks even me. "What are you? A hundred-year-old woman?"

His eye twitches. "Channeling my inner grandma. But seriously, it's cold and rainy."

Arguing with him is pointless. Especially since he's not wrong about the weather. And this way I can address the elephant in the room. I message Fee that I'll be home soon. Roman kisses Hammer on the cheek. I ignore the way my heart squeezes at the affection. He passes me his jacket.

"I'll be fine."

"It's pouring."

"You'll get soaked."

"I've survived worse." He nods to the bag. "Better soggy me than soggy dinner, don't you think, Coach Forrester?"

I stop arguing because his tone and his expression remind me of our weekend together. Even now, he could give me a look, or utter the simplest phrase, and turn me into his unapologetically willing cock slut.

I slide my arms into his sleeves, which are six inches too long, and pull the hood up, submerging me in his warmth. Roman holds the door open, and I step out into the rainy evening. The temperature has dropped several degrees, and the rain picks up the second we're on the sidewalk. Roman's hand settles on my low back as he stays close and guides me around the corner. The simple contact makes my body heat.

He doesn't utter a word and I'm suddenly too nervous to speak.

He's soaked to the bone when we reach his car, but he still opens the passenger door and waits until I'm settled before he rounds the hood.

He's wearing a pale blue shirt, and every single defined muscle is now highlighted by the translucent clinging fabric. And—*oh God*. I'd forgotten how good Roman smells. It's a combination of a very specific body wash, shampoo, and his aftershave. It made my knees weak back then, and now...sitting in the passenger seat of his car, I'm surrounded by his woodsy scent.

"Oh, fuck me." I swallow past the lump in my throat as I remember, vividly, what happened the last time I was in a car alone with him.

Roman slides into the driver's seat. Every part of him is soaked through. *Every part*. He slides the key into the ignition, turns the engine over, and adjusts the temperature so we're not blasted by the air conditioning. He turns to face me. I try to form a sentence, to say...something. Anything. But I'm frozen, heart hammering in my chest while my body remembers all the ways he made it sing.

"I have to grab my bag from the back." He leans in, his face only inches from mine. His chiseled jaw is so close I could brush my lips along the edge.

It's a challenge not to.

He retrieves a knapsack, unzips it, and produces a towel and an extra shirt. The towel he runs over his hair and face. And then he shucks off the soaked shirt.

"What are you doing?" Desire makes my voice waver.

He tosses it into the back seat—the interior is leather—where it lands with a wet thud. "What does it look like I'm doing?"

"Taking your clothes off." My whisper sounds horrifyingly needy.

I should get out and walk, fuck the soggy dinner. I should look away. I should not be staring shamelessly at his gloriously naked chest. That I've raked my nails over. That my lips have been on when I kissed my way down his body and he fed me his cock and his cum.

"I'm wet." He rubs the towel over his cut chest and arms. "Are you?"

I barely manage to keep from squirming under the intensity of his gaze. "What?"

He pulls the dry shirt over his head. "Wet, Lexi." Eyes on me as he slides his thick arms through the sleeves and covers his exceptional abs. "Are you?"

"I-I—" I tug at my collar and stammer, "I'm your coach. You can't—we can't."

His lip twitches. "I meant from the rain, but it's good to know where your head is."

I swallow my mortification and force my eyes to the windshield. It's officially a torrential downpour.

Roman sits on the towel, fastens his seat belt, and taps the GPS. "I need your address, Alexandria."

My pussy sobs at the rough sound of my name leaving his lips. With shaking hands, I type my address into the navigation system. I'll be home in nine minutes, according to the digital voice.

Roman pulls into traffic. I wish I had a bottle of water. My mouth is so dry. Seven painfully long minutes into the ride, I crumble under the weight of my regret.

"Roman, I—"

"Do *not* tell me you're sorry." The steering wheel groans under his grip.

"You don't understand."

"You're right. I don't."

He's a brick wall of…something. But I can't get a bead on his emotions. I sense his anger, but there's more. Is he upset? Hurt? Frustrated? All of the above? "Are you going to tell management?"

His jaw tics. "I won't ruin your career over a moment of weakness that happened three fucking years ago."

I wish I felt relief, but the sharp bite of his words is a fresh wound. It's dismissive. It cheapens the memories I've coveted the past three years. Taints them with bitterness.

"That's what you're worried about, right? Me ruining your career?"

"I didn't think you'd remember me," I whisper.

He scoffs and pulls up in front of my building. "You knew who I was the entire time."

"Not at first. Not right away." He'd looked so familiar. I couldn't figure out why—until he said his name was Roman. Then I'd realized who I was sitting beside, watching a baseball game with. I'd wanted to play it cool.

"But you knew by the time I asked you out to dinner." One hand stays on the wheel, gripping tightly. "And when I invited you up to my suite." His gaze shifts my way. "When you got on your knees for me. You knew."

This is why he's angry? Or at least part of the reason. I knew who he was and didn't tell him. And then I left without saying goodbye. "I'm sorry I didn't—"

He cuts me off before I can get the rest of the sentence out. "Have a good night, Coach Forrester. I'll see you on the ice tomorrow."

I want to tell him I didn't say anything because we'd already agreed not to talk about our jobs. I wanted to be me, and I wanted him to be a man I'd connected with. Genuinely. Authentically. But what will I accomplish by being honest?

"Thank you for the ride. See you tomorrow, Goalie." I grab

the takeout and exit his car. It isn't until I'm inside the building and on the way up to my place that I realize I'm still wearing his jacket.

CHAPTER 7

ROMAN

I should not have offered to drive Lexi home. Or opened the fucking can of worms by talking about the past.

I'm always stable. Steady. I don't lose control. I've spent the past twenty years focused on my career and making sure my daughter was raised in a loving home. There was no room for anyone who might upset the careful balance.

Except Lexi.

Every time I'm around her, my control slips a little more.

It was like that even when we spent the weekend together. I couldn't get enough of her—the way her skin felt under my hands, the sound of my name on her lips when I made her come, the way she fulfilled every depraved fantasy I'd ever had.

But it was so much more than that.

And now.

Now.

She's part of my every day.

And seeing her on the ice, learning my teammates, sharing her passion for the sport that's been my second love for two decades—is pushing me to the edge. I can't even deal when one of the guys smiles at her. I'm losing my damn mind.

I'm struggling most with knowing she *knew* who I was. Probably even understood the potential risk she was taking when she agreed to dinner. Ending up in bed with a player when her goal was to coach hockey probably hadn't been on her list of dicey choices. Maybe she didn't even realize this was a path she'd even end up on. But she took the chance. And then she ran out without saying goodbye. *And what the fuck does that mean*? How do I deal with that revelation? Especially now, when I can't have her.

DALLAS

Let's all play nice today.

ASH

No ice sprints please.

FLIP

I said I was sorry.

TRISTAN

My legs are sorry.

ROMAN

Deal with your shit, so we don't have to.

DALLAS

Team dad is in a mood.

ROMAN

I would not fuck with team dad today, if you all know what's good for you.

DALLAS

Disappearing GIF

I pocket my phone. I don't have the bandwidth for ribbing or being anything but a salty asshole this morning. And my sour mood turns downright bitter when I enter the locker room and find my jacket in my cubby. Folded exactly how I like it. *Because she paid attention to the small details during our weekend together.* Worse? It's freshly washed and smells like *her*.

Everyone gives me a wide berth as I change into my goalie gear. I need to compartmentalize. Keep my shit together. Not take my frustration out on my teammates.

This should be like exposure therapy. Over time, the effect Lexi has on me should dissipate. My body should calm the hell down.

Forrester is on the ice with Thomas and Boxer, clipboard in hand, hair pulled up in a high ponytail. Vander Zee skates next to her. Boxer has been with the team as long as I have, and has been working with me and Ryker while we prepare him to take over next year. The coaches have their heads together as we start warming up.

They break apart and Coach Forrester skates over, expression impassive. How she manages to maintain professionalism when I'm over here trying to control my hormones is a damn wonder.

"Grace and Palaniappa, bring it in, please." She motions for them to join us.

"Where's Boxer going?" I tip my chin toward the other net.

"Working with Ryker because he needs the attention, and you're a veteran. Your knowledge and skill set will be better utilized with the newest member of our team. Wouldn't you agree?"

Palaniappa taps his stick on the ice. "Coach makes a good point."

"What's your greatest strength on the ice, Grace?" Lexi asks. "Apart from your willingness to end up in the penalty box to save a shot from reaching the goalie."

"Reading plays and predicting outcomes," he says.

"And your weakness?"

Grace taps his stick on the ice. "Letting my emotions rule me."

"Connor Grace, get to know Roman Hammerstein and

Ashish Palaniappa. There is no one more controlled or more effective in the net and no defensive player in the league who has done a better job of helping our goalie protect the net. If anyone can teach you how to harness your emotions so you stay out of the penalty box and save your goalie from being overtaxed, it's these two." She skates backwards and bows, brow arched in challenge. "I dare you to prove me wrong."

"Goddamn she's intense, isn't she?" Palaniappa muses. It's not an insult, but pure admiration.

"Yeah." It's a smart strategy, appealing to our competitive nature and pushing Grace to work with us. And she's sexy as hell when she owns her role.

"Sorry you're stuck with me." Grace rolls his head on his shoulders.

"Just because you and Madden have issues to work out doesn't mean the rest of the team does, too. Let's run some drills." I pull my mask down.

Palaniappa and I work with Grace throughout the warm-up. He's an excellent player and knows how to handle the puck. I just wish he and Madden could figure their shit out.

Eventually, it's time to scrimmage. The puck drops, and the boys fight for possession. Bright snags it and heads down the ice, skillfully skirting players, moving with purpose as Grace gets into position, ready to enforce. And Madden, who apparently doesn't know what position he's playing today, gets in the way. He nearly trips Grace, and the two scuffle, their sticks inches from my face. In the distraction, the puck slides by my skate.

I shove Madden out of my space. "This isn't the fucking Madden show. Look where you are," I snap. "I already have two enforcers, I don't need another one. There's a whole team out there who wouldn't mind some practice." My words surprise even me. That isn't something I do. I'm always cool. Composed. Level.

Madden holds up both hands. "Whoa, I was just trying to get the puck to the other end of the rink."

The whistle blows, and Coach Forrester skates over. "Do we have a problem?"

"Everything's fine. Let's just play some hockey." I'm rattled by my inability to keep my shit together.

"You sure don't seem fine, Goalie." She motions between Grace and Madden. "Do you two want to air your grievances? Get whatever is eating at you off your chest so you can start learning how to work together."

"We're good." Madden focuses on the ice.

Grace dips his chin in agreement, face heated with embarrassment.

Lexi's nostrils flare. "Keep it up and there are more ice sprints in your future."

Coach Vander Zee skates over, glancing between Madden and Grace. "Do we have a problem, Coach Forrester?"

"No, sir," Grace says.

"All good here." Madden dips his chin.

"The three of us are having a chat after practice." Lexi motions between Grace and Madden.

Vander Zee gives her an approving nod. I want to knock his teeth out, which is completely irrational since he's just doing his job and he's a happily married man.

The rest of practice is an exercise in frustration. I can't protect my own net for shit, and Grace is a damn blessing with the way he deflects shots. He's a mouthy prick, but he's good at his job.

After practice, I pick up lunch and bring it back to the office so I can spend some time with my not-so-little girl.

Vander Zee pokes his head out as I pass. "Hey, Roman, you have a minute?"

"I'm sor—"

He holds up a hand. "We all have off days. This isn't about that."

I tuck a hand in my pocket. "Okay."

"Come in for a second." He motions me into his office.

"I'm having lunch with Peggy." I hold up the takeout bag.

"That's great. This won't take long."

I reluctantly follow him in, already certain I won't like whatever is coming my way.

Vander Zee leans against the edge of his desk. "I have a favor to ask."

"Shoot." I expect to spend more time with Grace, like I did today.

"It would be great if you could sit down with Alexandria and give her some insight on how to deal with the team from a player perspective."

One-on-one time with Lexi is the last thing I need. Strategizing, talking hockey and plays sounds like a bad idea. As if the practice boners aren't bad enough, sitting in an office with her, immersed in her scent, getting to know her better on a professional level, plus all the fucking memories? No thanks. "Can't anyone else do it? What about Dallas? Or Hollis even?"

"Dallas doesn't have the experience you do. And Hollis is pretty singularly focused these days." Vander Zee crosses his arms. "Are you okay? I know this is your last season, and you must be having feelings about that, but you're...not yourself."

I run a hand through my hair. *No, I'm not okay. Our new assistant coach is all I can think about these days. And I hate that I'm lying to everyone who matters.* "I've just got a lot going on, personally and professionally."

"I get it. But maybe helping Alexandria understand the guys she's working with will alleviate some of the professional issues," he urges. "I know bringing Grace on has been tough, but with you retiring and Ryker coming in to take your place, we need a strong defense. Aside from the hiccup with Madden this morning, things went well."

For Grace, maybe, not for me. But I get his point. Even though this team is tight, there's been a lot of change over the past couple of years. I can handle an hour.

"All right. I'll sit down with her. But I'm having lunch with Peggy first."

"Of course. I appreciate it." He taps on his desk. "Hammer's doing great, by the way."

"She's really embracing the job." Initially I wanted her to spread her wings, explore another industry. But this is her passion, and working with this team is her happy place.

"She is, and she has a great career ahead of her." Vander Zee claps me on the shoulder. "Thanks for agreeing to sit down with Alexandria. Let me know if you need anything, okay?"

"No problem, Coach." A lobotomy to remove the memories of that weekend would go a long way toward making this season manageable.

CHAPTER 8

ROMAN

I find Peggy in her office, sitting at her computer, dressed for business and looking like she belongs. Having her in the Terror office during my final season is the best gift. I miss the days when she needed to be taken care of, when she'd come to me with her problems and bounced ideas off me. But she's happy and thriving, and that's what's important.

"Got time for lunch with your dad?" I hold up the takeout from her favorite Thai place.

She smiles widely. "I sure do! Come on in."

We take a moment to rearrange her desk and make room to eat. "Hemi out today?"

"She's at a promo op with Kellan Ryker. He's been good on the ice so far." She hands me a set of chopsticks.

I pass her the yellow curry pad thai. "Yeah, he has a solid skill set and a good head on his shoulders. He'll be great in net."

She tips her chin. "How are you feeling about the beginning of the season?"

"It's a lot of change. Just getting my head around it." There are so many layers. I'm ending a twenty-year career, my daughter is moving in with my best friend, and basically already lives with him, and I have to work with the woman of my dreams for an entire year. There's no grand plan for what's next yet. My agent and I have discussed options, but I've shot anything down that would involve moving away from Peggy. I won't put physical distance between us. She's too important.

"Lexi seems like a good fit." Peggy twirls some noodles onto her chopsticks.

"She knows hockey, but she'll have to learn the team." I poke at my lunch, appetite waning as we veer into uncomfortable territory.

"That'll come with time." Peggy's tone shifts to empathy. "I can't even imagine being in her position."

"You mean being the first female assistant coach in the league?" It's a big deal—for Lexi, the league, women in sports.

"Obviously that, but I mean her family situation."

A hot spike shoots down my spine. "What about her family situation?" I didn't see a ring on her finger, but that doesn't mean she's single.

Peggy's brow furrows. "She has guardianship of her half-sisters. Her parents died last year in a boating accident. I mean, she still has her dad, thank God, but she lost her mom and step-dad. She's raising her sisters by herself. Can you imagine?"

That's a gut punch. When I looked her up, I was focused on her career, not her personal life. I'd thought it impressive that she chose to move from the Windsor team, which was performing well, to Niagara, who was at the bottom until she came on board, especially since it must have come with a pay cut. Now I wonder if that decision had to do with the loss of her parents.

I put my takeout container down. "I didn't realize. When did you find this out?"

"Yesterday, when we were at the Watering Hole," Peggy replies.

"I'm surprised Vander Zee hasn't said anything about it."

There were pictures of her and her sisters on her social media, but I just assumed they were close, not that she was functioning as their sole parent. If I'd been less focused on myself and my feelings, I might have learned this when I drove her home yesterday. But I didn't leave much room for sharing personal details. Especially not sensitive, emotional ones.

"It's not really his place to divulge that, is it?" Peggy asks.

"No. It's not. He asked me to give her some guidance." I pick up my takeout again, and continue pushing noodles around. "I'm supposed to meet with her after lunch."

"That's great! She can learn so much from you." Peggy's eyes light up. "And maybe she'll say something about her sisters. If anyone can empathize with raising a daughter on your own, it's you."

"Wouldn't trade it for the world." Peggy is the light of my life.

"Me neither." She hugs my arm. "Love you, Dado."

We shift topics, thankfully, and Peggy tells me about the promo ops she and Hemi are working on, but I'm reeling all over again.

Lexi and I talked a little about family during our weekend together, but it was surface stuff. She'd mentioned her mom and her younger sisters, and how she loved her dad—who had been at the game and left early because of work—but he was obsessed with his job. I'd talked about losing my dad when I was in my late twenties, and how tough that had been. I hadn't mentioned Peggy—not because I felt the need to hide her, but because I hadn't wanted to complicate the weekend. It had felt good to just be me for that short span of time. Not a hockey player, not a dad, just a man.

I wonder if Lexi hasn't said anything because she doesn't want anyone to think her family life will impact her ability to do her job. But I know it can. I wouldn't have been able to raise Peggy on my own without the help of the team.

It's with this new knowledge that I leave Peggy's office after lunch and head down the hall to Lexi's. I find her poring over files, a pen caught between her teeth. A green apple sits next to her coffee mug. Before that weekend, I liked the sweet-tart fruit, but since then, it's become a bit of an obsession. Logic and reason seem to go out the window every time I see her—even more so now that I know her situation—because all I want to do is gather her in my arms and feel the softness of her lips against mine. Which can't happen.

I know her, but I don't. I have intimate knowledge of her body, of the way she sounds when she's on the verge of an orgasm, of the things she likes in bed. Our passion for hockey matches. Huge pieces of what makes her who she is are now being jigsawed in. This new information about her family softens my initial shock and anger over her reappearance in my life. I'm still upset about the way she left, but I also haven't given her much of a chance to explain. Maybe because I'm afraid of the answer.

I'll give her an hour of my time, provide some insight to make her job easier. Then Vander Zee is off my back, hopefully she'll be armed with enough information to be helpful to the welfare of the team, and I can continue to work on keeping a safe distance. She's indicated that's what she wants.

I shove the past in a box as I knock on her door. I'm here as a resource. That's it. "Coach Forrester."

The pen between her lips falls to the floor. "Goalie."

"I didn't mean to startle you."

"You didn't." She bends to retrieve her pen—and maybe to avoid eye contact.

I arch a brow when she straightens.

"Okay. You did," she admits, then tacks on, "But it's fine."

She clasps her hands, unclasps them, then drops them to her lap. At least I'm not the only one affected. This thing between us holds so much power.

She squares her shoulders and puts on her professional hat. "What can I do for you, Roman?"

The sound of my name on her lips does things to me, things I don't know how to handle. "Vander Zee asked me to chat with you."

Her eyes flare. I can practically feel her anxiety from across the room, vibrating and electric. No one else would recognize it, but I see her. "Oh?"

"About the team. He thought I might have some valuable insight."

"Ah." Her shoulders relax a fraction. "If you'd rather not I'll understand. I can tell Vander Zee you followed through."

"But then it would be a lie, and we both know how I feel about those."

She bites her bottom lip, looking remorseful, and a whole host of other emotions that put me on edge. I might still be unhappy about the situation, but I also want her to find her footing.

"Besides, this is my team and my last season. I have a vested interest in how we perform." It's the truth.

"You've been with the team for a long time."

"I have."

She motions to the chair across from me. "Would you like to have a seat?"

No. "Sure."

I cross the room and drop into the chair across from her, bracing as I inhale her familiar perfume. She's no longer wearing athletic gear. Instead, she's in dress pants and a pale pink blouse. She looks stunning and professional. She crosses and uncrosses her legs, then grips the armrests. She's obviously nervous, and I was unkind and unyielding when I drove her home last night.

I'm practically jumping out of my skin with the sheer *need* to bury my face in her hair. To touch her. Calm her. And myself.

We stare at each other for a few long seconds. I'm trying to get my body under control while I'm this close to her.

"Where should we start?"

How about we go back in time and instead of leaving in the wee hours of the morning without so much as a goodbye, you stay? "Wherever you'd like."

"Okay." She closes the file folder and sets it on the pile. "I tried to talk to Grace and Madden after practice."

"Separately or together?"

"Together." Her hands stay clasped in her lap.

"How did that go?"

"Not fantastic."

"Elaborate, please." I don't mean for it to sound like an order.

A tiny sound escapes her, and she tips her chin down, while her eyes lift to mine. For a moment, the air is electric with tension, and I'm sure we're both suddenly lost in a not so safe for work memory.

She swallows thickly and her cheeks flush. "Neither of them were interested in sharing and they were insistent that they were fine, which we both know is bullshit." She punctuates the statement with a roll of her eyes.

There's the sass I remember. I can't help it, I laugh.

She crosses her arms, clearly annoyed. "I'm glad this amuses you."

"You amuse me, not the circumstances." I refocus and explain. "I understand wanting to get to the root of the problem, but they need time to get to know you before they'll feel comfortable with an intervention."

She sighs. "I can't afford to have them going after each other on the ice when it's game time. I can't afford to fail this team." Her eyes fall closed. "Oh my God. Why am I saying this to you?"

There's so much on the line for her. It's her first season and my last. We both want it to go well. It certainly takes a spine of steel to sit across from me and expose her vulnerabilities after the way I shut her down last night. "Because whether we like it or not, we have a connection."

"Goalie." There's warning in her tone.

I arch a brow.

She crosses her legs and exhales through her nose, as though she's working to maintain her composure.

I get it. I'm struggling not to reach out and touch her.

I save her from the awkwardness. "Tell me what you know about those two, apart from their stats."

She flips the pen between her fingers. "Madden's program at the Hockey Academy was fully subsidized."

I know some things about Madden's childhood, thanks to Peggy and Rix having lived together for a few months. "The Hockey Academy does that for a lot of their players."

"It's the best program of it's kind, and they've produced some of the most stand out players in the league," Lexi—*Coach Forrester*, I remind myself—agrees.

"Our team is proof of that."

"It absolutely is. The way Bright and Madden and Stiles are on the ice together is sheer magic. Those boys have a long history. They play like an extension of each other."

"They do." I cross and uncross my legs. This conversation is stimulating in ways that are becoming awkward and uncomfortable. She wears her passion for hockey on her sleeve. And that, along with my knowledge of how she sounds, tastes, and feels when she comes is a lethal combination for my hormones.

"From what I understand, Madden, Stiles, and Bright were well liked by the coaches and their teammates," I add evenly.

She leans forward. "But Grace wasn't."

"It doesn't seem that way, based on conversations with the other guys, but they're also biased and have a longer history together."

She taps her lips with her pen. "Grace is flashy and cocky."

I wish she'd stop drawing attention to parts of her body I've previously enjoyed. "He is."

"Grace has two sisters, but his grandmother is the only member of his family who appears on his social media," Coach Forrester shares. "And she's the only relative who attends his games, as far as I can see."

"I didn't realize that." *But it sure raises a lot of questions.* Connor comes from money. His family owns some of the most prestigious hotel chains in the world.

"Mmm... I noticed it when I did a social media scan. He clearly thinks highly of his grandmother, like Madden thinks highly of his sister."

"She's dating his best friend, so they're together a lot."

Coach Forrester leans back in her chair, expression pensive. "There has to be a way for them to connect."

"It might be easier if you try connecting with them individually."

"I do that on the ice with them every day," she says.

"Think about all your best coaches," I press. "What made them great?"

Her eyes flare and her cheeks flush. Flashes of our weekend together inconveniently float to the surface. *"Show me how. I want to learn, Roman."*

She clears her throat and looks away. "I saw them as people, not just my boss."

"So be the same. Share your story. That's the best way to learn something about Grace. What's he lost? What makes him who he is? You've overcome adversity, and maybe it's not the same as Grace, but it sure is relatable." I wait for her eyes to meet mine again. "You're the first female assistant coach in the league, Lexi. It's an incredible accomplishment. And it comes with its own challenges." *Such as me being a past hookup.* "But you've already proven you're tenacious and passionate about the sport. You wouldn't be here if you weren't. You're showing you care about more than team stats by having this conversation with me, because let's be honest, this isn't easy for either of us."

"I—"

I hold up a hand. I can tell I'm making her emotional, and if I break her, I'll break, too. I need to get the words out and get out of her office. "Show these guys who you are. Be real with them the way you were last night with my daughter and the other women who work for this team. You made an impression on them. You definitely made one on me. You're already making one on the team. Be more than their coach. You're a mother to your sisters. You're doing all of this on your own. *You* got yourself here." I motion to her office. "Your passion for leading is what brought you here. Have confidence in your abilities, and they will, too."

"You're being awfully kind to me today," she says softly.

"I wasn't my best self yesterday." I struggle to leave it at that and not bring up our past. "I'm sorry about your mom and your stepdad."

She smiles weakly. "Me, too."

"Are you and the girls managing okay?" I can't imagine how difficult this is for her.

"Most days, yeah," she replies.

"Being a single parent is hard, even when you're prepared for it."

"I want taking this job to have been the right move. Not just for me and my career, but for them, too. I wanted it to be a fresh start for all of us and I'm terrified that I'm going to fuck everything up. I don't want to do more damage than good." She shakes her head. "Why am I telling you this?"

"That you're worried Lexi means your head and heart are in the right place. I still worry that I'm fucking things up and Aurora is grown and self-sufficient, so you're not alone. Every good parent feels that way. I know you're here to support and guide this team, but if you let them, they'll show up for you and those girls." I grip the arms of my chair and let my eyes slide closed. I want so many things, and I can't have any of them. "I gotta go."

I stand and she does the same. "Roman."

I meet her gaze.

"I'm sorry I didn't warn you."

"I'm sure you are." I leave her office before I do something stupid—like ask questions that will only make keeping my distance harder.

CHAPTER 9

LEXI

"I'll do that for you." Roman's warm, calloused hands move mine away. I let mine fall to my sides and shiver as he finger combs my hair. It's devastatingly sexy to have this huge, imposing man french braid my hair.

I watch him in the mirror, my nipples peaking against my sleep tank. Not for the first time, I wish I'd packed sexy lingerie for this trip. Although I've spent the better part of the last twenty-four hours naked.

Roman's forearms flex as he gathers hair with his pinkie, feeding it into the braid. When he's finished, I pass him the hair tie, and he secures the end. Then he wraps it around his fist, tugging gently as his lips skim my neck. His other hand slides down my stomach to cup between my thighs. "I'm going to enjoy holding this when I ruin your pussy," he growls in my ear.

The sound turns into a grating beep. My eyes pop open. My sheets are twisted around my thighs, I'm sweaty, and my hand is in my underpants. "Seriously?" I shoot my phone a dirty look as I silence my alarm. I was just getting to the good part.

This is the fifth time in as many days that I've woken from an explicit dream featuring Roman. I thought they would settle down with time, not ramp up. Between ice time and the past two exhibition games, one of which we lost, I would have thought working together would dull his effect.

But apparently, my vagina is pining for Roman's cock.

I can't go to work like this. I need some release. But we're living in a three-bedroom condo. And half the time Callie crawls into bed with me around this time. The bathroom is the only place I have decent privacy. It's five thirty. I don't leave for work until seven, and Fee doesn't get up until six. Decision made, I grab my mini faux-makeup case of adult devices from my nightstand drawer—I learned to hide them after Callie almost found my clit sucker charging in the bathroom—and rush across the hall.

I lock the door and turn on the fan. The one in our old house sounded like a plane was landing in the bathroom, but at least no one could hear me moan. This one is new and unfortunately quiet. I strip out of my nightshirt and panties, grab my waterproof toy, and step into the shower.

And because I'm weak, I call upon the memories of my weekend with Roman. It's what I always do when I need a fast and dirty orgasm. I slide my vibrator inside me, turn it up to the highest setting, and let my eyes fall closed as the memories hit me—the phantom press of his hand on my hip, the other gripping my breast as I straddled his thighs and rode his gloriously thick cock. Or how he made good on his promise to hold my braid around his fist.

Orgasm one slams through me, and I sink to my knees. I'm all about stockpiling, because who knows when I'll have ten minutes to myself again? I go for orgasm number two, remembering the way he dragged me to the edge of the bed, dropped to his knees, and tongue-fucked my pussy until I was screaming his name. Then he flipped me over and pounded me into the mattress until I was delirious. Orgasm two hits like a lightning strike.

I let the water beat against my back as I catch my breath and try, desperately, to shut down the other memories. It hadn't just been sex. He'd ordered room service, pulled me into his lap on the couch, and fed me caramel-drenched apple slices. Which led to more sex and creative uses for the caramel sauce. And when we were both too exhausted to move, he curved his body around mine in the night and held me close. Possessive and tight.

That's enough fantasizing, I tell myself. *You can't be his.* I cut the water.

All my heat and need dissipate as I remind myself that I worked my ass off to get this job. Being attracted to Roman is an inconvenience I can't afford to indulge outside of the privacy of my own bedroom. Or the shower. We can't happen. Not now. Probably not ever. Besides, he can't be in the same room with me for more than five minutes without getting antsy. I assume it's because of the awkwardness and not because his memories of our time together keep popping up like an X-rated game of Whac-A-Mole. Which makes getting myself off to the memory of him even more pathetic.

I wrap myself in a towel, stuff my fun-time toys into my tote, and throw open the bathroom door. "Shit! What the hell, Fee?" My sister is standing outside the door, wearing her creepy smile—the one that makes her look like she should have a role in a horror film.

She glances down at the makeup case and arches a brow. "You better not have used all the hot water."

I roll my eyes. "I changed your diapers. You don't scare me."

She brushes by me, but before she closes the door she looks back, her grin positively evil. "I know what you keep in there." The door clicks shut and locks.

"I will one hundred percent embarrass the hell out of you with a pro-self-exploration talk, if you're not careful," I call through the door. It's so hard to be her sister and her pseudo mom.

I change into coaching attire and pad to the kitchen to put on a pot of coffee. While I assemble fruit and yogurt parfaits for me and the girls, I call my dad.

"Hey, Lexi. How's everything going?" he asks.

"Hey, Dad. Everything's good," I lie. "How about you? Did you get the pictures I sent of the girls' rooms?"

"I did! They look great! Did they like their housewarming gifts?" he asks.

"Callie is in love with her new bed, and Fee loves her art station. It was completely over the top and unnecessary, but we all appreciate it." My dad insisted on paying for a moving service, and he mined me for information on what I thought the girls would like or need for their new bedrooms. He bought Callie a hockey-themed bedroom set and a professional art desk for Fee. He also bought us brand-new, very expensive living room furniture. I'm used to his extravagant gifts. But since my mom passed away, I find I'd rather have more time with him than things. His life is busy, though. Being a fancy lawyer isn't a job, it's a lifestyle.

"I'm so glad. How are you settling in? How are the girls handling the change?"

"Condo living is an adjustment, but Fee loves her new arts school, and Callie's enrolled in an after-school hockey program, so I'll take the wins where I can get them."

"And the new job? It's going well? That exhibition game win the other night was clean. Lots of positive press for you."

His pride bolsters me. "Thanks. It's been great so far. Lots to learn, but management is super supportive, and the team is amazing." The only catch is having slept with the goalie.

"I know I've said it before, but I'm proud of you. You set a goal, and you achieved it."

I smile. It doesn't matter that I turn thirty next year; his approval matters—now more than ever since he's the only parent I have left.

"It's the opportunity of a lifetime," I admit.

"Just maintain your professionalism, and you'll do great," he says. "You've got a good head on your shoulders."

How disappointed would he be if he knew the truth? But three years ago, I never imagined I'd be here. "How's work? How's Jacqueline?"

"Work is good, and Jacqueline is also good. She says hello."

"Tell her I say hello back."

"We'll come to a game once the official season starts. Or maybe I'll come on my own, depending on her schedule," he amends.

"Whatever works. I'll get you good seats," I offer. It would be better if Jacqueline didn't come. She's not a bad person, but she doesn't have a maternal bone in her body, and she's about as interested in hockey as I am in hanging out with her lawyer friends.

We end the call, and I finish making breakfast.

My dad and Jacqueline are both career-focused and at the same firm, which is why their relationship works. I only see my dad a couple of times a year, and our visits typically include a sporting event that he works through, a distracted dinner, and a promise to spend more time with me next time.

I was barely two when my parents split, so I don't remember them together. But my mom was always focused on what she didn't get in the divorce, a.k.a. money. Eventually she met my stepdad, who doted on her and gave her everything she ever wanted. She expected to be taken care of, felt entitled to have her every whim provided for. That drove me to make my own way, and it was one of the reasons I never tried to contact Roman after our weekend together. He would have realized I'd known who he was. I didn't want to ruin that for either of us. Or for him to think I wanted something from him—*expected* something.

Back then I'd been coaching junior hockey. High level, but I was working to find my place in the sport. It was only a month later that I scored the job with the Ontario League. I made it here on my own merit.

Fee appears in the kitchen, phone in hand, dressed in all black, doing her best fair-haired Wednesday Addams impression. She used to wear bright colors and have the sunshiney personality to match, but the last year has been hard on her. I don't get on her case, even though sometimes her "dark" phase worries me.

"Are you reading your *Lord of the Rings* fanfic?" I ask.

"My favorite author updated last night." She pours herself a cup of coffee and tops mine up. "Oooh, look at the presentation on the parfaits. Mom could never even find the cereal."

"Because someone always put it in the wrong place," I add.

Our mom was the person to go shopping with, and she planned the best vacations, but her cooking skills started and ended with the microwave.

We both laugh until our eyes start to burn, and then she looks up to the ceiling. "Why are my feelings always on fire?"

"Hormones and grief, Fifi." I give her a side hug and kiss her temple.

She shakes it off. "I'm fine. It's too early to get sappy." She makes the sign of the cross. "Miss you, Mom. Miss you, Dad."

"Are you sure you're okay?"

"Yeah, a photo memory came up this morning, and those always hit differently."

I wish I could take her pain away, but it's a power I don't have. I wasn't close with our mom the way she was. My pain is different than hers, a black void instead of a raw wound. "I'm sorry."

"The only way forward is through. Any special instructions for Callie today? Practice as usual, right?"

"Yeah. Thank you. I know your schedule can be busy, and you want a social life, too." I feel guilty that she has to pick up Callie from hockey practice most days.

"I can hang out with friends at lunch." She points to the clock. "You need to get your ass in gear or you'll be late, Coach."

"Crap. Okay. See you for dinner. Text me your wishes, and I'll pick up supplies on the way home." I kiss her on the cheek, grab my messenger bag, slide my feet into my shoes, and head for the door. "Love you, Big Pheels!"

"Love you, too, Lex."

CHAPTER 10

LEXI

Practice goes relatively smoothly. I say *relatively*, because every time I look in Roman's direction, I'm reminded of what I did in the shower this morning. I need to get a grip. Maybe hypnotism would work.

Vander Zee skates up beside me. "Grace is open, don't watch him from the sidelines, try to connect with him whenever you have the chance. Take the initiative."

"Of course, yes." I want Vander Zee to see me as competent, not someone who needs hand holding.

I skate over to Grace who passes me the puck. "What do you want to get out of this season?"

"I'll be happy if I make it through without losing any teeth, courtesy of my teammates." The sarcasm is strong with this one.

"Really? That's your goal? Last year you were close to breaking records."

"I'm the outsider, so this year is about survival again." He flips the puck on the end of his stick, catching it twice before he flicks it to me.

His phrasing catches my attention. I know all about survival. I catch the puck before it touches the ice, tossing it up and letting it roll along the back of my stick before I pass it back. "What if it didn't have to be about survival? What if it could be about something else?"

He catches it easily, sends it up, spins his stick behind his back, and still manages to land the puck on his blade, tossing it in the air once more before sending it my way. "It's always survival for me, Coach Forrester. I get close to good things, and then they disappear." There's bite to his tone, but also another emotion. Sadness maybe. And resignation.

"Really?" I flip the puck back and forth half a dozen times before I flick it toward his non-dominant hand so he has to work a bit. "So you don't think five years in the pros counts as a good thing?"

"My family sure doesn't," he grumbles.

"What about your grandma?"

He fumbles, and I catch the puck before it touches the ice.

"Nice moves, Coach Forrester," Roman calls from the net.

I startle and almost drop the puck, but recover and shoot it instead. Even though Roman isn't expecting it he stops the shot before it crosses the line.

"Nice save, Goalie," I reply.

"I know what you're doing," Grace says.

"And what is that?"

"Trying to figure me out, get in my head. It's a losing battle, Coach Forrester. Not worth the effort," he replies.

"I can give you the name of a good therapist."

He throws his head back and laughs. "I'd rather eat a cactus."

"Good to know. Think about another goal. Survival is a start, but I want to see more from someone with your record on the ice, Grace." I pat his shoulder and skate over to retrieve the puck from Roman.

His gaze locks on mine as I approach, and I feel the heat in it course through my body. "That's some fan-fucking-tastic stick work, Coach."

How he manages to make that compliment sound illicit is beyond me.

I arch a brow and he grins, eyes darkening.

I hold out my hand and he drops the puck into it. His voice is low. "And good work with Grace. You're already making gains."

The praise settles low in my belly, igniting another fire. One I need to ignore. But his approval is something I still crave, and my breathy response gives me away.

"Thanks, Goalie."

Hemi pokes her head in my office later that afternoon. "A bunch of us are heading to the Watering Hole at five, if you want to join us."

"Let me check in with my sister. I want to make sure it doesn't conflict with her schedule." Fee is at practice with Callie until six. In theory, I could go for half an hour, still beat them home and have dinner started. Plus, it's another opportunity to connect with the team, but I want to make sure I'm not stepping over lines I shouldn't with Vander Zee first.

"Sure thing." Hemi smiles. "We're heading over in about twenty. If you can make it work, just pop by my office and we'll walk over together."

"Sounds good."

Hemi leaves to shut down for the day. Before I message Fee, I stop by Vander Zee's office. He's intense, but fair and I appreciate that about him. His door is open, but I still knock.

"Come on in."

He's standing at his whiteboard, players marked by their numbers.

"Planning out starting line-up for the Ottawa game?" I ask.

"Yeah. It works to keep Grace and Madden on separate lines for the most part." He taps Palaniappa's number on the board.

"But that will have to change eventually," I supply.

"It will," he agrees.

"Hammerstein gave me some good advice, and I'm working on Grace." I wish I could get to the bottom of this faster. It would be better for the team and could win me points with Vander Zee. It's a challenge, though, when I don't work closely with the variable who's been with this team longer.

"You mind me asking what the advice was?"

"He asked me who my best coaches were when I played. They were always the ones I connected with on a personal level. The ones who were relatable."

"That's true." He nods thoughtfully. "You know, when my daughter Tallulah came here for her co-op placement in high school it changed how the players saw me. They treated Tally like one of their sisters. Watched over her, took care of her. Hell, she's close with the girls in the office. And I'm more than just a guy barking orders and pushing them to play better and smarter."

"I can see that." It's the segue I need. "Hemi invited me out to the Watering Hole. I wanted to make sure it was okay before I accepted the offer."

"Yeah, of course it's okay. It's a good way for the guys to get to know you. And you know, if you can get Madden to open up, that'd be great."

"I'll see what I can do, but he holds his cards close to the vest."

"He sure does. If I didn't have two kids in opposing extracurriculars I would make the effort, but I can't clone myself or my wife."

"Fair. Is it okay if I head out?"

"Absolutely. I'm doing the same shortly."

"Okay, thanks Coach Vander Zee. Have a good night."

"You too."

I head for the door.

"Forrester."

I pause and turn back to him.

"It's good to get to know them. But when you're on the ice you're in charge and what you say goes."

"Yes, sir." There's a fine line between gaining their trust, being relatable, and still being in charge, and I want him to see me as capable of taking criticism without having to be babied.

He nods once and turns his attention back to the whiteboard.

I message my sister on the way back to my office.

LEXI

I've been invited to go out with some Terror staff after work. Same place as last time. Do you want me to bring takeout home or should we make something together?

BIG PHEELS

Takeout all the way. I'll have the same as last time. Also, take your time coming home. Callie wants to make cookies, so this is a good excuse for us to eat them all and pretend it didn't happen while you're out making friends.

LEXI

You should make plans with friends.

BIG PHEELS

I'm working on it. You know I take a while to warm up. ILY. Please have fun and don't come back too early.

LEXI

ILY back. Thank you.

I exhale the emotion that comes with her permission. She's been forced to grow up so quickly. I want to see her living, thriving in a way I never did.

I meet up with Hemi, Shilpa, and Hammer, and we pass Coach Thomas and Donnie on the way to the elevator.

"You on your way out, Forrester?" he asks, scanning our group.

"I am. Unless you need me for something?"

"You all heading to the Watering Hole?" Arnold asks before Donnie can reply.

"That's the plan," I say.

"You're welcome to join us, but I think your boys have practice tonight?" Hemi phrases it as a question.

"We're working on the next generation of Terror players, isn't that right, Donnie?" Coach Thomas claps him on the shoulder.

"Sure is." Donnie replies.

"You all have a good time. See you on the ice tomorrow, Forrester," Coach Thomas says before they continue down the hall.

We leave the office and head down the bustling street.

Hammer frowns as she consults her phone. "Tally can't come tonight. She has dance and an evening class."

"Her schedule isn't very forgiving this semester," Hemi says.

"She's a dancer? What kind?" I ask as we push through the doors to the Watering Hole.

"Modern contemporary. She's double majoring in dance and kinesiology. It's a big transition for her," Hammer says.

Dred, Rix, and Essie wave us over, and I'm welcomed with hugs.

Dred moves over, and I slide into the booth beside her. "I'm so glad you came tonight! Did dinner make it home okay last time?"

I smile. "It did, and it was a hit."

"You'll have to bring your sisters out so we can meet them," Rix says.

"I would love to. Callie plays hockey five nights a week, and Fee is a senior and has a portfolio class, so it's busy."

"Portfolio? Is she in the arts?" Rix asks.

"She goes to the Art Academy."

"What kind of art is she into?" Essie asks.

"She's a dancer, but she's also into mixed media art."

"We definitely need to get her out. Tally went to school there." Hemi accepts a glass of soda water.

I pass on the margaritas and order a ginger ale. "That would be a great connection for her." Tally seems nice, and Fee could definitely use some new friends.

The bell over the door tinkles, and the hairs on the back of my neck rise.

A moment later, Roman appears in my periphery. He stops to hug Hammer and say hi to everyone. He's so sweet with his daughter, and I once experienced that gentle side, but I also know how absolutely fucking filthy he can be when the clothes come off…

And when his gaze lands on me, I break out in goose bumps, and my entire body turns dewy. How can I spend the entire year like this? Always on alert. Always aware of his presence. Always turned on or anxious or both.

I give my attention to Dred, whose smile has turned sad as she watches Hammer and Roman. "It's pretty special, isn't it?"

"They're so close," I murmur.

"They are. They go out to bars and everything. They genuinely love spending time together."

"My stepdad was super involved with my sisters like that. Not the bars, obviously, but they did things together all the time." Maybe that's part of the reason my relationship with my dad is so difficult. I long for that closeness, and it's just not possible.

"I can't imagine losing that."

Flip, Tristan, and another man I haven't seen before come through the doors. They head straight for our table so Tristan can say hi to Rix.

Essie pulls out her compact and quickly applies some gloss.

Tristan introduces the other man as his brother Nate before they join the guys lining the stools at the bar. I want to find a way to talk to Flip without being obvious. It's impossible with so many of the guys around, though. I'm aware approaching him at the wrong time could make things worse instead of better.

I refocus on the girls, and making connections here, instead.

"How's Nate doing?" Hemi asks Rix.

She nods. "He's okay. It's an adjustment, but I think it's good for him." She turns toward me. "Nate was planning to pursue a master's, but he was offered his dream job, so he's living with us until he can find a place of his own."

"It's so great that you have the space," Hammer says.

"It is. And I think it's good for Tristan and Nate, especially with Brody close by at Tilton U."

"I'm kind of in love with the fact that my sister and Tally happened to find each other," Essie muses.

"Right? It's so perfect," Rix agrees, then turns to me again, probably reading the confusion on my face. "Sorry, you have no idea what we're on about, do you? Brody is Tristan's youngest brother. He's living on campus at Tilton this year, just like Tally and Essie's younger sister, Cammie. I'm attending classes there too, but I'm partly online, and it's a huge campus."

"Ah, that makes sense." I make a mental note that Tristan and Essie have university age siblings that go to Tilton.

"Lexi, we have something for you and your sisters!" Hammer passes a Terror tote bag down the table.

Dred does an excited seat shimmy. "It's your welcome gift!"

"You didn't need to do that," I say as the bag is placed in front of me.

"It's just something fun," Hammer explains.

I remove the tissue paper. Inside is a pink shirt with the phrase *Badass Babe Brigade*. There are more pink things folded below it. "This is so cute."

Hemi is all smiles. "Welcome to the Badass Babe Brigade. You're an official member now."

"We modified Callie's shirt, because she's eight, and we don't want her wearing swear words." Hammer winks.

"Smart." I laugh, but I'm a little choked up. "Thank you. This is really… Thanks."

Dred gives me a side hug. "Welcome to the Terror family."

It's terrifyingly amazing to be part of the group. And in the back of my mind, I wonder if Hammer would be quite so receptive if she knew the truth.

I'm folded into another hug by all the girls before I excuse myself to the ladies' room. I need a moment, because I'm suddenly overwhelmed. I'm so used to doing everything on my own. People can't accuse you of stepping on toes or climbing the ladder on the backs of favors if you don't accept help. I didn't realize how much I needed this camaraderie, to feel like I belong.

I'm not paying attention when I leave the bathroom and run right into a broad chest. I inhale deeply, breathing in the familiar scent of Roman's aftershave. His hands curve around my shoulders as if to steady me, and every part of me is electrified by the touch. Other than a handshake, and the occasional puck pass, there's been no physical contact. I should step back, separate myself from him, say something, do something. But I don't *want* to.

I tip my head up, and my heart stutters in my chest, then gallops. There's concern in his eyes, but the familiar heat is just as present. I need to keep my guard up with him, remain professional, but right now I feel so raw and needy. I long for the connection we shared. Ache for it in a way that's become uncomfortably familiar lately.

"You looked upset. Are you okay, Lexi?" His thumb sweeps along the exposed skin at the collar of my shirt, sending a shiver down my spine.

It's a damn wonder I don't moan at how *good* it feels to be this close to him again. I long to melt into him. To feel the strength of his arms around me. To not be the one holding everything together.

"No. Yes. I don't know." My eyes close, and I will myself to step back, but I can't. "This is...I shouldn't—" But even as I say it, I press my hand to his chest and feel his heart hammering just as hard as mine. "I can't be alone with you." Because I don't know if I could control the visceral need I have for him. With him, I belonged somewhere—even if it was brief, for a moment I felt like I was his. And I want that again, so badly.

His tongue drags across his bottom lip. "I'm trying to stay away from you, but I'm losing the battle." He drops his hands and fists them at his side, eyes full of the same desperate longing that makes my chest ache at what could have been, if I'd made a different choice all those years ago.

But then I wouldn't have this job.

"You should go," he says gruffly.

I nod once, but he skims the back of my hand as I pass. Like he can't help himself. Like his need matches mine and it's too strong to deny. He might still be angry about me showing back up in his life out of the blue, but we're both powerless against the pull. I keep walking, though, because screwing up my life isn't part of the plan.

CHAPTER 11

ROMAN

I pass the coaching staff as I board the plane for Ottawa. Coach Forrester is sitting in an aisle seat, dressed in a blue suit. Her long hair hangs over her shoulder in her signature braid, notebook open beside her, pen poised between her long fingers, New York's last game against Ottawa plays on her laptop. It's angled slightly so that Grace, who is in the seat next to her, can also watch.

"This right here." She pauses the game as Ottawa takes the shot on net. "What do you see?"

He rubs his chin. "I didn't read the play correctly."

"Oh, but I think you did," she replies. "And the deflection should have worked, but look what happens over here." Connor leans in as she resumes the game.

Pride makes my chest swell. She's making real progress with Grace on a game level, and I have confidence that the rest will follow. Especially because she lives and breathes the sport. In the weeks since she joined the Terror, she's been constantly throwing out new ideas and looking for ways the team can level up.

I take an aisle seat, facing her. Her gaze lifts to mine for a moment before she returns her attention to her screen and she and Connor continue to dissect the game. Her pen finds its way between her lips. And my cock stirs at the combination of her owning her role, leading her players as we discussed, while also looking like my favorite treat.

"You all right, man?" Hollis asks.

"Huh?" I look away from Coach Forrester.

"You seem like you're all up in your head. Last season reality hitting?"

"Oh. Yeah." My stomach twists as I swallow down the lie. This is not about my career. This season can't be over soon enough. "How was your meeting with your agent?"

"Good." Hollis taps on his armrest. "I talked to Alex Waters yesterday."

"Oh yeah? What'd he have to say?" Alex Waters, a legend of a player, runs the Hockey Academy out in Pearl Lake with a bunch of other retired players.

"They're in the process of opening a satellite campus in Toronto. His parents are out in Guelph, and he wants a reason to be closer," Hollis says. "They're looking for coaches."

"Really?" That's an interesting option.

"He's sending information next week. He asked what your plans were. Could be a good opportunity."

I rub my bottom lip as my heart leaps. My gaze drifts back to Coach Forrester. I could stay in Toronto. Next year I won't be on the team, and that means…she won't be off-limits. Dating her wouldn't be the issue it is now. We wouldn't be contending with red tape and bureaucracy. Now it could damage her reputation, not to mention her career. But after I'm retired, I could pursue her with much less recourse. *She could be mine*. "It could. I'll mention it to my agent."

"It'd be nice if we could keep working together next year, you know?" Hollis says.

"Yeah, it would," I agree. So much has changed in the past year, including our friendship, but coaching together could be a great next move.

It's a short flight to Ottawa. Soon we're getting settled in our room, and Hollis leaves me to my routine so he can "check in" on Peggy. I put all my things away, roll out my yoga mat, and do my post-flight stretch routine. When I'm done, I grab one of the green apples from the bowl I set out and head down to the lobby to meet Hollis.

But when I get there, the first person I see is Lexi. She's pacing an empty hall, phone to her ear, tugging the end of her braid. Something is clearly wrong. *I should leave her alone.* I shouldn't interfere, but the possibilities of what could be once the season ends make it impossible to walk the other way.

"How high is her fever?" She exhales a relieved breath. "Okay. That's manageable. And you already gave her something for the temperature?"

She spins around and nearly slams into me. I settle my hands on her shoulders to steady her. Worry creases her brow. "We don't want it to go over one-oh-three. I don't love that I'm not there when Callie's not well." She mouths, *I need a minute.*

"I'm not going anywhere," I murmur, hands still on her shoulders.

"Callie should stay home tomorrow. Crap. I don't want you to miss a test." She reaches out and skims my tie. I wore it when I took her out for a very private dinner in New York. "Maybe I can catch an earlier flight home. I'll check in with you after the game. I love you, too, Big Pheels. I'm sorry. Hugs for Callie." She ends the call and pinches the bridge of her nose. "How can I help you, Roman?"

"You can help me by letting me help you," I say softly.

"You need to get to the arena, and so do I," she replies.

"We do, but Callie is sick, and you won't be able to focus on the game if the situation doesn't get managed, which means neither will I, because I'll be irritated at myself for not stepping in when I could," I argue.

"Why are you being so kind?" she whispers.

"Because being angry about the past doesn't change anything tonight, and I feel better being a nice guy instead of an asshole."

I finger the end of her braid. "I presume Peggy and Hemi have already pulled you into their group chat."

"Yes, but—"

"You and Dred were talking the other day. Why don't you see if she's around?"

She frowns, like she's surprised I know this.

"I pay far more attention to you than I should, Lexi. If you don't pull up Dred's contact information, I'll get it from my daughter and do it myself."

"You're so bossy," she gripes.

"You love when I take control."

She gives me a look. "Watch yourself, Goalie."

"Pull up Dred's contact, Coach."

She worries her bottom lip. "I can't ask her to watch Callie when she's sick."

"Fine. I'll do it for you." I pull my phone out of my pocket.

"Don't." She grabs my hand. "I'll do it."

"Good girl." I don't mean for it to come out gravelly.

A shiver runs through her, but she doesn't say anything else, just sends the message. It takes all of three seconds for Dred to reply.

"She's done at the library at ten, and she's offered to stay the night."

"Perfect. Now the only thing you have to worry about tonight is the game, which I need to suit up for." I turn to walk away before I lose the battle with my body and pull her into my arms.

"Roman."

God, what it does to me when my name is on her lips. I glance over my shoulder.

"Thank you."

"You're welcome."

Despite feeling good going into the game, I do not play well. Nothing goes right for any of us. Grace is on second line with a less-experienced enforcer, leaving us vulnerable. But putting him on the same line as Madden seems to be asking for more problems than it's worth. That needs to end so we don't fuck up the season. As it is, I let in three goals while Ottawa shuts us out. I hope like hell it doesn't set the tone for what's coming my way for the rest of the season.

Peggy hugs me first when we exit the locker room after. I don't know if that makes me feel worse or better. "I'm sorry, Dado. I know that game was a hard one."

I pat her back. "Thanks, kiddo."

"You're coming out tonight, right?" She smooths the lapels on my suit jacket.

"Nah. I think I'll take it easy." I tip my chin toward the group, who look like they're figuring out where to go. "You have fun. Go burn some energy and take Hollis with you."

"Are you sure? We can stay back."

"I'm sure, kiddo. Go out. Have a good time. I'll see you in the morning for breakfast." If they stay back I'll have to make up more lies as to why I'm not in the mood, and I'd like to avoid that for the sake of my stomach and my conscience.

"Okay." She kisses my cheek. "I love you."

"I love you, too."

I return to the hotel, but I'm too on edge to relax, so I change and head to the gym to run out my frustration.

I'm 3K into a run when the gym door opens and in walks my wet dream and my worst temptation. Lexi pulls her cropped sweatshirt over her head, leaving her in a sports bra and running shorts. It's skin, skin, and more skin—all her toned, athletic, incredibly fucking bendy body on display as she crosses the room.

It's eleven, so the gym is empty apart from us. Our flight leaves at eight thirty in the morning. We should be getting ready for bed. *I'd love to give her a different kind of workout.*

She falters when she reaches the treadmills but steps up onto the one beside mine. "Didn't get enough of a workout on the ice tonight?"

"Apparently not." I fight to keep from looking at her, but I can't help myself as she winds her braid on top of her head and secures it with a scrunchie. I long to free that coil of hair, wrap it around my fist and kiss a path from her shoulder to her ear. I clear my throat and look away. "How's Callie?"

"The fever is down, and she's asleep, so that's good. Dred doesn't have a shift until the afternoon, so she can stay with Callie until I get back. That means Fee can go to school."

"That's good." I try to keep my mouth shut, to not say whatever the fuck is on my mind, but my self-restraint is a bag of shit. "So why are you here if Callie's being taken care of?"

"Probably the same reason you are." She starts her treadmill.

"Doubtful," I grumble.

She side-eyes me. "So this isn't post-game punishment?"

"Not entirely, no."

"So partially punishment."

I avoid the question and ask one of my own. "Why are you down here?"

"Trying to settle my mind. My goalie had a rough game, and it's my fault."

"How I fail to protect the net isn't on you." I increase my pace.

She hits the stop button and turns to face me. "Isn't it? I show up here, no warning, no explanation, in your last season. I know I fucked up, Roman. I knew the second I saw you that I'd made a mistake."

"You're a good fit for this team."

"I know. That's not the mistake."

My gut churns. I hop off the belt and hit the stop button on my treadmill. I should leave. Walk away. But I *can't*. "Me. I'm the mistake."

"I wish I could take it back," she whispers.

That hurts more than a puck to the chest. I take a moment before I speak. "At least look me in the eye when you tell me you regret me."

Her eyes move over my face, and I find that same desire I feel every time I'm close to her reflected back at me. "I don't regret you. At all," she says. "That's the problem, Roman. Every time you look at me, touch me—I relive what it was to be with you."

Fuck. I wish she was less beautiful, less incredible, less of a powerhouse woman, less of a siren in the bedroom. But she's all those things and more, and it's driving me up the fucking wall. "If that's true why did you leave with no note?" It's the thing that's been eating at me.

Her expression grows pained. "I thought I was just a fun weekend for you," she whispers. "That I was just one of many who got to warm your bed then be forgotten."

"And what do you think now?" I grip the rail, struggling not to reach out and stroke her cheek, feel her soft skin under my fingertips, to give in to this overwhelming need.

"That I was wrong."

Her fingers skim her collarbones, drawing my attention to her cleavage. Which I've had my hands and face buried in. And I also fucked.

I give her the *look*. The one that made her putty in my hands every fucking time. God, she's just so full of fire. So infuriatingly in control, while I'm over here fighting to stay on the right side of the line.

"Do *not* look at me like that, Roman." Her expression is resolute, but the waver in her voice tells a different story. "I'm your coach."

I step off my treadmill and onto hers.

She backs up until she hits the control panel.

"I think you like it when I look at you like this, Lexi." I grab the arm rails to keep myself from pulling her into my arms so I can reacquaint myself with her lips. Instead, I ask the still unanswered questions. "Why did you leave me in New York with cold sheets and no note."

"I didn't want to be just another woman after your fame." She glances away. "I was barely starting my career and you were...bigger than life. I didn't want to be a lifelong hockey fan who slept my way into my dream role." Her expression is pained as her eyes meet mine. "It was the best weekend of my life, Roman. I was young and I didn't believe you could possibly feel the way I did."

I motion between us. "Do you still feel this chemistry the way I do?"

I don't know what I was hoping for, but her guard goes back up.

"I'm your coach, Roman."

My gaze narrows and my next words sound like a demand. "That's not an answer, Alexandria."

She exhales a shuddering breath. "Roman."

"I want your truth."

"Yes. I still feel it. Whenever you're near me it's all I can think about. It consumes me. You consume me. I've played out every scenario in my head a thousand times. Do you have any idea how badly I'd wanted to stay that morning? But I didn't. All we have is here and now. You have to see how impossible this is," she implores. "It doesn't matter what I want anymore. My career would be over if I acted on these feelings."

"You're turning my world upside down."

Her bottom lip trembles. "So are you. Again. Still."

Knowing there's the possibility of a future with her that's currently out of reach is maddening. I want so desperately to find a way to have what I want. Her. Us.

We've both dropped our arms and moved closer, like our bodies know what they want and don't give a shit that acting on that impulse will blow our lives apart.

"Roman, please," she whispers.

I spin around and leave the gym before I give in and do something we'll both regret.

CHAPTER 12

LEXI

LEXI

Are you sure I can't bring anything else?

HEMI

Everything is covered. The dip and cookies are more than enough.

HAMMER

Hollis ate half the salad I made last night while I was asleep.

RIX

I tested a bunch of new recipes so I'm bringing a LOT of food. Sorry and you're welcome.

TALLY

No cucumber salad, though, right? :Giggling GIF:

HEMI

👀

SHILPA

😮

ESSIE

RIP cucumbers.

HEMI

:cucumber dancing GIF:

DRED

You're a bunch of deviants.

LEXI

???

A private message from Dred pops up.

DRED

Don't ask about the cucumber.

LEXI

Now I want to ask about the cucumber.

DRED

I promise you don't. Also, Hemi has these things catered, so don't stress about bringing stuff. See you soon!

LEXI

Looking forward to it!

I smile as I set the phone down and finish getting ready. I'm nervous about being around Roman without practice or a game to focus on, but I'm excited to spend more time with these women.

"The whole team is invited, right?" Callie has been bouncing on my bed for the last ten minutes while I agonize over the right outfit.

I've already answered this question several times. "Yup. The whole team is invited."

Hemi and Dallas have organized a team barbecue. The first official game of the season is two days away. The rocky exhibition games have leveled out, thankfully.

I've been working with Palaniappa and Grace, who seem to be connecting. And while I haven't managed to get either Flip or Grace to open up about their mutual disdain, I'm making gains with Grace on a personal level. He's used to being a scapegoat and a problem, and I've learned that calling him on the negativity and then praising his good work goes a long way. And Vander Zee approves which always feels good.

"I can't believe I get to meet Connor Grace and Roman Hammerstein! This will be the best day ever!"

Fingers crossed Connor shows, or I'll have one sad little girl on my hands. I mentioned during practice that my sister plays hockey and is a huge fan of his. He said he'd try to make it. Callie made him a card and is wearing her GRACE jersey. Although, she's almost equally obsessed with Roman, so he'll be a decent consolation prize.

Fee flops down on my bed. "Do I have to come?" She, too, has asked this question ten times. She's dressed in her uniform of darkness: black jeans, black shirt, black eyeliner.

"It'll be fun. You'll meet the head coach's daughter, and she went to your school last year, so you have something in common," I remind her.

"She won't want to hang out with a high school kid," Fee complains.

"Just give them a chance, okay?" I need the black cloud around her to lift a little.

"Okay."

How one word can be so heavily infused with disdain is a teenage wonder.

We drive the short distance to Dallas and Hemi's condo. The subway probably would have been quicker, but Callie made cookies, and I made BLT dip, so the car was easier.

The party room is hopping when we arrive. Upbeat music plays through the sound system, and the space is full of massive hockey players, the coaching staff, and Hemi and the girls.

Callie's face lights up as Dred comes over to greet us. "Dred! Yay!"

Even Fee perks up when she sees her.

Dred opens her arms and accepts a hug from Callie. "You look like you're feeling a million times better."

"I was only off school for one day, and I only missed one hockey practice," Callie declares. "When can I visit you at the library?"

"Whenever you want." Dred's attention shifts to Fee. "Love that shirt. Pierce the Veil will always be one of my favorite bands."

Fee's eyes flare, and she covers the band emblem with her hand. "You know Pierce the Veil?"

"I've even been to a concert. Best live performance ever."

"I would die."

Dred motions between them. "You and me, girl. We can go together—as long as that's okay with Lexi." She gives me an apologetic look while Fee gives me an imploring one.

"Yeah, of course it's okay." I'd rather her go to a concert with a responsible adult than a bunch of teenagers who have a questionable sense of self-preservation.

Callie starts bouncing and grabs my arm. "Oh my gosh, Lexi, it's Connor Grace. He's here. Can you introduce me so I can give him this?" She thrusts her card at Dred. "I made this for him. Do you think he'll like it?"

Dred manages to keep her eyebrows from touching her hairline. "Oh, absolutely. You're an incredibly talented artist. And I love the use of glitter."

Callie drops her voice. "I kinda traced it. I'm not good like Fee."

"Still awesome." Dred looks to me. "You want to introduce Callie to Connor, and I can introduce Fee to Tally?" She shifts her attention back to Fee. "She's dying to meet you."

Fee's eyes widen. "She is?"

"Yeah. This whole crew is all about hockey, and she's all

about dance. She's excited to have someone who loves the same things she does join the group."

"Okay."

Dred winks at me and guides Fee over to where Tally is standing with Rix, Essie, and Hammer. She's immediately greeted with enthusiastic hugs, and her entire face lights up. I send a thank you up to heaven for this remarkable group of people who have embraced us as their own.

Connor leans against the wall on the other side of the room, his phone in one hand and a bottle of water in the other. That he showed up says a lot about his desire to figure out how to mesh with the team. His head lifts as Callie and I approach. She's practically vibrating with excitement, but trying so hard to play it cool.

Connor slides his phone into his pocket and smiles as he notices the number 7 on the arm of Callie's jersey and the card in her hand. "Hey, Coach, this must be your sister. Calliope, right?"

"You know my name?" Callie stares up at him with awe-filled eyes.

He drops to one knee so they're at eye level with each other. "I do. And you know mine."

"You can call me Callie. You're my favorite player. I used to cheer for New York, but then you were traded, and my sister is your coach, so I asked for a Toronto jersey. Plus the mascot is funny," she adds.

Connor smiles, and it softens his otherwise regal, sometimes harsh features. "It is funny."

"Geese are always grumpy," Callie says.

"This is accurate. Maybe it's because they have to poop so much."

Callie giggles then grows serious. "You were really great during the last game."

"Thanks, and no penalty minutes," he says cheekily, but then his expression shifts. "You know your sister is probably the reason for that."

"She said you work together a lot because she's the defense coach."

His voice drops to a conspiratorial whisper. "What else has she said about me?"

Callie looks to me, as if asking permission.

I tip my head in encouragement.

"That you're one of the top defensive players in the league and she's excited about being able to help you harness your potential."

His eyes flare in surprise, and lift to me. "You really said that?"

"Yeah." I smile. "I did."

"Thanks, Coach. That—" He clears his throat. "It means a lot."

"Lexi's a great coach." Callie beams.

"She is," Connor agrees.

"Right, okay." I wave the compliment away and nudge Callie. "You have something for Connor."

"Oh! Right! I made you a card." She thrusts it at him and ducks her head as he takes it. "I traced you. I'm not that good of an artist."

"I don't know if I'd agree with that. Tracing or not, this is pretty darn awesome. And I love the glitter."

"I wanted it to look like there were sparks coming out of your skates because you're so fast," she explains.

"I think you did a great job. Is it okay if I put this in my cubby in the Terror locker room, so I can look at it before every game?" Connor asks.

And oh my God, my heart melts a little. If more people saw this side of Connor, wouldn't things be different for him? I tuck this moment away, because this is the connection Roman has been talking about. No amount of time on the ice can compare to a human moment like this.

"Oh yes! That would be great." Callie nods enthusiastically. She rolls her bottom lip between her teeth and looks up at me.

I give her a thumbs-up.

She twists her fingers together. "Would you sign my jersey?"

Another smile spreads across Connor's face. "Of course. I just need a pen."

"I have one!" Callie fishes it out of the pocket of her pants. It's maroon metallic, which I didn't even know existed until she showed it to me. Connor signs her jersey while Callie stares up at him with stars in her eyes.

When he's finished, he passes back the marker and holds up the card. "I'm going to put this in my car to keep it safe."

"Okay. It was really great to meet you. I'll come see you play this season."

"I would love that. Thank you for the card, Callie."

"You're welcome."

He gives me a chin tip and a small smile before he heads for the door, waving to a couple of the rookie players as he leaves.

"I can't believe he signed my jersey." She's all smiles and happiness. "Can you introduce me to Roman Hammerstein now?" She points across the room. "He's right there."

I swallow, force a smile, and battle against the way my heart races when I'm about to deal with Roman—especially after what happened in the hotel gym. I swear, if he hadn't walked away I could have made an untake-back-able mistake. "Of course."

She grabs my hand and tugs me toward Roman, who's standing with Hollis and Ash and Dallas. His gaze moves over me in a way that's all too familiar before it shifts to Callie a devastating smile crosses his beautiful face. I've been on the receiving end of that smile in the past, and the things I was willing to do to see it again would make my great-gran roll over in her grave. I still wouldn't take it back.

"You must be Calliope," Roman says, and just like Connor, he crouches so she doesn't have to crane her neck.

Callie's eyes are saucers. She'll probably talk about this day for weeks. "How does everyone know my name?"

"You're a goalie, right?" Roman motions between them.

"Goalies know goalies." He glances at the number on her shirt. "And you're a Grace fan."

"He's good at helping protect the net. And he's not afraid to get into it with players if it means they don't score," Callie says, almost defensively.

"That's absolutely true. He's a talented player," Roman agrees.

Callie's smile is radiant. "You're my second-favorite player. Fee and I watch all your games. Even when I was a New York fan because of Connor, I still watched your games, too. My dream is to be the first female goalie for the pros."

"That's a fantastic goal. You have to be really dedicated, don't you?" Roman asks.

"I have practice Monday through Friday, and games on Saturday," Callie informs him. "But I'm going to come and see you play on a weekend if I have an early Saturday game."

"Maybe I can return the favor, if your sister is okay with that." His eyes lift to mine, questions there. And maybe an apology.

"That would be…great." Callie's whole team will lose their minds. I'll have to sit next to him for an hour. It would be the most amazing torture.

"I would love that so much." And because she's eight, Callie throws her arms around Roman's neck.

His smile is soft as he squeezes her back. I'm pretty sure I just ovulated. Why does he have to be such a good guy? My heart clenches at how sweet he's being with her.

He's this massive, imposing man, a legend in his sport, someone so many look up to. That I spent a weekend with him, that he was mine so completely for that time, still feels like an impossible dream.

And to see him hugging my little sister, knowing what she's lost, being a role model and someone she admires, while also being the man who was viciously, ruthlessly thorough in his quest to bring me to orgasm any and every way possible… Well, that's a lot for any woman to handle.

He is the perfect man. I had him. And now I see his beautiful face every day, remember all the ways he made me feel so good, and watch him be this awe-inspiring father, player, goalie, peer, mentor, and friend. It's agonizing. Especially now that I know our time together meant something to him too. More than something, even.

When Callie finally releases him, I'm grateful that she grabs my arm and drags me over to where Fee chats with Tally, Rix, Essie, Dred, and Tristan. It almost looks like Fee and Tristan are having a moment. What's even more astonishing is that she's smiling and laughing and having a good time with surly as fuck Tristan. He's usually so serious all the time, but here he looks relaxed and happy.

How much do I want to embrace this team like the family they are? Become fully part of it. It's already happening.

I suddenly find myself on the edge of emotion, which occurs at the most inopportune times—like when I'm in a room full of my players. I can't afford weakness when I'm surrounded by the team and management.

"Are you okay with the girls for a minute?" I ask Dred. "I need to use the bathroom."

"Yeah, of course. You go ahead. They're in good hands." Dred squeezes my arm.

The signs for the bathroom lead me through the kitchen. I take a moment to collect myself. I don't know how to classify my emotions. There's real grief, in part over the loss of my mom, but beyond that, my chest aches at having had someone so wildly flawless and never being able to fully appreciate him for longer than a couple of days. Would things have been different if I stayed? I was so young. In my mid-twenties to his mid-thirties at the time. Green. New. How would he have taken me seriously? Why am I entertaining this when it's in the past?

I wet a paper towel and dab cold water on my neck. I'll go

back out there and stay close to Dred. She's a safe space. I'll keep my distance from Roman. I have to.

But I run into him as I pass through the kitchen. Every private moment with him feels dangerous. He's chipping away at my defenses, leaving me naked and vulnerable in a way only he's capable of. Every part of me yearns for him. For the easy smile that was once directed at me, for the feel of his body wrapped around mine. What I wouldn't give to be his again for one more night. But more than that, I long for the other parts of him too, for the intelligent player who so easily shares his experiences, who guides and encourages. I want that man, too.

He stops arranging broccoli on the veggie platter and plants his fists on the counter. "I shouldn't have offered to come to Callie's game. I wasn't thinking."

"She would love for you to come."

His jaw works. "And what about you? Would you love for me to come?"

My brain interprets that not at all the way he meant it, and before I can stop myself, I murmur a horribly moany, "Yes, please."

The right side of his mouth curves up. He picks up the veggie tray and heads straight for me. He bends until his lips are at my ear. "You're a little too tempting for your own good, Coach."

He leaves me standing there, wishing, not for the first time, that our paths had crossed again a year from now, after he retired—when wanting him wouldn't compromise everything I've worked for.

CHAPTER 13

ROMAN

Despite the ups and downs of our exhibition games and the tension between Grace and Madden, by some miracle we manage to get our feet under us during the regular season. We've been on a winning streak, riding the high. But tonight that broke, and we lost. It would have been fine if I'd been in net the whole game, but Ryker played the final period and let in two goals. I'm owning it, because it's on me to be a good mentor.

Lately I've felt like I'm failing at a lot of things. Maintaining my distance from Lexi has proven pretty fucking impossible, especially with her working so closely with the defensive line. All the self-control I usually possess when it comes to my career and my life seems to go out the window when she's around. It's no different tonight.

I should go out with Peggy and Hollis and some of the team. But I don't want to—and not just because I'm in no mood to watch my daughter and my best friend try to keep things PG on the dance floor. I'd rather hit the treadmill and run out my frustration, especially since there's a good chance my favorite coach will do the same.

"You sure we can't convince you to come?" Hollis opens the door for Peggy, who's club ready in her dress and heels.

"Why aren't you dressed?" she asks.

"I'm going to hang back tonight."

She frowns. "Again?"

"I'm just not feeling it, kiddo." *Not a lie.* Skipping nights out has become a habit of late. I don't need to watch over her anymore. And I want her to have fun with her friends.

"Come for one drink," Hollis suggests.

"Nah, I'm good." I rub my green apple on my T-shirt to shine it. "You have fun. I'll see you in the morning."

Peggy kisses me on the cheek, and they leave with Hemi, Dallas, Tristan, and Flip. I change into my workout gear and take the elevator to the hotel gym.

I'm not disappointed. Lexi is already there. But she's not alone. There's a guy chatting her up on the treadmill to her right. He's tall and lanky. Definitely a suit, based on his haircut and outfit. Lexi doesn't notice me at first. Neither of them do.

She's in her usual gym uniform of running shorts and a loose tank. Although when it's just her and me, as it often is these days, she loses the tank and runs in a sports bra. I like to think it's for my benefit, and also to torture me.

"How long are you in the city?" the guy asks.

"I fly out in the morning," she replies.

"How early? Maybe I can take you for breakfast?"

Lexi chuckles. "It's an early flight."

"You could come back to my room, and we could order room service instead."

Half of me wants to laugh at this guy's gall, and the other half would like to take Lexi back to my room, strip her naked and withhold orgasms until she's begging for release for giving this guy a shred of her attention. I stride across the room and hop onto the treadmill on the other side of her. "Did you make a new friend?"

She sucks in a shocked breath. "Roman."

The guy looks between me and Lexi, clearly trying to figure out who we are to each other.

I smile darkly at him. "You're not her type."

She gives me a disbelieving look that jacks me right up.

"Is this guy your boyfriend?" Business Guy asks.

I grin as Lexi stumbles over her response.

Business Guy stops his treadmill and grabs his towel with a shake of his head. "Careful with this one. She's a game player."

I laugh. "Don't worry. I can handle her." I grin at Lexi's incredulous expression. "Isn't that right, angel?"

Business Guy pushes through the door with a huff.

"Seriously? What the hell, Roman?"

"I'm not wrong. I can handle you."

"That was… You're so… That was out of line!" she snaps.

"I'm sorry, did I read that situation wrong? Did you *want* to go back to his room with him? Should I stop him?" I hop off the treadmill.

Lexi grabs my arm, her nails biting into my skin. "What? No! Have you lost your mind? What if he recognized you? Or me?"

I turn back to her. She's still holding my arm. "He probably watches golf, not hockey. And yes, Lexi, I'm losing my fucking mind over here. That guy is lucky he walked out with all his damn teeth still in his head."

Her eyes heat. "I'm capable of handling myself."

I smirk. "Not as good as I am."

Her mouth drops open. "Oh my God. What has gotten into you?"

"Isn't it obvious? *You* are what's gotten into me, Lexi. You think I like being like this? Always on edge. Out of fucking control?"

"What's your plan, Roman?" She props a fist on her hip, expression defiant. "Are you going to jizz a circle around me every time someone flirts with me?"

I arch a brow.

She frowns, but her eyes flare a moment later. "I mean piss a circle."

I give her a heated once-over. "Are you sure, Lexi?"

"You can't—" Her fingers flutter to her throat. "We work together."

I lean in, voice dropping to a whisper. "Doesn't change the fact that I know what you sound like when you come."

Her breath quickens. "You're playing dirty."

"And you're not? You were chatting up some guy, even though you had to know I'd end up on the treadmill next to you just to be near you."

She tips her chin up. "I was trying not to be rude, unlike you."

I make a noise in the back of my throat. "I dream about you almost every fucking night, Lexi." I let my gaze rove over her athletic curves, voice dropping at the next admission. "About the way you taste."

She swallows thickly. "Why are you torturing me like this? It's not fair."

"Oh angel, don't talk to me about fair." I lean in closer, my voice low and full of pent-up desire. "What do you think it's like for me, watching you own the ice every day. Having to stay quiet while you step into this role and fucking own it. Seeing all these sides of you. Knowing how different it could be when it's just you and me and all the walls are down. Every night I fall asleep thinking about you, and every morning I fuck my hand to the image of you just so I can control myself when I'm on the ice with you."

Her bottom lip slides through her teeth on a needy whimper.

"I can't get you out of my head. I can't escape you, and I can't stay the hell away from you." I drop my hands to my sides and clench them. "I don't have control when it comes to you. You shred it without even trying."

Inches separate us. She tilts her head up and settles one warm, soft palm on my chest. Her entire body relaxes, shoulders melting. "You're the only person I've ever felt like this with."

I need confirmation that I'm not alone in this. "Explain."

"You ground me." Her bottom lip trembles. "And it terrifies me."

"Why?"

"Because I don't want to lose it again."

"Why would you have to?" I cover her hand with mine. Even that innocent contact makes my body feel like a live wire. It would be so easy to give in.

"In what world do I get to have you and my career with no consequences?" she whispers.

We're both so close to breaking. I lift her hand and brush my lips across her knuckles. "Go to bed, Alexandria, before I entice you into mine."

She releases an unsteady breath and I let go of her hand.

"Now, angel. Go."

Her eyes soften. "Yes, Roman."

It takes every ounce of restraint I have left not to follow as she rushes out of the room.

CHAPTER 14

LEXI

"That was quite the win last night," Dad says.

"Oh, did you catch the game?"

"The highlights."

I shouldn't be surprised. The only thing my dad can do for three hours at a time is work. "The hockey-gossip sites have a lot to say."

"I thought you stayed away from those."

He's typing and talking. He never just has a phone call. I'm packing lunches, though, with Dad on speakerphone, so I guess I'm no different. "They come up in my feed because they're hockey and Terror related." And *me* related. "It's not unexpected, but it can be irritating."

We won the last game, but it was dirty. As good as Connor is on the ice, he still tends to play with his emotions. And I still don't have an answer to why he and Madden hate each other so much. Yes, I'm making gains, finding my footing, but it's infuriating to be unable to get to the bottom of this. And Thomas is all about protecting his center, which doesn't help at all.

"Are they blaming you for Grace and Madden?" Dad asks.

"I'm the new assistant coach and I work with the enforcers, there's speculation that I'm part of the problem."

"You don't control how the players behave on the ice," Dad argues. He's such a lawyer. And this is how he shows he cares.

"You're right, I don't. The chatter I can handle. I know Connor has a long history of chippy behavior, but he's been playing a lot cleaner lately. He has one bad game and everyone writes him off." And me. "He's so used to being a punching bag."

"Do you think he's turned it into a self-fulfilling prophecy?" Dad asks.

"Possibly. I need to pull him aside when the rest of the team isn't around so he doesn't feel like he has to save face." I drum my fingers on the counter, pondering. "Grace is my responsibility, and his actions reflect on me and the team." Getting him and Madden on the same line is imperative for a successful season—which means getting to the bottom of their sandwich problem. But Grace doesn't socialize off the ice, and Madden is always surrounded by his friends whenever we're at the Watering Hole.

Grace and I have a good rapport on the ice, and off it, but getting him and Madden to not just play nice but play together is the ultimate goal.

I realize there's been a pause in conversation. I still hear Dad typing, so hopefully he didn't notice. "Maybe you could fly out and catch a game soon? You could stay overnight?"

"My schedule is pretty packed," he hedges.

"We're two months into the regular season. You haven't even had a chance to see the living room you bought us." I hate that it feels like I'm begging. "What about Friday? Didn't you say you were only in court until Thursday? It could be a quick trip." That's two days from now.

Ophelia ambles into the kitchen and peeks over my shoulder, checking out my phone screen. Her lips push out, and she grabs a banana from the fruit bowl. She struggles to warm up to my dad. Callie, on the other hand, loves when he comes to visit. Probably because he brings her presents.

"I might be able to swing it."

Ophelia rolls her eyes.

I give her a look.

She gives me one back.

"I can get you box seats," I tell Dad. "I'll even book your flights. Just send me a link to your calendar."

"I guess that can work," he says after a moment. "Make sure it's business class, please. I'll send you money to cover the cost." He's typing again.

"Sure, Dad. The girls will be excited. They'll come to the game, too."

Ophelia gives me two thumbs down. A chunk of banana falls to the floor.

I hand her a damp cloth.

"It'll be nice to see them," he says, sounding more upbeat. "I can't believe Ophelia is almost through high school. Time really does fly. How are you doing for Christmas gifts? Can you send me a list for the girls and yourself? I can top up your account so you can get something special."

"You don't need to do that. This job pays really well."

"I know. But Toronto's expensive, and you're doing this on your own."

I take a breath. I know he means well. This is mostly how he expresses emotion. "We're fine. I promise." I practically raised myself, so I'm used to being self-sufficient. Taking money from my dad isn't something I enjoy.

"Okay, I'll stop pushing. You can add the flight details to my calendar once you've booked it," he says.

"Sounds good."

"I'll see you in a couple of days."

"Looking forward to it. Bye, Dad." I end the call.

Fee props her hip against the counter.

"If you don't have anything nice to say, don't say anything at all," I warn.

"We probably shouldn't tell Callie in advance, in case he cancels," Fee replies.

"Agreed." We've played in New York, but my dad got tied up at work. I get it, even though it's hard to always take a back seat to his job.

Fee's expression shifts. "It sucks that this is the first game he's been able to make."

I don't defend him to Fee, because she's right. "Yeah, it does."

"Doesn't it make you angry?" she asks.

I sigh. "It used to, but therapy helps. Some people just aren't designed to be parents, and they don't realize it until after they've had kids. He tries in the ways he knows how."

Her lips pull to the side. "Mom never had anything nice to say about him."

Phantom pain makes my heart ache. "I know. She wanted him to be someone he couldn't be, and that was difficult for her. You have to learn how to love people the way they are, not the way you wish they were."

"That seems hard."

"It is, but it also saves your sanity." I open my arms and make a bring-it-in motion.

She steps in and wraps her arms around me. "I miss them," she whispers.

"I know. Me, too."

"Kristoff! Yay! I'm so glad you're here for the game!" Callie throws herself into my dad's arms.

She only found out he was coming an hour ago, when I had confirmation that his flight had landed in Toronto. He pats her awkwardly on the back, then smooths his tie when she releases him. Other than the players, he's the only guy I know who would wear a three-piece suit to a hockey game. Although, he did leave New York directly from work and came straight here when he landed.

"My goodness, Calliope. You've grown at least a foot since I saw you last. How old are you now? Ten?"

"No! I'm eight!" She beams up at him. "We're going to have so much fun. They have snacks and drinks in the box, and they have a popcorn machine! Did you know Connor Grace is my favorite player and after that is Roman Hammerstein? I'm so excited to see them play!"

He nods knowingly. "Ah, that explains the jersey."

"Connor even signed it!" She shows him the signature across the shoulders.

Ophelia stands off to the side, dressed in her usual uniform of all black, but she is representing with a Terror hoodie. It's a special-edition one designed by a local tattoo artist. My dad bought it for her when I got the job with the Terror. He might not be around much, but he always pays attention when I tell him what she likes. She accepts an awkward hug from him, but perks up significantly when Rix, Essie, Tally, and Dred show up to escort them to the box.

At least I don't have to worry if Dad needs to take work calls. I wave goodbye and join the team in the locker room for the pregame strategy talk. We need more team cohesion if we want to win games. "I want clean game play tonight," Coach Vander Zee says.

"We need to remember what position we play," Grace mutters.

"You got something to say, Grace, say it to my face," Madden snaps.

"This, right here, is the damn problem!" Vander Zee booms. "Whatever your issue is with each other, iron it the fuck out *off* the ice. You're skilled professionals, and I want you to channel your energy into playing a good game, not trying to show each other up. Am I understood?"

"Yes, Coach," Madden and Grace say at the same time, ears a matching shade of red.

Vander Zee looks my way, giving me the floor.

I need to show him I can handle these boys and get them to play *together*. It's up to me to prove that he made the right decision by bringing me on the team, and this is one way.

"We need more of what we saw at practice today," I add. "You're a team, you need to support each other on and off the ice. Show up for each other, and more importantly, show up for *yourself.*" The room is pin-drop silent, every set of eyes trained on me. "When you step inside this locker room and suit up, you become brothers. You don't have to love each other every moment of every day, but you do have to have each other's backs. In this room, but especially out there." I point toward the door. "This team won the cup last year. That wasn't a fluke, that was *earned*. You fought for that. Be *that* team when you take the ice tonight."

"Well said, Coach Forrester." Roman claps and the rest of the room breaks into a round of enthusiastic applause.

I can't deny the way the look of pride on Roman's face bolsters my confidence. And lights up other parts of my body.

Coach Vander Zee gives me a rare smile of approval. "Let's get out there and play the kind of hockey that takes us to the finals again this year."

That gets a round of applause and *hell yeahs*. The players file out of the locker room, and I fall into step with the coaching staff. Coach Thomas is in the upper box with Fielding.

Vander Zee runs a hand through his hair. "Nice work in the locker room, Forrester."

"Thanks. I'm making headway with Grace, but we need those boys to sit down and deal with the issue." It's frustrating to feel like I'm at standstill. I can work with Grace as much as I want, but if I can't get Madden on my side, then where am I?

"Agreed. Every time I've pulled them in they say they're fine, but the tension is there." Vander Zee rubs his bottom lip. "I think you're right about Palaniappa and Grace on the same line, Forrester."

I made the suggestion this afternoon when I was rewatching

some of the practice footage. "Palaniappa is always level-headed."

"So is Grace when he's out there with him. He plays with skill instead of ego."

Last season I took a team at the bottom and brought them to the top. Toronto is already a strong team. We need Grace and Madden to bury the hatchet so there's no more team division. And the best way to make that happen is to talk to the guy who already has the team's loyalty, not the one fighting for it. Madden is the key to this, and if Thomas can't deal with him, someone else has to.

In the first period, Grace and Palaniappa help shut out Carolina, and Grace manages an assist with Bright scoring a goal for the Terror.

"Nice work out there, Grace. That's the kind of hockey I love to see from you," I praise when he rotates off after the goal.

"Thanks, Coach." A slight smile tugs at the corner of his mouth.

It grows larger when Bright echoes the statement.

The game unfolds, and Toronto manages to keep the lead, only letting in one goal at the beginning of the third period, giving us a 3-1 win. If we have a few more games like this, with Madden and Grace playing like they're on the same team, it could make sorting things out between them that much easier.

My phone is full of messages from Fee after the game.

BIG PHEELS

Callie is planning her wedding with Connor. They're getting married on the ice, obviously.

Kristoff left during the middle of the first period and came back in the last five minutes of the game. *eye roll*

But he bought us both new sweatshirts.

LEXI

I hope you said thank you.

BIG PHEELS

We both did.

LEXI

Also, a rink wedding is completely on brand for Callie.

I wish I couldn't empathize with my sister's irritation. But I never had the kind of parents she had. My mom didn't step up to the parenting plate until after my sisters were born. I'm glad things changed and that she gave them the attention they deserved.

Sure, they went on vacation often and left the girls with a nanny, but they never missed one of Callie's hockey games or Fee's dance recitals. My mom wasn't interested in my extra curriculars, mostly used my hockey games as excuses for dates with rich men. My dad just sent flowers or a gift card so I could buy myself something nice when he invariably had to miss an event. It's hard not to be disappointed sometimes, even though it's expected.

We transition to the Watering Hole to celebrate the win, and surprisingly, my dad agrees to come along. Fee is happy to join us since Tally is there, and Callie is in heaven knowing some of the team will be present.

We grab our favorite table and settle in, the energy positive after the win. I'm in the middle of introducing my dad to the team when Callie drags Roman over. He's holding her hand; my heart and ovaries are rioting. And then the panic sets in. But my dad was mostly checked out during the baseball game more than three years ago. He spent the first few innings on his laptop and then excused himself to take calls, until he left to handle some emergency. Surely he won't make the connection.

"Kristoff, this is Roman Hammerstein," Callie announces. "He's the Terror's goalie and my second-favorite player. Roman, this is Lexi's dad, Kristoff. He's a lawyer in New York, and he loves his job a lot."

I shoot Fee a meaningful look. She sips her soda and looks appropriately mortified.

"I'm so used to seeing you in the goalie gear." Dad shakes his hand, brow furrowing. "Have we met before?"

"Uh…" Roman glances at me.

I'm ninety percent of the way to a panic attack.

"Do you watch baseball?" Dad asks, completely oblivious.

"I mostly focus on hockey, but I've been known to catch a game."

Dad's brow smooths out. "Right. Yeah. We just…Lexi and I went to a game a few years back when she came to visit me in New York and for some reason…" He trails off and shakes his head, waving away the idea. "What are the chances you'd be in New York for a game and have seats right next to us, right?" He laughs, like the idea is ludicrous.

"It's not impossible, but unlikely," Roman says smoothly.

I don't know if I'm imagining it, or paranoid, but I swear Hollis is giving Roman the raised eyebrow. Roman is a huge New York fan. He wears their baseball caps all the time. Thankfully not tonight, though.

Dad rubs his bottom lip. "Lexi definitely would have mentioned it if we sat right beside a hockey player."

"I'm sure." Roman gives him a polite smile. "Anyway, it's nice to meet you. I hope you enjoyed the game."

"It was great." Dad's phone rings. "I'm sorry. I'm expecting a call. I need to take this. It was nice to meet you, though." He brings his phone to his ear and heads for the doors.

I heave an internal sigh of relief.

Roman gives me an unreadable look and excuses himself to the bathroom.

Dred passes me a glass. "You look like you might need this."

"What is it?" I sniff the contents.

"Just cranberry and soda water. You okay? You're a little pale."

"I'm fine." I sip the drink, my mouth ridiculously dry.

"Okay." She touches my shoulder. "But if you decide you're not fine, and you need to talk about it, I'm always here, and I'm a vault."

My dad returns a minute later. "I have to take care of a few things, but I'll call you first thing in the morning, and we can go for breakfast before my flight."

"Sounds good, Dad."

As much as I'm sad my time with him is cut short, it may be for the best. I can't have the people I work with figuring out what happened in New York three years ago. Not when we're this far into the season and I'm finally making the progress I need with the team.

CHAPTER 15

ROMAN

"I really hoped you'd bring a date this year." Peggy adjusts my tie as we take the elevator to the conference hall.

"And ruin my perfect record?" I joke. But not really. Next year everything will be different. I won't be part of this team. Hell, I could be coaching kids who might end up on the Terror. And all the red tape surrounding me and Lexi will have disappeared.

She rolls her eyes. "Seriously, Dado, you need to start dating."

"She's right," Hollis agrees.

I motion between them. "You two don't get to gang up on me."

Peggy slides her arm through Hollis's and rests her cheek against his biceps. "If you had a date, we'd be evenly matched and you wouldn't feel ganged-up on."

"I'm going home if you don't drop it." I almost mean that. Keeping stuff from my daughter and my best friend is high on the list of things I don't enjoy. But there's someone I want to see tonight more than I want to forgo the frustration that comes with Peggy and Hollis trying to set up online-dating accounts on my behalf.

"Don't be such a grump." Peggy pokes me in the side.

The elevator doors slide open, giving me an escape.

Tonight is the Terror's annual holiday party. Everyone on the team attends and brings their significant other, if they have one. Even the guys without serious girlfriends usually bring a date. But there's only one woman I want on my arm, and I can't have her.

As soon as we're through the doors, Peggy kisses Hollis on the cheek and tells him she'll find him at dinner. She flounces off, her gold dress billowing behind her as she rushes across the festively decorated room to be enveloped by her friends. My little girl is all grown up.

"They were together almost all day getting their hair and nails and makeup done," Hollis grumbles.

"They're not having a slumber party tonight, so you'll survive." It comes out with more bite than I intend.

Hollis turns to me. "You okay, man?"

"Yeah. I'm great." I'm the opposite of great. I'm on edge. It's almost five thirty, and I haven't seen Lexi since practice yesterday. I love practice as much as I loathe it these days. I can't escape her when I'm sleeping. She's on my mind every waking moment of the day. I'm jonesing, and I need a fix. I can't escape her, and I now know I really don't want to. The future possibilities hold too much allure.

"We gonna talk about this?" Hollis asks.

"Huh?"

He arches a brow. "Dude."

"What?" I wish I could shove my hands in my pockets, but I'm wearing a tux and that's impossible.

"You gonna tell me what happened in New York?"

"We beat them, but it wasn't clean." That lead weight is back in my stomach, but still, I try not to be obvious as I scan the room.

"Not what I'm referring to, and you know it."

The second I find her, I'm utterly transfixed. She's a fucking vision. Her hair has been braided and weaved into an intricate knot at the base of her elegant neck. Her dress is a pale, blush pink with a matching lace overlay that drapes across one shoulder and frames her cleavage, dipping low enough to be seductive, but still modest. The slit in the side shows off her toned leg from long days on the ice. It's very reminiscent of the dress I had delivered to our room during our weekend in New York. I took her out for dinner and dancing, and then brought her back to the hotel, peeled her out of the dress, and kept her in bliss for hours. The next morning I woke alone.

"Dude, you're as subtle as a fart in an elevator." Hollis pats me on the shoulder and walks away.

I barely spare him a glance, though it's highly problematic that he's noticed the way I look at Lexi. I don't know what she was thinking, bringing her dad to the Watering Hole last week with the whole team there. Hollis asked about it the next morning on the way to practice. I pretended I had no idea what he was talking about and switched the subject to holiday plans, all the while feeling like a hypocrite for doing exactly what he and Peggy did last season. I wonder if this is how he felt when he was hiding what was going on with Peggy at the start of their relationship. I'm not sure how I missed his caginess, or the way he looked at her. Maybe I didn't want to see it.

Lexi crosses the room, heading for the bar, so I do the same. I need to be in her orbit for a minute. Her head turns, as if she can sense my approach. Her throat bobs with a nervous swallow, and her tongue sweeps across her bottom lip.

"Hi, Coach Forrester." I prop my elbows on the bar top and try not to look directly at her.

"Hello, Goalie." Her gaze locks with mine in the reflection behind the mirrored bar. Her fingers flutter around her collarbones before she drops them and clasps her hands.

I order a scotch, neat. I need something stronger than beer with her looking the way she does. "Where's your date?"

"He's not available tonight. Yours?"

"Can't have her."

Just because we've acknowledged our mutual attraction doesn't mean she sees what we could be the same way I do. How I could be the one she spends her nights and mornings with. Though I can't imagine she's had time to date anyone since she arrived in Toronto. Not with an eight-year-old and a seventeen-year-old to take care of, on top of coaching a professional hockey team.

The bartender passes her a glass of ginger ale. Lexi isn't much for the taste of alcohol. We move away from the bar, and she turns to face me. "You can't look at me like that, Roman."

"We're not on the ice. You can't tell me what to do, Alexandria." I sip my scotch to hide my smile at her frustrated expression.

"Seriously, this needs to stop. I feel like I'm wearing a scarlet letter whenever you're around." She keeps looking to the side, clearly nervous to be seen talking to me.

"As far as anyone knows, we're just two people who work for the same team having a conversation. Unless you've told someone," I press.

"I haven't told a soul." Her emphasis is offensive.

"Why? Are you embarrassed?"

She rolls her eyes. "You players are all the same. Egos like eggshells. That has nothing to do with it. This is my job, Roman, and I've worked hard to be here. We can't keep dancing around each other like this. Someone will notice."

I don't tell her someone already has. I've considered confiding in Hollis, but he's dating my daughter, and I don't know if he'd be able to keep this from her.

"Whoa, this looks heated. You two debating the merits of Ash and Grace playing on the same line?" Flip asks. "Perhaps recognizing the error of your ways, Coach?"

I don't know where he came from, but the fact that we're having this discussion in the middle of a public place speaks to how fired up we are. I shift my attention to him. "It seems you have feelings about that."

Flip shrugs, attempting nonchalance. "Ash plays best when he's on the same line as Dallas. So yeah, maybe Grace is better behaved for the time being, but it's dragging Ash down."

I'm a second away from telling him to watch his mouth, but Lexi beats me to it.

"First of all, regardless of the casual setting, I'm still your coach. You don't get to tell me how to do my job. And secondly, it's your behavior that's problematic. Your negativity toward your teammate directly affects everyone's performance on the ice."

"But he—"

"I don't want excuses. You and Grace need to deal with your decade old grudge and get over it. This isn't high school, this is the pros, and I expect more from you. Especially since you'll be one of the more seasoned players on the ice after your goalie retires. What is the legacy you want to leave behind?"

Flip opens and closes his mouth. "I just want to keep the team intact."

Lexi's expression softens and her defensive posture relaxes slightly. "I get it. There's been a lot of change, professionally and personally for you. But we can't fight change. It happens whether we want it to or not. You can be part of the solution or part of the problem, Flip."

"I'm not the only problem, though," Flip states.

"No, you're not. But someone has to be the bigger man. And wouldn't you rather it be you?" Lexi arches a sexy, expectant brow.

"Coach has a point," I say.

Flip's defensive posture deflates.

"Think about it. And in the meantime, go enjoy your night."

"Yes, Coach." Flip heads toward the boys, rubbing the back of his neck as he goes.

"You're fucking gorgeous when you're schooling these boys," I say.

Her head snaps in my direction. "I need to use the ladies' room." She skirts around me and moves toward the hall.

And like the obsessed, completely out-of-control man I am, I leave my scotch on the bar and follow her. We're alone in the hall, so I grab her hand, tugging her in the opposite direction of the bathrooms.

"What are you doing?"

That's a great fucking question. "We need to discuss a few things."

"This is not the time."

"It's never the time, Lexi." I try the handle on a conference room door. It opens, so I push my way inside, but drop her hand.

The lights flicker on automatically. She crosses the threshold, eyes on fire, and the door falls shut behind her. Energy crackles between us, familiar and heavy and desperate.

"I don't know what you want from me, Roman." She crosses her arms.

For you to give in to this horrible, awful, unreal draw we both feel. "I don't know if you're ready for what I want."

"What does that even mean?"

"I wish like hell I had an ounce of self-restraint when it comes to you, Lexi, but I really fucking don't." I drink her in. She's stunning and heated and all I can think about is how good it would feel to snap this wire of tension between us.

Like every other time we've found ourselves alone together, we've gravitated closer. One step on either of our parts and the toes of our shoes will touch.

She tips her head up. "We can't be alone together like this. There is too much at stake for me. I have everything to lose."

"You think I don't know that? Messing up this opportunity for you is the last thing I want. I'm trying to stay away, but I'm powerless against the draw. You're everything I want and can't have. It's killing me, Lexi. *You're* killing me," I grind out.

"You think it's any different for me? You think I wouldn't love to spend hours talking game strategy with you? Or that I don't love it when I see the pride on your face after I make a good call? I miss the way your arms feel around me. And I desperately miss the way the world would fall away when it's just you and me. You being right in front of me, but untouchable is torture, Roman."

We're both so worked up. So frustrated. "I'm at my breaking point. You should walk away."

Her tongue sweeps along her bottom lip. "I should."

I clench my fists at my side. "Tell me kissing you is a bad idea."

"The absolute worst," she whispers.

I give in to the urge to skim the edge of her jaw.

She whimpers, and that one sound nearly brings me to my knees.

Her hand settles on my chest.

"You should go."

"I can't." She grips my lapel and tips her chin up. "Please."

"What do you want, angel?" I curve my hand against her delicate cheek, the relief in being able to touch her overwhelming.

"You." The whispered word floats between us.

I pull her against me. "Soften for me."

And she does. Instantly. Perfectly. Every curve melding to my hard lines.

Her lips part on a needy sigh, and I angle her head, taking control of the kiss. All the frustration slips away as she moans into my mouth. She loops her arms around my neck, holding me tightly as our tongues tangle and explore. Her mouth is bliss, the taste of her a balm for the ache that's been wrecking me.

The memory doesn't do the reality of Lexi justice. She's so soft under my touch, pliant and accommodating. Such a force on the ice and a pleaser in the bedroom.

"There you are. I've missed your sweet side," I praise.

She moans again, fingers sliding into my hair as she pushes up on her toes, fighting to get closer. I walk her back toward the conference table. Shoving a chair out of the way, I lift her, our mouths still fused as she adjusts her dress, and hooks one leg behind my knee.

She's as warm and rich as melted caramel on my tongue, and I can't get enough. Each seductive stroke takes me higher, makes me crave more. We're frantic—hands roaming, her heel digging into my ass cheek as I settle between her legs. We both groan when my erection presses between her thighs and she rocks her hips.

I keep one hand curved around the back of her neck. The other skims the outside of her thigh as I separate our mouths.

She makes a disappointed, plaintive sound.

"Are we done fighting?" I gently suck her bottom lip.

"So done." She moans and tilts her chin up, seeking more. "God, I've missed you so much."

I stroke her jaw with my thumb. "It's the same for me." It's a relief to be able to act on it, even if we shouldn't. "I've been dreaming of this tempting mouth." I drop my head, stroking inside once, twice, a third time, before I pull back again and press my hips into hers, eliciting a deep, primal moan. "Of those exquisite little whimpers when I made you come, of the scandalous things you can do with these pretty lips."

Our mouths collide again, hands gripping, bodies grinding. Somehow I knock one of the chairs over, and we both startle.

"Oh my God." Lexi's eyes dart around the room before settling on me again. "What are we doing?" She doesn't push me away, though.

"Giving in."

Her eyes fall closed as I run my thumb along the contour of her bottom lip, savoring what's left of this stolen moment.

When they open, they're full of the same yearning I feel. "I don't want to blow my life up, but staying away from you is breaking me apart."

I brush my lips over hers and straighten. I don't want to stop touching her, so I carefully smooth out her dress and help her to her feet. "We're almost halfway through the season. Once I retire, we're not breaking any rules."

"Six more months." She fingers the lapel of my tux. "I don't want to ruin this thing I've worked so hard for, but I don't want to lose the possibility of us either. I feel like I belong with you."

"That's because you do. And I belong with you. We can make it through playoffs and stay professional." *I hope.* "Go back to the party." I kiss her one last time, in case I don't get to do it again for several months.

When I try to pull back, she winds herself tighter around me. I gently pry her hands free and kiss her fingertips. It's agony to let her go again. If we stay in here much longer, I won't be able to resist her, and we risk getting caught. "Go find the girls, angel."

She nods, steadying herself. "Yes, Roman."

"Good girl." I press my lips to her temple and lead her to the door.

She runs her hands over her hips, smoothing out her dress. I make sure the coast is clear before she steps into the hall and heads for the ladies' room on not-entirely-steady legs.

I give myself a couple of minutes to get my body under control again before I leave the conference room. I pull my phone out and send Lexi a message.

ROMAN

Better than I remembered.

LEXI

I thought I'd romanticized how good it was. I was wrong. All I want is more.

ROMAN

Just a few months and we can have it all.

Waiting for the right time to show her how good it can be is the ultimate test of my self-control.

CHAPTER 16

LEXI

"Grace is playing clean tonight," Vander Zee observes as our enforcer gains control of the puck and shoots it to Bright, who takes it back down the ice, toward the opposition's net.

"He is." I follow the puck as Bright passes to Hendrix, then Grace, and back to Bright.

"The change up with Palaniappa was smart. I'm not the only one who's noticed," he adds.

I feel like I'm slowly earning my place here, becoming the asset he expects me to be. "They're playing with their skill set now, not their emotions."

It was a potentially risky move, especially with two less-seasoned players on the first defensive line, but over the past two weeks, it's allowed other players to shine, and Madden can handle the pressure. More than that, he needs to see how the rest of the players can elevate their game when given the chance, so he can do the same. If things continue on this trajectory, we could make some gains in the second half of the season. Two Cup wins in a row is rare, but making it to the finals would be great for team morale. And for Roman's final season.

The commentators have picked up on the shift, and while

they agree that it's been good for on-ice performance, they continue to bring up the glaring issue that Grace and Madden still aren't spending much time on the ice together. But during the last press conference, when Grace was interviewed, he credited me with the line change, and said he and Palaniappa work well together.

It makes what happened with Roman at the holiday party even more conflicting. Fraternization between staff and players is highly frowned upon. Being discovered could wipe out all the positive gains I'm making, yet my desire for him is a physical ache. I watched the situation with Hemi and Dallas unfold on social media last year, and while it was managed well, this is so much different. An assistant coach and a player in a relationship could jeopardize the entire team. Vander Zee and Fielding's leadership could be called into question. And if handled incorrectly, it will invariably ruin my career.

So there's really no choice but to give each other space until the end of the season. The holiday party was one transgression—a mistake made of hormones and pent up longing. *Once he's retired and there's distance between my role and his, we can pursue this.*

But can we be alone and not act on the chemistry? If he hadn't knocked over the chair that night, how far would it have gone? I shake my head and focus on the game, not the member of the team whose hands and lips I can't stop thinking about.

Toronto wins 2-1. It's particularly satisfying since we lost the last game against Detroit. I've learned that on nights like this, some of the players will hit the club. But Fee and Callie are here, so I fully expect to head straight home.

"I vote we go out for dessert tonight," Rix says.

Hemi perks up. "I'm a fan of dessert."

"There's a coffeehouse not far from my place that has the best cakes and ice cream sundaes. And I have class tomorrow at ten, so it'll ensure I get to bed at a reasonable time," Rix adds.

"Hemi and I have an early meeting with the women's team, so this is perfect," Hammer agrees.

"I never say no to cake and ice cream." Shilpa pulls out her phone. "I'll let Ash know, and he can tell the rest of the boys."

I send a message to Dred, on the off chance she can get out of work a little early. She couldn't make the game because she runs the adult evening literacy program.

LEXI

Going out for ice cream sundaes. Think you can join us?

DRED

☹ I'll have to take a rain check. One of my colleagues came down with the flu so now I have to close.

LEXI

Boo. Next time then.

DRED

10/10. Tell everyone I say hi and give Callie and Fee hugs from me.

LEXI

Will do! ♥

Half an hour later, we've taken over most of the cafe. Two of the girls behind the counter have died and gone to Flip Madden heaven. He signs hats and poses for pictures before he joins us at the table.

"This is ridiculously good. We should bring something home for Nate," Rix says as she passes the spoon back to Tristan.

"How's his hunt for an apartment going?" Flip asks.

"He's still looking, but we've told him there isn't a rush," Tristan replies.

Rix hugs his arm. "Bachelor apartments are small, and he's trying to save for a one bedroom. Finding something affordable is always the issue in the city."

"There's still a room at my place," Flip offers. "It's his if he wants it, for however long he wants it."

"Thanks, man." Tristan holds the spoon up to Rix's lips.

Knowing that Rix came from a house where they didn't always have enough makes me appreciate even more how soft Tristan can be with her.

Dallas and Hemi seem to be in a world of their own, while Ash and Shilpa trade their sundaes every few bites. Hollis sits with his arm across the back of Hammer's chair, his thumb sweeping back and forth along her shoulder.

There's so much love in this room, and so much pent-up tension flowing between me and Roman. He's seated across the table, and it takes all of my willpower not to cross my legs and brush my foot against his calf, just for the connection.

Callie is as close to him as she can be without sitting in his lap. *I feel you, girl.* She's abandoned her own sundae for his, and he doesn't seem to mind one bit. They're also playing tic-tac-toe on the back of a menu, and he lets her win every time. I'm doing my best to keep my eyes anywhere but on him. It's tough though, getting to see this soft side of him, while knowing what a filthy demon he can be behind closed doors.

Flip is next to me, shoveling ice cream into his face at a ridiculous speed.

"Are you even tasting that?" I ask.

"Fu–dge. I'm eating like I was raised in a barn, aren't I?" He sets his spoon down and wipes chocolate syrup from his chin.

"I mean, it is December. There's a pretty slim chance it'll melt on you."

He laughs. "Fair. I've been told I eat like it's always my last meal."

He glances toward the other end of the table where Fee and Tally talk animatedly. Tally's new boyfriend, who didn't come to the holiday party because he had a family thing, pokes at his cake and stares at his phone.

"I don't know about that guy." Flip stabs a chunk of brownie.

"Peggy says he's kind of quiet," Roman muses as he puts a green crayon O on the tic-tac-toe board.

"Tally's boyfriend?" Callie asks.

"Mm-hmm."

"He doesn't have a favorite player on the Terror. He said he roots for New York, probably because they have Kodiak Bowman," Callie says.

"Bowman is an excellent player," Roman says.

"He has pretty eyes and great scoring stats." Callie puts her hand on his arm and gives him an empathetic smile. "So you shouldn't feel too bad if he scores on you when you play them next."

"Are you expecting me to let a goal in for him?" he asks playfully.

"Of course not!" She huffs. "I'm just saying every game can't be perfect, and Kodiak has very strong stick-handling skills. Also, I heard he used to play hockey in his crib, so he was born to be on the ice."

Roman asks her what else she knows about Bowman, and I glance over at Tally. It doesn't matter how many games that guy comes to, he never really warms up. "Is this her first boyfriend?" I ask Flip.

"I think so. It's the first guy she's brought to games, anyway," he says. "I get that we all make mistakes, but I don't know. As someone who's made a ton of them, I'm not sure it was best for me to learn all those lessons the hard way." He sighs. "I don't want to see her get screwed around."

"We all experience heartbreak," I say, surprised at his openness and protectiveness for Tally.

"That's the truth. She has a real soft heart though. You just hope the person you fall for will give back what they get. It's a real taint punch when you realize you were the only one in it for love." He shakes his head. "Jeez. I need to stop watching reality dating shows with Dred."

I smile, but from the sound of it, someone hurt him. Badly.

"I miss Dred! You're so lucky you get to live next door to her," Callie says.

Flip smiles. "She's a good friend to have. Honest, loyal, and good at board games."

"I feel the same way. She's a rare gem. She's doesn't place expectations on people."

"She feels seen with you," Flip confides and motions to the table. "These girls have been good for her."

"She's been good for me and the girls, too," I reply.

"We all need a friend like her in our lives." I could try to use this as a segue to dig into his history with Grace, but I don't want to make it about that. Not when he's being real and honest and making me and the girls feel like part of their family.

"Ugh. I'm so full." Callie pushes Roman's sundae toward him and wilts against his side.

"You want me to finish my sundae for you?" Roman asks cheekily.

"Please." She slides her arm through his and hugs it, rubbing her eyes with her fists.

I'd be worried about her eating all this sugar so late in the evening, but they're off school for the holidays, so she can sleep in tomorrow morning.

Roman and I exchange a smile, and he digs into his dessert, finishing what she couldn't. Twenty minutes later, we're ready to go, but Callie is completely passed out.

"I'll carry her to the car. It's my fault she crashed so hard with all the sugar I let her eat," Roman offers.

"I could have stopped her," I argue.

"I'll own this one."

I quickly hug the girls goodbye before Roman scoops Callie up and carries her to the waiting car. Our fingers brush as I help secure her seat belt, and it's everything I can do not to huff his cologne. The memory of that kiss, of his hands on my skin and tongue sweeping my mouth still feels fresh.

"Thank you. You were really sweet with her tonight," I whisper as I carefully close the door.

"Honestly, it was my pleasure. Drive safe, Lexi." He holds my door open while I climb into the driver's seat. "'Night, Fee. I'll see you again soon."

She waves and smiles. "Bye, Roman."

He steps back and waves as we exit the lot.

"Roman's a really good guy, isn't he?" Fee muses.

"Yeah, he is." He's the complete package.

She glances over her shoulder, checking on her sister in the back seat. "Callie loves him."

"Yeah, she basically ate his sundae tonight, and he let her."

"Sounds like Callie." She leans her head against the rest. "This team feels like a family."

"It is." I give her a soft, sad smile. "I know no one can replace Mom and your dad, but it's nice to have people in our lives who fill some of those empty spaces."

"Yeah. I'm glad we moved here, Lex."

"Me, too."

And that's the reminder I need to watch myself with Roman. Fee and Callie have already lost too much. They can't lose this new family, too.

CHAPTER 17

ROMAN

ROMAN

Reason number 6982 why I can't wait for the end of the season.

I follow it with a picture of an oversized bathtub filled with bubbles and rose petals. It's the tub we spent a glorious hour engaging in the most torturous, incredible foreplay before I carried Lexi—soapy and needy—back to bed, where I fucked three orgasms out of her.

It's been sixteen days, seven hours, and five minutes since we shared that kiss at the holiday party, and I can't stop thinking about it—or every single other kiss, touch, and sensual moment we've ever had.

Lexi responds a minute later with an image of apple slices and caramel sauce. That weekend started my green apple addiction. That's when I learned exactly how much of a pleaser she is, and how amazing her sweet mouth felt when she was trying to swallow my entire cock, like a good girl.

ROMAN

You're killing me.

LEXI

You started it.

ROMAN

Hmm... True. I'll cease the torment for both our sakes.

Waiting for the season to end is increasingly challenging. If it was just sexual chemistry, it might be fine. But it's so much more than that. When she's in the room, my eyes are on her. We're on the ice together constantly.

She's smart, driven, and has quickly gained the respect of the team. Watching her confidence blossom as she leads this team is inspiring. I'm falling more for her every day. For her take-no-shit attitude on the ice, the soft moments when she gives a player a pep talk, the woman who has lost so much and puts everything she has left into her sisters, and the friend my daughter and the rest of the girls have embraced so wholly.

She would fit seamlessly into my life and world, and it's the most unreal mindfuck to be frozen like this. That we're adults with a history doesn't matter. Should something happen now, she'd forever be the assistant coach who was involved with one of her players.

Even if we don't make it to the playoffs, I have another four months of limbo ahead of me. *I could retire early*. It's not the first time I've rolled this possibility over in my head.

ROMAN

How are you and the girls holding up?

LEXI

That was a hard right.

ROMAN

I know. Don't evade the question.

LEXI

We're okay. It's just hard for them.

ROMAN

What about you?

LEXI

I'm managing.

Lexi is unaccustomed to asking for help, let alone accepting it. But it doesn't mean I have to sit back and let her drown in the difficulty of it all. I know what it means to miss the people you love during the holidays.

LEXI

Callie has a hockey party. Talk later. Thanks for checking in, though.

ROMAN

I'm around if you need to talk.

LEXI

I work out, manage some paperwork, call my mom who's on a cruise with one of her cousins for the holidays, and read some of the documentation Hollis sent me about the Hockey Academy. It's an increasingly attractive retirement option. Early in the afternoon, I place an order for all of Peggy's favorite things from our favorite Thai restaurant. I'm a glutton for punishment.

My phone chimes with new messages.

HOLLIS

It's not too late to change your mind and come to Niagara.

There's more than enough room for you at the table.

A picture of a smiling Peggy follows. She looks happy and beautiful and like she's having a great time with Hollis's family.

The invitation is enticing. But this is their first Christmas as a couple. I've spent more than enough holidays with Hollis's family over the years. Every other Christmas, Peggy would visit her mom and I'd go to Niagara with Hollis. But they need the opportunity to create their own traditions. And I need to step back and give them the space to do that, even though it's hard. We'll celebrate when they return.

ROMAN

Thanks for the offer, but I'm good. I'll see you two in a couple of days. Have a great time.

I slide my feet into a pair of boots, shrug into my winter jacket, pull on a toque, and head out to pick up my Thai. Light snow blankets the sidewalk. The streetlights are decorated with twinkling white lights and holly garland. Couples walk arm in arm, smiling and laughing. Businessmen rush down the street, laden with bags.

The familiar lightning bolt of loneliness strikes me. I've spent my whole adult life focused on Peggy and hockey, unwilling to put anyone else in front of her. I couldn't let someone else into my heart when I believed my daughter needed it the most.

I open the door to the Thai restaurant. Usually I find the rich scents comforting, but today it hits differently. This has been our tradition since Peggy came to live with me a decade and a half ago. The holidays were too quiet when she was living with her mom. When it was my year with her, we ate takeout on Christmas Eve and opened our stockings before bed. I still have a ton of presents waiting for her when she and Hollis get back. I'm beginning to understand why Peggy keeps pushing me to date. Spending the holidays alone is pretty fucking shitty.

The bell over the door tinkles, and I glance back to find Connor Grace brushing snow off his shoulders. He's polished and tailored, apart from the ball cap pulled low, the bill covering his face. I knew he lived somewhere around here, but I'm still surprised to see him. I assumed he'd be with family for the holidays. Or at the very least, his grandmother.

"Hey."

He startles, but when he realizes it's me, his shoulders come down from his ears. "Oh, hey, Roman. Picking up dinner for the fam?"

"Just for me," I reply. "How about you?"

His eyebrows rise. "Uh, same. Where's Hammer?"

"In Niagara with Hollis's family." I tuck my hands into my pockets.

"Ah." He nods. "That must be a change."

He's a perceptive kid. "Yeah. It's their first Christmas together. I want them to have time with Hollis's family."

"Makes sense." He shakes the snow off his ball cap. "Can't be easy, though."

I shrug. "It's an adjustment." After this season, my entire life will be an adjustment. Dad life? She doesn't need me like she used to. Hockey? I'll be retired. I need to make some decisions on what's next so I'm not completely untethered.

The door tinkles again. This time a woman wearing a burgundy knitted toque, complete with pompom and matching scarf that covers all but her eyes, joins us. She tilts her head when she sees us. For a moment I think we've found ourselves a Terror fan, but then she unravels the scarf.

"Dred?"

"Roman! Hey!" Her face lights up and then shifts to wary curiosity when she sees Connor. "And Grace. You're an unlikely pair."

"We're not together," Connor explains.

She makes a noise but doesn't comment further. "Looks like I'm not the only one who loves Christmas Eve Thai takeout."

The woman who runs the restaurant appears with three bags. "Sorry for the wait!"

We all murmur a variation of *no problem,* and Connor reaches for the bag with tamarind curry at the same time as Dred.

"Oh! Sorry!" Dred yanks her hand back and grips both ends

of her scarf.

Connor raises both hands. "My fault. I think we ordered the same thing."

We all peer at the receipts. The order is exactly the same, down to the sticky rice and mango salad sides.

"Huh." Dred picks up her bag and returns her attention to me. "I thought Hammer was in Niagara for Christmas Eve."

"She is." I grab my bag.

"So you're on your own?" Dred presses.

"Yup."

She looks to Connor. "And you?"

"Same."

"Me too. We're quite the trio of misfits, aren't we?"

"Why aren't you with your family?" Connor asks.

For a moment I feel bad. He doesn't know Dred or her history.

"I don't have any." She says this like she's giving a weather report.

"Shit. I'm sorry." He adjusts the brim of his hat.

"My parents were drug addicts, so I doubt Christmas would be all that enjoyable if they were still alive." She makes a face. "Oh my God. Sorry. Neither of you needed to know that."

"It's legit though," Connor replies.

"Mmm… And why are you solo on Christmas Eve?" Dred quickly shifts the focus away from her.

"My parents took my sisters and grandmother on vacation for the holidays and didn't tell me until last night, when they were already in Cabo," Connor says. "Not that it's the same, but still unfortunate."

If I didn't know he was the heir to a hotel chain, I might have assumed his family were long gone like Dred's too. Whenever they ask about his dad in interviews, he pivots or walks out.

"Yikes. That's rough." Dred and Connor look to me.

"My dad's been gone for a long time, and my mom and her cousin are on a cruise so the holidays hurt less for her." Apparently I feel like sharing today, too. "You can both come back to my place, if you want."

"You allowed to be in the same room as me?" Connor asks Dred.

She laughs. "I won't tell if you don't."

"I like my teeth where they are, so your secret is safe with me."

"Come on, kids. It's misfits' Christmas Eve at my place."

We grab our food and pile into Connor's sports car, with poor Dred crammed in the tiny back seat eating her knees. I offered her the front, but she just laughed and said no. A handful of minutes later, we're back at my place, gathered at my dining room table.

"We should have invited Lexi and the girls," Dred says as she uses chopsticks to move half the mango salad to her plate.

"Callie has a hockey party tonight," I say without thinking.

Dred lifts an eyebrow, like she's surprised I know this. "Of course she does. That girl lives and breathes hockey."

"She is so fucking adorable," Connor says. "And she has great taste in hockey players."

"Of course you'd say that," I tease. "But she is adorable."

"She has the chops for the Hockey Academy, if she keeps it up," Connor adds.

"She's an excellent goalie, from what I've seen," Dred agrees.

I set my fork down. It's an opportunity I can't pass up. "I have a question about the Hockey Academy."

Connor pokes at his mango salad, a flush working its way up his neck. "They have a great program, and it got me out of my parents' hair for the summer. It worked out well for all of us. Especially them."

"You were there at the same time as Madden, Bright, and Stiles, right?"

"Yup." He pops a bite of mango salad into his mouth.

"What's the deal with you and Madden's sandwich?"

Dred nearly spit-sprays her wine across the table. As it is,

Connor chokes on his food. Dred is out of her chair between one blink and the next, ready to take action.

Connor holds up his hand. "I'm fine." He coughs twice more. "Did Madden say something to you?"

I shake my head.

Connor rolls his eyes to the ceiling, the tips of his ears bright red. "Why can't I escape my past?"

"You have to deal with it to get past it," Dred replies.

For someone in her early twenties, she sure is self-aware.

Connor sighs. "Everyone loved Madden at the Hockey Academy. Everyone always loves Madden. Even when he does questionable shit. I was an asshole with a chip on my shoulder, and he was the golden boy. No one was ever going to be on my side."

"Have you tried to have a conversation?" Dred asks.

"What's the point? He'll believe what he wants. Doesn't matter if it's the truth or a lie." He pushes his chair back from the table. "I'm going to go."

"Please don't," Dred says softly. "Roman isn't trying to corner you. We just want to understand. But we can drop it, can't we?" She gives me an imploring look.

"Yeah. Absolutely. Sorry I brought it up."

"It's just... The Hockey Academy is what got me here, but the road wasn't easy. If it means I'm forever the villain, then that's what I'll be." He picks up his chopsticks.

"Noted. Leaving it alone." I change the subject. "What are everyone's plans for tomorrow?"

"I'm planning to stop by Lexi's with gifts for her and the girls at some point." Dred points a chopstick at each of us. "What about you two?"

"More of this." I point to my takeout. "Peggy and Hollis aren't coming back until Boxing Day."

"I plan to binge the *Die Hard* movies while drinking all day tomorrow and be hungover on Boxing Day," Connor says.

Day drinking alone on Christmas sounds like the opposite of

a good time. Being alone with Lexi will test my willpower. But if I have company…

"Could you put that plan on hold until later in the day?" I ask.

"I mean, it's a pretty depressing plan, so I'm up for alternatives," Connor replies.

"Great. I have an idea for Lexi and the girls, but I need both of you to pull it off." I look to Dred.

"Whatever it is, I'm in," Dred says. "Especially if it means we can make the holidays better for Lexi."

CHAPTER 18

LEXI

"Mommy, Mom! Daddy!" Callie bursts into my room, and the door bangs into the wall.

I sit up with a start, the hairs on my arms standing on end, a wave of goose bumps covering my skin. Callie stops short when she reaches my bed. Her lips pull down in a frown, and she hugs her stuffed axolotl to her chest.

"Did you have a dream?" It wouldn't be the first time.

She nods, and her chin wobbles. "It felt so real. I thought it was."

"I'm so sorry." I open my arms. Callie clambers up onto the bed and into my lap, her mournful wails making my chest ache. I stroke her hair while I rock her. Mom used to do it for her when she was little.

"I just want them back. That's all I wanted for Christmas. I wrote a letter to Santa and everything." She hiccups and sobs even harder.

This kind of pain is soul crushing. I'm angry at my stepdad for being reckless, for taking himself and our mother away from us. She wasn't perfect, but she was always there for my sisters when it counted. And now here I am, trying to fill her shoes and worried I'm failing.

I rock Callie until her sobs slow to a sniffle and the occasional hiccup. "Should I make you hot chocolate and we can eat sugar cookies for breakfast?"

She nuzzles into my neck. "Can we eat chocolate too?"

"I bought chocolate hazelnut croissants," I whisper.

Even though they're red-rimmed, her eyes light up. "Really? And we can have them for breakfast?"

Usually they're an afternoon treat, but I can't see her this sad on Christmas.

"Yup. Why don't you wake up your sister?"

"Okay." She slides off the edge of the bed, Axel still clutched to her chest as she rushes down the hall, calling Fee's name.

I flop down on my mattress and work to compartmentalize the pain in my heart. I need to be strong for the girls. *Please let that be the hardest part of today.*

I grab my phone from my nightstand and check my messages. I have one from my dad and Jacqueline, who are in the Bahamas because her birthday is on Christmas Eve.

There are new ones in the Badass Babe Brigade chat:

HEMI

Merry Christmas! I've already posted this to Dallas's feed while he was in a sugar coma last night.

A photo of Hemi with her family and Dallas's gathered in the living room of one of their houses follows. Dallas is dressed in an elf onesie, chatting with Hemi's brother.

HAMMER

I'm sure he'll appreciate all his new followers. Check out the sweater I made Hollis wear last night.

An image of Hollis wearing an ugly Grinch sweater, looking happily annoyed is under the message.

TALLY

10/10 on both of these! The boyfriend just arrived, and I'm still in my jammies. Merry Christmas! I need to get downstairs before my dad corners him.

RIX

Love you all! Hope today is wonderful for you! Look at these boys. 😍

A blurry close-up of Rix's eyes and the top of her mom's head in the foreground and Tristan and Flip surrounded by their respective dads and Tristan's brothers, all wearing holiday-themed Terror sweaters, pops up.

SHILPA

Merry Christmas!

Ash and Shilpa are cuddled on the couch, wearing matching holiday sweaters and drinking out of matching holiday mugs.

DRED

Good tidings from me and Dewey.

She adds a selfie of her and her hedgehog, both wearing Santa hats.

ESSIE

Me, my spiked coffee, and my sister all wish you the merriest of Christmases.

She has her arm wrapped around her half-asleep sister, who is dressed in pajama bottoms and a hoodie that has Gandalf from Lord of the Rings dressed as Santa on it.

It's our second Christmas without our mom, and it hurts just as much as it did last year.

LEXI

Happy Holidays, everyone! I'll send pictures once I've brushed my hair.

Hopefully by then Callie won't look like she's been crying.

I send a private message to Dred. She volunteers a lot around the holidays, so she may be already out and about.

LEXI

Merry Christmas. How's it going?

DRED

At the soup kitchen! Already made two hundred pounds of mashed potatoes. I should be done in a couple of hours.

LEXI

Super excited to have you here with us for dinner!

DRED

Same! I have a pie (made by Rix) in my fridge that I haven't touched.

LEXI

😮 I hear her pies are legendary.

DRED

I can confirm they are magical. Flip routinely makes himself sick on them.

LEXI

Are you sure you want to share it?

DRED

With you and the girls? Absolutely.

I already feel better. The girls love Dred, and she's become a good friend here in Toronto.

New messages pop up from Roman as I roll out of bed.

ROMAN

Merry Christmas. *holiday GIF*

If you and the girls need anything at all today, even if it's takeout, just message. I'm here. I know how hard today is.

I desperately want to invite him over. If he was here it would fill one of the gaping holes in my chest, but it will only make things more difficult. We haven't been in a room alone since the holiday party, and the idea of being in his arms again has been all-consuming. The end of the season is impossibly far away.

LEXI

Merry Christmas to you, too. Thank you for the offer. I'm hoping hot chocolate, croissants, and cookies for breakfast will win me some points.

I throw on a robe so I can put on a pot of coffee. I've just gotten started when Callie shows up in tears again.

"What happened?" I crouch so we're at eye level.

"I tried to wake Fee up, and she told me to stop being annoying and go away." She uses her sleeve to wipe her runny nose. "And then she said Christmas was canceled. Is that true?"

"Christmas isn't canceled." I grab a tissue from the counter and pull her into a hug. "Fee's just grumpy. She probably stayed up too late watching movies. I'll talk to her." I pile several cookies and croissants on a plate and fill Callie's mug with hot chocolate and marshmallows before I seat her at the table. "I'll be right back."

"Okay."

I kiss her on top of the head and leave her to eat sweets while I handle Fee. Dealing with hormonal, testosterone-fueled hockey players is easier than a sad teenager.

I channel the little holiday joy I have left and knock on her door.

"I'm sleeping," she gripes.

"I'm coming in anyway." I open her door in time to watch

her bury her head under her pillow. Undeterred, I sit on the edge of her bed. Coming in hot won't help. "I know today is hard."

She tosses her pillow aside and rolls over to glare at me, but her eyes are red-rimmed and puffy, like she's been crying for some time. "Christmas is supposed to be about family. Everyone I know is celebrating with theirs, and I just... I miss Mom and Dad so much. Mom used to take care of everything, and I didn't even realize it. I thought this year was going to be fun, but there's so much responsibility, and sometimes it's exhausting."

Pain makes my chest tight. I know that feeling all too well. All my failures are piling up, crushing me under their weight. I'm not doing a good enough job. My mom and my stepdad were both only children, and my grandparents are back in Niagara, so they can't be much help. Their old next-door neighbor, Donna a.k.a. Aunt Donna, is a nice woman, but she has grandchildren of her own and can't hold my hand. But what if I fuck up the girls beyond repair?

My own chin wobbles, because the weight of it all is crushing me. "I know, Fee. I'm so sorry. I wish I could ask what to do and how to do it better, because most of the time I have no idea. But Callie is out there crying because you told her to go away and Christmas was canceled."

"There's nothing to celebrate," she whispers, caught up in the emotion of it all.

I wish I could fix it, but I can't. "I know all you want is to be sad. But you can't decide for all of us if something is worth celebrating or not. You knew saying that would be hurtful to your sister, especially today. We are a family and we are still here. Missing Mom and your dad makes your heart feel like a giant skinned knee. There's a hole here." I tap over my heart. "And we miss them. But they loved you." I take in a deep breath, struggling to keep it together as tears track down her cheeks., wishing there was someone to hold me while I fall apart too.

"They loved you too, you know?" Fee links her fingers with mine.

My heart is a battered soda can. Knowing that's true and having felt it fully when they were alive is so different. With another deep exhale, I continue, "They loved us. We are alive and here, and we're going to be the kindest version of ourselves today that we can muster. We're going to be gentle with each other, which includes a little girl who doesn't understand that some days you just need to hide under the blankets and be really fucking sad. I love you, Fee. We've done a lot to survive, and I would say it is going to get easier and maybe it will, but mostly this is life now. There's no going back. But you can decide how you want to love the family you do have." I pass her a tissue and she dabs her tears away.

"I'm sorry I told Callie Christmas was canceled."

"I know. Just come out and do Christmas morning. If you need time after that, I'll totally understand."

She sighs. "Okay. Give me fifteen minutes."

I pat her leg. "Thank you, and I'm really sorry today hurts extra. I'll make you a mochaccino."

"With whipped cream?"

"As if I would leave out the whipped cream."

She throws her arms around me. "I love you."

"I love you, too."

I leave her room and pull the door closed behind me.

A wave of sadness threatens to pull me under. I'm so overwhelmed. I miss having a family, even though they weren't perfect. I'm drowning in the responsibility of all, choking on the loneliness. All I want is to curl up in bed and let my own tears fall. But I can't. There's one person I want more than anyone else right now. One person who seems to understand better than most how difficult today is.

But if I give in and call Roman, I'm not sure I won't give in to everything else, too.

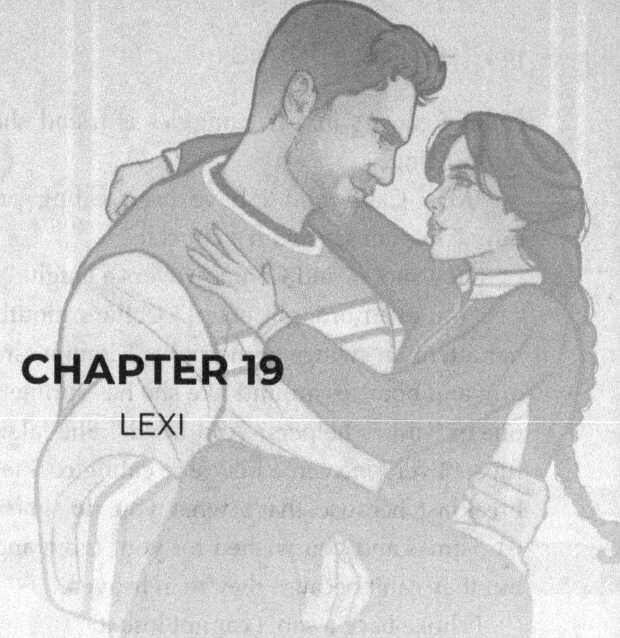

CHAPTER 19

LEXI

I've just managed to get my feelings back inside the box when there's a knock at the door. I frown as I check the time. It's barely nine. I'm so not prepared for company. I'm still in a robe, and I'm sure I look a wreck. But Callie is already rushing down the hall.

"Callie, wait until I'm with you before you open the door," I call after her.

As soon as I'm in view, she throws it open.

"Ho ho ho, Merry Christmas!" Santa and his two unlikely elves say.

"Santa? Oh my gosh! Lexi, Santa is here!" Callie exclaims.

I nearly burst into tears. Because standing in the hall is Roman, dressed as a very convincing Santa—minus the incredibly buff arms that pull at the seams of his red suit—and two elves in the form of Dred and…Connor Grace?

Dred is all smiles, and Connor is wearing his customary smirk.

Callie tips her head back. "Wow, Santa. You're tall. And not as friend shaped as I expected."

I almost die. "Friend shaped" is what her teacher calls her

chonky cat. As in, Mr. Snuggles is friend shaped and excellent for hugging.

"Mrs. Claus and I have been eating pretty healthy these days," Roman says with a chuckle.

Dred snorts, and Connor covers a laugh.

"You even brought elves!" Callie's mouth opens in an O as her attention swings to the right. "Connor Grace?" She grabs my arm and bounces around like she has springs in her feet. "You're one of Santa's helpers? And Dred!" She takes Santa's hand and tugs. "Everyone come in! We're eating cookies and croissants for breakfast because that's what you do when you wake up on Christmas and you wished for your mom and dad to come back but they can't because they're in heaven."

I choke back a sob. I cannot lose it.

Dred pulls me in for a hug. Roman gives me an empathetic, concerned smile and skims the back of my hand when he passes. Callie drags him and Connor down the hall, talking a mile a minute.

"You okay?" Dred asks, eyes full of concern.

"This morning has been rough, and it's barely started. I can't tell you how happy I am that you're here."

"Deep breath. We've got you." She hugs me again.

"Thank you." I squeeze and step back. "Where did you get these costumes, and whose idea was this?"

"The idea was Roman's, but we do a whole holiday-themed thing at the library every year, so I borrowed the costumes. As I'm sure you've noticed, the previous elf was a lot smaller than Connor."

I glance over my shoulder. His pants are capris, his socks pulled up to meet the cuff and the shirt sleeves are six inches shy of his wrists, exposing a hint of artwork. It's also at risk of busting at the seams across his shoulders. "Not too many six-three elves out there, I guess."

"Apparently not. How you hanging in there?"

"Close to breaking to be honest."

"We'll hold you together." She hugs me again.

"It means so much that you're my friend and you're here."

"There's nowhere we'd rather be. Also, Connor in an elf suit is pretty fucking spectacular, and I plan to take many, many photos." She inclines her head toward the living room. "Come on, let's make some new memories."

"Sounds good." I'm so grateful I don't have to handle today on my own.

"We've had this tree my whole life," Callie explains. "My mom was allergic to pine sap, so we couldn't have a real one. And all the ornaments are homemade. We make them for each other every year."

"We do the same thing at the North Pole, don't we, Elf Connor!" Roman exclaims.

"Yup. Sure do." Connor inspects a clay snowman. "It's a pretty bomb-ass tree."

"It looks like an art project gone awry," I whisper.

But I love it so much. Everyone else in our neighborhood had thematically decorated trees, and we had one in the front room that was for show, but we also always had the family tree after Fee and Callie were born.

"Can I offer anyone some coffee or hot chocolate?" I ask.

"I would love it most if you mixed the two together," Connor says.

"That sounds delicious." Roman pats his flat stomach and *ho hos*.

Dred helps me doctor up the coffees, and when we return, I pause at the threshold. "Why does he have to be so obscenely kind?" Callie is sitting on Roman's lap, telling him about her dream.

"Oh, my dear friend. What a complicated world we live in." She gives me a look. "I know you think you're not supposed to have feelings about or for that man, but Roman was born to do three things: play hockey, be the best kind of dad, and love people. As I mentioned, this was his idea."

"He's just being nice for my sisters."

"I've seen the way he looks at you, Lexi."

I side eye her.

"You deserve someone like him." She smiles softly. "But I'll pretend I don't see or feel the tension between you two."

We pass out the drinks, and I set a tray of chocolate croissants on the coffee table.

"Santa brought us presents!" Callie exclaims.

"I'll get Fee. She won't want to miss this." I head down the hall and knock on her door.

"I'll be out in a few minutes!"

"Can I come in for a sec?"

I hear her groan, but she follows with a yes.

I slip inside. "Santa and his elves are here."

She wrinkles her nose. "Uhh…"

"Let me rephrase that. Roman is here, dressed as a very convincing Santa."

Her brow furrows. "On Christmas?"

"Yeah. And Dred and Connor Grace are here as helper elves. Callie fully believes he's Santa, though."

Her eyes go wide. "Oh my God. Connor's so hot. Why didn't you tell me they were coming?"

"I didn't know until they showed up at the door. And Connor is way too old for you." He may also have done something to Flip's sandwich at some point that inspired a decade-long grudge, so I have questions, even if he's choosing to be a nice guy today.

She rolls her eyes. "Hammer is with Hollis, and he's twelve years older than she is."

She has a point. And I'm over here lusting over a man a decade older than me. But I'm closing in on thirty and she's still in high school. It's not the same. "They weren't dating when she was seventeen. In fact, they weren't dating until she was almost twenty-one. That's not the point. Just get your ass out there because Callie would like to open presents, and I'm sure you'd like to say hi to Dred since I'm not sure how long they're staying."

"Give me five." She pushes me out the door.

As promised, she joins us in the living room five minutes later, fully dressed, wearing makeup.

"Fifi, look! It's Santa! And Dred and Connor Grace are his helper elves!" Callie is happily perched between Roman and Connor. She's still wearing pajamas, but I stopped in my room to throw on jeans and a sweater and brush my hair—and teeth.

Fee waves and blushes.

Roman winks, and Dred gets up to give her a hug.

"Perfect! Now that everyone is here, you can open your presents!" Santa *ho hos* as he rummages around in his red sack and passes gifts to the girls.

Fee waits for Callie to go first. She tears into the paper and squeals with absolute delight. "I've been looking at these gloves forever! Thank you, Santa!" She squeezes Roman's neck.

"You're welcome, Callie. I'm glad you like them. Every goalie needs a favorite pair of gloves."

"These will be my lucky gloves! I just know it!"

Those gloves are unbelievably expensive. I've been waiting for a holiday sale so I can get them for her. She must have said something to Roman about it when we were out with the team for dessert. It's the only way he could have known.

Fee opens her gift next. "Oh my gosh! This is a bound edition of *Valiant*—I can't even." She flips the pages. "It's signed? To me? Oh my gosh! Thank you so much, Santa!" She rushes over to hug Roman, then stares lovingly at the book.

"And now it's your turn, Lexi." Santa passes me a small box.

"What's this?"

"Santa always brings gifts for everyone, even the biggest sister." He winks and sits back in his chair looking like he absolutely belongs here. Next year could be so different. I could be his again, and he could be mine. We wouldn't have to sit on opposite sides of the room, or fight this painful draw.

I focus on the gift, so I don't start crying, and tear through the paper, noting the care that went into wrapping the presents.

Inside is a gift certificate for three mani-pedis at the place Hemi always raves about. It's thoughtful, kind, and honestly a wonderful gift, because I can treat the girls to something fun. "Thank you, Santa. This is perfect."

I don't waste the opportunity to show my appreciation through a hug. Roman stands, and it doesn't matter that he's wearing a Santa suit, my entire body responds when his arms come around me. Like I've just found my home. "Thank you. You have no idea how much better you've made today," I whisper.

"It's better for me, too," he replies softly.

I release him, not wanting anyone else to pick up on the energy between us—especially because it feels very much like I'm falling for this man.

Santa and the elves finish their hot chocolate and croissants before Santa tells us he has to return to the North Pole or he'll be late for dinner with Mrs. Claus.

Callie wrings her hands. "Do you all have to go?"

"I can stick around," Dred offers.

"I'm off duty now, so I can hang out for a bit, too," Connor assures her. "But I need to change out of my elf gear so Santa can take it back to the North Pole."

Callie nods. "You should definitely get Connor a new elf suit. He's too big for this one."

"He had quite the growth spurt this year!" Roman claps Connor on the shoulder and tosses in another *ho ho ho*.

We all try not to laugh.

It's a flurry of hugs, and Callie rushes down the hall to change out of her pajamas.

I walk the three of them to the door. "Thank you so much for this."

"Way better than spending Christmas Day drunk," Connor says.

"Absolutely our pleasure. We'll be back in a few." Roman winks.

My heart stutters. I check to make sure the girls aren't in hearing range. "Where are you getting changed?" Hopefully not in a car.

"I live a couple buildings down," Connor says.

"Oh, I didn't realize."

"I moved at the beginning of the month. We'll be quick."

"Okay."

While they're off changing out of their costumes, my dad calls. "How are you and the girls doing?" he asks. "Have they had a chance to open their gifts yet?"

"Not yet. Santa stopped by with his elves this morning." I check to make sure Callie isn't around. "A couple of the guys from my team and one of my friends set it up. Callie was over the moon."

"I'm so glad to hear that. I'm sorry I can't be there with you."

I get it. They spent last Christmas with us, and it's Jacqueline's birthday, but it still hurts. "It's okay. Are you having a good time in the Bahamas?"

"It's beautiful here. Send me pictures of you and the girls when they open their presents."

"Of course."

There's a knock at the door, so I let him go with promises of photos from today.

"Look who I found!" Connor claps Roman on the shoulder. The three of them are laden with gift bags and food.

I usher them back into the living room, and Callie's eyes light up all over again. "First Santa, and now my two favorite hockey players are here? This is the best!" Callie hugs Roman, then turns to Connor, who has changed into jeans, a black button down that covers those tattoos on his arms, and a faux Santa hat with the Grinch on it. "I love the Grinch. I think he's misunderstood."

"I relate," Connor says with a wink and smile.

Roman joins us in the living room and listens raptly while

Callie tells him about the visit with Santa. There are more gifts for the girls—thoughtful, cute things that make them smile.

We play board games—Dred destroys all of us—and make the elaborate gingerbread Zamboni Roman brought over. What started as the second-worst Christmas of Callie and Fee's life, and probably mine, turns into a wonderful celebration and amazing new memories. I want this feeling to last, but I worry it will disappear when they all have to leave later.

When it's time to think about eating an actual meal, Roman helps me in the kitchen with dinner while the girls and Dred and Connor set the table.

"Thank you so much for doing this," I whisper as we stand side by side, assembling the stuffing. Throwing dinner together is easy since I ordered it from a local restaurant.

He covers my hand with his. "I'd rather be here with you all than at home alone. How are you holding up?"

"The start of today was rough, but it's better now."

He strokes his thumb along my knuckles. "Always so strong. You're a force, angel. I'm proud of the way you love these girls."

I tip my chin up, butterflies fluttering in my stomach at the praise. Having him here has made today not just bearable, but joyful, and I don't want it to end. "You don't have to go after dinner, if you don't want to."

"Do you want me to stay?" he asks.

My need for him wipes out everything else. "Yes, please."

He drops his head, eyes on my lips, but Callie rushes in to grab a paper towel because she spilled her water, breaking the moment.

"Sorry about that. I forgot myself," Roman says softly.

"It's okay. I did, too."

We bring the food to the table and finally sit down to our Christmas feast.

"Can we still say one thing we're thankful for before we eat?" Callie asks.

"Absolutely. Do you want to start?" I ask.

"Okay. Everyone take the hand of the person beside you," Callie instructs.

I slide my hands into Roman's and Fee's.

"I'm thankful for Lexi and all her new friends, because without you, this Christmas would have been sad."

My heart aches. Roman squeezes my hand.

Callie turns to Connor. "It's your turn."

"I'm thankful for being traded to Toronto, because it means I get to have Christmas dinner with my number one fan." He winks at Callie.

She beams up at him. The girl is totally smitten. Clearly I need to watch out, because she has a thing for bad boys.

Dred is next. "I'm thankful that the condo across the hall from me came up for rent and brought new friends into my life who fill my heart, especially on days like today."

Fee takes a deep breath and knocks her shoulder against mine. "I'm thankful for you, Lexi. You're a really good big sister, and I know it's not easy being our not-mom too, but you're doing a great job."

"I love you." I wrap my arm around her shoulder and kiss her temple.

"I love you, too."

Dred sniffs and looks away for a moment.

I make sure I'm composed before I speak. "I'm thankful for my sisters, who show me what perseverance and strength look like every day, and I'm thankful for this new job and all the wonderful people it's brought into my life."

Roman smiles, thumb brushing along my palm. "I'm thankful for takeout Thai, because without it, we might not all be together today."

Dinner is filled with smiles and more laughter. Roman tells stories about how Hammer would always try to stay up so she could see Santa when she was young. Dred entertains us with hilarious, outlandish things that happen at the library—that place is hoppin'—while Connor sits back and mostly observes.

After dessert—Dred wasn't wrong, Rix's pumpkin pie is to die for—Connor offers to drive her home. We send them off with hugs and thank yous, then gather in the living room.

I pop on a movie, and Fee's friend from school invites her for Boxing Day shopping, which turns into Fee asking if she can sleep over so they can get to the mall early, before the crowds. By the time her friend's mom picks her up, Callie is already fast asleep. Roman helps me tuck her into bed around nine, and then it's just him and me—and the wild sexual tension that's been building all day.

I should send him home. We shouldn't cross any more lines, but I don't want all the good of today to disappear when he walks out that door. "You can stay a little longer?"

"I don't want to be anywhere but here." His raw honesty is breaking me.

"What should we do now?" I give in to the urge to touch him. I'm tired of being good—of staying in control. I long for the past, when it was just us and the rest of the world didn't exist.

A roguish smile quirks the corner of his delightful mouth, and he leans down until his lips brush my ear. "It's time for me to unwrap *my* present."

CHAPTER 20
ROMAN

Lexi gives me a look that makes me want to take her directly to bed. "How am I supposed to resist you when you say things like that, Goalie?"

"I'm sorry. I wasn't thinking." *Not with the head on my shoulders anyway*.

Lexi fingers the buttons on my shirt. "I know what I'm supposed to say, but I'm having a hard time finding the will to say it."

I understand her conflict. I share it, even. But it doesn't stop me from wanting her. "Do you need me to make it easier on you? I can go."

She gently skims my throat with her fingertips. "I don't want you to, though."

"Good. Me either." I give in and stroke her cheek.

She leans into the touch, like it's exactly what she's been waiting for.

"Would you like to have tonight, angel? It can just be ours." I trace the contour of her bottom lip with my thumb. "Tell me what you want, Lexi, and I'll give it to you."

Her finger trails along my jaw, eyes full of conflict and longing. "I just want to be yours."

"I've been waiting to have you again for years." I brush my lips over hers. "You only had to ask."

She loops her arms around my neck, her body soft and warm. She's the perfect fit. The missing piece. She instantly fills the void her absence left all those years ago. I thread my fingers through her hair and deepen the kiss. When she moans into my mouth, I pull back. "Show me your bedroom so I can take care of you."

She glances around, maybe realizing we're standing in the middle of the hall. "Yes. Okay."

She laces our fingers and guides me through the condo. We pass Callie's room and continue to the end of the hall. She tugs me inside her bedroom, and I smile as I take in the space. Lexi is unyielding on the ice, a flawless example of a competent coach. Always confident and in control. But everything about this space is pretty and feminine. Ivory and pale gray with blush accents. This is where she's soft and unguarded. And I get to have that part of her all to myself.

Lexi flips the lock, grabs my shirt, and tries to pull my mouth back to hers.

"Ah, ah, ah," I chastise as I take her beautiful, flushed face tenderly in my hands. "It's been torture, being close to you, but unable to touch you like this."

"I need you." Her shaking hands slide up my chest.

I catch them and press my lips to her knuckles before biting gently. "I have three years to make up for. You're going to be my good girl and let me take my time with you."

Her breath leaves her on a soft whimper. "However you want me, you can have me."

"So compliant." She melts as my lips find the inside of her wrist. "Such a tempting treat." I kiss my way up the inside of her arm. "So many orgasms to coax out of you."

"Please, yes. I just want to disappear with you."

I ghost my lips along the column of her throat until I reach her ear. "But I decide when you get to have one and how many."

I grin darkly at her soft moan.

Fighting the draw has been agonizing. But I've had a chance to get to know *her* better, to see her shine as she owned her role as coach. I appreciate even more all the sides of her now. She's always poised and decisive on the ice and with the players, but here, in this space, she's finally mine to covet.

I dip beneath the hem of her shirt, skimming her side. "Arms up. I want to see you." She shivers and raises them. I pull it over her head, leaving her in a floral-print bra. Pale pink blossoms scatter across mint green satin, edged with sage green lace.

I trace the scalloped satin edge. "You still have this."

"It reminded me of our weekend together when I opened my dresser in the morning." She fingers the buttons on my shirt and bites her bottom lip.

"How often did you think about me?" My fingers glide along her collarbones.

"Every day." She fiddles with the button, waiting for permission.

"It was the same for me." I skim the length of her arm, reveling in the way it feels to finally be able to touch her again. "Would you like to take my shirt off?"

"Yes, please." And still, she waits.

"Go ahead."

She sighs with relief, working the buttons free with nervous efficiency. I reach behind her and flick the clasp of her bra open. It slides down her arms and catches in the crook of her elbows. She only let's it drop to the floor once all the buttons on my shirt are unfastened. Lexi runs her hands up my chest and pushes my shirt over my shoulders, tugging it free and tossing it aside.

I don't stop her, too enthralled with how good it feels to be with her like this again, without all the walls between us. Every touch and caress heighten our connection, easing the painful ache that's ruled me all these months.

"So fucking beautiful." I cup the generous swells, thumbs

sweeping across her taut nipples as I capture one stiff peak between my lips.

Lexi's hands slide into my hair on a quiet gasp, and she wraps her arm around my head, trying to keep me there. I chuckle, then bite as I carefully circle her wrists, pinning them to her sides.

She groans her displeasure when I straighten, lush bottom lip jutting out in an adorable pout.

I arch a brow. "Where's my sweet angel?"

"I need you. I missed you." She rubs her thighs together. "I missed *this*."

"Me, too." I curve my hand around the side of her delicate neck, her pulse pounding under my palm.

Her eyes flutter closed.

"Don't block me out, not when we're here and this close to finally having what we've been waiting for." I brush my lips over hers and press my thumb against the soft space under her chin. "Look at me, Alexandria."

Her lids lift with her shaky exhale.

"I feel it every time we're in a room together," I admit. "This unquenchable need to be near to you."

Her eyes soften. "The past few weeks have been so hard. That kiss unlocked a door I can't close, and I don't want to."

"We'll figure out tomorrow, but for tonight, you're mine." I search her eyes. There's no hesitation, no uncertainty, just the same longing and desire I feel.

"Only yours," she agrees.

I slant my mouth over hers and pop the button on her jeans. She grips my shoulders, nails biting into the skin as I drag the zipper down. I sweep a trail along the waistband of her panties as I kiss a path down her throat, over her collarbones to her breasts, pausing to devote attention to each nipple before I drop to one knee and press my lips below her navel.

Lexi's hands slide into my hair as I shimmy her jeans down her legs. I tap the top of her foot and she steps out of them. Next

I remove her holiday-themed socks, leaving her in panties. My fingers glide up the outside of her thighs, relishing the goose bumps that rise along her skin, proof that I affect her the way she does me.

I curve my palms around her ass and nuzzle against her panty-covered sex, inhaling deeply. "Smells like *mine*," I growl.

"Always yours, Roman." Lexi's fingers curl in my hair.

The things it does to me when she says my name like that. All my careful control finally snaps. I rise in a rush, wrap my hands around her waist, and toss her onto the mattress. She slaps a palm over her mouth to cover her shocked gasp. I move to stand at the end of the bed, drinking in the sight of her. Her gaze rakes over me, greedy and hot. She hooks her thumbs into the waistband of her panties.

"No." I shake my head as my fingers close around one ankle. "I get to take those off." I sink to my knees and bite just above the inside of her knee. "With my teeth."

"Oh fuck," she whimpers.

"Only if you're good." That's a lie and we both know it. It doesn't matter if she's naughty. I'll still give her whatever she wants, what we both want.

I fight to stay in control as I kiss an agonizingly slow path up the inside of her thigh. Her skin is warm under my lips, pebbling with each purposeful nip and kiss. When I reach the apex, I gently bite the satin covering her pussy, tugging before I let it snap back into place.

Her toes curl. "Roman, please."

I splay my hand across her abdomen. "What was that?"

"Please." She tries to roll her hips again, but I shake my head and she stills, breath leaving her in soft pants.

"Please what? What do you need?" I follow the edge of her panties along the juncture of her thigh.

"You. Your mouth on me," she whispers.

"My mouth on you where? Be explicit."

Her eyes light up with carnal excitement. "On my pussy. I

want you to fuck me with your tongue before you stretch me with your cock."

"That's my good girl." I kiss along the edge of her panties from one hip to the other. "Lift for me."

She complies and I tug the satin down a few inches with my teeth, before kissing the same path to the opposite hip. When I expose her slit, I slide my tongue between her folds—just a tease, a taste. My perfect little doll, ready for me.

I bar an arm across her hips, pinning her to the mattress as Lexi covers her mouth with her palm to muffle her moan. I continue the torment, dragging her panties down her legs with my teeth, until I discard them on the floor.

Lexi's eyes are full of heat and need as I pull her to the edge of the bed. "Hold yourself open for me."

She rushes to comply, parting her legs.

I settle my hands on the backs of her thighs, pushing them wider. "Look at you, spread out like a feast." I lean in and bite the inside of her thigh. "This pretty little pussy already weeping for me."

I slide my hands under her and lift her to my mouth, licking up the length of her.

Her head snaps back. "Oh fuck, thank you."

I bite the inside of her thigh. "Eyes on me," I order.

She lifts her head and moans when I brush my lips over her clit. She tastes better than I remember and feels like everything I've been missing. It takes what's left of my frayed restraint to not bury my face in her pussy and devour her. "Did you miss my mouth?" I suck on one soft, pink lip, reveling in the control she so willingly relinquishes for me.

"So much," she breathes. And what's left of the walls between us crumble, leaving only desire.

"This gorgeous, sweet pussy is mine." I drag my tongue through her folds. "And I'm done pretending it hasn't always been *mine*." I latch onto her swollen clit and suck hard.

She jerks and gasps, but her eyes stay where I want them, on me. "I'm yours. All of me. Every part. Only yours."

I relish her needy moans and soft sighs. There's no one and nothing more beautiful than Lexi open and on display for only me, struggling to stay quiet as I push her closer to an orgasm with each purposeful stroke of tongue and nip of teeth.

"Please, Roman, please," she whimpers every time I get her close to the edge, but keep her hovering there, the orgasm just out of reach.

I prowl up her body and cup her pussy, two fingers pressed against her entrance, but not penetrating. "I want to hear you beg."

She bites her bottom lip as she continues to hold herself open for me. "Please, Roman."

I tsk her, reveling in the power she lends me. "You can do better."

"Please let me come. Please fill me. I'm so close, I need to feel you."

I slide two fingers into her slick, wet heat, and her eyes roll up. I don't curl them until her eyes are back on mine.

"Please, please, please," she pleads.

I could hold her here, coiled tight, pussy clamped around my fingers teetering on the edge of an orgasm. She would be mindless with need, desperate for the release only I can give her.

I've been ravenous for her, desperate to have her again, waiting for her to give in and surrender control.

I curl my fingers and she moans, body trembling as the orgasm sweeps through her.

She curves a palm around the back of my neck, and I let her pull my mouth to hers, tongue sweeping inside on a needy moan.

Her other hand slides down my back, pausing when she realizes I'm still wearing my pants.

"I need you inside me." She slides her hand into my back

pocket, retrieving my wallet. "Please, Roman. I need you to fill me."

I need the same thing; proof I'm right. That she's meant for me, and I'm meant for her.

Her hands shake with anticipation as she finds the foil square. She groans her displeasure as I ease my fingers out, then groans as I bring them to my mouth and suck them clean.

Lexi passes me the condom and sits up. I fold back so she can unbutton my pants and push them over my hips, along with my boxers. My cock springs free, and Lexi skims the weeping tip. Her eyes lift as she leans in and rubs her cheek along the length, fingers curving around the shaft. Her lips brush the head and her tongue drags up the slit.

I press my thumb against her bottom lip to stop her from going any further, smiling at her disappointed expression. "I'll fuck your lovely mouth later. Right now it's time to feed this pretty little pussy my cock."

I pass Lexi the condom and she carefully rolls it down my length.

I move between her thighs, rubbing the head over her clit. Dragging it down, my cock sliding along all that softness as I grip her hip and position myself against her opening. I pause to savor this moment. Because the moment I push inside, she'll be mine again. Exactly as she should be.

She spreads her lips, fingers sliding on either side of my shaft. "Oh God. I forgot how big you are."

"Don't worry, we'll make it fit." I push in a couple of inches and her mouth falls open.

"Oh my fuck." Lexi rubs her clit, then traces the perimeter of my cock.

I push in another inch.

She shudders and groans, her hips rolling, and head falling back as I give her more, filling her.

"Open your eyes, Lexi. I need to see you."

She does as I order, bottom lip sliding through her teeth as I give her the final inch, then lean in, covering her body with mine, pressing my hips into hers as I cage her in place. I want to protect her, keep her safe from everything that comes after this.

"See, angel, I told you, it's the perfect fit." I savor the way it feels to finally be with her again. It's not just our bodies joining, it's the essence of us coalescing. For the first time in years I feel whole again.

Her fingers drift over my cheek. "Like we were made for each other."

Relief washes over me. I'm right about her, about this, about us. We finally have a reprieve from the agony of the last few months.

"That's right." I brush my lips over hers. "I'm going to fuck you hard and deep, Lexi, so the memory of my cock is imprinted in your pussy."

She moans and clenches around me. "God I love your filthy mouth."

I ease out, all the way to the ridge, already missing the feel of her surrounding me, and snap my hips forward. Lexi bites my shoulder as she winds herself around me. I hook her other leg into the crook of my elbow, opening her wider, allowing me to go deeper.

"You won't take this away again."

She shakes her head, eyes brimming with emotion. "No. Never. I don't want it to end. I never want it to end."

"Me neither."

I grip her ass and tilt her hips up, hitting that spot inside that turns her liquid under me.

"I'm so close."

"You don't come until I tell you." I need this from her, to give me the control I struggle to maintain whenever she's close but out of reach. I snap my hips forward.

She groans as I grind against her.

"Please, Roman. I need it. I need you." Her nails rake down my back, body trembling with the effort it takes to hold back.

I'm teetering on the edge with her. "Almost there."

I pump into her again.

She makes a plaintive sound and murmurs please one last time.

"Let go, angel."

My name is a guttural plea as she succumbs, pussy milking my cock, pulling me deeper, and I don't stop, don't give her time to recover. Instead, I keep her swirling in pleasure, wringing another orgasm from her as I follow.

A wave of calm follows, and I start to roll over, but she clings to me. "No, don't. Stay, please."

I pull back so I can meet her gaze. "I'm not going anywhere."

She runs her fingers through my hair. "You're the only person I can ever let go with. I want this feeling to last forever. I missed it so much." She cups my face in her palms. "I missed *you* so much."

"I missed you, too." I stroke her cheek. "Especially these past few months, when you were right in front of me but it felt like a million miles were separating us."

"I hated it."

"Me, too. So let's not do that to each other again."

"Never again."

I claim her mouth. We'll have to figure out tomorrow, but for now, I am lost in how good it feels to have her in my arms again.

CHAPTER 21

LEXI

"Afternoon, coaches." Roman dips his chin as he passes us.

"You feeling game ready, Hammerstein?" Boxer asks.

"Absolutely. Looking to shut New York out and remind them who kicked their ass last year in the finals." He winks and disappears into the locker room.

It's been nearly a week since the Christmas miracle. If my vagina could grow legs and follow him, she would. I exhale a tense breath.

Vander Zee claps me on the shoulder. "Have confidence in your decisions, Forrester. It's been a solid season. Roman's in net tonight, and Grace is playing cleaner and smarter."

"We're sure playing him on the same line as Madden is a good idea?" Coach Thomas asks for the third time.

"It's our best bet if we want to win against New York." Boxer comes to my defense. Again.

Last week I brought up playing Madden and Grace on the same line again. After I backed up my suggestion with data and a strategy, Vander Zee ran with it. Our team can handle New York, but I'm reasonably nervous. Bowman is proving to be one of the best players in the league and they've been dominating this season.

Vander Zee is showing me he values my input by allowing the line change. Now I just need the team to prove I'm right.

"Madden can handle it," Vander Zee assures us. "We discussed it earlier today. He understands what's at stake."

A win against New York will be good for team morale. And Madden and Grace have to play like they're on the same team. Madden has been better, but Grace has been off since the holidays. I can only guess as to why. I'm hoping this strategy works tonight. Either they'll get their shit together and be professionals or someone will end up on the bench. The former is preferred.

We join the team in the locker room for the pre-game strategy talk.

Roman is seated on a bench across the room, polishing a green apple on his jersey. A flush works its way up my neck. I look away.

How the hell do people have workplace romances without everyone finding out? I might as well be wearing a shirt that reads: *The goalie owns me.*

Two nights ago, Callie slept over at a friend's house and Fee had dance practice and went to a movie with her friends, which meant I had the condo all to myself for several hours. It took every ounce of restraint I had not to invite Roman over.

Every moment of my life I'm the one people look to for guidance and support. My job is to lead the team, to work with other leaders, to prove that I'm capable and that my emotions don't govern me when I'm on the ice.

But with Roman everything is different. I don't have to be in control. I can give it to him and trust that he'll take care of my every need. With Roman I finally feel like I truly belong to someone, mind, body and soul. I can forget who I'm supposed to be to everyone else because I'm just *his*. His to tease, to pleasure, to take pleasure from. Three years ago he opened the door to the possibilities and now… I'm falling for every single part of him. Not just the man who can bring me limitless pleasure. I'm in love with his hard and soft sides. And especially the man who makes me feel seen and worshipped and cared for.

My time with him at Christmas was a reminder of all the things I've been missing—and gave me a glimpse of what we could be when the season is over.

However, reality remains the same. Christmas was a weak moment for both of us.

When he's retired from the league, I'll have to contend with the backlash of being in a relationship with one of my former players. But that will be manageable. And waiting has to become manageable, because I've worked too hard to throw it all away.

The team files out of the locker room. "We've got this. Don't worry," Roman murmurs as he passes.

I'm not sure if he's talking about the game or us.

"What was that about?" Coach Thomas asks as we follow them out of the locker room.

"Just the line change." My voice comes out more confident than I am.

Thomas's lips thin. "Shouldn't he be talking to his coach about that instead of you?"

"We're all on the same team here," I remind him.

He grunts but doesn't respond otherwise.

I join Vander Zee behind the bench and Boxer and Thomas head up to the box to sit with Fielding and their families. I spot Richards and his boys up there, too, which happens often. I refocus on the ice and keep a close eye on Grace and Madden during the warm-up. This needs to work. I'm putting myself on the line here.

The game gets off to a rough start, with New York scoring a goal in the first three minutes of play, courtesy of Bowman. Grace rotates off the ice, his jaw set, lips in a line. New York came prepared. "He's got new moves," Grace grumbles as he takes a seat on the bench.

"He does," I agree. "Watch for those changes. We'll find the pattern."

Madden evens the score halfway through the first period. Roman is doing his best, but Bowman is skating circles around everyone, including his former teammate. I'd be more impressed if it wasn't my team he was shredding.

Grace rotates back in, and his frustration mounts with every shot on the Terror's net. So does Madden's. I am already rethinking strategy for the second period.

Madden chases the puck down as New York heads for Toronto's net. Before Grace can intervene, Madden slams into Bowman. He ends up against the boards, and players converge on them as they fight for possession of the puck. Grace is in there, trying to regain control, but it's almost impossible to see what's going on from where we're positioned, with sticks and arms and legs flying and flailing. Then three players go down, including Grace and Madden.

The refs jump in and clear the pileup, but the crowd is in a frenzy, especially with Madden and Grace shouting at each other while Madden struggles to his feet. He grips the boards, favoring his right leg.

"Fuck no," Vander Zee mutters.

I can see Thomas and Richards shaking their heads while Boxer runs a hand through his salt and pepper hair. This is the last thing I want. Regardless of data, this makes my call a bad one.

Madden makes it to the bench, shrugging off help from Palaniappa. Vander Zee calls in the team doctor.

"I'm fine." Madden winces as the doc palpates his ankle, then he shoots a glare at Grace. "This is your fucking fault."

"When isn't it?" Grace grouses.

"Enough," Vander Zee snaps. "Madden, you need to be looked at."

"This is bullshit." Madden is forced to accept Doc's help as he guides him to the locker room.

It's a blow we don't need. We're tied and our star center is out with an injury.

Bowman scores another goal in the second period, and with Madden off the ice, we can't recover the lead. We lose the game 2-1.

"It's not your fault," Vander Zee says as we head for the locker room for a post-game discussion. It doesn't matter that Vander Zee calls the shots, I made the suggestion, so I'll take the heat for this from the coaching side. Which is frustrating because Thomas isn't creating solutions, and all these boys have done with Vander Zee is give him lip service.

"You happy now, Grace? I'm off the ice thanks to you!" Madden shouts as we enter.

"You're the one trying to play defense!" Grace snaps back.

"Enough!" Roman roars. "The two of you are fucking the season for us. Deal with your shit! I don't care what the hell happened with your damn sandwich when you were at the Hockey Academy. Get the fuck over it!"

Grace and Madden's heads whip in Roman's direction, both wear mortified expressions.

Madden points at Stiles and Bright. "Which one of you said something?"

Bright raises his hand. "But I—"

"What the fuck happened to bro code?" Madden rages.

"I didn't—" Bright tries to defend himself.

"Get the fuck over it, Madden! So I fucked your sandwich. Big fucking deal. It was two slices of bread and a couple of slices of ham. All you had to do was throw it out. You're the one who fucked my damn shirt!"

"I cannot be hearing this right." Who fucks a t-shirt or a food item? These two, apparently.

The team seems to be frozen in shock.

Except Bright and Stiles. They don't look the least bit surprised.

"Everyone but Madden, Grace, Stiles, Bright, and Hammerstein get out," Vander Zee bellows.

Vander Zee crosses his arms. He waits until the locker room

is empty before he speaks again. His voice is quiet, but it wavers with barely contained rage. "Explain yourselves."

Grace and Madden glare at each other.

"I fucked Madden's sandwich at the Hockey Academy."

"Finally! You fucking admit it!" Madden fires him the bird.

"But only after you jizzed on my *last* clean shirt."

Coach Thomas coughs into his elbow. Coach Boxer does the same. Stiles rubs the back of his head, and Bright rubs his mouth to hide a smile. Roman bites into his apple with a loud crack.

I give him a look.

He licks his thumb.

"What the fuck is wrong with you two?" Vander Zee asks.

Roman and I both look quickly back to him. But of course, he's talking to Madden and Grace.

"We were living in Pearl Lake," Bright explains. "It was a small town, and half the population was the coaches' kids. We were a bunch of walking hormones with nowhere to blow off steam. Bread is a lot softer than our hands."

"Are you seriously fucking defending him?" Madden's voice is laced with disbelief.

Bright shrugs. "He has a point. You can throw out a sandwich. Who wants to wear a jizzy shirt?"

"Who wastes food like that?" Madden looks straight at Connor who doesn't respond.

"Why did you take Grace's shirt, Madden?" I ask.

Madden pokes at his cheek, which have both turned a wild shade of red. "It was an accident. I thought I had some privacy, and then I didn't, and I reached for the first shirt I could find which happened to belong to Grace."

Grace makes a sound that indicates he doesn't buy it.

Vander Zee pinches the bridge of his nose. "I can't believe this shit."

"I'd be pretty pissed if someone fucked my sandwich," Stiles offers, backing up his best friend.

"Shut the fuck up, Stiles." Vander Zee looks ready to bench every player in this room.

"Thanks, man." Madden tips his chin at Stiles.

I roll my eyes. Everything starts to line up. "Grace and Madden, apologize to each other. Now."

They glare at each other.

"Look, I think we all know that this isn't about fucking each other's food or clothing items." I shake my head. Seriously. What the hell?

They both frown in my direction.

"This is about wanting what someone else has. Madden, in your case it was Grace's financial stability and what that can afford you. Grace, you wanted Madden's ability to fit in wherever he goes." I'm sure there are layers to this, but knowing what I do about both of them, this definitely tracks. I just wish it hadn't taken this long to figure out. "The two of you have carried your anger at the seventeen-year-old versions of each other through a decade and onto this team, where it doesn't belong. Let it go. Stop hating each other for things you can't control or change, and apologize for being teenage idiots," I order.

Bright claps. "That was well said."

"It really was. I should have asked you to do that weeks ago," Vander Zee agrees.

"I tried earlier in the season, it wasn't the right time," I offer. And now I wish I'd tried again before tonight.

Vander Zee turns back to the boys. "You heard Coach Forrester."

Madden sighs.

Grace shakes his head.

Roman takes another bite of his apple.

"I'm sorry I fucked your stupid sandwich," Grace mumbles.

Vander Zee gives him a look that would bury most men. "Try again."

"I'm sorry I fucked your ham sandwich," Grace grits out.

Madden looks everywhere but at Grace. "I'm sorry I jizzed on your last clean shirt."

"Look at you two! This is some serious progress," Bright says jovially. "It only took you a decade to sort your shit out. We should grab some beers to celebrate this milestone in your relationship."

"Don't push it, Bright," Madden mutters.

"We lost this game because of some of the dumbest shit I've heard in all my years," Vander Zee states with ire. "This entire season has been a nightmare over a fucking sandwich and a t-shirt. Once Madden is healed up, the two of you will be doing ice sprints after every practice together for the rest of the season. You have both put this team under undue stress. You will be professionals and learn to work together or I will be taking a good hard look at this roster."

The room drops ten degrees by the time he's done. I don't dare make eye contact with anyone outside the rest of the coaching staff.

"I think it goes without saying that this stays here, between the people in this room," Vander Zee tacks on.

"And the sandwich and Grace's shirt," Bright adds, all fucking smiles and zero self-preservation.

"I threw it out," Grace replies.

"Probably for the best," I mumble.

Roman snickers.

This game has been a disaster.

CHAPTER 22

LEXI

The following day, after practice, I stop by Flip's. I'm surprised that he lives in a regular condo unit. It's nice, but he could afford a much more exclusive building. It explains how Dred ended up as his neighbor.

He opens the door, crutches tucked under his arms. He looks tired, and like last night wasn't the best for him. "Hey, Coach. You here to check up on me?"

"Yup. And I brought you snacks." I hold up a bag.

"You bring me KD? I'll let you in if you brought KD."

"Sure did." I was told by Dred that his go-to favorite food is neon noodles, which he buys by the case. But when the extra-creamy variety is on sale, he'll splurge, so that's what I brought. And a few other things.

He moves aside. "I was kidding. I would have let you in anyway, but I appreciate the comfort food."

Empty bowls sit in the sink, and a pile of mail litters the counter. The couch is set up like a bed, with a pillow at one end and blankets hanging off the other. A laptop sits on the coffee table. There's a loft space with a huge TV, but instead of stairs, there's a retractable ladder. That's one hell of a design oversight.

"How are you feeling?" I ask.

"Like an idiot." His cheeks flush. "You wanna sit? You want coffee? I can put on a pot."

"I'm good. I won't keep you long. I just wanted to see how you're holding up and make sure you're okay. I feel partly responsible because I put you on the ice together." Although it needed to happen, and so did the airing of grievances.

"Our history isn't your fault. Grace and I should have dealt with it at the beginning of the season, uh, if not before. It's not like you didn't try." He unpacks the bag I brought and chuckles when he finds a two pack of white t-shirts and a box of tissues. "You got me the tissues with lotion, huh?"

I shrug. "I figured you could use a laugh."

"Not sure how either of us will ever live this one down." His face turns the customary shade of red I've grown accustomed to whenever Madden and Grace have been faced with their history.

"You may not, but at least it's just your friends who know. Besides, I imagine your actions didn't come out of nowhere."

"What we did to each other…it was a storm brewing." Flip looks to the ceiling. "He seemed like he had everything. Rich family who could afford all the best things, and he loved to rub that in my face. Always acted like he was hot shit who didn't care about anyone but himself." He runs a hand through his hair. "But we're all covering for something, aren't we? Hiding behind masks so people don't see our weaknesses. He isn't any different. I just think his mask comes with thorns, and they hurt him as much as other people."

"Is that what you do? Hide behind a mask?"

He nods slowly. "The way we acted back then was juvenile, but we were kids." He rubs his bottom lip. "And my actions after I made the pros weren't much better. All the women…" He shakes his head and averts his gaze again. "I don't have a problem with people doing what makes them feel good. It's not my place to pass judgment. I wasn't doing it just because I love sex though, and I pulled people into it who I shouldn't have. I didn't see it until I almost blew up my relationship with my sister and my best friend."

I don't know the details of his exploits, but I've seen enough of them on the gossip sites to have an idea. "You and Rix seem to have a good relationship now, and you and Tristan are tight."

"We're good now, yeah. But I made a lot of mistakes Rix had to pay for. I should have helped her more when she needed it, and I should have considered how my actions off the ice affected her, and my best friend. Anyway, that's for my therapist to deal with, not you." He smiles wryly. "I'm going to ice this ankle and elevate it so I can get back on the ice and do my job as soon as possible."

"Want help?"

He starts to shake his head but stops. "You know what? Yeah. Please. There's a soft gel pack in the freezer."

"You want me to bring over any snacks while I'm at it?"

"You gonna get on me for eating crap while I feel like crap?" he asks.

"You get a pass for a couple of days," I reply.

"An ice cream sandwich would be awesome. There's a box beside the gel pack. And maybe a bag of buffalo-wing chips. They're in the cupboard to the right of the fridge, first shelf."

"On it."

He stuffs a box of candy-coated black licorice into his pocket and crutches to the couch while I gather the requested items. I find it interesting that his cupboards and freezer are stocked with the same stuff I buy: mostly the generic brands. I feel like I've learned a lot about Flip in a few short minutes.

I set everything on the coffee table. "You need anything else?"

"Nope. I'm all good here. Going to eat my feelings and watch something other than hockey. Thanks for stopping by, Coach. I appreciate it. I know you've been trying this season, and I'm sorry it took this long to get to the bottom of things, but I think we were mostly embarrassed. Or at least I was. Still am, to be honest. Owning my stupidity and jealousy is something I'm clearly still working on, and I wish I could have done it earlier in the season. The team needed someone like you. You've got all the best parts of the other coaches and a side of empathy that gives you an edge. We all see it." He gives me a chagrined smile. "And it wasn't your fault I got hurt. It's on me and Grace. I know you're probably getting heat on the hockey sites. It's just noise. You gotta block it out."

"Thanks, Flip, I appreciate it." More than he knows. It's validating. Affirming when I need it the most, but it also shines a light on the things I'm not doing right. Like what happened at Christmas with Roman.

I leave him to his emotional eating and let myself out. I'm on my way to the elevators when I run into Dred.

"Hey! Were you visiting the broken hockey boy?" She pulls me in for a hug. "You know that's not on you, right? He was acting like he suddenly played defense and isn't a center."

"Were you at the game?"

"No. I was at work. I was secretly watching it on my phone behind the desk." She tilts her head. "You want to come in for a minute?" She does a full-body shimmy. "You look like you've got a lot going on."

I check the time. Fee is with friends today, and Callie has hockey until six. "Are you sure you're not busy?"

"Not at all. Come on." Dred slides her arm through mine and leads me back down the hall.

Once we're inside, she drops her purse and kicks off her shoes. She motions to her khaki pants, burgundy turtleneck, and cream-colored sweater. "Give me a minute. I need to change out of this."

"Sure."

She disappears down the hall. Her apartment is modestly furnished, with shelves lining one wall. Most are filled with books, though one contains all manner of board games. A couch and two chairs take up most of the small living room.

There's no dining table, but the small kitchen island has two stools.

Dred reappears a minute later in a pair of black jogging pants and a Badass Babe Brigade shirt. "Can I offer you something to drink?" She wrinkles her nose. "Flip left two beers behind the other day. Otherwise I have pomegranate juice and ginger ale."

"Ginger ale works for me."

"Flip told me you finally know what happened between him and Connor." She pulls two glasses from the cupboard.

"Gotta say, it wasn't what I expected, but it does explain a lot."

"Yeah. I think Flip was more frustrated about the waste of food than he was the actual sandwich defilement, but it's hard to tell with him sometimes. Anyway, now that they've aired their grievances, maybe they can start to move past them."

"I'm hopeful, too." I don't know if I should ask, but I do anyway. "Have you and Flip ever…? Because I know you're best friends. I could understand the appeal."

Horror crosses her face. "Never. Gross." I swear she starts to gag. "Friends. Only friends from now until forever. Like a brother if I had one."

"You sound sure about that."

"The first time I met Flip he asked me if I wanted to fuck."

"That was his line?" I ask.

"Oh yeah, it was a special low for him, I think. I've witnessed him be smoother, but I see that now for what it was. He'd had a bad practice that day and wanted to disappear. I said no. He said okay, cool. Then we hung out like it'd never happened. He came over and I kicked his ass at Connect Four. From that moment on, we were only ever going to be friends."

"Very grown up of you."

"As the kids used to say, the sex vibes between us are not vibing. I'm proud to be his very platonic friend because it's a special thing to love someone without romance or sex." She passes me a glass of soda. "So how are you, really?"

"I slept with Roman." I bite my lips together. "I did not mean to lead with that."

Empathy softens her features. "Been holding on to that for a while, huh?"

"Yeah."

"Recently or before you came to the Terror?"

"Both," I admit.

"Well, that explains the tension between you two."

I feel a panic spiral coming on. "Do you think anyone else knows?"

Dred holds up a hand. "No one else suspects anything."

"Are you sure?"

She leans against the counter. "I had to learn how to read people at a young age. It was a self-preservation kind of situation—suss out the bad guys so I knew who was a friend and who was an enemy. There's been a vibe between you two. You're guarded with him, more than you are with everyone else, and he looks at you like you're an ice cream cone he wants but can't have. Which is quite accurate." She sips her soda. "Did you sleep with him on Christmas night?"

I nod.

"Yeah. He was killing it with the hot-Santa Daddy thing, and then the way he is with Callie..." She sighs. "He really is a great guy all the way around. Don't feel too bad about giving in to temptation. That man would be hard to resist. Especially if you've ridden that ride before and it was a good time."

"It's the best sex of my life. Then and now." God, it feels good to tell someone about this. I didn't realize how heavy it was. "But we can't do it again. I shouldn't have allowed it in the first place."

"Because you're his coach."

"Exactly." My mouth has turned into a desert, so I chug the ginger ale. "You can't tell anyone, Dred. Especially not Flip. Or the Babe Brigade. If Hammer found out—or Hemi. Or Shilpa. Or

Tally. Or Rix and Essie." I bite my lips together. "Shit. I should've kept my mouth shut."

"Take a breath." Dred meets my eyes. "I promise this stays between us, and you and Roman."

"It could ruin my career if people found out."

"How are you going to handle the rest of the season?" Her tone holds concern.

"We can't give in again. *I* can't give in again. It would probably be fine for him, but not for me."

"And of course he understands that." It's not a question.

"Absolutely. He knows how hard I worked to get here." I explain how we met a few years ago and spent the weekend together, and how it ended. "When the season is over and he's retired, we can pursue this. It'll still be hard. I'll still get flak, but then we're not blatantly breaking rules. He won't be a player anymore, and I won't be his coach."

"And you think you can do that? Stay away from him until June?" Dred asks. "Provided they make the playoffs."

"Oh, they'll make the playoffs," I assure her. "And I have to. There is no other choice."

CHAPTER 23

ROMAN

"Knock, knock."

Peggy leans around her computer monitor and a smile curves the corner of mouth as she spots the edible bouquet in my hand. "How did you know I needed cookies today?"

"Hollis might have made an offhand comment about picking up supplies, and I read between the lines." I set the cookie bouquet on her desk. "How are you feeling? You need these too?" I pull a pack of painkillers from my pocket.

She laughs. "You're already dad of the year. You don't need to bring me PMS meds. And besides you, Hollis is the only other man in my life who's offered to get me supplies."

"He's a keeper, then."

"He is," she agrees and pushes out of her chair. She wraps her arms around me. "Thank you for being so thoughtful."

"Thank you for giving me a reason to smile every day." I squeeze her. "You got time for lunch?"

She glances at the clock. "I have a meeting at two thirty, but that'll give us plenty of time. I'll just let Hemi know." She grabs her purse, coat, scarf, and toque and pops across to Hemi's office before we head for the elevators. We pass the coaching staff on the way out, and I try my best not to let my gaze linger on Lexi.

Peggy and I make the short walk in the blustery January afternoon to our favorite lunch spot. They serve the best homemade soup and sandwiches.

We settle in at one of the tables by the window after we order. "Are you glad Flip is back on the ice tonight?" Peggy asks.

"Definitely. We've beat New Jersey once already this season, so we're in a good position to do it again. Hopefully he can play the entire game."

"How's he been at practice since the talk?" She stresses the word *talk*.

As much as Flip and Connor would love for their secrets to remain in the locker room, all the girls with partners who were there for the come to Jesus talk are now also in the know.

"Good. They've both been better. I think they're equally mortified by their actions."

The server drops off our soups and sandwiches.

"I'm really glad we both decided on grilled cheese." She presses her lips together, fighting laughter.

After a moment we both lose the battle and end up in tears over it, garnering looks from several patrons.

"Teenage boys do such stupid things." I wipe under my eyes with my napkin.

"This is so true." Peggy picks up half of her grilled cheese and dips it in her tomato bisque. "And probably one of the many reasons I barely dated in high school." She rolls her eyes.

"I'm glad you didn't date jerks in high school." I dip my bacon and grilled cheese sandwich into my loaded baked potato soup.

"Oh, I did. I just broke up with them before you met them." She eyes me from the side. "Speaking of dating…"

I give her a look.

"Seriously, Dad. You need to put yourself out there. You have so much to offer. You're the most amazing parent. The team loves you; you love the team. You deserve someone to share life with."

I desperately want to tell her I've already found the perfect woman. That I'm in love. But I can't do that to Lexi, and I can't put that on Peggy. It's bad enough that I've been lying to her for months, I don't want her to carry around this sick feeling in the pit of my stomach, or keep my secrets.

So I say the only thing I can, "Let me retire. Then I'll start dating."

"How long before the girls get here?" Hollis asks for the third time in ten minutes.

"Text my daughter." I sip my scotch. He convinced me to come out for a drink.

"I did. She's not responding." He arches an expectant brow.

"I'm not checking my app for you. It's your own damn fault that you haven't asked her to add you to the circle." I fight a smile at his irritated expression.

"They're here." Flip squints. "Who's with them?"

I follow his eyes. Dred, Hemi, Rix, Essie, and Peggy, plus one, are heading our way.

"Oh shit. Is that *Coach Forrester*? Wow. Just…okay." Flip refocuses on his beer.

The girls must have persuaded Lexi to come out tonight. And they clearly dressed her up, too. She's wearing a deep rose slinky number that conforms to every single one of her curves. All the years of hockey and her time on the ice with us have sculpted her into a masterpiece. If she turns around… *Do not think about fucking her from behind*. It's too late, though. The memory of her french braid slipping through my fist slams into my brain. I tighten my grip on my scotch. I'm so fucked. So, so fucked.

Her gaze catches mine for a moment, and she fiddles with the clutch hanging from her wrist. What I wouldn't give to get out there on the dance floor with her. To put my hands on her, to feel her body melt against mine. To take her home so I can experience the soft and sweet sides of her. But we have months until the season ends.

"You okay, man?" Hollis asks.

"Fine. Great."

"Aurora will be fine. Dallas and Tristan and I will keep an eye on the girls," he assures me.

"Yup."

"But that's not what this is about." He focuses on his glass.

I say nothing. Hollis watches out for Peggy these days. But Lexi is a new problem. She looks incredible, and if Flip's reaction is anything to go by, we won't be the only ones to notice.

Peggy and the girls stop by our table. It seems Shilpa and Ash opted out because Shilps wasn't feeling the best. But I still wonder how they persuaded Lexi to come. Did she leave Fee in charge tonight? Her phone is clutched in her hand, and she checks it every few seconds. I get it. She wants to have a life, but she feels guilty for having fun.

"You're coming out to dance with us later." Peggy points a finger at me, then leans in to kiss Hollis on the cheek.

I look away, because I don't need to see them making eyes at each other. Once again, my attention shifts to Lexi. She gives me a small smile. Dred glances between us. Her expression makes me question whether Lexi finally cracked and confided in her. And if so, what exactly has she said? Dred waves at the table, then links her arm with Lexi's and pulls her toward the dance floor. Unfortunately, I have an excellent view of them. And now my head is spinning worse than it already was.

Drinking my feelings away won't help, and it certainly won't make me an asset on the ice tomorrow, so I switch to water and try my best to keep my eyes to myself.

After a few minutes, Hollis, Dallas, and Tristan head for the dance floor to play bodyguard and get up close and personal with their significant others. Flip stays behind with me.

"You don't have to hang back if you want to get out there."

"Just saving my ankle for the ice."

"You still hurting?"

"Nah, just want to be an asset to the team and make good choices when it comes to taking care of my body. Besides, I feel like I have some making up to do for all the stress I caused in the first half of the season."

"The issue seems to be resolved," I reply.

"Yeah. Seems pretty fucking stupid in hindsight." He slaps his thighs. "Anyway, Hollis and Hammer seem good. You handling that okay?"

"My daughter is happy, and that's all that matters."

"Yeah. Changes things, though, doesn't it?" Flip muses.

"Yeah, it does," I agree.

I watch Lexi part from the group and head toward the bathroom. At least half a dozen heads turn as she passes. I hate that I have to sit back and do nothing when the mere *idea* of her getting hit on makes me twitchy—especially by drunk idiots with dicks for brains. "You mind holding the table for a minute? I gotta use the bathroom."

Flip nods. "Sure. No problem."

"Thanks."

I slide out of the booth and walk the perimeter of the dance floor, positioning myself across from the bathroom to wait. Lexi appears a few minutes later and weaves between the press of bodies, but she pauses to check her phone. She worries her bottom lip as she scrolls through the messages. As predicted, some young douchebag approaches her. He's probably her age—in his late twenties, still all balls and no brains.

There's no way I won't do something regrettable if I see some guy flirt with her. So I step up behind her and skim the length of her arm. She startles, and goose bumps rise along her skin. She nearly drops her phone, but I catch it and slide it back into her hand.

The guy's expression shifts above her head, and his eyes flare.

"She's with me," I grind out.

He raises his hands. "Sorry. I didn't realize."

He backs away as Lexi spins around. If I wasn't fucked before, I certainly am now. Her braid hangs over her shoulder, begging to be wrapped around my fist. Her eyes are on fire, her lips glossy and pink and entirely too fucking enticing.

"What are you doing, Roman?"

Digging my hole deeper, apparently. "He was hitting on you."

She props a fist on her hip. "I'm fully capable of handling myself."

"I know. I can't, though," I admit. "I just saved him from a broken nose and me from an assault charge. Not proud of my complete lack of control when it comes to you, but at least I can admit I have a problem."

Her eyes narrow, and she pokes at her lip with her tongue. "I should not find that sexy."

"I find you sexy." I give her a heated once-over.

Her fingers flutter near her throat. "You have to stop looking at me like that."

"Again, I know, but I can't." She's so fucking full of sass; beautiful and brilliant. She's right in front of me, but I can't have her. "This is torture."

She scans the room. "This was such a bad idea."

That's a gut punch I'm not sure I'll ever recover from. I don't know what my expression must be, but her fingers curve around my wrist.

"Coming out tonight, I mean," she clarifies.

"Because I'm here."

"No. Yes. Not because I don't want to see you, Roman, but because I *do*. And it's so hard to stay away, especially when you're being all alpha possessive and you look like this." She gestures to me and seems annoyed.

"Look like what?"

She rolls her gorgeous, expressive eyes. "You hardly need me to spell it out."

"Maybe I do. Maybe I need to hear that you're struggling the way I am. Because I'm losing the battle here, Lexi."

"Every room you walk into, you're all I see." Her expression is pained. "Every time my phone goes off, I hope it's you. When I feel your eyes on me, I want to beg you to take me to bed so I can be yours again."

My relief that she feels the same is tempered by all she stands to lose.

"I should go." Even as she speaks, she takes a step closer. "Before someone notices us. I need to get back to the girls anyway—my sisters, I mean. Callie's having trouble sleeping."

"I could drive you. I've only had one drink. Let me take you home, Lexi."

"It's too risky."

I tip my head in understanding. It is, but we'll have a moment alone. Many moments. No text messages to delete right away. No one watching us. No one to stop us from acting on the feelings we've been fighting.

"I have to tell you something important." She fiddles with the collar of my shirt, eyes on her fingers. Her inability to meet my gaze tells me whatever she's about to say makes her nervous.

"Okay. I'm listening."

Her eyes lift. "Dred knows."

"Knows what exactly?"

"That we slept together before I joined the Terror and then again at Christmas. She said she picked up on a vibe, but no one else suspects anything. She won't tell anyone."

Dred is as loyal as they come. "Okay."

Her hand settles on my chest. "You're not upset?"

"I know this isn't any easier for you than it is for me. You need someone to talk to. I'm glad you have her." And it gives me hope that we want the same thing, which is more than a stolen night together.

"Who do you have?" she whispers.

"My position is different than yours." I give in to the urge to skim her hip, just the hint of connection. "Let me take you home. We can talk without an audience."

She drops her head and sways into me. Her forehead rests against my chest and her hands curl around my biceps for a moment, nails biting into my skin. I stroke her cheek and press my lips to the top of her head. Holding her in my arms makes me feel like a king. I would fight a thousand armies just to have this moment with her.

She grips my shirt and spins us around until her back is against a wide column, obscuring her from view. I brace an arm above her head, and she looks up at me. Conflict is written all over her face—the weight of our feelings pushing us to the edge of our limits. "I can't, Roman."

"I'll stay in the car."

"I'm worried about what will happen when we're in the car." Her fingers drift up my chest. "I will break if I'm alone with you. I'm breaking now."

I search her eyes. It wouldn't be hard to convince her that I'll keep her from making a mistake she can't take back. But it would be a lie. "I understand."

I start to step back, but she fists my shirt, eyes darting to my mouth. The tension between us is electric. "Give me permission, angel."

Her eyes lock with mine, and she mouths the words, *Kiss me, please.*

I angle my body, making sure she's completely hidden before I cover her mouth with mine. Desire runs through my veins like fire as her lips part and our tongues tangle. Brushing and whispering with all the words we can't say. Her soft body presses closer. It's weeks of pent-up need, lust, longing, unquenched desire. It's bliss and agony.

But we're in the middle of a nightclub, and the longer we stand here, the more at risk I put her. Every taste, every touch leaves me craving more. Eventually I pry my lips from hers. "You need to go, Lexi. You are a temptation I don't want to resist."

Her lips brush across my throat as she slips out from between me and the column and disappears into the crowd. The end of the season has never felt so impossibly far away.

And early retirement has never seemed so appealing.

CHAPTER 24

ROMAN

"Stop eyeing my sausage." Peggy elbows Hollis in the ribs. "You're the one who ordered peameal."

He purses his lips. "I thought you'd be willing to share."

She scoffs and points her speared sausage at his plate. "Your peameal. My sausage." She nibbles the end of the link.

I barely resist the urge to tell her to use her fork and cut it up like a normal person, but I'm also aware she eats it like this to irk me. Otherwise she has impeccable table manners. Besides, mostly I'm thankful our tradition of breakfast at the Pancake House after an away series has remained intact, despite all the other changes in our lives.

Hollis stares at her and says nothing.

"Get a side, if you're desperate for your own." She turns to me. "You were great during the away series. How does it feel to almost have a total shutout over the last three games?"

"Amazing, to be honest." I was legitimately worried about how I would perform, especially with the constant tension between me and Lexi. But I managed to keep my head in the game. We returned with three wins, shifting us back into the top ten teams.

"I love that you're both having such a great season. Especially with it being your last. And maybe yours." Peggy rests her cheek against Hollis's biceps.

"Probably mine," Hollis says.

"They could extend," I argue.

"Doesn't mean I have to accept the offer, though." He pokes at his food.

It's looking more likely that he'll hang up his skates at the same time as me. Not being alone as I navigate what's next sounds nice.

"We'll figure it all out." Peggy pats his arm and directs her next question at me. "Are you any closer to making a decision on what you want to do next year?"

"I talked to my agent about the Hockey Academy satellite campus opening here and I reached out to Alex Waters." I won't move away from my only daughter. And I have no plans to leave Toronto when Lexi is here.

Peggy reaches across the table to touch my arm. "It would be so good if you stayed close. Both of you would be great coaches."

"I would never leave you. You're my baby." It doesn't matter that she's self-sufficient, she'll always be a top priority. "They have a summer program for university students that they hope to start in May." I'm testing the waters.

"It's too bad we'll be in playoffs then." Hollis sips his coffee.

"Unless I take early retirement."

Peggy laughs. "As if."

Rainbow, our regular waitress, stops by to freshen our coffees. "Is everything okay with the hash today?" she asks Hollis.

"Oh, yeah. It's great as usual," he assures her. "Just overdid it on the snacks before I got here."

Peggy gets a message, distracting her from the Hockey Academy conversation. "Looks like you can finish my sausage after all. I need to head over to Rix's." She shoves her phone in her banana duck bag.

"Everything okay?" I ask.

"Mostly. Nate is moving in with Flip next week so they need to get his stuff out of storage and Rix is stressing about the wedding. Summer is basically tomorrow in her head. It'll all be fine, but she needs some girl time." She kisses Hollis on the cheek. "Love you."

Hollis arches a brow. "I love you too, Princess."

"I know. It's written all over your gorgeous face every day." She squeezes his arm. She slides out of her seat and comes around to hug me from behind and kiss my cheek too. "Love you, Dado."

"Are Rix and Tristan okay?" I ask once she's out the door. Tristan, who is known for being a notoriously surly fucker is the happiest I've ever seen him. But I know they've had some ups and downs, especially with all the damage Tristan's mother left behind.

"They're good." Hollis stabs Peggy's sausage and transfers it to his plate. "Rix is a bit overwhelmed about planning a wedding and being full time in university and trying to work part-time, though."

"Why is she still working part-time with all that going on?" She also preps meals for a bunch of us on top of everything else she does.

"I guess Tristan has been topping up her account, but instead of using it, she's invested it, which sounds like a Rix thing to do. But also, she's running herself a little ragged. She's terrible at accepting help, always wanting to be self-sufficient. Aurora is trying to be a sounding board. She knows what it's like to be surrounded by big earners and be in a job that doesn't have the same kind of potential." He drags the sausage bite through Peggy's pool of maple syrup.

"Is Peggy struggling?" I ask.

He shakes his head. "No. I mean, she thinks it's pretty comical when we compare bank statements, but she's used to it because she's grown up in it. Rix is still trying to catch up."

Rainbow stops by, and Hollis asks for a takeout box. We settle the tab and leave the Pancake House, crossing the street and pushing through the doors of our building.

"You busy, or uh…you got a little time to hang out?" Hollis asks as we step into the elevator.

I swipe my fob and hit the button for the penthouse floor. "I can hang out."

"Great. Cool." He leans against the rail and runs a hand through his hair. Then shoves his hand in his pocket.

"Everything okay?" I ask.

"Yeah. Good. Great." He nods a bunch of times.

He's cagey as fuck. The elevator stops, and a couple joins us —from the gym based on their workout clothes and slightly sweaty appearance. They get off a few floors before us. Again, Hollis waits until I get off before he does. He follows me into my penthouse, sets his takeout bag on the entry table and wipes his hands on his jeans.

Hollis and I have been friends for a long time. I can read him pretty easily, and while I missed a lot of signs when he and my daughter were sneaking around last season, it's pretty obvious he's nervous about something. "Okay, man, what's going on?"

"We need to talk."

His tone makes my heart beat double time. "Not a good sentence to start with. I swear to fucking God, Hollis, if you've gotten my twenty-one-year-old daughter pregnant—"

"No! She's not pregnant. She's on the pill. We're super careful. We use extra protec—"

I hold up a hand. "I don't need more information about that."

"Fair. Right. Yes. I'm sorry." He exhales a long breath. "We've been together for a year."

"Openly for a little better than six months," I point out.

"It's more like nine," he argues. "She's it for me, Roman. I love her more than life. More than hockey. I know this has been hard to get used to, and that you've got a lot going on already, but I can't see a future without her. There's a good chance I'll retire at the end of this season with you. I just want to be prepared, you know?"

"For?"

"The next step. I want her to be my wife, and I know it seems fast, and I'm not saying I want it to happen right away, but the past couple of years... We've been through a lot together." He rubs his bottom lip. "I'm asking for your permission."

"To propose?"

"Yeah. Not like next week, but at least within the next year. Probably more like six months."

"I need a drink." I cross to the bar and turn over two crystal glasses. They were my dad's. My mom gave them to me when he passed away and she moved to Arizona to be closer to her cousins.

I pour both of us a scotch. Three fingers. I pass him a glass and take a hefty gulp of mine. It's two in the afternoon.

"Roman?"

"Just give me a second, please." I take another gulp. "She's my baby."

"I know." He sips his scotch.

"She's...so young."

"We can have a long engagement," he bargains.

I hold up a hand. "I'm not going to stand in your way, Hollis. I know how much you love her. And I know she loves you back just as fiercely. She's always been sure of her path in life. You have my permission. I just..." I swirl the amber liquid in my glass. "Didn't think this was coming so soon. I thought I'd be settled. I thought maybe..." I shake my head. "I thought I'd be in this position before my daughter."

"Well, to be fair, you haven't put a whole lot of effort into meeting someone."

"I wanted to be done with the travel." I move to one of the armchairs and sink into it.

Hollis does the same. "No offense, Roman, but that sounds like a convenient excuse not to get into something. And I get it.

For a long time I used my breakup with Scarlet as a reason not to get involved—just like not wanting to upset your relationship with Aurora was yours. But she's settled. Hell, she settles me. You'll never stop being her dad, but I'll take care of her. I'll love her and be devoted to her. You're good to focus on you."

"I can't have what I want right now, anyway," I retort.

"You want to talk about that?" Hollis sips his scotch and gives me the eyebrow.

I blink at him.

He blinks back.

It's a standoff.

"It'll probably feel good to talk about it. This is me, Roman. I'm still your best friend."

"You're dating my daughter. The dynamics have changed. Your allegiance is to her now." It sounds harsher than I intend, mostly because I feel like a bag of shit for lying to him for as long as I have.

But this is Hollis. He doesn't take offense. "To a certain point. But if you tell me something in confidence, I'll keep it to myself."

"Like you kept the sandwich and shirt fuck to yourself?" I inquire.

"Dallas told Hemi first. Probably so she wouldn't make him dress up like a clown for keeping it from her for so long," he grumbles.

"That's fair." And I had Lexi to talk to. Besides, I'm tired of the lies and the way they make me feel. "Remember that weekend you and I were supposed to go to New York, but Micha went into labor?"

"Yeah, of course. You went on your own." His expression turns knowing. "And met Lexi."

"I met Lexi," I agree.

"Fuck. I knew something was up when her dad came to the Watering Hole. Did you two spend the night together?"

"The whole weekend."

The weight in my stomach lifts as I unravel the lies I've had to tell him. I fill him in on everything, right down to the kiss we shared last week at the club before she went home. I messaged to make sure she got back okay. She did. And she also said that it couldn't happen again.

"Well, that's fucking messy," Hollis says. "That makes what happened with Dallas and Hemi last year seem like a walk in the park. How are you going to deal with this?"

"We wait until I'm retired before we pursue it."

Hollis blows out a breath. "What if we make it to the final round of the playoffs again? I know what the odds are, but it could happen. Do you think you can toe that line until then?"

"I won't ruin her career. And that's exactly what would happen. It'll be hard enough when I'm not playing anymore. It would ruin her if it got out now. I can't do that to her."

Hollis takes a long swig of his scotch. "I see what you're saying. But as someone who tried to stay on the right side of the line, even knowing what I stood to lose, eventually I broke."

"It's a handful of months."

"Can you both keep your distance for that long?"

"I know what the optics are. What other choice do I have? Unless I retire early."

His brows rise. "I thought you were joking earlier. Is that something you're considering?"

"It could solve the problem."

The question is, would it create new ones?

CHAPTER 25

LEXI

My desk is covered in paper, my whiteboard looks like my brain exploded all over it, and Fee's school just called asking me to pick her up, because she's been suspended. Today has been a clusterfuck.

I save all my work and make sure it's on the cloud. At least it's not a game day, or I'd be totally screwed. I slide my phone and laptop into my bag, pull my door closed behind me. "It'll be fine, just explain the situation. He has kids, he'll understand," I mutter to myself as I walk down the hall to Vander Zee's office. My stomach flipflops anyway. I hate that I don't have the strategy plan finished, but I've been agonizing over it for three hours, hung up on the little details. Second-guessing every decision. Not wanting to disappoint Vander Zee, or the team.

I knock on his door, and he calls me in. "You ready to talk through your plan? I didn't see it come through my email yet."

"I'm almost there, just a few pieces to iron out, but Fee has an emergency at school, and I need to pick her up. I know we're supposed to meet before I leave to discuss it, but I might need to send it from home later tonight, if I can't make it back here."

He nods. "That's fine. As long as I can look it over tonight, we can meet in the morning to talk it through. Is everything okay?"

"Yeah. Everything's fine," I lie.

He narrows his eyes, obviously questioning the truth of my statement. "Let me know if you need help with anything."

"Will do. Thanks. And I'm sorry about this."

"No problem."

I rush down the hall and wait impatiently for the elevator.

And of course, because today isn't hard enough, I run right into Roman when the doors finally open. He's not alone, though. Donnie also steps out. In the months since I've been here, he hasn't warmed up to me in the slightest. Thankfully our interactions are limited and I'm meticulous about logging the equipment.

"Hey." Roman's eyes light up for a moment before his brow furrows. "Are you okay, Le—Coach Forrester?"

I force a smile. "I'm fine. Just a minor school emergency." I brush by him and step into the elevator, glancing at Donnie, who seems far too interested in this interaction. Or maybe I'm being paranoid. "Have a good afternoon." I punch the close-door button, cutting off Roman's concerned expression.

Dred knowing is one thing, but if someone in the office finds out, I'll be in so much trouble.

I don't have time to worry about that, though, not with whatever is going on with Fee. It's well past the end of the school day by the time I arrive. At least Callie takes a bus directly to hockey practice, so she's fine for now. I'm escorted into the principal's office to have a conversation about Fee's recent concerning behavior, and the resulting five-day suspension.

Not for the first time, I question whether I can handle this, if I'm equipped to be my sisters' guardian, if all I'll do is mess them up. Here's hoping a therapist can fix what I might be breaking.

I assure the administration team that I'll handle things and usher Fee into the car.

"Possession with intent to distribute, Fee? What the hell were you thinking?" I grip the steering wheel as I drive to Callie's hockey practice.

Her arms are crossed, she's slouched in her seat, and her hood is up. "It's not that big a deal. They're making it seem like I was dealing drugs. It's just vapes."

"Hood down so I can see your face."

She sighs dramatically.

"Hood down."

She yanks it off but drops her head so her curtain of hair covers her face.

"If it was one vape, I might be able to get over it, but you were carrying *several.* So either your friends are using you as their keeper, or you *are* intending to sell them. Either is bad. So which one is it?"

"My friends aren't using me," she snaps.

"So you planned to sell them, then."

"No! Oh my God. I'm not selling vapes."

"So why were you carrying all your friends' vapes?"

"Because that's what we do. One person carries them, and we trade off every day."

So only one person takes the heat. It's smart and stupid at the same time. "When did you start vaping?"

"Just like…this year."

"You're a dancer, Fee. It's a terrible habit."

Her head bangs against the seat, and she rolls her eyes. "I don't need a lecture."

"Well, apparently you do, because you're now suspended from school for the next five days! You're grounded until further notice."

"You're not my mom! You can't ground me!"

I know it's not personal, but it still hurts. "I may not be your mother, but whether you like it or not, I'm responsible for you. Do you have any idea how hard life will be if you end up with a criminal record, Fee?"

"They're fucking vapes!" she shouts.

I pull into the arena parking lot and find a spot, shifting into park before I turn to her. "Do not yell at me. I get that nothing about life is easy for you right now, but I didn't make this bad decision for you."

"You're the one who moved us to Toronto!"

"You were on board with this move," I remind her, then sigh. "Look, this isn't a productive conversation. I'm heated, and you're heated. But you can't get suspended from school and expect there to be no punishment."

"The suspension is the punishment."

"The suspension is the consequence. The punishment is a result of the suspension." I cut the engine. "Come on."

"I'm staying here."

"It's minus fifteen. I'm not leaving the keys, and you'll be frozen in five minutes. While I appreciate that you're also unhappy with the situation you've put yourself in, I will not have you dying of hypothermia because you have the same stubborn gene as me," I snap.

Her chin wobbles, and she dashes her tears away. "I need a fucking minute, okay?"

I struggle to keep myself in check, to not cry along with her. "I'm coming back out to get you in ten minutes if you're not in the arena by then."

"Fine."

I open the door. "I might not love your current choice, but I love you, Fee."

She sniffles but doesn't say anything.

"I'll check on you in a bit."

I leave her in the car and head inside, where I stop in the bathroom and take a moment to get myself under control. I'm so close to a complete breakdown. I want to call Dred, but she's at work, and calling Roman will add to the layers of complication I'm already buried under.

I get my shit together, leave the bathroom, and go to Callie's rink. But when I get there, Callie isn't in the net. She's not even in her goalie gear. Instead she's sitting in the stands behind the bench with Glenda Barton, one of the assistant coaches.

"Is everything okay?"

Glenda gives me one of those smiles that tells me everything is *not* okay. Callie's arms are crossed, and she's slumped in her seat. She looks like she's on the verge of tears. Glenda pats her on the arm and meets me at the end of the row, motioning for me to follow her down the hall.

I don't know what to do with my hands so I stuff them in my jacket pockets. When we get to her office, Glenda looks like this is the last thing she wants to handle.

"What did Callie do?" That's the only reason I can see her being off the ice. If she was hurt in some way, Glenda wouldn't have pulled me aside.

"She got into it with one of her teammates," Glenda says.

"Got into it how?" I ask.

"She shoved him and pinned him to the ice when he went down."

"Oh my gosh. Why would she do that?"

"He was chirping her. He absolutely said things that weren't acceptable, and he's been removed from practice today, too. But if we hadn't pulled her off, we were worried she would have hit him."

"I'm so sorry." Callie is a lot of things, but violent isn't usually one of them.

"Me, too. I wish we would have caught things sooner, and I feel awful. I know how important hockey is to Callie, but we have zero tolerance for physical violence."

"I get it. How long is she out?" It's her one escape, and I worry about how she'll deal—and how I'll manage without an after-school program for any length of time.

"Three practices."

"Is she allowed to watch?" I ask.

"We're asking the other player to stay home for the next two practices, and we'd ask that Callie do the same, just for some cool-off and reflection time. But after that, she can support the team by sitting in the stands if she wants."

At least Fee will be home to help manage, so there's that. "Okay. I understand. I'm sorry about this. I'll have a talk with her."

"I know you have a lot on your plate. This can't be easy for your family."

"I appreciate your compassion, but it certainly doesn't excuse Callie's behavior. I'll impress upon her the importance of handling interactions like these with words instead of aggression."

I return to the rink to gather Callie and her equipment, and we go out to the car.

Unlike Fee, she doesn't give me sass. She follows along, side-eyeing me as I stride through the parking lot. I just need to get them home, dole out punishments, and have a private emotional breakdown of my own.

Fee is in the front seat, trying to use makeup to hide the fact that her eyes are puffy. "I was just coming in." She frowns. "Practice isn't over yet."

"It is for Callie." I direct her into the back seat and round the driver's side.

"What happened?" Fee asks as I close the door behind me.

"Callie got into a fight, so she has a few days off from hockey practice."

"But he—"

I hold up my hand. "Not now. Let's get home, and then we can deal."

Callie bites her lips together.

I turn the engine over and focus on getting us back to the condo. I'm so out of my depth. I have no idea how to deal with a teenager who was caught vaping and an eight-year-old who's picking fights with her teammates.

The drive home is tense. Every part of me feels like it's

sparking. My dad won't be any help. He basically moved to New York when I was a toddler, and I only saw him on holidays and for a month in the summer. He had me in hockey camp out there, and I spent almost all my time on the ice when I visited him. He didn't have to parent me. I was too busy to find trouble.

Callie is crying as silently as she can by the time we get home, and Fee isn't much better. She helps Callie out of the back seat, I grab Callie's hockey equipment, and we pile into the elevator. I'm choking on the silence, on the certainty that I'm messing these girls up. That I can't hack it. That I'll crack under the pressure.

My phone buzzes with new messages. "Fuck." I still have to finish the strategy plans for Vander Zee tonight.

Callie's head snaps in my direction.

I don't apologize for the swear. I'm exhausted, overwhelmed, and terrified that I'm headed for a cliff with no brakes. I pull my phone from my pocket. There are new messages in the Babe Brigade chat, which is normal, but I also have new messages from Roman—one from more than an hour ago, and one recent.

ROMAN

Hope everything is okay. Message when you can.

Followed by the recent one:

ROMAN

I've got the best pizza in the city on speed dial if you need dinner sent to you.

I look toward the ceiling, trying to keep my emotions in check. I'm reaching my breaking point, and here he is, being so sweet and thoughtful.

"Lexi?"

"I'm fine," I croak.

I type a quick reply.

LEXI

All good here!

We're barely in the door before my phone rings. Of course it's Roman. "I need to take this," I tell my sisters. "I would like both of you to go to your rooms. I'll call you when I'm ready to discuss your choices today." I wait until they've disappeared down the hall before I answer the call. "Hey."

"You never write text messages with exclamation marks. What's wrong?"

And that's all it takes for the dam to break. The first sob escapes, and I slap a palm over my mouth and rush down the hall to my bedroom. Throwing the door closed, I lock it and disappear into the closet so my sisters can't hear me losing it.

"Lexi, angel, I'm on my way over. I'm leaving now. I'll be fifteen minutes at the most."

"You d-d-don't—"

"No arguments. I'm already on my way. Take a breath. I'm not hanging up, the reception might be crappy for a minute, and if I lose you, I'll call back as soon as I'm out of the parking garage. Breathe with me, okay?" He counts to four and back down to one.

I follow the soothing cadence of his voice. "This is so hard, Roman."

"What happened? Are your sisters okay?" he asks.

"Yes. No. They're okay, but they're not coping. I'm not coping. I feel like I'm drowning," I whisper.

"I'll be there soon, okay? And we'll figure it out together." A car starts. "You don't have to do this on your own." He keeps talking, assuring me I've got this, and he'll help me through it.

My walls are crumbling. Having Roman come here is the wrong thing to do. But I need him. So I don't lie and say I'll be fine. I stay on the line while he drives to my place.

"Okay. I'm here and parked. Just buzz me in, and I'll be up in a minute."

CHAPTER 26

LEXI

I'm under control enough to pick myself up off the closet floor and buzz Roman in. When I open the door, he takes one look at me, steps inside, and folds me into his strong, warm embrace. "I've got you. Whatever it is, we'll figure it out."

I grip his jacket and hold on for dear life, like he can stop me from sinking. Like he's a life preserver in rough waters. Like I finally have permission to be vulnerable. With him, I don't have to be strong and in control all the time. "I don't know how to do this. I'm failing them."

"Oh, angel, no you're not." He tips my chin up. "Tell me what happened. What's going on?"

I recount the whole story through stuttered breaths and hiccups.

"This doesn't sound like you're failing. It sounds like two kids who lost their parents are struggling with how to handle their emotions. Should we get them out here so we can talk it through?"

"They can't see me like this." I dash tears away.

"Yes, they can, and they should. You're hurting too. You're not their parent, you're their sister, and they need to understand that this is just as hard for you as it is for them. It's okay for them to see you upset. It's how you connect, and heal." He presses his lips to my forehead, then guides me to the living room.

I sit on the couch, and he crouches in front of me, his hands on my knees. He's just so incredible. Kind and gentle when the circumstances call for it, intensely focused and ruthlessly competent when it comes to his job and…other things. He knows how to handle this situation and how to calm me. I'm falling deeper every day, and I'm powerless to stop it.

"I'm sorry," I whisper.

"For what?" He tucks my hair behind my ear.

For so many things, starting with the morning I left him sleeping in that hotel bed without saying goodbye. "For being such a hot mess. For dragging you into this."

"No one dragged me here. I called you. I didn't ask if I could come over; I told you I was. I was showing up no matter what, Lexi. Staying away from you, maintaining a veneer of professionalism, I do those things for *you*, not me. But when you're hurting, I can't toe that line. I won't. And I will face whatever consequences there are for that, because *not* being here when you need me isn't something I can handle."

"Why do you have to be so amazing?" My bottom lip trembles.

"Why do you?" He passes me a tissue.

"I'm trying so hard not to need you, Roman."

He strokes my cheek. "That's because you always have to be the strong one. It's okay to need someone. It took me until you showed up to realize that."

I exhale a steadying breath. There are so many things I want to say, but the words won't come.

"We can figure us out later, when you're not in an emotional tornado."

I laugh, and he smiles.

"You let me know when you're ready to handle the girls."

I nod. "I'm ready."

"You've got this, Lexi. Take a few deep breaths. I'll get Callie and Fee. It's okay for them to see you cry." He kisses me on the cheek and stands.

I watch him walk down the hall, wondering what the hell my sisters will think when he comes knocking on their doors. I guess I'll find out soon enough. He returns a minute later with Fee and Callie. Both look like they've been crying, and both are wide-eyed.

"Lexi?" Callie runs over. "I'm sorry! I didn't mean to make you cry!" Her tears start all over again.

Fee drops her head and peeks up at us through her curtain of hair. I hold out a hand, and she comes around to the other side. And then we're a mass of limbs and tears. Roman takes a seat on one of the occasional chairs. He's so calm, composed, completely in control—the opposite of how he is when we're fighting the draw. But all these sides of him, all the versions I've come to know these past few months create a man I desperately want to be with.

I'm past falling. I've fallen. That realization is sobering. And damning. But I don't want to undo it. Not when he's here, trying to keep us from shattering. Eventually the tears stop.

The intercom buzzes.

I frown, and the girls look confused.

"That's dinner," Roman says. "It's hard to have a productive conversation when everyone is upset and hangry." He excuses himself to get the door.

"I really like him a lot," Callie says.

"Me, too," I whisper.

"Me three. Having him around makes me miss Dad a little less," Fee admits.

And my heart cracks in two all over again.

Roman returns with pizza, boneless chicken wings, and double-chocolate cake. The girls help set the table and dig in. Of course Roman knows all our favorites. Because he pays attention. Because he cares.

"Okay, let's discuss what happened today that resulted in everyone in tears," Roman says once we all have food.

"I'd like to hear your side of things, not just what I've been told by someone else," I add.

Callie takes a deep breath. "Eddie has been chirping me a lot. He wants to be the goalie, but he's not good enough. At first he would say things when I let a goal get by, but lately he's started saying other stuff."

"What kind of other stuff?" I ask.

She ducks her head and picks the burned cheese off her crust. "About me not having parents, and that they only made me goalie because they feel sorry for me."

"Did you tell any of your coaches about this?" Roman, bless his gorgeous heart, looks like he wants to flip the table.

Callie shakes her head.

"Why not?" I ask.

"Because I don't want to cry in front of my team. So I keep it inside until I'm in my bedroom, and then I let the feelings out," she admits softly. "But today they came out in the wrong way, and now I'm in trouble."

My stomach twists, and my heart squeezes. This poor little girl is struggling to keep it together, and I had no idea. "I can share this with your coaches, Callie. They should know what's going on."

"I don't want it to get worse," Callie admits.

"You've done a great job being level-headed on the ice," I assure her, glancing at Roman, looking to him for support, for assurance, because I'm so new at this and he has experience I don't.

He dips his chin in agreement. "It's an important job when you're the goalie."

Callie peels a pepperoni off her pizza. "You never lose your cool."

"I've had a lot of years to practice," he reminds her. "And

sometimes I do lose my cool. Ask Lexi. She's had to school me more than once this season during practice."

"Really?" Callie's eyes are wide.

"A couple of times, sure. No one is perfect," I explain. "I understand that you want to prove you deserve your place on the team, Callie, and that this boy is jealous because you have the position he wants. But not telling your coaches means he thinks what he's doing is okay, and it's not."

"He makes me so angry I want to cry," she says.

"Your teammates are supposed to be an extension of your family, so it's okay to cry in front of them," I explain.

"Tears make you human. And we all cry," Roman adds.

"Even you?"

"Yup. Even me." Roman turns his attention to Fee. "Your turn."

She sinks in her chair. "Lexi can just tell you."

"We'd prefer to hear your version," I press. Having a partner to do this with is so much less stressful. I don't feel like I'm second guessing every word that comes out of my mouth. And I trust that Roman will redirect if it's necessary.

She sets her pizza on her plate and gives me an imploring look.

I shake my head. "Why don't you want to explain what happened?"

"Because I feel stupid."

"Callie, do you have ranch dressing?" Roman asks.

"I dunno." She shrugs and lines all her pepperonis up on one end of her pizza. It's what she always does.

"Can you check the fridge for me, please?" he asks.

"Okay." She slips off her chair and heads for the kitchen. Roman waits until she's out of earshot before he drops his voice and addresses Fee. "When I was your age, I got my high school girlfriend pregnant because neither of us thought to read the fine print on her birth control pills. So whatever life changing thing you think you did, I'm pretty sure I have you beat. Now, Peggy is hands down the best thing that's ever happened to me. I wouldn't change having her for the world, but it definitely would have been better for her if I'd been about ten years older and a lot more settled before I brought her into the world. However, that's not how it went."

I didn't think I could find him more endearing, but this absolutely takes the cake.

Fee wrinkles her nose. "You were my age when Hammer was born?"

"I was eighteen. I'd just been drafted. It was quite the eventful year." He leans back and crosses his arms. "The floor for questionable choices is now yours. See if you can one-up me."

"I got caught with all my friends' vapes in my backpack."

Roman props his chin on his fist. "Why did you have all your friends' vapes in your backpack?"

It's the old repeat-the-statement-back-to-the-person trick.

She cringes. "Because I'm an idiot."

"Try again."

She sighs. "Because I wanted to fit in."

"And do you fit in now?" He's so calm about it. So unruffled.

Seeing him like this should *not* get me hot, especially under the circumstances, but damn, he's good at this.

She focuses on her plate. "Only, like, one of the girls in the group has messaged, and it was to see if I still had their stuff."

"They sound like a bunch of assholes and not great friends," Roman observes.

"They're not." She sighs. "I don't know where I fit anymore. I wanted to leave my old school because I was the girl whose parents died at the lake. And now I'm the girl who got caught with vapes."

"Here's the ranch dressing!" Callie plops back into her seat.

"Thanks, kiddo." Roman winks, then looks to Fee. "Why don't you just be you?"

"I don't even know who that is anymore! Other than my fandom friends online, I don't feel people at school even want to make room for new friends. I think those kids just want to be my friend because I get to hang out with you and the other guys on the Terror. I can't talk about my weekends or who I'm with without it sounding like I'm bragging. Tally gets it, but no one else does, and she's already in university, so we can't hang out all the time. And it's not like she wants to spend all her time with a high schooler. It's my last year, and everything is hard, and I wanted it to be fun, but it's the opposite." She deflates like a balloon.

"Tally has been hanging out with my daughter and the other Terror women for the past two years. She was a high school senior last year, and my daughter, who will be twenty-two soon, spent loads of time with her. Very willingly. They'd happily welcome you, if that's where you feel the most comfortable. Rix, Peggy, and Tally understand your situation, and it makes sense that you want to spend time with people who get you just as you are."

"That's all I want. Just for people to get me." Fee turns to me. "I love you, and I'm super grateful that you let me and Callie come live with you, but things are so different. You're not just my sister anymore. And then we moved, and I wanted it to be a fresh start, but sometimes I don't know what to do with myself. I know you're already stressed out because of this new job, and I didn't want to add to it by dumping my problems on you."

"Talking to me when you're having a hard time isn't dumping your problems on me. I'm here for you, both of you," I assure her. "And I know our relationship has changed a lot, but I will always be here to help and listen. And Roman is right, the Terror girls are great, and if you want to spend more time with them, we can make that happen."

"I think you and Peggy probably have more in common than you realize," Roman says.

"Really? How?" Fee asks.

Roman tells her about how Peggy came to live with him when she was six, and she was basically raised by him and the team. He ended up hanging out with a lot of the older players who had families, because it made more sense after he had full custody of Peggy. Every word he speaks, every story he shares, every moment of connection he forms with my sisters winds him tighter around my heart.

"Did Peggy ever get in trouble?" Fee asks.

"Everyone gets in trouble. It's about learning from your mistakes," Roman replies.

"Did you ground her?" Callie asks, eyes wide.

"Depended on the circumstances. Sometimes I asked her what her punishment should be."

The girls look to me. "Do you think we should try that?" I ask.

They glance at each other.

"It's worth a shot," Roman offers.

In the end, they're harder on themselves than I ever would have been. Eventually I send them to their rooms because it's getting late. Callie needs to go to bed, and Fee has homework. Callie is wiped from all the emotion, so it only takes one story for her to fall asleep.

"Why are you made of magic?" I ask Roman when I return to the kitchen and find the leftovers already put away and the dishes done.

"I have experience raising a girl in this environment. And I fully admit, I leveraged my power with them, which makes it easier. But you did great. You're not failing, Lexi. Your instincts are spot on, and you love them so much. That's what matters most." He leans his hip against the counter. "I have a question, though, and it's personal."

"Okay."

"Have the girls gone to therapy at all?"

"They did some grief counseling, but neither of them stuck with it," I admit. It was tough that first year. I was pulled in so many different directions, and neither of them really connected to the grief counselor.

"I have a name of a great therapist. Peggy's been seeing her for years, and she's wonderful with kids. You have good coverage. It might be helpful for them to have a sounding board that isn't their friends or you."

I sigh. "You're right. I know you're right. I'll suggest it." It's been on my mind a lot lately—not just for them, but for me, too. I saw someone back in Niagara, but not since I moved to Toronto.

"They know you love them," he says. "And they adore you." He runs his hands up and down my arms.

"Thank you. This is so hard. I sound like a broken record." I pinch the bridge of my nose. "Shit. I have a strategy plan I need to finish for Vander Zee, and it's already after eight. I was supposed to have it done before I left, and then all this happened."

"I can help you."

"You've already done more than enough tonight."

He gazes down at me and the intensity makes my knees weak. "I'm already here, and I have twenty years of on ice experience. It's okay to take advantage of me in this situation." He smirks and winks.

I laugh and lift a hand to block out his face. "You have to behave yourself and not look at me like that."

His fingers wrap around mine and he presses my palm to my chest. "Take me to your office, Coach."

"Yes, Goalie."

He makes a sound in the back of his throat and leans down until his lips are at my ear. "You know I'm keeping track of all *your* bad behavior so I can dole out your punishments one at a time when the season is finally over."

"Things to look forward to," I murmur pushing the door to

my office open. It's so hard not to forget myself when we're alone like this.

He frowns when he steps inside. "This is a storage closet, not an office."

There's not much room to turn around with the two of us in here, especially since Roman is so tall and broad. "It's better than working in the living room or my bedroom." I pat the executive chair. "Have a seat."

"What about you?"

"I have a wobble stool under the desk." I drag it out. It has a round bottom and I use it sometimes when I have more hours in a chair than I'd like.

"I'll take the stool, you sit in the chair." He motions for me to sit. His expression doesn't leave any room for argument.

It's almost comical how much he dwarfs the stool. He moves in close, one arm stretched across the back of my chair as I pull up the strategy plan and try not to focus on how close Roman is.

He takes control of the mouse, scrolling through the document. "This is fantastic, Lexi. You're capitalizing on everyone's strengths, giving rookie players time on the ice, rotating in seasoned players to make sure the lines are balanced. It's a top tier strategy plan. All it needs is a few minor tweaks and you're good to go."

His praise makes my heart race. Next season I won't have to worry about being alone with him. We could do this together all the time. He could be my partner in all ways. "You really think so?" I turn to look at him.

"You've got this," he assures me.

"It's nice to hear it from you," I admit.

His expression softens. "You are brilliant, Lexi. A born leader on the ice. That I get to witness you soar during my final year with the Terror is an absolute honor. This is just the beginning for you."

"I couldn't do any of this without you," I whisper.

"You could and you have." His gaze heats. "And if I didn't

want to fuck you senseless all the time, I'd be sorry that I don't get to stick around to see you really shine."

My breath leaves me on a whoosh. We're so close. Inches apart. If either of us leaned in we could deal with the wild, unceasing chemistry between us. But we can't. Not again.

His eyes slide closed. "Fuck. Sorry. I'm not doing a great job of being on my best behavior." He shifts his position, removing his arm from the back of my chair and refocusing on the screen. "What's your plan if we're leading in the third period?"

It takes a moment to switch back into professional mode. "Rotate Ryker in, if we're leading, Palaniappa and Grace on the same line as Madden to give us the best scoring shot and the strongest defense."

"Excellent. That's smart strategy. It works with the teams' strengths." His smile is beautiful and affirming and sparks the neediest places inside me.

"Thanks." His pride settles the deepest fears in me. He makes me feel capable, strong, sure of my path.

"See? You didn't need my help. Trust your gut."

"But it's nice to have someone to toss around ideas with. And even nicer to have you here." I make the tweaks to the strategy plan and email them to Vander Zee.

Roman stands and holds out a hand, pulling me to my feet. He wraps his arms around me, and I do the same. We stand there for a long time, neither of us willing to let go. I feel his lips on my crown. "I have to go."

"I know. I can walk you out."

He cups my face in his hands, eyes roving hotly over my face. "It's better if you don't."

"Are you okay?"

"Hitting my limit on self-control. Counting down the days until I don't have to put up walls when I'm around you. Be a good girl and wait until you hear the door close." He presses his lips to my forehead. "Night, angel."

"Night, Roman. Thank you for everything."

"Thank you for trusting me." He leaves me standing in my office, heart drumming in my chest, body aching. We didn't cross the line, though. It should feel like a win, but all it does is make me long for what could be, if we can just make it to the end of the season.

CHAPTER 27

ROMAN

"Alex, it's great to see you."

"Thanks for agreeing to meet with me." Alex Waters, hockey legend and huge inspiration, steps inside Hollis's penthouse.

"It's an honor." Hollis shakes his hand.

"Hi. Hello. I'm Aurora, Roman's daughter and Hollis's girlfriend. We met last year at the gala." Peggy is practically vibrating with excitement.

Alex's smile widens. "I remember. That was a really fun event. My wife and daughter, Lavender, talked about it for weeks. We're looking forward to attending again this year."

"We're so thrilled you're coming back! Why don't you all get comfortable, and I'll bring out refreshments." She flits off to the kitchen.

"She's a big fan." Hollis leads us through the penthouse into the living room.

Postie and Malone, his rescue tabbies, come out to greet us. Alex takes a seat in one of the chairs, and Postie immediately jumps onto the arm, looking for pets.

"This guy is a bit of a lover," Hollis warns.

"I like cats." He scratches Postie's head.

"Just don't let him straddle your arm. He'll treat it like it's his girlfriend."

I cough to hide my laugh and take a seat in the other chair.

"Good to know." Alex doesn't seem fazed in the slightest. Although I've read some of the things his wife says in interviews, so I doubt much shocks him.

"I'll just go help Aurora. She kind of went all out." Hollis excuses himself.

"Were they together at the gala last year?" Alex asks.

"Not publicly yet." I rap on the armrest. "How's the family? How are your kids?"

"They're great. Lavender loves New York, and my son Maverick has really stepped up and taken an active role in the Hockey Academy. My youngest boy is working on his PhD, and he's getting married this spring. I'm just waiting for my oldest to get tired of the West Coast and move back this way with my granddaughter."

"That can't be easy." I can't imagine Peggy being on the other side of the country. It was hard enough when she was living with Zara and they moved around for those few years before she came to stay with me full time.

"We visit them often. But I can't lie, I'd love to have everyone closer," Alex replies.

Hollis and Peggy reappear with a charcuterie board and an array of drinks, including coffee, beer, sparkling water, and soda.

"You weren't kidding about going all out," Alex says. "This looks great."

"It's no problem!" Peggy sets the tray of drinks on the coffee table. "I'll leave you guys to it."

Hollis catches her hand. "You can stay, Princess."

"Are you sure?"

"You're more than welcome," Alex agrees.

I give her an encouraging smile. She and Hollis take a seat on the couch.

"I'm excited about your plans for the Hockey Academy," I say.

"We've been floating the idea of expansion for a few years." Alex scratches Postie when he headbutts his hand. "I grew up not far from here."

"In Guelph," Peggy supplies.

"That's right." Alex turns his sportscaster smile on my daughter. "My parents still live there. They love visiting Pearl Lake, but they're getting older, and I want to make it easier to spend time with them. Opening a satellite campus here is a great way to accomplish that and grow the program."

"There's definitely demand for it." Hockey camps fill up quickly around here.

"There is. But to make it work, I need a staff with the same kind of passion as my team in Pearl Lake. I know you're retiring this year, Roman, and Hollis, your contract is up, although I'm sure Toronto will want to extend. But if you decide you want to go in a different direction, we'd love to recruit you. No pressure. Just an option to consider."

"What positions are you looking to fill?" I ask.

"Recruiting, management, coaching. We'll need a full staff. Some are already in place, but we want to prepare for as much growth as possible," Alex says.

"That sounds fantastic." Peggy hugs Hollis's arm.

This is exactly what I've been hoping for. "I'd love to prepare up-and-comers for the pros." Lexi can stay with the Terror, and we can be together without bureaucratic red tape.

"This is absolutely something I would consider," Hollis says. "You know what it's like to have a serious injury. I won't jeopardize my body more than I already have."

"I get it." Alex nods. "It'll be big change for the team if you're both done at the end of the season."

"Ryker's already in position to take over for me," I say.

"And me leaving will give a rookie more ice time," Hollis adds.

"Maybe Fielding and Vander Zee will be interested in picking up Quinn Romero," Alex muses.

"That kid's got skill. I'm surprised I haven't seen him on a roster yet." He's the son of Lance Romero, another legend in hockey and one of Alex's good friends.

"Fingers crossed. I'd take him on as part of my team at the Hockey Academy, but I'd hate to see that talent squandered."

"Agreed." My wheels are already turning. "How soon are you looking to onboard your coaching staff?"

"The sooner the better, but I'm aware you're mid-season."

"You'd want to start before the season ends?" I press. This could be the excuse I need.

"If you're interested in coaching, we'll wait for you. Having you as our lead goalie coach would be phenomenal for the program." Alex continues to scratch Postie's head. The alternative is being swatted.

"You have a high school and a university summer program slated?" I tap the armrest.

"That's right. The university program begins in early May, and high school in early July," Alex replies.

I glance at Hollis. "Ryker could handle the playoffs."

Peggy's eyes flare. "You can't retire before the end of the season."

A knock at the door saves me from answering.

"I'll get that." Peggy crosses the room, eyeing me as she goes.

I give her a reassuring smile, though that's exactly what I'm considering.

"Some program graduates wanted to say hello," Hollis explains.

Alex grins. "I was hoping to see some of the boys while I'm in town."

Tristan, Flip, and Dallas file into the penthouse, Rix trailing behind them with Peggy.

Rix stops short when she sees Alex and grabs Peggy's arm. "Oh! Oh my God."

Tristan frowns and looks over his shoulder. "You all right, Bea?"

"I'll be right back! I have to grab my Alex Waters milk ad!" She spins around and heads for the door.

"What is she talking about?" Tristan's brow is extra furrowed.

"Didn't you do an ad for milk back when you were playing for Chicago?" Flip asks.

"Yeah. But that was like…a really long time ago," Alex says.

"She has that magazine," Peggy replies helpfully.

"Since when?" Tristan asks.

Peggy shrugs. "Dunno. But she put it in a plastic sleeve to preserve it."

"Huh." Tristan scrubs his chin.

We spend the afternoon chatting with Alex. The guys reminisce about the Hockey Academy, and Alex talks about the plan to open a second campus here. Eventually he excuses himself, citing a late lunch with Connor. We invited him over, but while he and Flip are currently managing, he didn't want to dredge up the past.

"Wills will be so disappointed she missed this." Dallas pops the cap on a beer. "What a cool opportunity."

"Callie could spend a summer there when she's old enough!" Peggy grabs my arm. "She would love to have you as a coach."

"I'd love to coach her." To have a hand in helping her develop her skill set would be so rewarding.

"Isn't her birthday coming up?" Tristan asks.

"I'm pretty sure you're right." I'm actually positive. It's marked on Lexi's calendar, which I saw when I was over there last week.

"We should plan something big for her," Tristan declares. "It's her second birthday with no parents. It needs to be something to remember."

"Let's make a list." Rix pulls out her phone.

"I'll grab my laptop, and we can start a spreadsheet." Peggy rushes down the hall and returns a moment later, laptop already open.

We spend the next half hour lobbing ideas back and forth, making lists, assigning tasks, and getting things organized. Tristan is determined to go all out, as is his way when it comes to birthday celebrations. I let him take the lead, mostly so I don't draw attention to how much I know about the things Callie loves.

When all the tasks have been allocated, we disband, and I message Lexi. She's at hockey practice with Callie, so I hop in my SUV.

With Lexi's permission, I stopped by the arena the day after Callie jumped on that kid and had a conversation with the coaching staff. Then I helped her mediate a discussion between Callie, the coaches, and the kid in question. The kid's eyes seemed like they were on the verge of falling out of his head the entire time. I'm not above using my hockey fame to make an impression.

I also sat with Lexi while she called Fee's vice principal. They had a frank discussion about the school's responsibility to check in with a new student who's lost both of her parents and support her during the transition. Fee finished the rest of her suspension in school.

I run into Donnie on my way into the arena. He's toting two hockey bags and a pair of four-year-old boys.

"Coaching tonight?" I ask.

"Yeah, gotta get the experience somewhere, right?" He glances behind me. "What are you doing here?"

"Here to watch a game."

He nods, maybe waiting for me to elaborate. His son tugs on his sleeve. "Dad, we're hungry, can we go now?"

"I should get in there. See you tomorrow, Donnie."

"Yeah, see you later."

I head inside and find Callie's rink, scanning until I locate Lexi. I slide into one of the slightly too-small seats beside her.

"Hey." I skim the back of her hand, just for the contact.

She flips it palm up. "Hey yourself."

I lace our fingers briefly and squeeze before I reluctantly release her hand and clasp mine together. I glance at the scoreboard. "Looks like the game is going well." Callie's team is up by two goals.

"It is. How was your meeting with Waters?"

"He wants Hollis and me to join their coaching staff at the satellite campus in Toronto."

"Oh wow, that's—wow. What did you say?"

"That I'm definitely interested." I rub my bottom lip.

She tracks the movement. "What are your concerns?"

"About the job? None. The Hockey Academy has a great mission, they're one of the most renowned hockey programs out there, and they've produced some of the best players in the league. It'll be a pay cut, but I've had twenty years in the pros, so I'm not concerned about that."

"You're concerned about something, though?" she asks.

Might as well feel her out, see what she thinks. "If I want to coach the university program, it starts in May."

Her eyes flare. "We'll be in the middle of playoffs."

"Ryker could handle the playoffs."

"There has to be another option."

"The summer high school program starts in July."

"You'd be able to finish out the season, then."

"Early retirement would mean we could be together sooner. We could stop fighting the draw." I wouldn't have to keep lying to the people I love.

Her conflict is written all over her face. "It's only a couple more months, Roman. The team needs you."

I want to tell her I need *her*. But I don't want to put that kind of pressure on her, or us. So I let it go. For now. "Okay. We'll get through the season."

But I keep that card in my back pocket. Because the longer we do this, the harder it becomes to deny the truth.

I'm in love with Alexandria Forrester.

CHAPTER 28

LEXI

I head down the hall to Hammer's office. Callie's hockey practice was canceled because there's a problem with the rink. The cancellation email popped up just before I went into a meeting. Fee has dance rehearsals, so Hammer graciously offered to pick Callie up and bring her here.

My heart stutters when I reach her office and take in the scene before me. It's a snapshot of what the future could look like. Hammer sits behind her desk, typing away on her computer. Callie is seated at the small conference table homework spread out, a carton of chocolate milk and a half-eaten scone from the bakery across the street on a napkin next to her. And beside her is Roman, arm stretched across the back of her chair while they work through her math problems.

How would Hammer react if she found out we've been lying to her and everyone else? It makes me feel like trash, especially with the way this team, and especially the women on staff, have showed up for me and the girls since we joined the Terror family. The fear of losing all of this is terrifying.

I push those thoughts away. The end of the season is coming, and with that will be freedom. "Hey, how's it going?"

All three heads turn my way.

"Lexi!" Callie's chair screeches obnoxiously across the floor and she rushes over, throwing her arms around me. "Hammer and Roman picked me up from school! And the head secretary took pictures with Roman, and he gave autographs and everything. We stopped at a bakery, and I tried a scone. And Roman has been helping me with math and I'm almost finished with all my homework! Roman said you have ice time with Connor Grace soon. Can I come to the rink and watch you practice?" She's flying high on the thrill of it all.

"Wow! Sounds like an eventful afternoon, of course you can come to the rink."

"Yay! I'll pack up my stuff!" She bounces back to the table.

"Thank you." I glance between Hammer and Roman. "Both of you. I really appreciate you coming to the rescue."

"It was really no problem," Hammer says with a smile.

"Gave me an excuse to spend some time with Peggy and my favorite goalie before we hit the ice." Roman winks at Callie who beams up at him.

I move in to help put her things back in her pencil case. The guilt is real and heavy as Hammer comes around to help, too.

"I'll see you before the game?" Hammer asks her dad.

"Absolutely, kiddo."

He gives her a hug and she kisses his cheek.

Callie skips over to Hammer and wraps her arms around her waist. "Thanks for picking me up, and for bringing Roman with you."

"It was my pleasure. Next time you come to a game we'll sit together in the box, okay?" Hammer asks.

"Okay!"

Callie slips her hand into mine and Roman slings her backpack over his shoulder. It's comically small compared to the size of him.

"See you later!" I glance over my shoulder to find Hammer smiling softly.

And I wonder, again, how upset she would be if she knew the truth.

"I'm going to watch the game at home tonight. Or at least the first period and maybe part of the second because I have school tomorrow and if I stay up late, I'm grumpy the next day."

"I get grumpy when I stay up late, too," Roman commiserates.

"You do? I've never seen you be grumpy. Except on the ice when someone scores on you. I don't like it when someone scores on me either."

We round the corner and my stomach lurches as Donnie walks out of Thomas's office. His eyebrows rise as he takes in the three of us, walking down the hall together, Roman still holding Callie's backpack.

"Hey, Donnie. How's it going?" Roman is all smiles and friendliness.

I'm in a mild panic spiral, worried that Donnie will jump to accurate conclusions.

"Good, good." He nods slowly, attention shifting to me. "Forrester, I think there's an error in the system. Roman's equipment is logged under you this afternoon."

"It's not an error. I'm heading to the rink shortly with Hammerstein and a couple of the enforcers for a little extra practice."

"Right before a game? Shouldn't the guys be resting up?" he asks.

"We'll be fine," Roman assures him. "I'm going to head down to suit up." He passes Callie her backpack. "I'll see you down, there, okay?"

"Okay! Thanks for helping me with my math homework."

"Anytime, kiddo." Roman turns to Donnie. "You coming to the game tonight?"

"Sure am."

"See you there." He waves and heads down the hall.

"You have a minute?" Donnie asks.

"Sure." My mouth is suddenly bone dry. "Callie, why don't you drop your backpack in my office."

"Okay!" She skips down the hall.

He waits until she disappears into my office. "I see what's going on here."

Heat rushes down my spine. "I'm not sure what you mean."

"You've got our goalie helping your kid with homework?"

"Callie is my sister."

"Right. Whatever. You're clearly taking a page from the other office girls."

"Excuse me?"

"Nothing. Never mind." He shakes his head. "Just remember, everything has to be inventoried properly for cleaning. When you go around Boxer, it becomes your responsibility."

Before I can explain that I didn't go around Boxer, he turns and walks away.

His insinuation hits hard, mainly because there's merit in it. Is that what everyone else will see next season when we're together? That I was just after a player? But I don't have time to fixate on it, because I need to get on the ice.

Callie sits in the seats behind the bench, thrilled to watch her favorite players practice. She's all waving arms and excitement as Grace skates over to accept a hug from her.

"Shouldn't she be at practice?" Grace asks.

"They had an issue with the rink," I explain.

"Ahh, well, that sucks."

"This seems like a decent consolation prize."

We start with a short warm-up before we move into more complicated stick work. It's no longer enough to be fast and agile. Stick work is where it's at.

While Roman has years of experience to help anticipate what's coming at him, Ryker has exceptional agility and the ability to read a player's intentions before he makes the move. It's why Vander Zee brought him to the team. And why we're on the ice hours before a game, hoping to put Ryker in net for the third period.

As much as Grace can be a brute, the guy is fucking magical with stick and puck handling. He can catch a puck midair, flip it, deke around another player, and nab it out of the air before shooting at the net. It's pretty damn spectacular.

I'm about to tell Ryker to protect his left shoulder, because I see what Grace is planning, when Roman shouts, "Ryker, your five hole!"

The puck goes sailing past Ryker's left ear.

I blow the whistle directly at Roman.

He raises both hands. "Sorry, Coach."

"Can you repeat that for me, please, Goalie?"

The corner of his mouth twitches, like he's trying not to react. But I see the heat in his eyes and hope like hell no one else can. "I'm sorry, Coach Forrester." His voice is all gravel.

I stay firmly in coach mode, the interaction with Donnie still sitting heavy in stomach. "Don't apologize to me; apologize to Ryker for giving him the wrong cue. You know as well as I do that Grace doesn't need to wait until the puck hits the ice to shoot it. Those fractions of a second are all it takes for your opposition to score a goal and put our team at a disadvantage."

Roman lowers his head in deference. "Sorry, Ryker. That goal is on me."

I give Roman my back. "Ryker, if Hammerstein hadn't been playing armchair coach, what would your instincts have told you to do?"

"Protect my left side, because Grace has mad stick-handling skills, and he was moving right, which tells me he'll likely try to fake me out."

"Good call. Trust your gut, Ryker." I toss a puck to Grace. "Let's try that again."

The rest of the session goes smoothly, and I'm feeling positive when the guys hit the locker room.

Dred stops by to pick up Callie and brings me a sandwich so

I'm going into the game tonight with food in my stomach. I'm lucky to have made such wonderful, supportive friends.

We still have a few hours before the game, so I decide to head up to my office to review strategy. If all goes well, we'll pull out a win tonight against Philly.

"Forrester, I'd like to speak with you," Vander Zee barks.

Heat works its way up my spine and my stomach twists at the look on his face. I step inside the office. "Sure. What can I do for you?"

"Did you come from the ice?"

"Yes, sir."

He crosses his arms. "Why wasn't that run by me first?"

"I checked with Boxer—"

He cuts me off. "I've already talked to Boxer about this. You're an assistant coach, Boxer is the goalie coach, I am the head coach. If you want to put guys on the ice for extra practice on a game day, you run it by me first. Boxer might agree that the guys need the time, but the final say is ultimately mine. Don't go around me again, do you understand?"

If I could sink into the floor I would. "Of course, sir. I'm sorry. I just…I thought…I'm so sorry. My intention wasn't to go over your head on this. I honestly just wanted to give Grace a little more time to work on stick handling."

"I know you're working hard to prove yourself, but this isn't the way to do it. I'm always the last person to sign off on things like this. These guys get on the ice in a few hours. They need to be rested, and they need time to get into the right mental headspace."

"It won't happen again, sir," I promise.

"It better not. I expect you to learn from your mistakes." He taps his pen agitatedly on his desk. "Go review game strategy. I'll see you in a couple of hours."

"Yes, sir." I leave his office, feeling a lot like I might vomit.

I stop at Boxer's office and knock on his door. He looks up from the papers on his desk and his expression turns to empathy.

I don't know if that's a good or bad thing. "Come in and close the door."

I do as he asks. "I'm so sorry. I did not mean to get you in trouble."

He raises a hand. "This is on me. I assumed you'd already cleared it with Vander Zee when you suggested the extra ice time."

"I got ahead of myself," I admit. It was a stupid error. One I wish I could take back.

He rubs his chin. "We all fuck up, Forrester. Don't be too hard on yourself. I know Vander Zee's approval is important to you like it is to all of us, but the world isn't going to end over one mistake. Learn from it and move on, okay? Chin up. You got this."

I nod. "Thank you. I'm still sorry. I won't make the same mistake again."

"I know you won't. Go get your head on straight and be ready for game time."

I leave his office and head down the hall to my own.

Despite Boxer's kind words, being chewed out by my boss and mentor puts me in a bad headspace. I should have double checked and not made assumptions. That paired with the conversation with Donnie has me on edge. And it feels like a punishment when I get to watch the game from the box instead of behind the bench. By the third period, we're down two goals and Ryker is in net. They start out strong and close the lead by one goal, but it all goes sideways and Ryker misreads a shot on net, giving Philly back the two goal lead.

Vander Zee puts Roman back in net, but the damage is done, and the Terror can't recover. We lose the game, and I feel responsible. I overtaxed our goalies and best defensive players and lost us the game. Vander Zee is in a particularly somber mood during the post-game team talk. I keep my mouth shut.

"Lesson learned, I guess," Thomas mutters, wearing the same black cloud as Vander Zee.

"It'll be all right," Boxer assures me.

"I'm still sorry." He might feel some kind of responsibility for this, but I'm the reason we lost this game.

Roman tries to make eye contact. He doesn't look particularly happy about the loss either, but his brow is furrowed in concern. I don't want to draw more attention to myself, so I stay focused on my clipboard while Vander Zee talks about being game ready and in the right physical and mental state for the game.

Hemi and the girls invite me to the Watering Hole, but I'm barely holding it together, so I decline the offer. I need to get home so I can have a little emotional breakdown. And Dred is with the girls, she came over to help Fee with an essay. I've told her she doesn't need to stay until I get home, but she often does anyway.

I drive home on auto pilot and manage to get the car parked before I lose it. My phone keeps buzzing with new messages.

The Babe chat is full of sympathy messages over the game and virtual hugs that the next one will be better.

Dred sent a picture of a gorgeous bouquet of flowers and a wrapped gift followed by the message:

DRED

Your secret admirer has great taste in flowers.

No card but pretty sure I can guess who they're from.

That just makes the tears fall harder. I need to get my shit together. Fee can't see me like this post a bad game. But I'm spiraling, and there's only one person I want, and I can't have him.

Roman has sent me a slew of messages:

ROMAN

Talked to Boxer, this isn't on you.

Hemi said you went home, please message when you see this.

It's been half an hour. I'm worried.

Instead of sending him a message, I call.

"I'm so sorry," I croak. For not being strong enough to sort out my own shit, for compromising the game, for needing him. "I hardly deserve flowers after tonight."

"Those were for playing armchair coach with Ryker earlier. But Lexi, angel, this is not your fault," he says gently.

"I'm the one who put you on the ice too close to game time, so it is most definitely on me." I hiccup and dash away the tears.

"I'm coming over," he states.

"You can't. Dred is here and Fee will ask questions and I can't be trusted with you right now," I admit. "I won't want you to leave, and that is definitely not something I can explain to Fee or Callie. I fucked up so hard today, Roman. What if I can't do this? What if I'm not cut out for this job?"

"You are absolutely cut out for this job. This is not our first loss and it won't be the last. You're building rapport with Grace and Ryker. They're seasoned players who will be there next year, and that's bigger than one game. Vander Zee is upset about not being in the loop, and that's on all of us who have been doing this job far longer than you and didn't ask the right questions."

I hiccup again. "I made the mistake."

"You're a first year assistant coach, of course you're going to make mistakes. But it wasn't because your heart or your head was in the wrong place, Lexi. You care. You're an amazing coach. I know you feel bad, but don't let this shake your confidence."

"I don't feel like an amazing coach."

"Fuck. I hate that I can't be there with you. I wish you would have waited for me so we could have this conversation in person and not over the phone. I just want to hold you."

"The end of the season seems so far away," I whisper. He's the only person I don't have to be strong with all the time. With

Roman I can be afraid, and uncertain. I don't have to fake confidence. I can share my fears and worries, and I know he'll be there to talk them through. I can let go of all my careful control, give myself over completely and feel safe and cared for.

"What do you need? What can I do for you?"

"I don't know. I just need..." *Him*. "I'm trying so hard not to need you."

"I know. It goes both ways. We could have a night. Just to get us through the next few months. I can take you somewhere private and secluded. We have three days between this game and the next. We can go north, get out of the city, just you and me. Let me take care of you. I can't carry the responsibilities for you, but I can give you a break from them. Give us both something to hold on to while we wait the season out."

"I want that so much," I admit. Dred will stay with the girls if I ask.

"It's okay to want something for yourself, Lexi. I need you as much as you need me. Please let me do this for us."

Roman commands, orders, directs, but this gentle request is what tips me over the edge. I can't say no, and I don't want to. "Yes. Okay. Let me talk to Dred."

"Good girl," Roman replies in that tone that promises a reprieve from the painful longing.

"She's with the girls now. I'll go up and clear it with her. I'll message soon."

"Okay. Deep breaths, angel. Soon you'll be all mine."

I make the trip up to the condo, already relieved that I don't have to wait another three months before I feel his arms around me. It's been so hard to be just the assistant coach. For one night I won't have to fit inside a box. I can be Roman's and he can be mine.

I let myself into the condo and Dred pokes her head around the corner.

"Are the girls asleep?" I ask quietly.

She gives me two thumbs up, but her expression shifts to

concern. "Are you okay? Oh my gosh, is this about the game?" She opens her arms and I accept the hug.

I explain what happened and how my mistake cost us the game.

"I think it's easy to blame yourself, but the four guys you had ice time with do not make up the entire roster of players on the ice tonight."

"I feel responsible. Vander Zee has never been that…upset with me and it just hit differently." I swallow past the lump in my throat. "Roman wants to take me away for a night."

She doesn't even hesitate. "I'll stay with the girls."

I fiddle with the end of my braid. "Do you think it's a bad idea?"

Her expression fills with empathy. "I think you deserve a night off from being responsible all the time. I also think you both need this time."

"I really do," I admit. "I need him. The end of the season is too far away."

"I've got you. Your secret is safe with me."

CHAPTER 29

ROMAN

"This is beautiful." Lexi's eyes are wide as I follow her into the cabin.

Should we be here? No. Can I find it in me to feel bad for giving in? Also, no.

Lexi needs a break from all the responsibilities, and I need *her*. I drop our bags and close the door behind me, locking out the cold. It's warm and cozy, a fire already crackling in the fireplace.

"There's a hot tub in the four-seasons room, and it's very, very private." Which is why I booked the place. Privacy and luxury.

Lexi links her fingers behind my neck. "I love private."

"So do I." I finger the end of her braid. "Because it means you can be exuberant and vocal." I brush my lips across her cheek and whisper in her ear, "And no one can hear you beg for orgasms but me."

She tugs at the zipper on my jacket. "I can't wait."

"Ah, ah." I capture her hands and kiss her knuckles. "You don't get to undress me yet."

"But I had to behave myself for an hour and a half." Her

bottom lip juts out. "You wouldn't even entertain road head or a handy."

"It's snowing," I remind her. Besides, if her mouth is going to be on my cock I don't want to have to pay attention to anything but her.

"I know. You're frustratingly responsible." She attempts to free her hands, but I circle her wrists. Her eyes light up with excitement. "I'm dying to get my hands and mouth on you."

"You'd like to start our night on your knees then?"

Her smile turns devilish. "With a mouth full of your cock? Yes, please."

This is the version of Lexi I spent the weekend with in New York: sexy, uninhibited, such a pleaser. I pin her wrists at her sides and slant my mouth over hers. She melts into me, gives herself over. All it takes is one kiss to make me ravenous for her. All the texting in preparation for tonight, followed by an hour and a half of Lexi practically begging me to let her suck my cock, has pushed me to the edge. I had a plan for tonight, and she's already derailed it.

I break the kiss and release her hands. Before she can reach for me, I give her a look that freezes her in place. "Get naked."

She shrugs out of her jacket and drapes it on the entry table. I drop to one knee and work on unlacing her boots as she pulls her sweater and shirt over her head, tossing them aside. She braces a hand on my shoulder and lifts one foot at a time so I can rid her of her boots. As soon as they're off, she shimmies out of her leggings and panties, leaving her gloriously naked.

I smooth my hands up her hips as I rise, cupping between her thighs while I give her braid a light tug. "So fucking beautiful."

She moans when I wrap it around my fist and tip her head back. I press two fingers against her entrance. "So wet and ready." I give her pussy a gentle slap and she moans softly. But she doesn't try to touch me. Not yet. She needs an escape from all the decision making and I need to be the one who gives her what she craves.

I grab a throw pillow from the closest chair and drop it at my feet. "On your knees, angel." We're still standing in the entryway.

She sinks to the floor, braid still fisted in my hand, eyes on mine, waiting for the next order. She's such a force on the ice, such a powerhouse of a woman, talented and driven. Capable, competent and in control. But here, when it's just us, she lets it all go. Just for me. And I fucking love it.

"Get my cock out."

She quickly unbuckles my belt as I pull my shirt over my head, finds the button, and drags my zipper down. Her warm hand slides into my boxer briefs and curves around my erection, freeing it.

Her eyes lift as she gives me a slow stroke, lips brushing over the head. "I've been dreaming about this for months. Years, even."

"That makes two of us," I admit. "Now show me how much you've missed my cock."

A satisfied grin tips the corner of her mouth as she leaves open-mouthed kisses along the shaft. Lexi hums her contentment, beautiful and naked and finally fucking mine. At least for tonight. She sucks and nibbles, her little moans and whimpers driving me wild.

"Enough teasing." I keep a firm grip on her braid and fist my cock, tapping her bottom lip with the tip. "Open that pretty mouth."

She parts her lips and I push inside.

"Suck," I order.

Her eyes stay on me as her lips cover the head and her cheeks hollow out.

I give her another inch, skimming her bottom lip as it slides over my shaft. "So fucking beautiful."

She moans and rubs her thighs together. One hand lifts from

my thigh and I give my head a quick shake and pull out of her mouth. "Who do your orgasms belong to tonight?"

"You."

"That's right. Your hands stay on me. Do you understand?"

"Yes, Roman."

I push back inside her mouth. "Are you going to be my good girl and take it all?"

She nods as much as she can with the way I'm filling her mouth and holding her braid. I keep her still and fuck her sweet mouth, going deeper with every pass. When I hit the back of her throat her nails dig into my hips, so I pull back. I stroke along her throat. "Relax, angel."

She breathes through her nose and this time when I shift my hips forward, another inch disappears between her swollen, flawless lips. She's a damn revelation.

Determination flashes in her eyes and she shifts her hands, curving them around my ass as she urges me deeper. A dark satisfied smile curves my lips and I caress her cheek again. "Such a fucking vision, my perfect little slut swallowing down my cock."

She moans and rolls her hips, seeking friction against nothing.

She's too exquisite, her mouth is too damn good, and she does that thing with her tongue that makes my knees nearly buckle. "Enough, Lexi."

I tug on her braid, but her eyes light up with devilish intent as her nails sink into my ass. I don't stop her when she pulls me deep again. The orgasm slams through me, vicious and overwhelming. Her satisfied gaze stays locked on my face, even as my eyes roll up.

As soon as I can do something beyond groan her name, I pull her off my cock. "You are a gift." She sucks in a gasping breath as I slide my hands under her arms and lift her to her feet.

"I was good?"

"Phenomenal."

I take her mouth. I don't care that she tastes like me, that my cum is still coating her tongue. Kicking off my boots, I pick her up, wrapping her legs around my waist as I carry her to the bedroom. Another fire crackles on the far side of the room, and a bottle of champagne chills between two occasional chairs. Rose petals dot the comforter.

I toss her on the bed, slide my wallet out of my back pocket and set it on the nightstand, then rid myself of my pants.

"This is beautiful, Roman." Lexi looks around, her eyes come back to me as I climb up after her.

"You are exquisite." I run my hands over her shins and up the inside of her thighs, spreading her wide so I can kiss the sensitive spot close to her knee. "You deserve a reward." I drop my head and lick up the length of her sex.

"Oh god, thank you." Lexi's hands slide into my hair, and I stretch out, getting comfortable. I take my time, licking, nibbling. I slide a single finger inside, curling once before I withdraw.

"Roman, please." She writhes under me, breath leaving her in pants and soft moans.

"Please what?" I lap at her.

"I need to come. Oh god, I'm so close."

"I don't think you want it enough." I withdraw my fingers and roughly suck her clit.

I've missed this side of her. Of us. Of the power shift. She owns me, heart and soul. And the way she gives herself so completely, without reservation, is humbling. I want to keep her. Protect her. Revere her above all others and not just here, but in life.

She rolls her hips and I bar an arm across them, pinning her to the bed. I suck her labia this time, biting gently. "Please, Roman."

I lick her again. "Beg for it."

"Please, please, *please*," she pleads. "I need you. I need you to fuck me. To make me come. To fill me, please."

I spread her, tongue dipping inside, and I feel the flutter.

"Right on the edge." I suck her clit again, addicted to the taste of her, to the way she feels under my tongue, how completely she gives herself over to me.

Her head whips back and forth. "Oh god, just please," she begs, then bargains. "You can fuck me any way you want. Whatever you want, Roman. Just, *please,* make me come."

I smile darkly. "That's a dangerous offer, but I think I'll accept it anyway."

Goose bumps rise along her skin as I slide three thick fingers inside her, stretching her. She moans and gasps as I pump fast and hard, wetness coating my fingers and dripping into my palm. Lexi bows up off the bed when I latch onto her clit and suck, my name a loud, deep moan tumbling from her lips as she bucks against my mouth.

"You're fucking gorgeous when you're coming apart for me," I growl. And I can't get enough.

She rides out the orgasm, body quaking, pussy contracting around my fingers. The aftershocks come in waves as I withdraw them one at a time and reach for my wallet.

She covers my hand with hers. "Can you go bare? Even if it's just for a minute. I'm on the patch. I want to feel you."

I'd do anything for her. Give her anything she wants. I grip her thighs and pull her closer, arranging her legs so they're draped over mine. "I'll give you the world, angel." I drag the head of my cock through her slit and push in an inch as Lexi props herself up on one arm.

She bites her lip, fingers drifting over her throat and down her chest, skimming a nipple as she goes lower, until she reaches the apex of her thighs. She circles her clit and spreads her pussy, fingers sliding on either side of my cock. I withdraw, then push back in again. "Look at how perfectly you stretch around me." I slide in another inch before I pull out again, the head coated in her juices. "At how ready you are for me." I cover her body with mine. "I'm going fuck you until you're screaming my name and creaming all over my cock."

"Yes, please."

I sheath myself inside her in one smooth stroke.

She winds her arms and legs around me, body already trembling, pussy contracting.

"Are you coming for me already?"

"Oh God, I can't stop." She moans, hands in my hair, nails running down my neck, biting into my shoulders.

I pull my hips back, and she groans at the loss, then moans wantonly when I snap forward, filling her.

"Thank you." Her knees clamp against my hips. "Oh fuck."

I start a punishing rhythm, fucking her into the mattress, wringing cries from her lips. There is nothing that compares to this. To her. To the feel of her surrounding me, milking my cock, her greedy moans and pleas for more humming over my lips.

"Please don't stop." She grips my shoulders. "I don't want it to ever end."

"I have all night to whisper dirty things in your ear while I fuck endless orgasms out of you," I promise.

She groans, still quaking underneath me. I fold back on my knees and pull out, fisting my erection as my own orgasm rolls through me. She slides three fingers inside as I paint the inside of her thigh with cum.

Lexi slowly withdraws her fingers and drags them across her cum-soaked skin. She lifts them to her lips and licks.

"Such a filthy girl." I stretch out next to her. "You were made for me."

"Only for you," she whispers.

"And so damn sweet." I slide an arm under her and move her so she's sprawled across my chest.

Lexi straddles my hips, her palms on my chest, her smile matching mine. "We're a little messy."

I tap her ass. "Let's shower. Then we can unpack our groceries and cuddle by the fire."

"That sounds great."

I follow her into the bathroom, and a shower turns into more sex.

Afterward, I towel her off, and she nabs my T-shirt, pulling it over her head. The sleeves nearly reach her elbows, and the hem skims just below the curve of her ass. "Please wear nothing but this for the rest of our time here."

"I packed sexy lingerie."

"Amendment, please wear nothing but this and your sexy lingerie, independently and possibly at the same time."

She tosses me my boxer briefs. "Please be shirtless as much as possible for the rest of our time here."

"Deal."

I pull my boxer briefs up my legs and follow Lexi out of the bathroom. I grab the cooler bag while she picks up the tote of nonperishables. We set them on the counter and unload our food supplies.

"I like this." I pass her the coffee creamer and eggs to put in the fridge.

"Me in your shirt with nothing on underneath?" She shoots a saucy grin over her shoulder.

"That's a bonus. I just mean this." I motion between us. "Domestic comfort, I guess. I haven't had someone to do this with since, well…never, really."

She empties a bag of green apples into a bowl and sets them on the counter. "Not even when you were with Peggy's mother?"

"We were kids, and I was drafted in the middle of her pregnancy. She moved with me to Vancouver when I started playing for the farm team, but it was hard on her. She was on her own a lot, and I was on the ice all the time, so after a few months she moved back to her parents'. We tried again after Peggy was born, but we just…didn't fit. She thought the travel would be fun, but it was a challenge with a baby, and she spent all her time in hotel rooms, trying to cope. I also don't share well, and my brand of sex didn't work for us. I didn't want to feel bad about what I need, and I didn't want her to feel bad for not liking it."

"That must have been hard for both of you."

"We realized early on that we would be better as friends."

"What about since then? You must have dated." Lexi puts the bottle of wine in the fridge to chill.

"I did for the first few years. But Peggy stayed with me in the off-season, and I wanted my focus to be on her," I explain. "Zara moved around a lot and it was hard on Peggy. She wasn't thriving and Zara realized she would have more stability with me. So when she was six, Peggy came to live with me full time. I didn't have room in my life for anything but her and hockey."

Lexi props her hip against the counter. "You didn't have room, or you didn't make room?"

"Hmm..." I mirror her pose and drag my finger along the edge of her jaw. "The latter more than the former. When I was home, I wanted to be with Peggy. Her first six years I missed a lot. I wanted to be present when I wasn't traveling. I tried a relationship once, but my daughter was my priority."

"And now?"

I smile. "She's settled. In love. Hollis has already asked permission to marry her, so it's only a matter of time." I finger the end of her braid. "Peggy has been so adamant that I start dating I kept putting it off. I was so afraid I'd bring the wrong person into our lives, or that I couldn't give enough of myself to someone else. But she doesn't need me to take care of her the way I once did. So now I get to focus on myself and what I want for my future."

"And what do you want?" she asks softly.

"You."

"You have me."

"Mmm..." I grab the hem of her shirt and pull her closer. "I want more than a stolen night with you, Lexi."

She loops her arms around my neck. "Me, too."

"I'm falling for you." If I leave the game, we would have every night together.

"I'm falling for you, too." Her voice is a barely audible whisper. "But it's already February." She smooths her hands over my chest. "Just a few more months. Then I'm not your coach, and you're not my goalie, and the red tape disappears."

"I know it won't be easy." I brush my lips over hers. "And that there will be challenges, but I can't lose you again, Lexi."

"You won't." She takes my face in her hands. "I promise we will find a way through this, together."

CHAPTER 30

LEXI

"I'll see you after the game." I hug my sisters at the private entrance to the arena, reserved for injured players and staff.

"You ready for popcorn and snacks?" Dred links arms with Callie.

"Yes! Do you think I'll get to say hi to Connor after the game?" Callie asks.

"Definitely. You're his favorite," Dred replies and winks at me.

"Try to keep her away from the caffeinated beverages," I whisper to Fee.

"I'll do my best."

"Good luck tonight, Lexi." Tally smiles and waves.

Tally's boyfriend, who's been hanging in the background, gives us a chin tip and follows the girls down the hall.

Vander Zee sighs. "I can't believe that kid has lasted this long. Here's hoping he goes home for the summer and things fizzle out."

I clap him on the shoulder. "Let's manifest that into existence."

"I just don't get it. He's just…flat? He's been to dinner at our house three times, and all I know about him is that he's an engineering major, he has a younger brother, and his dad is also an engineer. I don't even know what kind of engineer."

It's not my place to judge, but Fee doesn't have a lot of nice things to say about him either. "He is a—uh quiet one."

"There's quiet, and then there's this chucklehead." Vander Zee sighs. "Madden would be a better option than this guy."

I arch a brow. "Seriously?"

"Fuck no. But this kid gets two thumbs down."

I pat him on the shoulder. "She'll figure it out."

"I sure hope so."

We head to the locker room for the pre-game pep talk.

"Family's here tonight?" Boxer asks Thomas.

"Yeah, and we brought Donnie's youngest along. His oldest has a tournament tonight," Thomas replies.

It's interesting that Donnie was all over me about my relationship with the office staff and team, and here he is doing the same thing. I keep my mouth shut about it, though, because I don't want to draw unnecessary attention to my situation. *Only a few more months...*

I take my spot with the rest of the coaches behind the player bench and wave when I spot the girls in the box with Dred, Tally, Hammer, Rix, Hemi, and Shilpa.

"Your sisters have been at the games a lot lately," Boxer observes.

"The home weekend ones, yeah," I agree.

"I guess it saves on babysitting, eh?" Thomas quips.

I can't tell if that's a jab or I'm being extra paranoid. "Tally and Fee are friends."

"I noticed." Thomas rubs his chin. "Those girls are all tight."

"They are. It's nice to know my sisters have people looking out for them, especially when so much of our job takes place outside regular hours."

"It gets easier when they're older," Boxer assures me. "And it's good that your sisters get to see you in action. I bet it's real inspiring to see you behind the bench."

"Thanks, Boxer." It's nice to have affirmation from my colleagues, especially Boxer, since he and I work together so often.

The guys file off the ice and onto the bench, ending that conversation.

First period puts us ahead by two after Madden and Stiles score a goal apiece. Defense is playing tight, and Roman shuts out Tennessee, giving us the win. It feels good, like the extra practice is worth it. And not just because it means more time with Roman.

Fee, Callie, the girls, and Tally's boyfriend come down to meet us while the team showers and changes. Callie is bleary-eyed, having fallen asleep during the third period. "I'm tired, and my tummy is sore." She wraps her arms around my waist and buries her face against my stomach.

I stroke her hair. "Too much candy?"

"Maybe."

Dred mouths, *Sorry*.

"Bet it seemed like a good idea at the time." I rub her back. I can't be angry at her for having a good time, or Fee and Dred for not noticing. At least she's happy and had fun, even if the aftermath isn't so pleasant.

"Some of the guys from res are at the Brass Taps, and Braydon is on the door, so we can get in no problem," the boyfriend mutters to Tally.

She gives him a look. "Can we talk about this after?"

"It's Friday night, Tally. I'd like to hang out with some of *my* friends," he grumbles.

"Just give me a minute, okay?" Her irritation is obvious.

He sighs but continues typing on his phone.

Tally gives us all hugs and tells Fee she'll see her tomorrow afternoon, then turns to me, expression apologetic. "Can you tell my dad I said bye and that I'll call him tomorrow?"

"Of course."

The guys come out of the locker room as the boyfriend

follows Tally down the hall. Callie, who was falling asleep standing up moments ago, perks up when Connor appears.

He gives her a hug. "How's my number-one fan?"

"I'm good. You were great out there tonight. And no penalties!"

"I was keeping it clean just for you." He winks. "Is it still cool for me to come to your next game?"

"Only if you're not busy." Callie twists her fingers together.

"Never too busy for you. One more hug?" He opens his arms, and she wraps hers around his neck.

"See you later, Coach." He gives me a chin tip and continues down the hall.

Callie's eyes light up all over again as Roman approaches. My ovaries get all excited about him in a suit, and my heart turns mushy when he crouches in front of Callie. His brow furrows. "You look like a tired little girl."

"I ate too much candy," she admits.

He opens his arms, and she snuggles right into him. "It's hard to resist, isn't it?"

"I couldn't say no to the gummy bears. They're my favorite."

"I have trouble saying no to those, too," Roman commiserates.

"Can you come to my game again this weekend? Dred said she can come, and Connor is coming, too."

"If Connor can make it, I'm pretty sure I can."

Callie smiles hopefully. "Really?"

"Yeah, I need to support my favorite goalie," he says with the utmost seriousness.

"I'm your favorite?"

"You are."

"Sometimes we go out for chicken fingers and french fries after. You could come with us, if you want."

"That sounds perfect." Roman winks at me.

The rest of the group make plans to go to the Watering Hole, but I need to get Callie home. Otherwise she won't get enough sleep, which could make tomorrow's game tough. She always wants to play her best, especially when Roman or Connor comes to watch.

"You want me to carry you to the car?" Roman asks Callie.

"Yes, please."

"See you all later," Roman tells the rest of the group.

Dred hugs me and whispers, "Stay strong."

Roman picks Callie up and she wraps her arms around his neck. She rests her head on his shoulder.

"This is too cute." Hammer pulls out her phone and snaps a few pictures before she hugs me and kisses her dad on the cheek.

"Did you have a good time with the girls tonight?" Roman asks Fee as we head for the car.

"The game was so good! Tally and I were talking about next year, because I applied to the same program she's in. I know she's a year ahead, but it would be so cool to know someone on campus already. Especially since we love the same things."

"I think that's great. Peggy loved university."

"Tally says it's the best!" Fee exclaims. "And like, the people in my art program this semester are so fun, and I'm making better friends now."

"It's nice to feel understood, isn't it?"

"It is. Like so great."

Callie's out cold when we reach the car, so it takes the two of us to get her buckled in. I nearly melt when Roman kisses her on the forehead and tucks her stuffed axolotl under her arm.

Roman waits until Fee is in the passenger seat and the door is closed before he murmurs, "Message when you're home."

"Aren't you going to the Watering Hole?"

"Not tonight." His fingers brush the back of my hand.

"I wish I could invite you back to my place." There's an ache building low in my stomach.

"Me, too. Not long now, though. Then I won't have to resist those gorgeous lips of yours." He winks and walks away.

I slide into the driver's seat and turn the engine over, adjusting the radio so it doesn't wake Callie.

Fee fiddles with the snap on her purse. "Sometimes I feel bad for liking Roman as much as I do."

I grip the steering wheel. "How do you mean?"

"He's such a great dad. Like, he's so close with Hammer. I mean, they work together and everything, and then the way he is with Callie..." She tugs on the string of her hoodie. "He goes to her games. He asks me about school and stuff. He really cares. It's like we're part of this big family, you know? It makes me miss Mom and Dad. And sometimes I feel guilty, because no one can replace them, but at the same time, there are holes in my heart, and I want to fill them. Does that make sense?"

"It absolutely does, Big Pheels. And I feel the same way."

She looks over her shoulder and drops her voice. "Callie says sometimes she wishes Roman was our dad."

My heart clenches. "I can understand that."

"She told me she was going to wish for it when she blows out her candles this year on her birthday," Fee says softly. "I didn't have the heart to tell her it's impossible because he's a player on your team."

"Until the end of the season, yes." I swallow the guilt that follows on the heels of hope. I want the same things she does.

"But then he's retiring, right?"

I swallow. "He is."

"What will he do after he retires? Will he have another job?" Fee presses.

"Probably. A lot of teams would love to have him as a coach. He could end up anywhere." The Hockey Academy satellite campus seems like a real possibility, but I can't tell Fee that. Not yet.

"Oh." Her disappointment makes my heart hurt. "But Hammer is here. He wouldn't leave her, would he?"

"Probably not," I agree.

"Okay." She rolls her bottom lip between her teeth. "You like him, don't you?"

"He's been very kind to us." I hate that I can't be honest with her, that I have to deflect.

"Yeah. He has." She's silent for the rest of the ride home.

Fee helps me get Callie up to the condo and into bed before she disappears into her room. Apparently her favorite *Lord of the Rings* fanfic author just updated, and she needs to read it *right now*.

I wait until I'm in bed before I snuggle up with my phone. Roman has already messaged. I worry that we're not hiding things as well as we should. But I'm weak for him.

ROMAN

I hope you got Callie to bed okay.

LEXI

I did. She's out like a light. You had a great game tonight.

ROMAN

Those strategy talks of ours have been helpful this season.

Although my favorite talks have been when you're naked and sprawled across my chest.

LEXI

Those are my favorite, too.

ROMAN

Walking away without kissing you nearly broke me tonight.

The end of the season can't come soon enough.

I love working with him, seeing him every day, but it's as painful as it is wonderful.

LEXI

I feel the same.

ROMAN

I didn't think a handful of weeks could feel this endless.

Early retirement looks better every day.

The selfish part of me loves this idea, but the coach in me knows how much it will devastate the team. They're his family and they're already sad enough to see him go at the end of the season. I need him, but…

LEXI

The team needs you.

The dots appear and disappear three times.

LEXI

We're so close.

ROMAN

I know. I'm just impatient. And on nights like tonight, I'd rather be curled up on the couch with you in my arms than sitting alone in my living room.

I long for the comfort of his closeness, and our easy conversations.

LEXI

I would tell you to come over, but I worry that one of us will break.

ROMAN

I know I would.

My heart aches at his raw honesty. And truthfully, I doubt I have the strength to say no to him if he showed up at my door tonight.

ROMAN

When the season is over, I'm taking you away again, but this time it will be for more than a night.

LEXI

Somewhere private again.

ROMAN

Middle of nowhere. Just the two of us.

Pretending he's just a player and I'm just a coach is breaking me down. If I have something to hold on to, even if it's still weeks away, then maybe it will get easier.

LEXI

I miss you.

ROMAN

I miss you, too.

Stay strong for me, angel. 🖤

CHAPTER 31

ROMAN

"Do you think it looks good? Do you think she'll like the cake?" Tristan's hands are on his hips and he's wearing his customary scowl. He's standing in front of a table set up just inside the rink, surrounded by decorations. The whole room has been transformed.

"It's a pretty kick-ass cake," Nate assures him.

Tristan ignores his brother. "Roman, what do you think?"

I clap him on the shoulder. "It looks awesome. She's going to love it."

"Should we check with Coach Forrester?"

"Bro, chill out. It's not like you're going to have another one made between now and when everyone starts showing up. The cake is a masterpiece." Nate doesn't seem the least bit fazed by Tristan and his mild freak-out.

"It's exceptionally cool," I add. And it is. The cake is shaped like a hockey rink, and it boasts an entirely edible net and a miniature sculpture of Callie in her goalie gear that she can take home.

"Do you think the balloon arch is big enough?"

"Yeah, dude. The arch is big enough." Nate rolls his eyes.

He moved in with Flip at the beginning of the month and seems to be roped into everything involving the team these days.

"It's perfect," I agree. It's her team colors and takes up almost an entire wall. There's also a photo booth, complete with dress-up options.

"Okay. Cool. Did you get your shirt? There's a special one for you. You should change into it." He checks his watch and runs his hand over his chest. It reads #TeamCallie Birthday Crew. "The kids are arriving any second. Bea? Babe, do you think there are enough balloons marking the entrance?"

"Tris, babycakes, take a breath." Rix hugs his waist. "There are more than enough balloons. This birthday party will be fabulous, and Callie will love it." Her shirt reads #TeamCallie Party Brigade.

"I want it to be a good day for her, you know? She doesn't have a mom or a dad, and not because either of them sucked as parents, but because they're fuckin' gone." He takes a calming breath. "Sorry. I just know how hard birthdays were after our mom bailed."

Nate mumbles *excuse me* and disappears down the hall to the bathroom.

"I know." It's a sore spot for him, but he's been channeling it into something good, and this party is one of those things. "You've done a fantastic job, Tristan." I assure him. "I'll put my shirt on."

I leave him with Rix and move to the table with all the shirts. Peggy, Hollis, Dred, and Connor are already wearing theirs. Connor's reads: Callie's Favorite Player.

He grins at me. "No hard feelings, right, Roman?"

I laugh. "None at all." Because if all goes according to plan, I'll get to take that little girl on family vacations. I'll be the one who reads her bedtime stories, gets on the ice with her, goes to parent-teacher interview nights, and cheers her on at games. While I'll never replace her dad, I'll sure as hell do my best to fill the void his loss has caused.

I'm falling just as hard for those girls as I am for Lexi. I'm excited about the possibility of stepping into the role of parent again. Unconventional, maybe. But this time I'll have a partner who feels the same way about me as I do about her.

I grab my shirt and chuckle. Mine reads Callie's 2nd Favorite Player. The "O" in *favorite* is replaced with a sad-face emoji. It's perfect. Everything about the party is.

Callie's school friends and teammates arrive, along with her grandparents from Niagara. Lexi's dad is in the middle of a huge court case, so he's planning a visit in the next few weeks, but he sent a gift to Tristan and an apology that he couldn't make it work. Hopefully the party will make up for it, but I wish he was more present for them.

The kids are so excited, especially when they realize they each get a jersey and will meet a bunch of Terror players. They're already familiar with me and Connor, since we've both attended Callie's games.

Flip, who's been helping organize the food with Rix and Essie, hands me a napkin with a cookie. "This is looking good. When does the birthday girl arrive?"

I check the scoreboard instead of my phone for the time because I don't want Flip to see my messages with Lexi. "Soon." He's just another person to add to the never-ending list of people I'm hiding the truth from.

He frowns as he scans the room, stopping at Tally, Dred, and Connor, who are busy making sure the loot bags are all tagged. "Talls's boyfriend didn't make it today, eh?"

"Doesn't seem like this would be his thing."

He crosses his arms. "I don't think anything is that kid's thing. What's his name again? I always forget."

I shrug. "Dunno. Peggy just calls him Tally's boyfriend."

"Well, I'm glad he's not here. He's a wet blanket, and Tally can do better."

"I think the girls would agree."

"Why don't they say anything?" he asks.

"Because it's Tally's decision who she dates, and they want her to feel supported and not judged. Or at least that's what Peggy told me when I asked."

"Makes sense, I guess." He rubs his bottom lip.

"You and Grace seem to be getting along better these days."

Flip makes an irritated sound. "I'm going to go help Rix in the kitchen. See you later."

He hustles off.

My phone pings.

LEXI

In the parking lot.

I whistle shrilly to get everyone's attention. "They're coming in! Take your places!" We cut the lights when everyone is in position and wait for the doors to open.

"Why's it so dark?" Callie asks.

Dred flicks on the light, and we yell a collective, "*Surprise*!"

Hemi is ready with her camera, snapping photos as Callie's friends converge on her. The way her face brightens makes my heart swell. Fee's smile is wide, and Lexi looks like she's on the verge of tears. I want nothing more than to be able to go to her, to wrap her in my arms and tell her I've got her. But I can't. Not yet.

Dred is the one who steps in and hugs the three of them. It's a flurry of excitement as Callie and her friends suit up to take the ice. Connor, Tristan, Hollis, Dallas, Ash, Flip, and I all suit up as well, and we spend an hour on the ice, shooting the puck around with Callie and her teammates. Even Fee, who doesn't normally get excited about being on the ice, comes out and plays with Tristan's encouragement.

After hockey and games, we feed the kids. Tristan sits beside Fee, and Connor takes the seat beside Callie, who keeps looking up at him with moon eyes.

"She's so happy," Lexi says softly.

"She is. How was the morning?" I ask.

"It was hard. There were some tears, and for a while I was worried she wouldn't come around, but Fee made her chocolate chip pancakes and told her we had big plans and that Mom and Dad would want her to have a fun birthday and not be sad." She pinches the bridge of her nose.

I covertly skim the back of her hand. "I wish I could hug you."

"I wish you could, too," she whispers.

"Next year it'll look a lot different, and I'll be able to," I murmur.

She smiles up at me. "I'm really looking forward to that."

"Me, too."

Dred approaches with a smile plastered on her face. "Lexi, they're almost ready for cake. Do you want to come to the kitchen with me?"

"I can help," I offer.

"It's less conspicuous if it's me who goes." She threads her arm through Lexi's and guides her away.

Hollis sidles up next to me. "Dred stepped in to make sure you two didn't look too cozy."

"Mmm..." Two of our people have noticed now. I glance around, stomach rioting.

"Getting harder to stay away?"

"Yup." Harder than I realized, maybe.

He claps me on the shoulder, his expression pained but also empathetic. "I'm sorry. Especially because I know exactly where you are right now."

I tuck a hand into my pocket, the guilt heavy on my shoulders. "I wish it was me who stood to lose, instead of the other way around."

"It's a tough place." He sighs.

I watch Callie and her friends laughing and smiling. "I don't want to make Lexi's life harder, but I don't want to be without her."

Understanding crosses his features. "That's good, man. You

both deserve to have someone to share this life with. You have a huge heart. More people should get to fit inside it."

Dred and Lexi return with the cake, a number 9 candle burning brightly. Essie, Peggy, and Rix follow with ice cream, plates, and silverware. Tristan hops up and starts belting out "Happy Birthday." He's completely out of tune. Rix jumps in, her voice a melodic counterpart to Tristan's pitchiness, and we all join her.

"Did you know Rix could sing?" Hollis asks.

"I did not," I reply.

Callie's smile is so wide and beautiful, her joy and excitement infectious. She bounces in her seat and screws her eyes shut tight before she blows out the candle.

Dred and Lexi cut the cake and pass it out to the kids and then the adults.

After cake, Callie digs into her mountain of presents.

She tears through the paper of Connor's gift, bottom lip pushed out as she tries to figure out what it is. Connor steps in to help her set it up.

"Oh wow! Can I keep this in my room, Lexi?" Callie bounces up and down and wraps her arms around Connor's waist. "This is the best!"

"If that's where you want to keep it, absolutely." Lexi gives her two thumbs-up, all smiles.

Taking up more space than is reasonable are life-size cutouts of the two of them. Callie's dressed in her hockey gear, and Connor's wearing his #1 Fan T-shirt. It's fantastic, and I almost wish I'd thought of it.

Callie opens gifts from her friends, oohing and ahhing over the stuffies and games and toys. Lexi hands her the gift from Kristoff, and Callie tears into it.

"Oh this is so cool! I love it!" It's a special-edition Connor Grace jersey, complete with sequins. He probably had it custom embellished.

The girls pamper her with more fun gifts, and she rushes

over and gives me a huge hug after she opens mine. Callie is big into Legos, and I picked up the Terror hockey rink kit.

"Can we build it together?" she asks.

"Absolutely."

I exchange a look with Lexi, hoping Dred and Hollis are the only ones who pick up on that.

The final gift is from Tristan. It's huge with a big bow.

She tears through the paper and opens the box. "Oh my gosh! No way!" She pulls out brand new goalie gear. Top of the line. It's extravagant, especially for a kid who will grow out of it in less than a year, but her joy and Tristan's are worth it.

"Dude, that's like five grand in gear," Nate mutters to his brother.

"I bought you a car," Tristan counters with a furrowed brow.

Nate opens his mouth to argue, but shrugs instead. "True."

When all the presents are unwrapped, Callie passes out the loot bags, which again, are ostentatious and over the top.

"I will never be able to top this birthday," Lexi says as she surveys the mountain of gifts.

"You won't have to, now that you have us," Tristan assures her. "We take care of our own. You're family, Coach. We've got your back."

The girls hug Lexi, echoing Tristan, and I stand back, knowing how emotional this makes her. I want to say *fuck it* and step in. But I'd be doing more harm than good.

I have a deeper appreciation now for how hard it must have been for Hollis last year when he was in this position—feeling like he had to hide his feelings for Peggy, wishing he could love her the way he does now, afraid to blow up our friendship, unsure if I'd ever get over the betrayal.

But they made it out the other side, which gives me hope for me and Lexi.

Once all the kids have gone and we've cleaned up, we take the gifts out to Lexi's car.

We're halfway to Lexi's vehicle when we run into Donnie

Richards and his kids. "Hey, how's it going?" I rearrange the gifts so I can shake his hand and say hi to him and his boys.

"Roman? Hey, this is a surprise. Someone have a birthday?" He glances between me and Lexi. "Hey Forrester."

"Hey Donnie." She smiles, but it looks strained. "My youngest sister. She plays at this arena."

"Right, yeah." He nods slowly. "I didn't realize that."

His son tugs on his sleeve. "Dad, we gotta go in or we'll be late."

Donnie thumbs over his shoulder. "We need to head in."

"Good luck on the ice today," I say.

"Yeah, thanks. See you tomorrow. Happy birthday to your sister," Donnie says.

"Thanks," Lexi replies.

Donnie corrals his boys and heads for entrance.

She tosses a worried glance over her shoulder. "I don't love that he's seen us together outside of the arena."

"All the guys are still in there, and he's about to run into them, too," I remind her.

"Right. Yeah. I'm being paranoid."

"Don't forget that Donnie and Arnold are friends outside of work." I don't say anything about having run into Donnie here before, though, because I don't want to cause her unnecessary stress. "Come on, let's get these presents in your car."

She pops the trunk, and we pile gifts inside.

"I don't think all of it will fit," she notes.

We haven't even loaded half of them and her trunk is almost full.

"I can take the rest and follow you," I offer.

Lexi scans the parking lot, like she's nervous we'll run into someone else we know. "Are you sure you don't mind?"

"It's not a problem. My SUV has loads of space."

"Okay. Great. Thank you." We load both vehicles, and there's another round of hugs and happy birthdays for Callie. She comes to me last, and I crouch so I'm at eye level for a hug.

"I have a question," she whispers when her arms are wrapped around my neck.

"Okay." I pat her back.

She backs up and looks over her shoulder, maybe making sure we have a little privacy. "We're going to watch a movie when we get home. Will you stay and watch it with us?"

"Sure. I'd love to. Is that your question?"

She shakes her head and twists her fingers. "I made a wish today when I blew out my candles, and I know I'm not supposed to tell anyone, but I told Fifi, and now I'm worried it won't come true."

"It can still come true," I assure her.

"Really?" Relief crosses her face.

"Most of the time, yeah." Unless she's wishing for her parents to come back. That's not possible, and I don't want to give her false hope.

"Okay, good. I'll see you back at the house for the movie."

"You don't want to tell me what the wish was?"

"Not yet." She kisses me on the cheek and skips back to the car.

Lexi and I exchange a smile.

I'm in so deep with these girls.

I can see the future unfolding, and the more the vision forms, the harder it is to hold back. But we're almost there. I just have to remind myself of that.

CHAPTER 32

LEXI

ROMAN

Your ass in those pants is a revelation.

I'm fantasizing about bending you over your desk.

And my dining room table.

And the arm of my couch.

Only a handful of weeks before fantasy becomes a reality.

Unless you're on board with Ryker handling the playoffs.

I can have my paperwork filed by the end of the day.

This has become a regular habit of Roman's. He sends me texts about my outfit, his future plans for getting me out of it, and how it could happen sooner if he retires early, all while we're standing right beside each other. It would be an appealing option if it wouldn't break the entire team's heart. I'm about to say something, but the elevator doors slide open.

I almost opt for the stairs because Donnie is leaning against the wall inside the elevator. But Roman steps inside and puts his hand over the sensor, so I have no choice but to join him. Donnie glances between us and says hello.

I smile and say hi, moving to stand on the opposite side of the elevator.

"How you doing, Donnie?" Roman asks, always the conversationalist.

"Good. Getting close to the end of the season. How are you feeling about that?" he asks.

Roman pockets his phone. "Good. Ryker has really stepped up, and he'll be ready to take over come fall. Coach Forrester has been instrumental in making sure the defensive players are prepared for the shift."

Donnie's gaze slides my way. "I'm sure you've made that easier, seeing how involved you are."

Roman narrows his eyes. "I've always worked closely with the enforcers. It's a symbiotic relationship."

"Yeah, of course. Gotta work together to keep the team strong." Donnie seems to backtrack a little.

The elevator doors open, and all three of us step into the hall.

Donnie dips his chin. "Have a good day. You know where to find me if you need anything."

"Sure do," Roman replies.

Donnie disappears around the corner, and Roman turns to me, but before he can say anything, Hemi appears.

"Lexi! Hey, Roman." Her smile widens.

"Hey, Hemi. See you on the ice later." Roman touches my shoulder before heading down the hall to Vander Zee's office.

"Sure thing." I wave and focus on Hemi. "How's it going?"

"Fine. Good. Sorry, I didn't mean to interrupt you and Roman."

I wave the comment away. "You didn't. What's up?"

"I was just talking to Hammer about lunch today. If you're around, you should join us."

"I'd love that. What time are you thinking?"

"How's one-ish? I'm heading to a promo op with Hammer now, but we'll be back by noon."

"That sounds perfect."

"I'll pop by when I'm back." Hemi heads down the hall, and I go to my office to check emails and review the plan for today's practice. At ten, I stop by the break room to make myself a coffee before I meet with Vander Zee and the other coaches.

Donnie walks in as I finish doctoring up my coffee. "Hey, how's your morning?" I ask. It doesn't hurt to be pleasant.

"Decent. Yours?"

"Good. I should get back to it." And away from him and his gray-cloud aura. I turn toward the door.

"You should be careful, Coach Forrester," he says to my back.

I stop and turn to face him. "I'm sorry?"

He arches a brow. "I'm not the only one who sees what you're doing."

I force myself to remain impassive. "Excuse me?"

"You and all your office friends."

I hate that he's jumping to conclusions and that they're accurate. "They're my colleagues, and yours."

"And they're all involved with players. You taking notes?"

"Why are you—"

He cuts me off. "I'm not the only person who's noticed. People are talking. Especially about you and the goalie."

"I work with the defensive players." Sweat trickles down my spine. *Maybe I'm overreacting. Maybe it's nothing but jealousy.* I have the job he wants.

He scoffs. "You think we don't see what's going on? You aren't the only woman who applied for the job. Which shouldn't be a surprise after the past couple of years. The new PR girl is the daughter of the goalie and dating Hendrix. Head of PR is engaged to a player, and the team lawyer is married to one of your enforcers. It's like a fucking incest fest in here, and management signs off on the paperwork. And then you come in with your rise-from-the-ashes story." He crosses his arms. "I mean, honestly, I can't blame you. Roman is a stand-up guy. Fucking dad of the year, managing to keep his shit together when his best friend starts dating his daughter. Pretty much a saint, if you ask me. Twenty-year career. A veteran in the league. Must have at least fifty mil in his bank account."

My stomach twists. I thought we were being careful, that we had a plan, but everything he's saying is exactly what I was afraid of. "You're out of li—"

He holds up a hand. "Don't try to deny. He threw your sister a damn birthday party. You're with him and his crew all the time. I'm not stupid. And neither is the rest of management. And when I tell them what's going on, what's been going on, your coaching career is over. Enjoy what's left of it." He brushes by, leaving me reeling.

He's right, except about the birthday party. That was Tristan's doing, and everyone pitched in. Not that he'll care. He's clearly determined to take me down any way he can.

There is nothing worse than a coach who gets involved with a player. I knew this. Know this. And I did it anyway.

And now I stand to lose everything.

My dignity included.

CHAPTER 33

ROMAN

LEXI

Donnie knows, and he plans to tell management.

It's been hours since that message landed on my phone. I've been waiting all fucking day to have a conversation with Lexi. It isn't until Callie is at practice with Fee that I'm finally able to go to her place so she can share the details.

She tells me what happened while pacing the living room, her fingers at her lips. "I'll lose my job, Roman. I'll be fired."

"I'll retire early. If I'm not on the team, they can't fire you." It would solve the problem. "I've already floated the idea with Vander Zee."

"What? When? Why didn't I know about this?"

"Because I didn't want you to panic. I mentioned the Hockey Academy option, mostly to feel them out and see if they thought Ryker was ready."

"You can't. There's a month left in the season. We're on track to make the playoffs, and Ryker needs the time to prepare."

"If I had an injury, he'd have to be ready," I point out.

"You will not hurt yourself to get out of the playoffs! Besides, if you retire early for me, it will make things worse," Lexi argues.

This will already have backlash. There's no way it won't. But there must be a way out of this that doesn't ruin her career. "I love you," I state.

She stops pacing and turns to face me. "I love you, too." Her eyes roll up to the ceiling. "This is not how I wanted to tell you that."

I move to stand in front of her and take her hands in mine. "It doesn't change the weight of those words."

"I know, but management won't care that we've fallen in love, Roman. I'm in a position of power, and I'm engaging in a romantic relationship with a player. Full stop. The story ends there. No one cares that we're both adults. No one cares that you're retiring this year or that you're a decade older. I'm a first-year assistant coach, and I disregarded one of the fundamental rules. There is no getting out of this without a shitstorm."

I hate that I've put her in this position. I should have kept my distance. Should have made it easier for her to stay away from me. But I didn't, and we're here, in this place I never wanted her to be.

There is a solution, though. "Let's get married."

Her eyes flare. "What?"

"If you love me, and I love you, why not get married? They can't fire you if you're my wife."

"I don't know if that's true," she whispers.

"The rules say no fraternizing with players. But if you're my wife, that can't apply."

"Roman—"

I gently kiss the knuckle on her bare ring finger. "I want you. I want to be with you. I want to take care of you, and love you, and support you and the girls. I'm head over heels for you, Lexi. I'm desperate for the season to be over so we can be together. I think about early retirement on the daily because I want you more than I want to finish the season. You are what makes coming to the rink worth it every day. We get married, and we save your career, and we don't have to hide anymore." No more guilt. No more lying. The freedom to love her openly and protect her is all I want.

"I don't want to throw your entire world into upheaval." She settles a palm on my chest. "I don't want the start of your retirement to be a media nightmare."

"And I don't want to be without you," I reply.

"I don't want to be without you either." She exhales an unsteady breath. "I love you; I want a life with you. I just don't want to create a rift with all the people *you* love if we do this. There will be consequences."

"Teenage dad, remember? I can handle consequences, especially if it means I get to spend the rest of my life loving you. That's bigger than some blowback from head office."

She nods slowly, hand still pressed against my chest, like she needs grounding. "If I have to choose between my job and you, I will always choose you, Roman. I would rather have to start over in a new career then spend another three years regretting my choices." She looks so scared, but under that is hope and the love I feel for her reflected back at me. "Are you sure this is what you want?"

"Yes. Absolutely. Unequivocally. I've been searching for this feeling since I found you all those years ago. I was going to ask you to marry me once I retired, anyway. Now I don't have to wait." I squeeze her hand, wishing I had a ring to put on her finger. "Let me stand beside you. Let's build our future together."

"It'll be messy," she whispers.

"Stop trying to give me an out I don't want, angel. I'm not scared of messy. I raised a daughter on my own who ended up falling for my best friend. I can handle messy. I can handle anything, as long as I get to do it with you. Marry me, Lexi. Be my wife."

"Why are you so amazing?" A single tear tracks down her cheek.

I brush it away. "Is that a yes?"

"Yes." She pushes up on her toes, whispering the words with a smile against my lips, "I'll marry you."

CHAPTER 34

LEXI

"It'll be fine." Roman kisses the back of my hand.

Most of the time I can channel confidence, but nerves are winning. I've just said yes to marrying the man of my dreams. I'm head over heels in love with Roman and I can't wait to spend the rest of my life with him. But we've been hiding this from all the people we care about. Telling them we're together is one thing, but explaining that we're getting married as soon as possible is entirely another. I have a lot of feelings and they are all over the place.

Hammer and Hollis are on their way over, along with Dred, because if ever I needed the support of my friend, it's now. Fee and Callie will be home from practice any minute. Roman ordered pizza, boneless wings, and dessert from Callie and Fee's favorite restaurant. Hollis and Hammer are picking it up.

I don't know if I should be calling her Peggy or Aurora now. I'm about to become her dad's wife. And I'm only eight years older than she is.

Roman cups my cheek in his palm and looks down at me with compassion and love. "We will get through this, angel. No matter what, I will stand by your side and do everything I can to help you realize your goals. It doesn't matter how messy it is. We'll have each other."

He's my one constant in a sea of uncertainty. I voice the fear that's been eating at me ever since he called his daughter and asked her to come over. "What if Peggy isn't okay with this?" Losing my job would be a blow, but this worries me the most. She's his number one, as she should be. What if she can't accept this? What if she believes, like Donnie, that I'm in this for the wrong reasons? "I can't come between you."

He brushes his lips tenderly over mine. "My daughter is living with my best friend, and he's planning to propose sometime soon. If anyone will be annoyed, it'll be Hollis because I've stolen his thunder. But he's pretty used to it by now, considering Tristan and Dallas also beat him to the punch."

I chuckle a little. "That's not what I mean."

"What's the worry, then?"

"People will make assumptions about our relationship and my motives."

His smile is soft and sure. "My daughter won't be one of those people. And the ones who do can fuck themselves. We know how we feel about each other. The people who care about you and me and who we care about will see the truth and that's what's important. The rest is noise."

"You're so calm." I wish it would rub off on me.

"If we had more time, I'd help settle your anxiety," he murmurs.

"I'll take a rain check on that." We haven't even had time to celebrate the fact that we're engaged. It's been triage since he walked through the door. Telling his daughter and my sisters makes it so much more real. And the stakes that much higher.

The condo door opens, and Callie comes barreling down the hall like a miniature hurricane. "I had a total shutout today during practice! Roman! This is the best surprise! Hi!" She launches herself at him.

"Way to go! A shutout is awesome!" Roman scoops her up

and gives her a huge hug. "We ordered pizza from your favorite place. It should be here soon."

Fee comes down the hall, a questioning smile on her face. "Hey, Roman. I didn't know you were coming over. You two having a strategy meeting?" She glances between us.

"Sort of." I laugh, and it sounds reedy. "Dred, Peggy, and Hollis are coming over, too."

"Oh yay! I love Dred." Callie is all smiles.

"Why don't you put your backpacks in your rooms, and you two can help me set the table?" I need to do something with this nervous energy. The girls love Roman. But it's one thing to love having someone around sometimes, it's another when they're suddenly part of their everyday, though.

"Sure." Fee gives me a funny look, and she and Callie disappear down the hall.

"I'm freaking out," I whisper.

He brushes his lips against my temple. "It'll be fine. You'll see."

Dred shows up first, takes one look at me and says, "Shit's about to go down, isn't it?"

"Yeah." I hug her. "Hollis and Peggy should be here soon."

"Okay. Whatever you need. I've got your back." She looks to Roman. "And yours, too, obviously."

The pizza and Hollis and Peggy arrive a minute later. "Dred! I didn't know you were coming over, too. I brought wine." Hammer-Peggy-Aurora holds up a bottle of white. She hugs me and steps back, brows furrowing. "Is everything okay?"

"Everything is great!" Yeah, I'm not convincing anyone. I'm thrilled that the man of my dreams is finally going to be mine, but I wish we didn't have to spring the news on the people we both care the most about and hope they understand.

Hollis and Roman exchange a look.

Callie reappears, bouncing over to hug Hammer-Peggy-Aurora and Dred and tell them about her shutout today. Roman and Hollis continue to communicate with their eyebrows.

We bring the food to the table, and Hammer-Peggy-Aurora pours the wine. Roman and Hollis have beer, Callie has chocolate milk, and Fee sticks with water. I don't know why I'm so focused on what everyone is drinking, other than my stress levels are through the roof.

"Okay. As cool as this is, what's the vibe going on here?" Fee is frustratingly perceptive and yet totally clueless.

"We have something we need to tell you," I blurt.

"We as in…?" Fee glances around the table.

"As in Lexi and me." Roman covers my hand with his.

All eyes at the table focus on his fingers curved around mine.

Hammer-Peggy-Aurora's eyes flare, and her back straightens. Hollis stretches his arm across her chair and gently runs his finger down the nape of her neck. Fee says nothing. Callie looks gleeful. Dred looks like she's ready for anything. That makes one of us.

"I've asked Lexi to marry me," Roman states, calmly, matter-of-factly.

"And I said yes."

"Yeah, you did." Dred nods her approval.

"Uhhh…" Hammer-Peggy-Aurora's eyes are uncommonly wide.

"Holy shit," Fee mutters.

"My birthday wish came true!" Callie claps.

"Who found out?" Hollis asks.

"Donnie," Roman replies.

Hammer-Peggy-Aurora's head whips around. Her jaw goes slack as she registers Hollis's lack of surprise. "Found out what?"

"That guy's been gunning for Lexi's job from day one," Hollis says flatly.

"Found out what?" Callie echoes.

"That Roman and Lexi are in love. She's not supposed to be in love with a player on the team," Fee says helpfully. "Do I get to be a bridesmaid?"

"Can I be the flower girl?" Callie bounces in her seat.

"You knew about this, and you didn't tell me?" Hammer-Peggy-Aurora crosses her arms and gives Hollis an unimpressed look.

"Princess—"

"Don't you dare Princess me! We just went through this! You kept this from me!"

"Peggy, honey, you have to understand—"

"Oh, I understand all right. Hollis gets to know, and I get to be the one in the dark." She gives her father and Hollis a look that would incinerate most men. Then she scans the rest of the table. "And Dred doesn't look surprised either!"

"We were hoping to avoid this until the season was over. It's not personal, Ham—Peg—I don't know what I'm supposed to call you, and Hammer feels really weird," I admit.

"You can call me Aurora."

My chin wobbles. For a moment I try to compose myself, but then I remember the conversation I had with Roman about it being okay to show my real feelings in front of the people I care for the most. And if ever there was a time to let my feelings show, it's now. So when that tear made of fear and worry slips out, I don't try to hide it. "I am so sorry your dad had to keep this from you, and completely understand if you feel blind-sided. But I also feel like you might understand how difficult this has been. We tried so hard to *not* fall, but it just became—" Roman squeezes my hand and settles my nerves with one touch. "—impossible. And Dred isn't in the Terror office, so she felt safe. She also figured it out without me even saying a word."

"I'm an annoyingly perceptive observer." Dred steps right in to defend me.

"I'm sure you're shocked and hurt. It's reasonable if you need time, Aurora, but please know that I love Roman, and he loves me. I wish the timing was different, but it doesn't change the fact that I want to spend the rest of my life with him. I already lost him once, the idea of losing him again is unfathomable." *More than the idea of losing my job.*

She straightens. "What does that mean? You already lost him once?"

I exchange a glance with Roman.

"I met Lexi at a baseball game in New York. You were visiting your mom, and I decided to take a trip."

Aurora looks between us, and her brow arches, then her eyes narrow. "How long ago was this?"

"Three and a half years," I reply.

"In the summer between first and second year?" Understanding dawns. "You were so broody when I came back from my trip with mom. Wow. You've been holding a torch all this time."

"Basically, yeah," Roman and I say at the same time.

Aurora's face softens, and she reaches across the table, taking my other hand. "I get it. He's a great guy."

"The best," I agree.

"This still hurts," she whispers.

"I'm so sorry," I whisper back.

She gives me a watery smile, then turns that brokenhearted expression on her dad. "I am so, so sorry for keeping you in the dark for as long as I did last season. I understand now in a way I couldn't before."

"Kiddo," Roman says softly.

"You're an amazing dad. I adore you. And this—" She motions between us. "—this is wonderful. I've been secretly shipping you for months."

"Wait, what?" Roman looks confused.

"I've been shipping you too!" Callie adds.

Fee raises her hands. "Also, same."

"Does this mean Hammer will be our sister, too?" Callie is practically out of her mind with excitement.

Aurora turns her bright, beautiful, and slightly wobbly smile on Callie. "That's right. We'll all be a family."

"I can't even process that." I don't just gain a husband, my sisters gain a father figure and a sister, and the entire, wonderful support system of love that comes with them. It's more than I've ever dared to dream of.

"I love this team so much," Dred says.

Aurora rolls her shoulders back and taps her lip. "So, just for the sake of clarity, how many years are there between you?"

"I'm twenty-nine and I turn thirty in the summer," I say.

"And, Dad, how about you?" She props her hands on her chin and smiles angelically.

"I know where you're going with this, Peggy."

"Just humor me and answer the question Dado."

Roman gives her a look. "I'm forty."

"Oh dude, this is gold," Dred chuckles.

"Huh." Aurora bats her lashes. "So you're a *decade* older than Lexi. Interesting."

"Why is that interesting?" Callie asks, so sweetly unaware.

"Because Hollis is twelve and a half years older than Hammer," Fee says helpfully.

Roman opens and closes his mouth. Shakes his head. "The irony is not lost on me, kiddo."

"I accept your apology," Aurora says cheekily. "So, how soon are you tying the knot?"

"As soon as possible." Roman squeezes my hand.

"Like, this needs to happen ASAP?" Aurora clarifies.

"Ideally, yes. We want to get ahead of Donnie and the no-fraternization policy." Roman explains. "And the fewer people involved the better."

"So only the people at this table who know?" Hollis asks.

"We're the only ones who know the secret?" Callie seems to love this idea.

"That's right. But it won't be a secret for long." My stomach twists uncomfortably. This is getting really real. But the most important people are behind us. And that's what matters.

Roman and I will belong to each other, and whatever happens after that...we'll handle it.

Roman slides his hand under my braid and gives the back of my neck a light squeeze.

"I'll be right back." Aurora pushes away from the table.

For a moment I think she needs a minute because she's emotional, but she returns with her phone. "We need to make a list. I'm assuming we're either going to a justice of the peace or having a friend perform this ceremony." She slides back into her chair beside Hollis.

She hasn't looked at him once since we dropped this bomb and she found out he already knew. I sincerely hope the secret he's been keeping hasn't done damage to their relationship. The ripple effect has the potential to be huge in so many ways. I desperately want to limit the pain we cause the people we love.

"My sister has a friend who works at the courthouse. I can make a call now, if you want," Hollis offers.

"That would be great," Roman replies.

Hollis excuses himself.

"You have practice until, what? Eleven tomorrow?" Aurora asks us.

"That's right."

"Okay." She taps her lip with her stylus. "I'm clearing my schedule tomorrow."

"What will you tell Hemi?" I ask.

"That I need to take a personal day. Which isn't a lie, and by the time I'm back at work, this will all be out in the open. I'll come up with a PR plan to help mitigate, but this will likely be a bit of a sh—poopstorm. We'll deal with that as required. While you're at practice in the morning, I'll take the girls dress shopping."

"I have tomorrow off already, so I can come with you—or tackle whatever else needs to be done," Dred offers.

"Great. It'll be easier with the two of us. We can grab flowers and all the other important things we'll need. How does that sound?" She directs the question at Callie and Fee.

"Do I get to wear a fancy princess dress?" Callie is all enthusiasm.

"You sure do," Dred replies.

"Sounds good to me." Fee nods, eyes wide.

"Perfect. We'll have a great time." Aurora taps away on her phone. "Dad, when we get home, we'll take your tux down to get steamed and your shoes polished." She adds that to her list. "Lexi, after practice the five of us will get you a dress off the rack, and I'll make hair appointments. While we're doing that, Dad, you can take Hollis with you to pick out an engagement ring and wedding bands."

Hollis returns, phone still in hand. "How is four o'clock at city hall tomorrow?"

I look to Roman.

"Does that give you enough time to do everything?" he asks.

"I have to defer to Aurora on this, because I have no idea."

"We'll make it work," she promises.

Hollis squeezes her shoulder. "Four works. Thanks. We'll see you then." He ends the call. "You'll be married tomorrow."

CHAPTER 35

LEXI

"Lexi! You should see our dresses! They're so pretty. And we went for lunch, and I had sushi, but not the raw fish. Did you know not all sushi is raw fish? They have a roll with sweet potato in it, and it's really yummy. And I had green tea ice cream and red bean ice cream, and I like them both! Ice cream with beans in it! Isn't that funny?"

"Sorry. She maybe had some of Fee's cola while I wasn't looking." Aurora gives me an apologetic smile.

"I was also not paying attention. We were very dress focused this morning," Dred adds.

"No apologies necessary. Thank you both for doing this. I know we're throwing a lot at you, and I sincerely appreciate all your help." Marrying Roman today feels like it's the best roller coaster I've ever been on. In a matter of hours, he'll be my husband. We'll be starting our future together. Even under these less than ideal circumstances, he's everything I've ever wanted.

"I need to use the bathroom," Callie announces.

Fee glances at me. "I'll take her."

"I'll come too," Dred offers.

Aurora waits until they're out of earshot before she asks, "How are you doing? How was practice?"

"Practice was okay. The anxiety was something else. But now I'm excited and a little nervous. I'm also so grateful for your support today."

"You're making a big decision under a lot of pressure." Aurora's smile is empathetic, with a hint of worry.

"I know. I'm in love with your dad, though." He's the only person who's ever made me feel like I truly belonged. "He sees me in a way no one else ever has. And it's not just that we have the same passion for hockey. It's so much more. Until he came into my life, I didn't know what it felt like to be so completely loved, or to love so deeply. I feel like I finally understand the concept of a soulmate and that I've found mine in him."

"I believe you." She pulls me in for a hug. "And I know he feels the same way about you. I can see it on his face every time he says your name. He wouldn't do this if he wasn't sure. I have faith in his decisions. Even his accidents tend to have positive results."

She winks and we both chuckle.

"How are you and Hollis?" I've been worried about it all day. "I'm sorry I put Roman in this position where he couldn't be honest with you. I know how important you are to him."

Aurora gives me another squeeze and waves it away. "Oh, we're fine. I was...shocked, and a little hurt at first, but mostly my reaction came from a place of deep understanding. Because I did that to my dad last year—kept things from him out of what felt like necessity at the time but was mostly based on fear. Your situation is different, but it hits the same emotions. I expressed my feelings about it, and Hollis listened, and we talked it through. I know this is a precarious position for you. It has the power to be divisive. But I won't let hurt feelings interfere with my dad's happiness or my relationship with him."

"How are you only twenty-one?"

She smiles softly. "Almost twenty-two, actually. But I grew up in this world, and my dad is a huge believer in the benefit of therapy, so I've spent a lot of time talking about and understanding my feelings. That's not to say I haven't had my struggles. Falling for my dad's best friend was a challenge. I worried about the impact it would have on our relationship, but also on his relationship with his teammates, and with Hollis. We're mostly okay now, but it's taken some time." There's so much compassion in her eyes. "My dad wouldn't promise you forever if he didn't mean it, and he wouldn't choose someone who didn't love him back with the same ferocity. He loves hard and so do you, I see it with your sisters, with your dedication to the team. I know the circumstances are a challenge, and that this is a solution, but I also know it's about much more than that. You're protecting each other because that's what partners do."

Fighting the tears is pointless because I've already lost that battle. "You don't know what a relief it is to hear you say that, Aurora. I love Roman. That man owns my heart, and I'm so grateful to have you behind us. I tried so hard to keep my distance, but he's just...easy to fall in love with."

"He was built to love people. I'm happy that he's happy. And I like you, Lexi. A lot. The only thing I'm nervous about is what's on the other side of this. For all of us."

"Me, too," I admit.

"It's clear he pursued you when he shouldn't have. Seems to be a family trait, since I did it too." She rolls her eyes.

"Turned out good for you. Hopefully, it'll be the same for us," I say as Fee, Callie, and Dred make their way back to us.

"It will." Aurora gives me a side hug. "Now, let's find you a very pretty dress so you can marry my dad."

Aurora takes us to a very swanky, very expensive boutique dress shop with name-brand, top-of-the-line dresses.

"Um, this place is nice, but I don't know if I can afford anything in here," I whisper before one of the sales associates reaches us.

Aurora pats my hand and laughs. "You're not paying for the dress. My dad gave me his credit card, which is something you'll have to get used to. He's a bit extravagant with gifts. It's part of his love language." My dad is the same. I consider calling him, but he won't be able to make it.

"Hi, you must be Aurora." The sales associate shakes her hand.

"Thank you so much for fitting us in. This is Callie, Fee, and Dred—the wedding party—and this is Lexi, our bride to be." Aurora squeezes my shoulder.

"It's lovely to meet all of you. I'm Sariah, and I'm excited to help you find your perfect wedding dress today."

"I'll need to be able to wear it right away." I can't believe I'm having a shotgun wedding. And yet, I'm more ready than I ever thought I'd be to walk down the aisle.

Sariah doesn't miss a beat. "Of course. Shall we get started?"

"That would be great, yes, thank you."

We follow Sariah to the back of the store. We're the only people here. The girls are given sparkling grape juice, and Aurora, Dred, and I are handed champagne. I don't drink often, but I accept it as we browse dresses, already pulled in my size.

"I can come in and help you, if you want," Dred offers once we've collected a few possibilities.

I nod. "That would be great."

"We'll be back!" Dred calls over her shoulder as Sariah brings the first two dresses to the room.

I strip down to my bra and panties. Having spent years in locker rooms with a team of women, I tend not to be shy about my body.

"How are you doing?" Dred helps zip me into the first dress.

"This is the right decision," I whisper.

She turns me around to face her. "You love him."

"So unbelievably much."

"And you want to be his wife."

"A thousand percent yes. Today, tomorrow, six months from now, the answer would be the same."

"Then this is the right decision." Dred is an amazing best friend, but I still wish this was a conversation I could have had with my mom. She couldn't be the mom I wanted her to be, but I yearn for that mother daughter connection. She'll never see me in my wedding dress or her other daughters. Now we're building another family, and my chest aches a little. I resolve, in this moment, to be the mom my sisters need, and to show up for Dred if she ever walks down the aisle and needs me in the same way.

"Thank you for being here."

"I got you, girl. How do you feel about this dress?"

I smooth my hands over my hips and look at my reflection. "I like it, but I don't think I love it."

"We should show the girls anyway." She opens the door, and I step out.

They ooh and ahh but agree that it's not quite right.

The second one is the same.

"How about this one?" Aurora points to a simple, elegant dress.

"It's pretty." Callie has said this about every dress.

"I like it." Fee gives her approval.

"It's understated, and I love it," Dred weighs in.

It's not flashy, but it has the potential to be stunning. "I'll try it."

I disappear into the changing room and carefully slip into the beautiful blush dress, dotted with simple blossoms. The back is corset style and laces up. Dred expertly tightens it and ties a bow at the base of my spine. "If I could get a boner over a dress, I would have one now." She steps back and turns me toward the mirror.

"Oh my gosh. This is…"

"It?" She arches a brow.

"Yes." I can see myself walking down the aisle in this, envision Roman waiting at the altar for me. Warmth spreads through me and my heart swells, knowing that soon, I'll be standing in front of the man I love, promising him forever. For all the heartache this season and the potential for more fallout, knowing

I'll finally be his brings me such peace. "This is the dress I'm getting married in."

"Let's show the girls," Dred suggests.

I step out of the dressing room, and the girls suck in a collective gasp.

"That is..." Aurora presses her hand to her heart. "Wow. Just wow."

I'm unable to contain my smile as Sariah sweeps in with a veil, shoes, and a bouquet of flowers to complete the look.

"You're so beautiful," Fee says.

"Like a princess," Callie agrees.

"Stunning." Dred arranges my train.

"This is the one." My nerves vanish and in their wake is giddy anticipation.

"My dad is going to lose his mind when he sees you." Aurora's smile is huge.

She snaps a few pictures before I disappear into the dressing room and put my regular clothes on so they can steam the dress.

I just about pass out when the sales associate rings up the dress, shoes, and veil. I grip Aurora's arm and whisper, "Maybe I should try on something else."

She gives me a look. "That dress is perfect for you. Trying on more is pointless. Just do what I do when Hollis decides he needs to outfit me in a dress that costs three months' salary: pretend there's one less zero at the end of the price tag."

"This will take some getting used to," I murmur.

"I know." She passes over Roman's credit card.

Our next stop is a salon down the street. I'm prepared with pictures of what I'd like. The stylist braids my hair, weaving it through with baby's breath, while my sisters, Dred, and Aurora get light curls and their nails done.

It's nearly three by the time we're finished with hair and makeup. We pick up the dress and flowers and return to the condo to get ready.

When I reach my bedroom, I find a huge gift box in the

middle of my bed. Aurora hangs my dress and squeezes my arm. "I'll give you a minute. Just call if you need me." She pulls the door closed behind her.

I run my damp hands over my thighs and pick up the card lying on top of the wrapped box, smiling at Roman's neat handwriting.

Lexi,

I know this isn't how we expected things to go, but I can't wait to make you my wife. The moment I met you, I started falling. And in the years between then and now, the longing to find someone who made me feel the way you do kept growing. But that hole in my heart could only be filled by you. I can't wait to spend the rest of my life loving you, caring for you, standing beside you.

All my love,
Roman

I tip my head back, overcome with emotion at how thoughtful and kind this man is. And he's about to be mine. "Get it together, Lexi." I reach for a tissue so I don't ruin my makeup before I even put my dress on.

I pull the satin bow, lift the lid, and peel back the tissue paper. On top is another note from Roman.

I can't wait to take these off you when you're my wife. With my teeth, of course.

Love, Roman

I smile at the satin-and-lace panty set. It's sexy, classy, and pretty—everything I'd expect from Roman. I strip out of my clothes, carefully rinse off from the neck down with the handheld showerhead, apply lotion, and then slip into my new lingerie. It's the most beautiful set I've ever had the pleasure of wearing.

My phone pings with a message.

ROMAN

How's my almost-wife doing?

LEXI

Getting ready to put on my dress.

ROMAN

I can't wait to see you in it. Did you happen to get my gift?

LEXI

I'm wearing it right now.

ROMAN

I look forward to taking it off you later tonight.

LEXI

Would you like a preview?

ROMAN

sweating GIF *nail biting GIF*

So very tempting, but I think I'd like to wait until I'm peeling you out of your wedding dress.

LEXI

Fair. Not long now.

ROMAN

Hollis and I are leaving for City Hall shortly. Your car will be there in about twenty, but they'll wait as long as you need.

LEXI

I'll be ready.

ROMAN

I'm calling you.

I answer on the first ring.

"Talk to me. I need to hear your voice."

"Hi."

"Hi, beautiful. Tell me how you're doing," he says.

"Excited to have you as all mine, nervous because of the circumstances, guilty that I'm about to make your life a lot more complicated."

"My dear, sweet, sexy, incredible almost-wife, I want you—all of you and everything that comes with you, including complications. I wouldn't have asked you to marry me otherwise," he assures me. "What else do you feel guilty about?"

"That I'm getting married and I haven't even told my dad. And you haven't told your mom." I put the phone on speaker and set it on the bed as I run my hands over my dress.

"My mom is on a two-month cruise, and she'll be ecstatic that I'm not single anymore. But we will have a proper wedding in the summer, with all our friends and your dad in attendance. And if he needs to have words with me for marrying you without asking his blessing first, I'll gladly accept his wrath," he says as I loosen the corset. "How does that sound?"

"Like you know exactly what to say to calm me," I whisper.

"Good. Later I'll wind you right up. Sound like a plan?"

I laugh. "Sounds like a wonderful plan."

"I think so, too. I'll see you soon, okay?"

"Okay. I love you."

"With all my heart. Deep breaths, angel. We're almost there."

There's a pause before I say something scarier than even those three little words. "Marrying you feels like a dream I was too afraid to hope for. You make me feel like I'm the most precious thing in the world. I never worry you'll disregard me or prioritize something else above me. I've never had that before, Roman. I've never had someone love me the way you do. You are the most caring, wonderful man I've ever met, and that I get to give you my heart is the best gift in the world."

His breath comes heavy through the line. "You were always meant to be mine. I was always meant to be yours. I love every part of you, and I've never felt so wholly loved in return. I can't wait to be your partner in this life."

"Same. See you soon?" My eyes burn as I think about the man I'm about to call husband.

"I'll be there."

We end the call, and I step into my dress, then call Dred in to help me lace it up.

"You are absolutely radiant." Dred ties a bow at the base of my spine for a second time today, then helps me with my shoes before she opens the door.

Callie comes bounding in, her poofy dress swishing and curls bobbing. "Oh wow! You look like a princess, Lexi!"

Aurora gives me a soft smile. "You are beautiful."

"You really are." Fee's chin wobbles. "I wish Mom were here to see you."

That's one thought I've been shoving down all day. I miss her, and I wish she was here to fuss over my hair or my lipstick. "Me, too, honey." I open my arms, and my sisters fall into them.

Dred pulls a tissue from her purse and dabs under my eyes. I laugh, and the girls laugh, and Aurora dabs under her eyes, too. "We need some pictures, and then we need to get you to City Hall."

Aurora snaps a bunch of photos of me with the girls, then sets her camera on a tripod in the living room so she and Dred can be part of it, too.

They make sure we have everything we need, and the five of us take the elevator to the lobby and climb into the waiting limo.

It's really happening. I'm getting married. To the man who's starred in my dreams for the past three years and become the man I want to spend the rest of my life with.

CHAPTER 36

ROMAN

"You gotta stop pacing, man," Hollis says. "You're making me dizzy."

"She said they were on their way fifteen minutes ago. Shouldn't they be here by now?" I've read over Lexi's contract four times, and Hollis had a lawyer friend check it over, too. Marrying her is the best way to keep her job safe. I love her, and I would do anything to protect her.

"I'll check the family circle." Hollis had Peggy add him as soon as I mentioned it last time. He consults his phone, which I could have done if I wasn't stressing so hard. "Based on Aurora's phone location, they're two minutes out."

"Okay. Good. That's good." I check my breast pocket for the engagement ring and wedding ring. I went shopping for both after practice this morning. It was a challenge not to show Donnie what happens to people who cross me when I saw him talking to Vander Zee before I left. But we're so close to having what we want, and with that comes a weight lifted.

"I don't think I've ever seen you this nervous in my life." Hollis is infuriatingly calm.

"I've never been married before." My anxiety is at an all-time high, but I'm not afraid. I just want this to be perfect. I want her. I want her to be mine. No reservations.

My phone buzzes, and I almost drop it. *What if she changes her mind?*

It's not a message from Lexi or Aurora, though. It's from Vander Zee and Fielding. "Fuck."

Hollis straightens. "Are the girls okay?"

"They're fine. Vander Zee and Fielding want to see me tomorrow morning."

"It could be about anything."

"Maybe, but I saw Donnie talking to Vander Zee after practice."

"You'll be married within the hour, Roman. It's legal and binding. So whatever the meeting is about, Lexi should be covered."

"I fucking hope so." But no matter what happens, I'll take care of her. Of the girls. We'll be partners. She won't have to go through this alone.

Peggy messages to let me know they've arrived. I try not to sweat through my tux as Hollis and I take our places at the front of the room. The music begins, and Callie is first to walk down the aisle, all smiles and adorableness in her mint-green dress. She rushes over and gives me a big hug as Fee comes in after her. Dred is next, and her smile is wider than I've ever seen it. And then Peggy appears. She looks beautiful. Hollis can't take his eyes off her, and I'm sure he's imagining what his own wedding will be like.

My mind trips on that for a moment, but then Lexi appears, and I feel like my heart is about to burst out of my chest. She's just so gorgeous in her blush-colored dress, hair cascading over her shoulder in a braid woven with flowers, a bouquet of lilies clasped in her hands. Today is without a doubt one of the best days of my life, because this stunning woman, who I can trust with my heart in a way I never have with anyone else, is about to be mine.

I must take an unconscious step toward her because Hollis puts his hand on my chest.

Lexi's smile lights up the entire room. "I'm coming for you," she calls out with a saucy wink.

"I'm ready for you." My answering grin widens with every step she takes. I hold out my hand when she's within reach, and she slips her fingers into my palm.

Peggy takes her flowers, and I kiss the back of Lexi's hand. "You look radiant."

"You look devastatingly handsome," she whispers.

"I love you." I kiss her bare ring finger.

"I love you, too," she echoes.

"Before we get this party started, I have something for you."

"Okay." Her eyes light up with the same excitement I feel.

I pull the small velvet box from my breast pocket. "I know I already asked, and you already said yes, but I didn't have a ring." I drop to one knee in front of her and flip the box open. The emerald-cut diamond, set in rose gold, nestled in the velvet cushion, glints in the light.

"Oh, Roman." Her eyes flare and her fingers go to her lips.

"Alexandria, you are a force and the most amazing woman I've ever known. Since the moment we met, my heart knew it belonged to you. Will you allow me the honor of loving you for the rest of our lives? Will you marry me?"

"Yes, Roman." Her smile is soft and warm. "You are everything I've ever wanted. It would be the most wonderful honor to marry you."

"I'm happy to hear that." I slide the ring onto her trembling finger.

"It's beautiful," she whispers.

"You're beautiful," I whisper back.

Dred hands Lexi a tissue when she fans her face.

"Thank you."

"We got you, girl." Dred steps back with a soft smile.

Lexi dabs under her eyes, then tucks the tissue away in a hidden pocket.

"Okay." She takes a steadying breath. "I'm ready."

"Me, too." I wink, and she laughs.

The justice of the peace smiles. "Now we can proceed."

I hold Lexi's hands. I've never felt so steady, so sure of anything. Lexi is what my heart has been missing.

I barely listen to the officiant as I soak in the woman before me—so beautiful, so inspiring in every way. And she's about to be my wife. Mine to have, hold, and protect. And then no one can fuck with her. Not Donnie, not the head office. Not Fielding or Vander Zee.

When it's time for her vows, Lexi grips my hands tightly and exhales a steadying breath. "You are the most incredible man, and your heart is one of the most beautiful things about you. It is an honor to be loved by you, and even more of an honor to love you. I will guard your inner most thoughts like they're my own. Your soft spots and gentleness will always be protected. When you're trying to hold everyone together, I will remind you that you are always more than enough and that you are so very loved. I promise that I will do everything in my power to be deserving of the love you give so freely and without reservation. I will always stand by your side, and no matter what challenges we face, we'll do it together. And I promise to be your partner and your confidant, your friend and your strongest ally, your very best student, and your most supportive coach."

I smirk, and she grins and blushes.

Hollis coughs into the crook of his elbow, and Peggy snickers.

"From this day forward, until the end of this lifetime and whatever lies beyond, I take you, Roman Hammerstein, to be my husband, my soul mate, my forever."

With unsteady hands, Lexi slides the ring onto my finger. I start to pull the cue card from my pocket but decide to speak from the heart. That's what brought me here today.

"Lexi, I will never forget the moment I met you. You lit up

the world for me. And for years I thought you would forever be a memory. But then you came back to me, and I realized that the space in my heart was waiting for you to fill it again. I promise to love you, to cherish and revere you, to keep you safe, to be your partner, your best friend, your confidant, your cheerleader, your student, and your coach. Whatever you need, I will be it for you, because you're it for me. I am whole with you, and wholly in love with every part of you. From this day forward, until my very last breath, I take you, Alexandria Forrester, to be my wife, my soul mate, my one and only."

I slide the wedding band onto her finger. "My wife."

The officiant barely had time to make the pronouncement before I sealed our vows with a kiss. Alexandria is mine.

CHAPTER 37

ROMAN

After the ceremony, we go to Eliza Van Horn's for a private, celebratory dinner. Before she opened her restaurant, Eliza was a chef who worked with the Terror, among other pro teams. She even made us a mini wedding cake, and Lexi and I shared a first dance.

Hollis and Peggy take the girls home for the night—or what will be their home until they move in with me, something we have yet to discuss—and Lexi and I head to my place for a celebration of our own.

I kiss her knuckles and admire how perfect my ring looks on her finger. I love that she's wearing a symbol of my commitment to her, and that we're done hiding. "Have I mentioned how stunning you look today?"

"Several times, yes." She smiles. "But feel free to tell me again, if you like."

"You are an absolute vision. This dress was made for you. But if you want to wear something different when we have a ceremony with our friends and family, we'll get you a new one."

"This one was plenty expensive. There's no need to buy another. Especially since so few people saw me in this one."

Of course she'll be practical about it. She's used to having to manage on a budget. She's accustomed to *not* asking for things, including help. "I would buy you a hundred dresses, if it made you happy. And to be quite honest, I don't mind that very few people have seen you in this dress. In fact, I prefer it."

"Feeling a little covetous?"

"Absolutely." I kiss a path up the inside of her arm. "All these months of having to stay away from you when we're around other people has been hell. All this wishing you were mine, and now you are." I kiss the dip in her elbow. "All mine. Only mine. To dote on, to love, to please, to spoil." I tuck a finger under her chin and brush my lips over hers. "And tonight I get to do all of those things for the first time with you as *my wife*."

Her lips curve up in a sultry smile. "I really love the way that sounds, *husband*."

I nuzzle into her neck and kiss up to her ear, nipping at the lobe. "I can't wait to hear you say that again, but as a moan."

The car stops, and the driver announces our arrival, waiting until I give the okay before he opens the door for us. I help Lexi out and guide her to the elevator.

Fortunately, we make it to the penthouse floor with no stops. I hand her my fob and sweep her up in my arms. She laughs and wraps her arms around my neck.

I nod toward the door. "Let us in before I make a scene out here in the hallway."

"It's not like there's anyone to catch us with Hollis and Aurora at my place."

"I have plans for you that do not include sex in this hallway," I murmur darkly.

"Fair." She swipes the fob, and I carry her inside. I don't put her down after I cross the threshold.

"Aren't you going to let me look around?"

"You'll see it every day when you live here. First I want to show you exactly how much I love you." I carry her through the living room, past the kitchen and dining room, and down the hall.

"This place is huge."

"Lots of room for our family," I agree.

"I can't believe we're really married," she says softly.

"This is the beginning of our forever." I push through the doors to my bedroom.

"Oh, Roman." Lexi gasps. "This is a fairytale."

My bedroom has been transformed. Rose petals are scattered across the floor and my bed. Champagne and green apple slices with salted caramel dip sit on the table next to an armchair. Candlelight glows from every surface.

I set her down, only because I can't get her out of this dress if I don't. The low strains of music filter through the speakers. Lexi settles her hands on my chest. "This is otherworldly romantic." There's awe in her expression, and a flash of sadness. "I'm sorry we couldn't share this day with our friends."

"We'll do it all again," I promise. "But on a much grander scale, with a real honeymoon. We'll spend two weeks somewhere that makes you happy, half of it in bed, enjoying each other, the other half making memories we can share with the people we love."

"I adore you." She loosens my tie and bites her lip. "Thank you for making today so special. I'm sure it isn't how you envisioned your wedding."

I stroke her cheek. "My darling wife." I trace the contour of her bottom lip. "I didn't know I wanted a wedding day at all until you walked into my life—" I follow the edge of her dress and tap gently over the part of her that I reside in now. "—stole my heart and never gave it back." I curve my hand around the side of her neck, the thrum of her pulse grounding me as I slant my mouth over hers. Lexi loops her arms over my shoulders. I force myself to slow down, to savor the moment as I skim her satin-covered curves.

"You're all mine," I whisper, so in awe of this woman. She trusts me to be her person, to give her everything she needs, to grow and learn and live and love with her.

"All yours," she agrees, one hand sliding down to work my tie free. "And you're all mine, too."

"Only yours." I skim along her spine until I reach the bow at the base and pull the tie free. "Turn around for me."

She shivers and complies. Her braid hangs down her back, threaded through with baby's breath. I skim it gently with my fingertips. "So beautiful." I lean down to kiss her shoulder. "I couldn't stop thinking about how pretty this braid would look when it's wrapped around my fist."

Lexi tips her chin up. "I hoped you'd like it."

I let the rope of hair slide through my hand once, then grip it at the nape of her neck and give a tug, angling her head so I can kiss a path to her ear. "I'm going to take my time undressing you. And when you're naked, I'm going to worship every inch of your beautiful body with my mouth." I bite the edge of her jaw. "Until you're begging for my cock."

"Sounds like heaven."

I turn her head and brush my lips across hers, taking in her flushed cheeks, and parted lips. I want to remember every moment of this night with her. This first. To claim and be claimed by each other. "I love you, angel."

"I love you too, Roman."

I loosen the corset, dipping down to pepper kisses along her shoulders. "This is like unwrapping my favorite gift." I work my way down the dress, exposing the blush satin and lace bra I picked out for her earlier today. "Such a pretty, tempting treat."

I pull the final loop and the bodice falls away, revealing the delicate lace and satin bra and panty set that matches her dress. My lips coast along her shoulder as I move in front of her and drop to my knee. I press a kiss below her navel. "I can't wait to taste my sweet wife."

Lexi settles a palm on my shoulder for balance as she steps out of the layers of satin. I lay it across the closest chair and take her hands, kissing her knuckles as I drink her in. This beautiful, strong woman, so soft for only me. "You are beyond exquisite."

"I'm glad you like it." She pulls her braid over her shoulder, bites her lip, and fingers a button on my shirt. "Is it my turn to unwrap you?"

"Almost." I reach around behind her and flick the clasp on her bra. She lets it slide down her arms, dropping to the floor, before she pushes my jacket over my shoulders. It joins her dress on the chair. My tie goes next. When she starts on the buttons on my shirt, I tease her nipples, skimming them with gentle fingers, then tugging lightly. She groans and rubs her thighs together. But finally, she rids me of my shirt.

She moves on to my belt, then pops the button on my dress pants as she drops to her knees to remove my pants and socks. When she reaches for the waistband of my boxer shorts, I shake my head.

"But there are green apple slices and caramel dip." She gives me doe eyes and strokes her braid. "Pretty, please?"

I lean down and slip my thumb between her parted lips. Her tongue presses against the pad and she sucks softly. "How can I say no you when you're being so polite."

Her eyes light up. There were so many memorable moments when we spent that weekend together in New York. But those green apple slices and caramel dip were unforgettable.

Lexi tugs my boxers down my thighs. Once I'm rid of them, I step back and drop into the chair next to the champagne and apple slices. I crook a finger and feel like a God when my gorgeous wife crawls to me. She runs her hands up my thighs, her braid dragging across my skin and she pulls herself up, brushing her lips over mine.

"Thank you for indulging me." She sucks my bottom lip, then kisses her way down my chest.

"I'll fuck your sweet mouth, but I come in your pretty pussy, understood?"

"Yes, Roman." Lexi reaches for an apple slice and drags it through the caramel dip. She carefully positions it over my throbbing, frankly painful erection, drizzling caramel sauce onto the head and down the shaft.

She nibbles the end, then holds the rest of the slice out to me. I take it with my teeth, the sweet tart flavor bursting on my tongue and bringing back memories of the last time we did this.

"Such a mess you made," I tsk.

She blinks innocently up at me. "Can I lick it up?"

She's beyond beautiful, on her knees for me, so eager and ready to please. "Be thorough."

Lexi grins as she braces her hands on my thighs and drags her tongue around the head. She laps at me, teasing, placing open mouthed kisses along the shaft.

I hold out my hand and she places the end of her braid in my waiting palm. I plan to buy baby's breath and weave it into her hair every chance I get. I wrap the length gently around my fist, not wanting to crush the fragile blooms.

"Be a good girl and suck it clean."

I marvel at how perfect she is, how much power she wields as she takes me in her mouth and brings me to the edge. And I get to spend the rest of my life loving her, adoring her, and being loved and adored in return.

When I hit the back of her throat, I pull her off my cock. "That's enough."

She grins up at me. "Caramel drizzle dick is my favorite."

I laugh and pull her into my lap, kissing her roughly. "You can have it for dessert any night you want."

I slide my arm under her knees and she wraps her arms around my neck so I can carry her to the bed.

She tries to wind her legs around my waist, but I bracket her thighs with mine. "Ah, ah, ah. What did I say I was going to do?"

"Kiss every inch of me until I'm begging for your cock."

"That's right, angel. You got what you wanted, now I get what I want."

Stretching out over her, I make good on my promise. I suck

and bite her nipples, kiss my way across her stomach, down to her satin covered pussy. I lick the damp fabric, then tug her panties down her thighs with my teeth as I spread her legs wide.

"Hold yourself open for me," I demand.

She parts her lips with two fingers and I lave her clit, teasing and nipping. I loop my arms around her thighs and fuck her with my tongue, swallowing down the taste of her.

"Roman, please," her voice is rough with need.

"Those are the pretty words I've been waiting for." I lick up the length of her, desperate for more of her soft moans and pleas for more.

When her legs start to shake and I'm as mindless with desire as she is, I cover her body with mine and settle between her hips. My cock slides between her slick folds and we both groan.

Her hands slide into my hair, eyes searching mine as she whispers, "I need you inside me."

I shift my hips forward, filling her in one smooth stroke, connecting us, making us one.

Her trembling fingers drift down my cheek. "I love you so much."

"I love you, too. More than I ever thought possible." I brush my lips over hers.

She bites her way across the edge of my jaw until her lips are at my ear. She takes the lobe between her teeth, then whispers, "Please fuck me with your fat cock, *husband*."

I pull my hips back. "Anything for you, *wife*."

Her breath leaves her on a high-pitched gasp as I fill her in one rough stroke.

Lexi grips my forearms, eyes hot with desire. "Please, more."

I ease out and snap forward.

Her head falls back on a low moan. "Thank you."

All the softness fades, and we come together like a storm, desperate to claim each other. I can't get enough of her deep moans, her high-pitched cries, and the sound of my name tumbling from her lips—or the way her pussy grips me like a fist when she comes.

This is the first night of our forever, and I never want it to end. I slow my strokes, fighting to stay in control, to postpone the inevitable. "You're mine," I growl against her lips. "To love." I grind my hips against hers. "To cherish." I suck her bottom lip. "To worship." I pull my hips back. "To fuck." And slam back in.

"Always yours," she groans.

Her body quakes with the force of her orgasm. And I fall too. Into bliss. Into her. We stay wrapped in each other, bodies twined, my lips pressed against her temple.

I want to stay here, in this perfect place where reality can't touch us. Where there are no consequences for falling in love with the right person at the wrong time.

CHAPTER 38

LEXI

I wake up to breakfast in bed, served by my husband. He's dressed in nothing but blue boxer briefs with the team logo stamped on the peen pouch.

"Morning, angel."

I grin. "I could get used to this."

"Good. Because it's going to happen often—although likely minus me in only boxer shorts when the girls are here."

I pull myself into a sitting position so Roman can set the tray over my lap. "We have a lot to figure out, don't we?"

"We do," he agrees, climbing into bed beside me. "Optics wise, it's probably best for you and your sisters to move in as soon as possible. But I also understand they may need time to adjust." He sips his coffee. "So maybe we can start by inviting them over so they can get comfortable, and we'll go from there."

"That sounds good. To be honest, I think Callie will want to move in right away, but Fee might take more time to warm up."

"That's understandable. Asking her to move again so soon is more change on top of change, so we can go at her pace," Roman says.

Emotion clogs my throat. I know in my heart I've made the right decision for me, but I want it to be the right decision for all of us. And here's my husband, showing me once again, that he'll stand by me. "You are beyond remarkable."

He settles a finger under my chin and brushes his lips over mine. "I know you're used to handling things on your own, Lexi, but we're partners. So we do this together, okay?"

"I'm not accustomed to relying on other people, but I'm learning how. There's just so much going on—personally, professionally." My stomach flips. "I should check my phone." I turned off my alerts yesterday afternoon so it wouldn't be a distraction and forgot to turn them back on last night, for obvious reasons.

"Have something to eat first." His expression and tone set me on edge.

I sit up straighter. "Did something happen?"

"Vander Zee and Fielding asked to see me this morning. Privately. I assume they'll ask the same of you."

"I really should check my messages." I start to move the lap tray, but Roman holds up a hand.

"Have some toast. I'll get your phone for you." He kisses me on the cheek and disappears down the hall.

My appetite has disappeared, but I take a bite of toast, aware that going in with an empty stomach won't help. I've eaten half a slice when Roman reappears with my clutch. As expected, I have an email from Vander Zee and Fielding citing a meeting this morning.

"We'll do this together, Lexi. They won't divide and conquer." His conviction grounds me.

"We present a united front. There's no more hiding. We tell them the truth and own the choice. They can disapprove, but we're legally married, and they can't take that away from us." I worry my bottom lip. This morning won't be easy.

He takes my hand. "You freaking out?"

"A little, yeah," I say honestly.

"Do you regret marrying me?" he asks gently.

"No. Of course not. This won't be a comfortable conversation, and I'm at peace with that and my decisions." Regardless of how this impacts my career moving forward, he's what matters most. "But my biggest worry is how it will affect you, and the rest of the team, and what it could mean for the end of your final season. I don't want your legacy in the hockey world to be overshadowed by this."

"My hockey legacy has nothing on marrying the love of my life. As for the team, they're my family, and they might have some feelings about this, but we back each other up." He presses a kiss to my temple. "We should get ready so we can deal with this."

Roman moves the lap tray for me and refrains from commenting on the mostly full plate.

"Roman?"

When his eyes lift, I see his love for me. "What is it, angel?"

"I would have married you any day. You're more important than this job. I'd trade it all to spend the rest of my life with you."

He crosses the room and with strong hands and a delicate touch, he tips my chin up. "I would do the same for you. You're everything I've ever wanted." His lips are a balm filled with promises only our souls know.

I disappear into the bathroom to shower. Roman is already dressed by the time I'm done, and my outfit is laid out on the bed. It's my standard tracksuit for ice practice. Roman helps me into my clothes, then turns me around and expertly french braids my hair. It settles me in a way only he can.

He presses a kiss to the side of my neck. "Tonight, we can work out some of this nervous energy."

"Something to look forward to."

He links his fingers with mine and I follow him through the penthouse, taking in the massive space as we go. I slip my feet into my shoes and, hands still joined, we take the elevator to the parking garage.

Roman, ever the gentleman outside of the bedroom, opens

the door for me and helps me in. Then he takes his place behind the wheel.

"How are you feeling?" he asks as he shifts the car into gear.

"Like I'm going to vomit," I admit. The toast I ate sits like gravel. The unknowns are scary, but he's my one constant.

He leans over and kisses my temple. "Everything will be okay."

What will my future look like? I don't want to start our life together unemployed. I don't want to end up like my mother, who always had to rely on her partner to provide financial stability. There will be other opportunities, though. Other paths I can take if I need to.

He pulls into the parking lot at the head office. Regardless of Roman's assurances and my mental pep talks, my stomach still feels like it's trying to turn itself inside out. "Lexi." He squeezes my hand. "I'm with you on this. You're not alone, and you never will be again."

"I love you so much," I whisper.

"And I love you." He presses a kiss to my lips before he gets out of the car.

I meet him at the hood and fall into step beside him. My mouth is dry, and my heart is a drum in my chest. I rub my rings as we step into the elevator.

We don't speak as we watch the numbers climb. I'm sweaty and anxious by the time we reach our floor. But I roll my shoulders back and channel confidence I don't feel, as Roman's fingers press lightly into the dip in my spine, and we walk down the hall together.

The scarlet letter on my forehead is burning. Shilpa, who is carrying a file folder and a sleeve of crackers, frowns as we approach each other. She's always been kind to me. Professional and polite in the office, and chatty and friendly when we're at the Watering Hole. But she's the team attorney, and currently she looks less than impressed.

"Morning, Shilpa," Roman says jovially, like we're not about to drop a giant bomb on the head office.

Her eyes drop to his left hand and then to mine. "Roman, Lexi. I'll see you both shortly." She disappears into her office.

"This is going to be rough," I mutter.

"We'll get through it," Roman assures me.

We will. I know that's true. It just doesn't *feel* true.

Roman knocks on Vander Zee's open door. The head coach drags his gaze away from the computer screen, glancing between us. The disappointment on his face is cutting in a way I didn't expect.

"You wanted to see us?" Roman asks.

"Have a seat. Forrester. Hammerstein." He motions to the conference table, then picks up the phone and dials an extension. "They're here."

Roman pulls out a chair for me and takes the seat beside me. He folds his hands on the conference table, wedding band clearly on display. I do the same and try not to crap my pants.

A moment later, Jamie Fielding enters the office and closes the door behind him. "There have been some allegations, which I questioned strongly. But if you're coming in together, should I assume there's merit in them?" Fielding slides into the chair across from us.

Vander Zee focuses on Roman's clasped hands and then mine, eyes flaring. "You gotta be fucking kidding me."

Fielding frowns at Vander Zee.

Vander Zee's teeth grind together. "How did this happen?"

"Do you want to fill me in?" Fielding looks lost.

Vander Zee taps his own wedding band and nods to our hands.

Fielding follows his gaze. His eyebrows shoot up as he glances between us. "Well, shit. Is this for real?"

"It is," Roman replies.

"When did this happen?" Vander Zee asks.

Roman drapes his arm across the back of my chair. "Does the when matter?"

Vander Zee pins him with an irritated glare. "If the two of you are married, we need to know. We have a process in place that's been blatantly disregarded. Did you learn nothing from your daughter?" He scrubs his face with a palm. "We need to bring Shilpa in."

Fielding dials Shilpa's extension. They speak for a moment before he hangs up. The silence in the room is tense as we wait for her to join us. Fielding and Vander Zee both look like they're trying to keep it together.

Shilpa takes the seat next to Fielding. I don't know if it's just me, but she looks as green as I feel. She sets a thick folder on the table in front of her and motions between us. "Is this real? Are you legally married?"

"Yes," Roman and I say at the same time.

She pinches the bridge of her nose, then levels me with a look that speaks volumes. "You I'll get to in a moment." Her attention shifts to Roman. "You're retiring in a couple of months."

"I'm aware." He's so calm, unruffled.

I want to channel some of that, but there's a storm brewing and we're in the middle of it.

Vander Zee clicks his pen in agitation. "Of all the players on this team, you've been the one who can prioritize the game and the welfare of the team over your personal relationships. Why, in the final weeks of a twenty-year career, would you choose now to change that? And with the only female-identifying assistant coach in the entire league. Do you have any idea how difficult you've just made our jobs, and Shilpa's? Hemi is going to shit a brick."

Shilpa looks like she could spit nails. I don't love being on her bad side.

"Do you think I fell in love to spite all of you? That I did this on purpose?" Roman motions to our superiors and crosses his arms. "Do you have any idea how hard this has been for Lexi?

The challenge this poses? It's my fault she's in this tenuous position. I pursued Lexi, not the other way around."

"Are you saying this was coercion?" Fielding crosses his arms.

"Is that a serious fucking question?" Roman snaps.

"What the hell are we supposed to think? Yesterday Donnie came in with allegations, and today you show up married." Vander Zee points to our hands.

"Think whatever you want, but Alexandria is my *wife*. That should tell you everything you need to know about our feelings for each other. Lexi and her personal welfare take precedence above all others, except for my daughter. They sit at the same level."

I cover his hand. "I'd like to hear these allegations."

Fielding sighs, and Vander Zee shifts around. Shilpa rolls her eyes.

"Donnie expressed concern that Lexi only took the job for financial opportunities," Vander Zee says, keeping his face carefully neutral.

"Because it's a better-paying job than my last one?" I ask. "Isn't that how the job market and career growth work? Did he completely disregard the fact that I took a position in Niagara that paid significantly less than the one I had in Windsor so I didn't have to uproot my sisters after we lost our mom and their father?"

"I'm explaining the allegations, not telling you I believe them." Fielding's jaw tics. "Donnie suggested that your friendships with the office staff and some of the personal ice sessions that included Roman were meant to..." He clears his throat. "... seduce him."

I scoff. "Because seducing him in front of his teammates wouldn't have garnered negative attention from the other players? Talk about ludicrous. Not to mention that Roman is a forty-year-old man with the ability to control his hormones, especially when he's on the ice. We are both professionals who can and have separated our personal feelings from our professional duties." I turn to my husband. "Would you agree?"

His lip twitches. "I would."

I turn back to Fielding. "What else did Donnie say?"

"He believes you've been planning this for some time. That you targeted Roman specifically and curated your friendships to get you closer to him."

"Wow. That's just...wow." I can't believe what I'm hearing. "So from his perspective, I'm what? A sociopath? Do you believe your star goalie, who mentors his teammates and who you regularly talk through game strategy with, would fall for someone with no moral compass?"

"This sounds like someone reaching because they didn't get what they wanted." Roman rests a protective arm across the back of my chair. "Lexi is a remarkable leader and an inspiration, which is what I and everyone sees when we look at her. She came to this city as the sole guardian of her two grieving sisters, while also grieving the loss of her mother. She made hockey history when she became an assistant coach. Do you not agree that it would be impossible to bear that load of responsibility alone?"

Shilpa turns her head and swallows thickly.

"Are you okay?" Vander Zee asks.

"I'm fine." She takes a sip of water then turns her attention to Roman. "Do you understand the implications of your actions?"

"Absolutely," Roman replies. "Donnie has been gunning for Lexi's job from day one. He's made a point of giving her his unsolicited advice about who she should be associating with more than once. Yourself included, Shilpa. Lexi and I have spent a lot of time together this season on the ice—because of her role, not some outlandish plan to seduce me. She's an outstanding coach and member of our team. Our current position in the standings affirms that. Off the ice, she's a dedicated sister, parent, and friend. I fell in love with all of Lexi. I didn't intend for it to happen. I tried to keep my distance, but she and I have history and a connection that is clearly impossible to deny, since we're sitting here as husband and wife."

"If the roles were reversed, this would be grounds for automatic dismissal," Vander Zee says.

"You mean if I was the player and Roman was the coach?" I ask.

"I would have retired early to make this happen," Roman jumps in.

"That's why you came in and asked about the Hockey Academy and Ryker being ready," Vander Zee muses.

Roman nods. "I floated the idea, but ultimately we decided, for the good of the team and Lexi's well-being, that this was the better course of action."

"You said you have history. What does that mean?" Shilpa asks.

I swallow my anxiety over this revelation, but I have to own it. "We met each other years ago, before I took the job. I didn't believe it would interfere with my ability to handle my role with the team because it was so long ago, and brief."

"Knew each other in what capacity?" Shilpa demands.

"We spent time together." Roman remains evasive.

Shilpa looks to me. "Did you have an intimate relationship with Roman prior to accepting the position as assistant coach?"

"We did," I admit.

"Why is this relevant?" Roman asks, trying to keep me from being interrogated most likely.

I squeeze his hand. "They're trying to ascertain whether I joined the team with ulterior motives, as intimated by Donnie."

"Couldn't you have asked the same thing about Hemi or my daughter?" Roman snaps.

Shilpa leans back in her chair. "This is not the same, Roman. Aurora went through the proper channels *prior* to joining the Terror, and she proved that she was committed to the team, and the welfare of the team, when she brought her concerns and her relationship to management *before* she even applied for the position. Dallas and Hemi's situation is vastly different. Hemi is not in a position of power over Dallas, and while the way that rolled out was not ideal, it doesn't pose the same level of challenge as this."

Shilpa's gaze shifts to me. "It's my job, as the team lawyer, to assess the facts and determine what the next steps should be. But your relationship with Roman should have been disclosed prior to stepping into your role as assistant coach?"

"I understand, but I didn't believe it to be relevant as it was one weekend, three years ago," I explain. "I didn't think Roman even remembered me."

"Well, you were obviously wrong since you're sitting here as a married couple." Shilpa taps her pen on the conference table. "I'll need legal documentation, including your marriage certificate. Alexandria, you'll be on a leave of absence while we perform an internal review."

"You will not fire her over this," Roman says hotly.

"You are not in a position to make demands, Roman," Fielding barks. "And an internal review is standard protocol under the circumstances."

"This puts the team and the leadership under a microscope," Shilpa adds. "The problem is the lack of forthrightness."

"Dallas wasn't very forthcoming about being in love with Hemi from jump," Roman states.

"Again, Roman, this is not the same. Lexi is a coach. You are a player. The lines are very clear."

"I retire in two months and would have handed the net to Ryker to save Lexi from this bureaucratic bullshit if I'd known this was how it would go down, regardless of how ready Ryker is."

"But that's not what happened, so here we are." Shilpa replies evenly. "My job is to take care of the team, and that includes management and the players. It's my duty to ensure that the people who work for this team also have the team's best interests in mind."

Before Roman can go off again, I hold up a hand. "I understand the need for an internal review. I expected this, and if I were in your shoes, I would do the same thing. I am very aware of the challenges I'm up against because of this. If I could have shut off my feelings for Roman, I would have. The easier route would have been to let him retire early, but I didn't want that for Ryker, or for the team, and especially not for Roman. I hope the review gives you peace of mind, and you'll see that my allegiance is to the players and the welfare of the Terror."

"We'll keep your leave quiet while the review is being performed," Fielding says. "In the meantime, please hand over your keycard, and I'll escort you out of the building."

"Is that necessary?" Roman asks.

"It's okay." I squeeze his hand.

"You're treating my wife like a criminal."

"We're treating her the same way we would any coach who marries a player without going through the proper channels." Shilpa pushes her chair back and looks at Lexi. "You being married to Roman might save your job, but I sincerely hope you're ready for the battle you're about to face."

"I know. And he's worth it."

"That's the right answer." Shilpa leaves the office.

Vander Zee exhales harshly through his nose. "I need to brief Boxer and Thomas before practice."

I pass over my keycard and ID badge.

"I'll walk Lexi out," Roman declares.

Fielding gives him a look. "I have to function as an escort."

"That's fine," I say, trying to keep everyone level.

Roman is on the edge, and the last thing we need is him doing something that will get him benched. He takes my hand and leads me down the hall. And of course we run into Dallas and Ash on the way out. Their instant jaw drop is a sign of the challenges to come. At least their surprise means we did a mostly good job of hiding what was going on. *Fucking Donnie*...

Roman dips his chin. "I'll see you guys shortly."

I feel bad for them, because we've created one hell of a headache for both of their significant others.

The elevator doors open, and Kellan and Connor step out. Their smiles drop as they process the scene.

"Oh fuck. Holy shit." Connor's gaze volleys between us. "Wow." He runs a hand through his hair. "I guess the heat is off me."

"If you know what's good for you, you'll watch your mouth, Grace," Roman grinds out.

"I'm already down a coach. I can't afford to be down a goalie and an enforcer." Fielding ushers us past them and we step into the elevator.

The descent to the parking garage is tense and silent.

"Take my SUV," Roman says while Fielding stands guard by the door. "I'll get a ride to your place when practice is over, and we'll figure things out, okay?"

I nod. My head is spinning, my stomach in knots.

"We're in this together."

CHAPTER 39

LEXI

I drive home on autopilot. Aurora and Hollis took the girls to school, so the condo is already empty when I let myself in.

Everything is the same but different. I drop onto the couch. I need to call my dad. He'll see that I'm not behind the bench tonight and have questions. I hate how much I don't want to disappoint him. I pull up his contact and dial before I lose my nerve.

"Hey, Lexi, this is a surprise. Shouldn't you be on the ice now?" Dad says in greeting. The clicking of fingers on a keyboard comes through the phone.

"Uh, yeah, but uh…things are a bit complicated." Understatement of the year.

The clicking stops. "Is everything okay?"

"Um… Well, I have some news, and I'm not sure how you'll feel about it." My entire life I've sought his approval. If I could make him proud enough, he'd magically turn into the dad who would show up for me in ways that aren't financial. But that's an impossible ask, and I need to make peace with it, starting here.

"Are you and your sisters okay?"

"Fee and Callie are fine. I'm…I got married," I blurt.

Silence follows. Long and heavy. "Did I hear that right? You're…married?"

"Yes." I explain what happened—although I gloss over what happened three years ago and focus mostly on joining the team, spending all this time with Roman, and my colleague going to management, which led us to yesterday.

"You want to be married to Roman, though?" Dad clarifies.

"I'm in love with him. Obviously, it would've been better if we could've waited until he was no longer with the team, but this seemed like the best way to protect ourselves and my career." Although, at this point, I'll accept whatever the consequences are. "We'll have a ceremony in the summer with friends and family. I'm sorry I didn't tell you before it happened."

He's quiet for a moment. "It's okay, Lexi. I wish I could've been there with you. I wish you felt you could have come to me first." He clears his throat. "But if you're in love and this was the plan regardless, then I'm glad you took action to protect both of you. How does this impact your role as assistant coach."

"I'm on leave while they perform an internal review, and I'm not sure what will happen. We've gone against the team's no-fraternization policy. It's made that much more serious because I'm a coach and in a position of authority. And I'm a woman."

"Your gender should have absolutely no bearing on this. But since you've made history as an assistant coach in your specific industry, you'll be under a microscope." He makes an irritated sound. "Aren't there several players on that team who are in relationships with other members of the office staff?"

"The team lawyer is married to a player, but they were married before she came on board. And two of the PR reps are also in relationships with players," I explain.

"Didn't one of the players propose on national TV? Dallas Bright? I doubt the paperwork had already been filed when that happened," Dad muses.

"I'm not sure how that all rolled out." But Shilpa and Hemi are best friends.

"Still, there are examples of players dating staff over the past three years that have been overlooked. Roman is at the end of his career. By June, he'll no longer be a member of the team and all of this will be moot."

"But it's not moot now." Being incomeless for the remainder of the season is another wrench. I don't want Roman to be my keeper, as well as my husband.

"Do you have your contract available? And the no-fraternization policy? I'd like to have a look at them."

"Sure. One of Roman's friends looked them over, but I'll email that to you now."

"I would have done that for you. Give me an hour. I'll give it a quick once-over and check for any loopholes."

"Are you sure you have time?" I wish it didn't take my life falling apart for him to step up, but I need his help.

"You're my daughter, Lexi. Of course I have time for you. I'll call back as soon as I've been through these documents."

"Thanks, Dad."

Once we hang up, I call Dred, who messaged this morning to check in.

"I'm coming over," she says after I explain what happened. "I'll be there in twenty."

"I'm sure you have things to do besides watch me have an emotional breakdown." I dab at my eyes.

"Roman is at practice for the next few hours. The last thing you need is to be alone with your worries. I'm on my way." I hear the elevator ding.

"Thank you for being my friend." I hate being emotional, but I'm spinning.

"You don't have to hold it together, and you don't have to do it all on your own. I'll be there soon."

As I end the call, an alert from my bank pops up. I log into my account to find my dad has sent me ten thousand dollars, and promptly burst into tears. This is how he shows he cares.

I allow myself five minutes to break down before I splash

cold water on my face. This isn't how I envisioned the day after my wedding. I have no idea how long I'll be on leave. The coming weeks won't be easy. Not for me, not for Roman, and definitely not for the girls.

But I can't undo any of this. And frankly, I don't want to. I wouldn't trade his love for the world. Roman has been instrumental in making this season bearable in so many ways.

Dred shows up with ice cream and hugs. I'm grateful for her presence, even if it's just to keep me company. We've just settled in the living room when my dad calls back.

I put him on speaker and let him know Dred is with me and that she knows everything. "You didn't need to give me money," I tell him.

"I'm your father. I'm allowed to give you money if I feel like it. Consider it a wedding gift, if you need to, but you're under enough stress as it is. You don't need to be worried about whether you can pay the bills."

"I just married a millionaire hockey player." And Donnie believes it was my nefarious plan from the start. *How many other people will believe the same?*

"And you hate being dependent on other people emotionally and financially," he counters. "So as your dad, I'm providing you with your own cushion. If you don't need it, that's fine. You can put it in savings for your sisters. Are you done arguing over money?"

Dred squeezes my hand. She understands the complexities of my relationship with my dad.

"I guess I don't have much of an option, do I?" And I'm probably only doing it because I'm terrified of what he's about to tell me.

"Nope. You don't. And I mean that with love. Anyway, I have some fantastic news for you," he says.

"I could use some of that."

"There is nothing in your contract that says you can't be married to a player."

"But I can't date a player," I confirm.

"That's correct. You can't date a player—not without going through the proper channels and filing the appropriate paperwork. But if you're married to a player, none of that paperwork is required. All you need is a marriage certificate and a written agreement between you and the administrative team that when a conflict of interest arises, another member of your team will step in and mediate."

That's a comfort, but I hope none of Donnie's allegations become the new reason I end up unemployed.

CHAPTER 40

ROMAN

"It sure is tense in here," Grace observes as we suit up for practice.

A shitstorm is brewing—well, actually, it's brewed. I just hope my teammates can handle it.

"Where's Coach Forrester?" Madden asks as he finishes lacing up his skates.

"She won't be joining us today," Vander Zee snaps.

Madden frowns. "Is she okay?"

"Why don't you ask our goalie? He might know."

I give Vander Zee a look. "Really, man?"

"Fuck." Hendrix shakes his head.

"This is about to get nasty." Palaniappa focuses on his gear.

"What's in the air today?" a rookie asks.

"I wish I had some popcorn," Bright whispers, but he's not nearly as quiet as he thinks.

Vander Zee's head whips around. "You think this is funny?"

"Nope. Just hungry." Bright goes back to lacing up his skates.

Ryker looks anxious, and Stiles seems like he'd rather be anywhere else.

"Someone want to explain what the fuck is going on?" Madden asks.

I cross my arms. "This is how you thought the team should find out? While you're still pissed off and being reactive? You've been my coach for the past nine years. Where's the respect?"

"I could ask you the same question," Vander Zee fires back.

"Is there a full moon or something?" Stiles mutters.

I hold up my hand with the ring on it and glare at Vander Zee. "Coach Forrester is my wife. She's not here because *someone* has an axe to grind. Happy now?"

Vander Zee's nostrils flare.

Murmurs of "holy shit" and "no way" and "what the fuck?" ricochet through my teammates.

"All right, guys. Let's get on the ice and give these two a minute, yeah?" Hendrix makes a circle motion with his finger. Coaches Thomas and Boxer step in and usher the team out of the locker room.

Hendrix hangs back, arms crossed.

"Of course you knew about this," Vander Zee says to him.

Hendrix sighs and pins Vander Zee with an unimpressed stare. "I get that you're not happy about this, Coach, and I respect that you've been blindsided, but I'm a little concerned you're going to say the very wrongest of things, and then our goalie is going to be out for a five-game suspension for punching you in the mouth."

"I can handle myself," I say through gritted teeth.

"Under normal circumstances, I would agree. However, these are not normal circumstances," Hendrix argues.

"We'll be fine," I assure him.

"You can go," Vander Zee agrees.

"Okay." Hendrix raises his hands. "Please don't break your hands on each other's faces."

He leaves the locker room.

Vander Zee grips the back of his neck. "Why, Roman? You've kept your dick in your pants this entire time. Why fuck the team now?"

"First of all, Lexi is *my wife*. Not some bunny I decided to have a good time with," I grind out.

"She said you met three years ago, and she didn't think you would remember her. So what was that about?" Vander Zee asks.

"It's none of your fucking business, Coach."

"It is when my assistant coach is suddenly married to my goalie! Do you have any idea what the heat is going to look like coming down from the top? This isn't just about the two of you breaking every fucking rule we have."

"The team lawyer is married to a player, and two of the PR staff are involved with players," I point out. Again.

"This isn't the same. We've been over this already." Vander Zee slices his hand through the air. "Every time something like this happens, who do you think gets to deal with the team owner? It's not you who will end up on the chopping block. It's me and Fielding. I bring Lexi to the team, and you can't find the self-control *not* to go after her until the season is over? What do you think this will look like, Roman? Like bringing Lexi on wasn't enough of a risk without this?"

"Lexi was an excellent choice for assistant coach, regardless of her gender." I hold up a hand. "And my relationship with Lexi has nothing to do with her effectiveness in her role."

"To you, maybe. What do you think it looks like to those guys out there? To the fans? To the people who have been waiting for something like this to happen? You think she won't be called a bunny? Or that they won't question whether this was her motivation from the start, like Donnie did?"

"Watch your mouth, Vander Zee. That's my wife you're talking about. Our being married doesn't change all the positive things she's done for this team this year."

He scoffs. "Get your head out of your ass, Roman. Alexandria just married a twenty-year veteran player during her first season as assistant coach. It doesn't matter what's true and what's not. She could be the best assistant coach out there, but all of that is eclipsed by this." He motions to me. "You might have saved her job by marrying her, but how will you protect her from the media? Are you ready for the backlash, Roman? Because I'm not."

I suppose he's right. Gaining the support of the team will be hard enough. But the rest of the hockey-watching world is a whole different beast.

CHAPTER 41

LEXI

BRIGHT

We've got your back.

MADDEN

Seriously. If it weren't for you, Grace and I probably would have unalived each other by now.

PALANIAPPA

We're on your side. Shilps too, even though she can't tell you right now.

HENDRIX

The team is rallying for you.

RYKER

Miss you at practice, Coach.

STILES

Can't wait for this shit to be resolved so we can have you back on the ice.

GRACE

Practice is a bag of balls without you. Thanks for having faith in me as a player. You're more important to this team than you know.

Messages from the players have kept me afloat the past few days. Not being able to attend practices, see my players, do my job, is a horrible kind of torture. I worked so hard to get here, and now I'm in limbo. But Roman has been a rock through it all. And the outpouring of support from the team has been humbling. So has the support from the Badass Babe Brigade. Dred has been a constant, and the rest of the girls have been so good about daily check-ins. Well, except for Shilpa, but that I understand.

Today Roman is meeting with the Hockey Academy staff, and because I'm not at work, it means I'm very available for Callie and her hockey practices. I'm grateful no one seems to have clued in as to *why* I've been here the past few days. Still, it's only a matter of time before the rest of the world finds out. I'm preparing for the worst, but I honestly have no idea what I'll be up against.

I refocus on the rink. Callie is having an off practice. She's let in three goals, which isn't like her. She usually has more energy. Maybe she hasn't been sleeping well either. I'm sure my stress is rubbing off on her.

After practice, she comes out of the locker room, dragging her bag behind her.

"You okay, kiddo?" I ruffle her hair.

"My tummy feels yucky," she mumbles.

"Let me carry your bag. Maybe you're hungry? Did you eat all your lunch?"

She shakes her head. "I didn't feel like pizza today."

Pizza is her favorite. She loves leftovers for lunch the next day. "Should we grab something from the snack bar on the way out? It might help."

She shrugs. "Okay. Is Roman coming over?"

"He should be at our place around seven."

"Do you think he'll read me stories tonight? He always does different voices for the characters."

"I'm sure he will." We stop at the concession stand. "Do you feel like a hot dog?"

She wrinkles her nose. "Maybe just some pretzels."

"Okay. And how about a ginger ale?"

I pay the teenager working the cash register and tuck the snacks into my purse until we're in the car. Callie is quiet on the ride home, but she polishes off the pretzels and half the can of soda. As soon as we get on the elevator, she buries her face against my stomach. "I really don't feel good, Lexi."

I smooth her hair back. "Maybe you're coming down with something."

She's been tired the past couple of days, falling asleep in the middle of a story. I chalked it up to all the stuff going on in our lives. But maybe it's more than that. I bend and press my lips to her forehead. "You're warm. Let's get you into the condo, and we'll take your temperature."

I barely have her in the door before she throws up all over the wall. Exorcist style. And promptly bursts into tears. I get it. I want to do the same.

"Lexi, I feel really awful," Callie moans.

"I know, honey." I hustle her down the hall to the bathroom, and she unleashes the demons in her stomach while I hold her ponytail and rub her back.

"Lexi! What the heck happened in the hallway!" Fee shouts.

"Callie's not well!" I call back as another round of heaving begins.

But there's nothing left in Callie's stomach, so she just keeps retching and crying.

"Oh wow. Someone has the flu." Roman's voice brings equal parts relief and anxiety.

I don't know if he has the best or worst timing. I'm over here holding myself together with duct tape and a prayer.

"Lexi, angel?" He appears in the doorway. He's wearing a suit, looking far too put together for this nightmare.

"Can you grab us a glass of water, please? She's dry heaving."

"Absolutely. I'll be right back." He returns seconds later with a glass of water. "Give your mouth a rinse, kiddo," he instructs Callie.

She spits the water out, then does it again and follows with a small sip.

"Don't guzzle it, even if you want to, okay? A little at a time." He looks to me. "Do you want me to take over here or would you like me to tackle the hall?"

I shrug and shake my head. Neither seems appealing.

"I'll deal with the hall and come back to check on you." At least one of us can make decisions.

He kisses my temple and leaves me with Callie, returning a handful of minutes later, which seems impossible considering the mess. Thankfully, Callie has stopped heaving.

"How are my girls?" he asks.

"I think I have the flu." Callie lets him pick her up and rests her head on his shoulder.

"I think maybe you're right." Roman carries her out of the bathroom. "Should we get you into some jammies and have a little snuggle on the couch?"

"What if I'm sick again?" she asks.

"We'll have everything we need, just in case."

I trail behind them, feeling wildly incompetent.

He sets Callie on her bed. "I'll get everything set up in the living room." He kisses my cheek and leaves me to help her change.

"I'm sorry I threw up in the hall," she says as I tuck her feet into slippers.

"It's okay. It's not your fault." It feels like mine thanks to the stress we're all under.

Roman knocks on the door. "How's it going in there?"

"You can come in!" I should be able to handle a sick little girl on my own, but I'm barely coping.

"Want a ride to the living room?" he asks.

Callie grabs her stuffed axolotl as he swoops in again to pick her up. Out in the living room, a towel covers one arm of the couch, a blanket laid out beside it. Close by is a bowl and a glass of water, along with some children's flu medication. Callie's favorite movie is cued up. Roman settles her on the couch and starts the movie. Half an hour in, I get a delivery alert.

"I ordered some stuff. I'll go down and get it," Roman offers.

Two pillows are stacked on his lap, and Callie is snuggled up with him, her feet tucked under my leg. He gave her some flu medicine, and she's already half asleep.

"That's okay. I'll grab it." I leave the two of them on the couch and take the elevator to the lobby.

Of course Roman thought of everything. The bag contains soda crackers, plain noodles, ginger ale, a gel ice pack, and electrolyte-replacement freezies. I love how thoughtful and action-oriented he is. But I worry that I'm starting to see a pattern. He keeps saving us, especially me, and I don't want that to unbalance our relationship. But I can't decide if it's rooted in my fear of ending up like my mother, or that I'm just particularly sensitive because of my current situation.

Callie has passed out by the time I return, so I gather her up and put her to bed. Fee is holed up in her room, uninterested in getting the flu since she has a math test tomorrow.

I motion for Roman to follow me down the hall to my bedroom.

He pulls the door closed and pushes my hair over my shoulders. "How are you?"

"Okay." I fiddle with the collar of his shirt.

"You don't seem okay. Callie being sick is stressing you out on top of everything else?" he asks.

"Yeah." I blow out a breath.

He tips my chin up. "What aren't you saying, angel?"

"I can handle Callie when she's sick. I've done it before. I mean, you've probably done a lot more of it than I have, and I absolutely appreciate you stepping in and helping…" I pause, hating my own vulnerabilities. But he's my partner and saying nothing won't make anything better.

"But..." He strokes my cheek, encouraging me, telling me with actions that honesty isn't just okay, it's essential.

"I'm not used to being saved all the time, Roman, and you are very good at it. Part of that is my own issue. My mom had a lot of hard feelings when she and my dad split up, and I realize that to stay on her side, I avoided asking him for help. I need to work on that, but when you come in and try to fix everything, I feel like I don't have a handle on my own shit."

He fingers a tendril of my hair. "You absolutely have a handle on your shit, Lexi."

"Do I, though? We got married to save my job. And I absolutely want to be married to you, but now I'm on leave and I feel...I don't know. Like I've lost my agency, maybe? You're running interference with the Terror while I'm here, just sort of paralyzed. Now Callie is sick, and again, you show up and save the day. I love that you're a problem solver, Roman, but I want to feel like your partner and not someone you need to take care of."

He frowns, absorbing. "Do you feel steamrolled?"

"Not steamrolled. You're just so capable, and I love that about you. It's easy for you to step in and fix things. You're ruthlessly competent. But sometimes, like tonight, I question my ability to handle things. I worry I won't measure up. I know part of this is me and my own hang-ups, but with the girls I need to be your equal. Especially right now."

The hurt on his face makes my chest ache.

"That's not what—" He runs a hand through his hair. "Shit. I totally take over. How long have you felt like this?"

"I just noticed the pattern. Like a minute ago." I don't want to hurt him, but keeping my mouth shut the way I used to when it came to my parents isn't helpful for either of us.

"So you haven't been holding this in? Feeling like you can't tell me how my actions affect you?" he presses.

"No. I literally just made the connection."

"Okay." He nods once. "That's good. I need you to tell me when I'm being overbearing. Or make you question your capabilities." He tucks my hair gently behind my ear. "This was a big thing with me and Peggy last year, and a major reason she and Hollis felt like they had to keep their relationship a secret." His anguish is real, and so is his vulnerability. "I overcompensated and over-parented her to the point where she believed I'd be so upset with her that I'd stop loving her. I could have saved us all so much heartache if I'd realized sooner what I was doing."

He's showing me the soft part of himself. Giving me the pieces that make up the whole, letting me see his fears, just like he did at the cabin.

"Oh, Roman." I cup his face in my palms. "You love so completely. I promise I'll tell you, as gently as possible, to step back when I feel like you're veering into fix-the-problem mode, so we can have balance."

"Okay, good." He wraps his arm around my waist and pulls me closer. "I'm sorry I took over."

"I appreciate you cleaning up all the gross stuff and ordering supplies for Callie, though." I link my hands behind his neck. "It was thoughtful."

"I'm used to taking care of everything on my own. I mean, I had the team's support when Peggy was growing up, but it was mostly a me show." His fingers drift up and down my spine. "I don't want you to ever feel alone in this."

"I get that, and I welcome you in my life. I'm used to taking care of myself, too. But you make me feel secure enough in myself and our relationship that I can be honest about things like this. We just have some adjusting to do to make it all work."

"We'll figure it out together." He kisses me softly.

"Just to be clear, inside the bedroom I'm all about you taking complete control." I finger the hair at the nape of his neck. "Nothing makes me happier than being yours to do with as you please."

His smile grows wicked, and he captures my braid in his fist, but he doesn't have the chance to utter something wicked, because my phone rings. "You could ignore that and let me make up for being an overbearing husband," he murmurs darkly.

"I would love that, but it's my dad."

He releases my braid and steps back. "We'll pause this until later."

"I'm sorry."

"No apologies." He strokes my cheek. "Talk to your dad."

I answer the call. "Hey, how's it going?"

"Good. I wanted to check in. Any movement on you going back to work? Do you need me to top up your bank account? Do the girls need anything?" Dad rapid-fires questions, but I can hear him typing in the background. Attention divided.

Roman kisses my forehead and leaves my bedroom, closing the door behind him.

"No news on when I'm going back to work. They're in the process of interviewing the team, and that will take some time." Although based on Roman's reports and my text messages, we have the overwhelming support of the players. "And Callie's sick," I tack on.

"I'm sorry to hear that," Dad says. "I've called the team lawyer. She's a sharp one. She also knows they can't fire you. This is all standard protocol. It's only a matter of time before you're back on the ice. Did you take Callie to the doctor?"

"It's the flu, so it just has to run it's course. But maybe when she's feeling better you can come out for a visit." Callie would be excited, and Lord knows she could use something to look forward to with all the shit going on.

"I can check my calendar and get back to you on that."

"Why don't you check it now?" I press.

"It depends on my cases, honey. It's a busy time of year."

"It's always a busy time of year." I'm too tired of fighting for his attention to bite my tongue anymore. "You know what?

Don't bother. You'll just work the entire time and leave early, like always."

"That's not fair. You know how important my job is."

"More important than me, every single time," I fire back. Apparently, I'm in full confrontation mode. And as much as I might love my job with the Terror, I won't put it in front of the people I love. I won't do that to the people I care about the most, because I've had it done to me my entire life.

"That's not true."

"Isn't it? I've been put on leave, and I got *married*, to one of the players no less, and not once have you suggested coming to see me, or even formally meeting Roman. I'm parenting my sisters, my life is in upheaval, and you're calling me while you're writing an email, or a report, or who the fuck knows what. Like a phone call to your daughter is something to tick off on a list."

"Lexi, it isn't—"

"It's not what, Dad? It's not true either? Tell me there isn't a paper list sitting beside you with my name and *phone call* at the bottom of it."

He sighs.

"God, it sucks that I'm right." Here I am getting upset with Roman for overdoing it in the taking-care-of-me department, and now I'm upset with my dad for never making me a priority. I'm a hot mess of conflicting emotions. But it all makes sense. It's rooted in my fear of losing my independence, my desire to have a partner who sees me as their equal, who I would give it all up for, because Roman would do the same for me. I want the kind of love that's worth fighting for. I want to be worth fighting for. And with Roman, I am.

"I'm not a good father," Dad says.

"That's—"

"Let me finish. I know I haven't done a great job being your dad, Lexi. And I know your relationship with your mom was strained because of me. I tried to give you space because I didn't want to come between you. Or that's what I rationalized. But it doesn't excuse my lack of presence in your life. And I'm sorry for that. Emotionally, I don't think I'll ever be able to give you what you need, what you deserve. And you deserve a dad who can drop everything and be there for you. But if I did come to see you, all I'd be doing is setting us both up for disappointment. I'm good at being a lawyer. I'm good at solving legal problems that involve logic. But I'm not good at emotional support. And I'm so sorry for that."

"I'm sorry, too." It's not what I want to hear, but at least it's the truth and not lip service.

"I wish I was better at being a parent. I know it's a shortcoming."

"I love you anyway, Dad." And I do, even though sometimes it hurts.

"I love you, too, honey. More than I'm capable of expressing most of the time. I'll come for a visit. Maybe I can time it so I can be there for your first game back with the team. If you want me there?"

The girl in me who forever wants her dad's approval rejoices. The rest of me realizes I should probably make a therapist appointment so I can find a healthy way to deal with these feelings. "That would be good."

"And I can get to know your husband a little better."

"We'd like that." The tears start to well, so I clear my throat. "I should check on Callie. Make sure she's doing okay."

"Okay. We'll talk soon."

"Sounds good."

I end the call and look at the ceiling, willing the tears to stay put. But they fall anyway. I open my bedroom door as Roman steps out of Callie's room. He's changed into a plain white shirt and plaid pajama pants. He puts his finger to his lips and slips back into my bedroom.

He takes one look at my face and gathers me in his arms. "You okay?"

"Nope. But I will be." I loop my arms around his neck.

"Do you want to talk about it?"

"Not right now."

"What can I do?" He strokes my cheek. "Tell me what you need."

"Just you."

CHAPTER 42

ROMAN

I hold the door open for the guys as they file into my penthouse.

"This one says Callie's bedroom," Flip's voice comes from behind a large cardboard box.

"Second door on the right," Peggy replies. "It's a pink room. You can't miss it." She was the one who suggested it for Callie.

Tristan and Nate are on his heels. "We're heading there, too."

Hollis and Ash are next. "We have stuff for Lexi's office."

"Those can go in my office."

"Got it." They keep moving.

"I'll show Dallas where Fee's room is." Peggy motions for him to follow her.

I put the door stopper down and check on Lexi in the kitchen. "How's it going?"

"I can't believe how much stuff we have." Her hair is pulled back in a ponytail, flyaways sticking to her temples. She props her fists on her hips, surveying the stack on the floor. "I don't know why I bothered to pack any of this. You already have a stocked kitchen, and your stuff is way nicer than mine."

A week or so after the wedding, once Callie had recovered, we broached the subject of the move with the girls. As predicted,

Callie was all for it, and Fee was less excited. We brought them to my place for dinner the next night so they could see the house and the spare rooms. Peggy is thrilled that Callie fell in love with the princess pink space that was once hers. Fee grudgingly admitted she liked the room we suggested could be hers.

With Lexi on leave until the internal review is complete, she's had more free time than she'd like, so it took less than a week to pack up the contents of their condo. Today is move-in day.

"We'll sort through it, and whatever we don't need we can donate." Or we can put it in storage depending on what Fee's post high school plan is. "We're almost done unloading the truck, and the girls are picking up the food. We don't have to unpack everything today."

"I know. As long as the girls' rooms are set up, I'll feel reasonably settled, and hopefully so will they."

"It's okay if it takes some time for them to acclimate."

"The housewarming committee has arrived!"

Rix, Essie, Hemi, Tally, and Dred appear, laden with not only takeout bags from Callie and Fee's favorite restaurant, but also wrapped gift boxes.

"What's all this?" Lexi's brows furrow.

"Housewarming gifts for the girls," Dred explains. "We know this has been a lot for all of you and we wanted to get them something special for their new home."

"You're doing so much already. You didn't need to buy presents." Lexi bites her lips together. It's what she does when she's fighting to keep her emotions in check.

"We brought food and went shopping. The guys are doing the hard work." Hemi gives me a side hug. "Besides, they'll use it as a workout replacement."

"And honestly, I'll find any reason I can to order a cake from Just Desserts," Rix adds.

"I've considered pretending to be engaged for an excuse to test their cakes," Essie admits.

"I'm zero percent surprised to hear this," Rix deadpans.

"I happen to love their cakes—and also unpacking," Dred says.

"Can you point me in Fee's direction?" Tally asks. "I want to see her room."

"Third door on the right, just after Barbie's dream bedroom." Peggy motions toward the hall.

Shilpa appears in the doorway and walks directly to Lexi and me, offering us both an uncertain smile, which is unusual for her. "I know I've been quiet in the Babe chat, but I have a line to toe."

Lexi's expression softens. "I understand that your allegiance is to the team."

"It is." Shilpa takes Lexi's hands. "But outside of the office, you have my and Ash's full support, okay?"

Lexi exhales what seems to be a steadying breath and smiles. "I appreciate that, and that you're in a difficult position."

"Even though this review is a pain in all our asses, mostly yours, I'm still glad you took the steps you did to safeguard yourselves. I also love the two of you together, and off the record, so does the rest of the team."

"Thank you. That means a lot."

Her expression shifts to chagrin. "I'm sorry for how salty I was with both of you when I initially found out."

"We understand it threw you for a loop," Lexi replies.

"It did," she agrees. "But I'd also just found out I was pregnant, and I was trying not to barf every five minutes."

"Oh my gosh! Congratulations! That's fantastic news. How far along are you?" Lexi hugs her. "I'm so sorry we caused you added stress!"

"I'm used to stress. You should have seen me last year with Dallas and Hemi." She chuckles and rolls her eyes. "We passed the eleven-week mark and heard the heartbeat yesterday, so we're in the clear to share the news with our friends," Shilpa explains.

"What news?" Hollis appears, carrying another box marked *kitchen*.

"Is it finally sharing time?" Hemi's eyes light up as she hugs Shilpa from the side.

"It is." Shilpa is all smiles.

"Let me get everyone together." Hemi calls the group into the room.

The rest of the guys put their boxes down, and the girls come out of their rooms to join us.

Ash is beaming as he puts his arm around Shilpa and announces, "We're having a baby!"

The room turns into a flurry of excitement and congratulations, and not for the first time, I consider what it would be like to start again, with a partner this time—how different it would be, how much I'd love to have the chance to do this with Lexi.

Post baby announcement, we set up all the food on the kitchen island, buffet style, and everyone grabs a plate. After they're loaded up, we sit in the formal dining room. The table is huge, but it's still a tight fit.

Callie is between Peggy and Dred, talking a mile a minute. Fee is sandwiched between Tally and Tristan.

"Fee seems okay," Lexi observes.

"She does," I agree. But she's been moody and quiet the past couple of days. She could be putting on a brave face because of our company.

"This team is so special." Lexi dabs at her mouth with her napkin.

"Yeah. It's a great group. Everyone looks out for each other." I kiss her temple.

"They really do. Not every team is like this."

"There's a reason I wanted to finish my career here."

When everyone's plates are empty, Peggy taps her glass with her fork. "Before we have cake, it's time for presents!" She pushes back her chair, and Hollis and Tristan do the same, following her out of the room.

Callie's mouth hangs open. "Presents? Whose birthday is it?"

"We're celebrating the new move," Dred explains.

"Oh wow. I think I like moving parties!"

That earns a collective chuckle from the table.

Peggy, Hollis, and Tristan return with stacks of boxes.

Most of the gifts are for the girls' rooms, to make them feel more like home. Fee unwraps the lava lamp she's been in love with forever, and Callie is thrilled about the giant axolotl to go with her small one.

"Connor wanted to be here today, but he had to take his grandma to an appointment," Tristan explains as he passes Callie a very large, very flat gift wrapped in unicorn-printed paper. "He said he'd come to your game tomorrow, though."

"He loves his grandma." Callie opens the card first, grinning and blushing as she reads it, then sets it aside. Dred holds the gift steady while she carefully peels the tape free and reveals the contents. Callie bursts into a fit of giggles.

"Seriously, man?" Flip mutters.

"That's awesome." Nate snorts a laugh and Flip side eyes him.

"Oh, that is magical," Rix snickers.

"So magical," Dred agrees.

"We all need your talent in our lives." Essie points at Peggy with her lip gloss wand.

"Thank you," Peggy says, smiling widely.

"You helped with this?" Flip looks put out.

"It's sweet," Tally says defensively. She turns her unimpressed gaze on Flip. "You don't have to like him to acknowledge that."

He holds up his hands. "You're right, Talls. I'm just jealous I didn't think of it myself."

"Oh, I can make this happen for you, too." Peggy grins.

Mounted on a board the size of a movie poster is a picture of Connor, dressed in full hockey gear, wielding his stick like a sword, riding a unicorn up a rainbow. It's been signed by Connor as Callie's number one fan.

"Can I ride a dragon instead?" Flip asks.

"You can ride anything you want," Tally pipes up. Her eyes go wide, and she sinks into her chair.

"She means I can photoshop you riding any animal, mythical or otherwise," Peggy clarifies. "I can even make you ride a dinosaur, if you want."

"I want in on this," Dallas says.

"Of course you do, honey." Hemi smirks.

"Should I jump in on this, Callie-wallie?" I ask.

She shrugs. "If you want. But I don't need a picture of you on my walls because now I get to live with you and see you all the time when you're not traveling, and you're going to be my dad, which is the best present of them all."

"He's married to our sister, Callie. He's not our dad. Our dad is gone!" Fee snaps.

The room is silent for a moment. Her face turns red, and she pushes her chair away from the table, rushing down the hall to her bedroom.

Callie bursts into tears.

Lexi stands, rounds the table, and hugs her sister. "She's not upset with you. She's just overwhelmed, Callie. It's a lot of change."

"I could see if Fee's okay?" Tally offers.

"She probably needs a minute to herself, but you could text her later," Lexi replies, still hugging a tearful Callie.

Tally nods, and everyone rises to help clear the table. Once everything is put away they excuse themselves shortly thereafter, despite there still being cake and more housewarming gifts to open.

"I'll be right next door if she needs someone to talk to later," Peggy offers as she and Hollis follow the rest of the crew to the door. "I know it's not the same, but I understand that the change is hard."

"I'll let you know how things go," I assure her.

By the time everyone leaves, Lexi has calmed Callie down, helped her bring all her new gifts to her room, and goes to check on Fee. I meet her in the hall, looking frantic. "I can't find Fee. She's not in her room, and she's not answering when I text."

"Let me check." I remember how hard it was for Peggy when she first moved in here.

I knock on Fee's open bedroom door and call her name, not expecting an answer. Empty boxes have been broken down and left in a pile in the corner. More boxes litter the floor, clothes are piled on the bed—half of them on hangers, the rest waiting for the same treatment. Her phone sits on her nightstand. At first glance, the room appears empty, but the closet door is ajar. I hold up a finger to Lexi and cross the room, poking my head inside.

She's exactly where I expected she would be, curled up in the corner of the closet beside the laundry hamper, head resting on her knees, shoulders shaking.

"Hey, you're having a tough time today, eh?" I say quietly.

She dashes away her tears. "I'm embarrassed."

"You don't need to be. Everyone understands that this is hard," I assure her.

"We love you, Fee. And we know this is a struggle," Lexi adds.

"Lexi! Can you help me make my bed?" Callie calls.

I squeeze her hand, gauging what she needs from me. "I can go if you want, or I can talk to Fee. It's up to you."

"You stay with Fee. I'll help Callie." Lexi kisses the edge of my jaw and leaves me.

"Can I come in?" I ask.

Fee lifts a shoulder and swipes at her tears again. I grab the tissues from her nightstand, set the box beside her, and sit down on the closet floor across from her. "When Peggy first moved in with me, she used to hide in her closet. Scared the crap out of me when she fell asleep in a pile of stuffed animals and I couldn't find her for twenty minutes."

"I'm sorry if I scared you and Lexi."

"I had a solid idea where you were. My phone gets an alert

when someone enters or leaves this place, so I knew you couldn't have gone far."

"Is Callie okay?" She sniffles and picks at a loose thread on the sleeve of her sweatshirt.

"She's all right. Lexi has it handled. I want you to know that I understand how hard this is. You've lost a lot in the past couple of years, and so much has changed in a very short time. You're going to have some big feelings about that. But it's important that you talk about those feelings. It doesn't have to be to me, or Lexi. You can talk to your friends, and Peggy can be a great sounding board. She's had a lot of experience dealing with me, and while her mom is still alive, she can relate to how hard this all is."

"Her mom lives in California, right?"

"For now she does. They move a lot. Which is why Peggy came to live with me when she was six. It was tough for her and her mom, but it was best for Peggy. She needed a home base, and Zara couldn't give that to her," I explain.

"Why not?"

"Because Zara needs frequent change. Some kids can roll with it. Peggy wasn't one of those kids. It took her over a year to really settle in with me. She was so used to moving every few months. She didn't trust the stability at first."

"Oh. I didn't realize that." She dabs at her eyes with a tissue. "It's not that I don't want to live here with you, or that I don't like you." She bites the inside of her cheek. "But I just got used to living with Lexi, and now Callie and I have to get used to living with you. And I feel bad because it's so nice here, and I know you're trying hard, and you're such a good dad, but I miss *my* dad." She sucks in a shuddering breath.

It's a pain I'm familiar with and I want to give her hope that it will get easier. That even though these deep wounds leave real scars, they hurt less with time. "I know you do, kiddo. I get it. I lost my dad more than a decade ago, and it still hurts. I still miss him. But you're not betraying his memory or your love for him and your mom by allowing yourself to find the joy in this new life, either."

She lifts her head, eyes wide. "That's it. That's what's so hard. Because this is such a nice place, and I really like you, Roman, and I love my sister, but I feel like I'm not supposed to like it as much as I do. Everyone on the Terror is so kind, and it feels like this big family I've never really had before."

None of them have, I realize. Especially not Lexi. I want this for them, for us. To have this tight knit group who will love and support them. "It's tough, isn't it? Wanting to embrace it, but feeling like you shouldn't?"

She nods.

"I have a tendency to overdo it. I just want to be enough, you know? And I want to be loved like everyone else. When Peggy was young, I wanted to make up for the years that were hard for her, and for the fact that she couldn't be with her mom."

"Peggy adores you. Everyone does," Fee says.

"I don't want to lose that, though. So I overcompensate. I understand that it can be hard to trust that this won't disappear on you, but as unconventional as we are, we're a family, Fee. We don't bail on each other. Even when it's hard, we'll stand by each other, okay?"

"Okay." Her bottom lip trembles.

"You want a hug?" I offer.

"Yeah."

I extend a hand and pull her to her feet, then wrap her in my arms. "We'll get through this. That's what families do."

I help her unpack for a while, and it's late by the time I finally leave Fee's room. I find Lexi and Callie cuddled up in her princess bed, both out cold. I carefully gather Lexi up and carry her down the hall to our room.

"I fell asleep in Callie's bed, didn't I?" She nuzzles into my neck, all warm and groggy.

"You did." I pull the comforter back and set her down. Lexi lets me pull the covers over her.

"How's Fee?" she mumbles.

"She's okay. We talked it out. She was just overwhelmed."

"Thank you for being there for her, for all of us."

"I'd do anything for you and the girls." I press my lips to her forehead. "I just need to brush my teeth. I'll be right back."

Two minutes later, I slide under the sheets next to her. She snuggles into me. "I love you," she mumbles.

"I love you, too." I press my lips to her temple and marvel at how much my life has changed and how I wouldn't trade it for the world.

CHAPTER 43

ROMAN

"Can you pass me the syrup, please?" Fee asks.

"Absolutely. Whipped cream, too, right?" I pass her both.

"Oh, and the blueberries." Fee reaches across the table for them. She's in much better form this morning.

"Can I have more bacon?" Callie asks.

"Can I have more bacon, *please*?" Lexi adds another slice to her plate.

I set my knife and fork down. "Okay, now that we're all here, Lexi and I wanted to let you know that we're starting family therapy next week."

Lexi and I discussed it this morning, and she agreed that it's something the girls need. We all do. These girls are grieving the loss of their parents, and they need a sounding board who can help them deal with their feelings and all the changes they're managing. And I need to learn not to overcompensate.

"Therapy?" Fee looks nervous.

"We're an unconventional family, and we all need a safe place to talk about our feelings. We'll see one therapist together, all four of us, and then if you girls want to talk to someone on your own, we can do that too," Lexi explains.

"I'm sure Peggy's therapist would be happy to take you girls on," I add.

"Aurora's in therapy?" Fee seems shocked.

"She has been since she was six. She started with art therapy and progressed. She goes every other month now, but for a while she went weekly."

"Was there something wrong with her?" Callie asks.

"Nope. She just needed someone to talk to when she was having a hard time with her feelings and didn't know what to do with them. I see one, too. I started going once a month this year because I'm retiring, and I have some feelings about that." I want therapy to be normalized for them, like it is for Peggy.

"Okay. If Peggy can handle therapy so can I," Fee says decisively.

"Can I try art therapy?" Callie asks.

"Sure. We can give that a shot." Lexi squeezes my hand.

"Great. I'm glad we're all on board." I look to Lexi, and she smiles, giving me the go ahead. "Now that you girls are moved in, Lexi and I thought it would be a good idea if we came up with a list of house rules."

"House rules?" Callie parrots.

"Yup. I think it's important, now that we're the Hammerstein-Forrester clan, that we have our own set of rules."

"We get to help make them?" Fee asks skeptically.

"We're a democracy, so we should all get a say," Lexi confirms.

"Like if the dishwasher isn't running, put your dishes in it instead of leaving them in the sink." Fee gives her sister a look.

"Sometimes I'm in a hurry," Callie says defensively, while grinning.

"The kitchen can have its own set of rules," Lexi clarifies, "which are different from our family rules. So what are the things we want to make sure we always do or don't do when it comes to respecting each other?"

"Never go to bed angry?" Fee asks.

"I love that one. Peggy and I had the same rule when she was growing up." I write it at the top of the list.

"Okay, Callie, your turn," Lexi says.

"Be kind and use kind words."

"That's a great one," Lexi says.

"I didn't make it up. It's a rule in my class." Callie drags her bacon through her maple syrup. I'm pretty sure she learned that from Peggy.

"Definitely a great class rule and house rule." I add it to the list.

"Is it Lexi's turn?" Callie asks.

"It sure is." This feels good, like we're part of a new team, working together to figure things out.

"Be accountable. That means when we do something wrong, we own our mistake and try not to do it again," Lexi explains.

"It's okay to make mistakes, though. We're all human," I add. "But when we say we're sorry, we should always mean it."

"Those are rules three and four, right?" Fee pops a blueberry into her mouth.

"Yup. Your turn again, Fee." I write down rules three and four.

"Um…" She taps her lip. "How about always be honest with each other?"

"Love that one." I jot it down.

Callie bounces in her chair. "Oh! Never say it's too hard or I quit!"

"You sound like a true goalie." I wink.

"It's Lexi's turn again," Fee says.

"We always keep our word, to ourselves and to others," Lexi adds.

I dip my chin in agreement. "It's okay to fail, as long as we learn and try again. Okay, Fee and Callie, last two rules, what should they be?"

"Always have fun!" Callie shouts.

"Yes to that. I love it. Fee, what's rule ten?"

"Listen to each other?" she asks.

"That's perfect. I think we have a great list." I read them over, before I ask, "Are we missing anything?"

"I think it's good," Callie says.

"I like it," Fee agrees.

"Me three." Lexi smiles.

"It's unanimous, then. I'll get Peggy to help me turn it into a poster."

"I could do that! I'm good at graphics," Fee offers.

I grin, it's amazing to be surrounded by so much love. "Even better."

We finish breakfast, and the girls help clear the table before they go to their rooms. Lexi wraps her arms around my waist. "I adore you."

I stroke her cheek. "And I adore you."

"Thank you for making them feel heard."

"We're a family. Families make decisions together." I kiss her softly, marveling at how lucky I am to have found Lexi, and that against all odds we came back to each other when we needed each other the most.

"How do you always know what to do and say?" she whispers.

"I don't. I just know that the first time around, I didn't have a partner to do any of this with. And this time I do. So I want us to make decisions as a unit, and the best way to do that is to ensure everyone has a voice."

She fingers the hair at the nape of my neck. "I'm a little obsessed with how incredible you are."

I pull her tighter against me. "I'm a little obsessed with everything about you."

"Kiss me, please." She tips her chin up, and I drop my head, covering her mouth with mine.

"Oh. Ew. No. New rule! No making out anywhere that isn't behind a closed door!" Fee groans. "I'll be in my room, rocking in the corner, if you're looking for me!"

"Add it to the list," I call over my shoulder.

CHAPTER 44

LEXI

"Thank you so much for coming tonight. It really means a lot, Dad." I usher him into my hotel room here in New York. I leave for the arena soon, but we're managing a short visit before he fits in another quick meeting prior to the game. How much of it he'll actually see is a question mark, but he's here supporting me, and that's the most important part. I'm learning how to accept his limitations and appreciate these moments for what they are.

Having Roman definitely makes it easier.

"I'm glad I could make it work." He hugs me tightly, then holds me at arm's length. "How are you holding up?"

I'm sure I look tired. Sleep hasn't been the greatest the past few days. "Okay. Happy to be back at work, but nervous about the media after the game."

There will be questions. I've been on leave for almost three weeks while they performed the internal review. Evidently Donnie threw everything he could at trying to discredit me. He said I was biased because I was in a relationship with the goalie, and favoring Roman. Thankfully, the defensive line shot holes in that theory by saying Roman had been helpful in supporting me—and them, as he has for years—rather than the other way around. As a veteran player, his knowledge base is far more expansive, and his willingness to share it has helped the team.

The support from the players has been a balm. Every time a player is questioned, he has the nicest things to say about me and my role as an assistant coach. The same goes for Vander Zee. It's been rough watching games from the couch, but I've finally been cleared to travel with the team. Head office is still in the process of filing the paperwork, but they've deemed Donnie's allegations unfounded. With playoffs coming up, and the importance of having the full coaching staff available, I've been allowed to return to work.

"Your team supports you," Dad reminds me.

"I know. But playing against New York is always tense," I admit. Bowman continues to be a dominating force on the ice this season.

"How's Roman?" Dad asks.

"Good. Protective. Worried about me more than anything." I smile at the memory of breakfast in bed this morning and how he takes care of me. "He has my back every step of the way, though, and it's just…so nice to have him to lean on."

"I'm glad you found each other." He means it, but there's sadness in his eyes. "How are the girls? Are they settling in okay?"

"They've been great. Callie is in love with her bedroom, and Fee and Aurora, Roman's daughter, are really connecting, which is good for all of us." Being away from them is tough, but Dred sleeps over when we have away games and Aurora is traveling with the team. She's a great friend, and I'm so thankful for her.

"I'm so glad to hear that. And the girls like Roman, too?"

"They adore him as much as I do. He's fantastic with them. He's an incredibly supportive partner."

Dad smiles. "I know this hasn't been easy, but I'm proud of you. And I will always be proud of you, no matter what. I haven't always showed up the way you need me to, but I'll try to be the best dad and grandpa I can to you and those girls," he says.

"It means a lot that you're here now."

His phone buzzes with a call.

I give him the permission he needs. "You should check that. I need to head to the arena anyway." I can love him, and love that he's trying, but he's still a workaholic lawyer. That won't change.

He pulls his phone from his pocket and glances at the screen, his expression apologetic. "I should take this."

"Go ahead."

"Kristoff here. Can you hold for a second, please?" He mutes the call. "I'll be cheering you on rinkside, okay?"

"Sounds great."

He kisses me on the cheek. "I love you, Lexi."

"I love you too, Dad."

He unmutes the call as he leaves my room. He's showing up the way he knows how. And that's the important part.

"Do you want to talk anything through before you're behind the bench?" Hemi asks as we head to the arena. "Any direction you need regarding the interview after the game."

"I should stay focused on the game play and my role as an assistant coach." I recite what Vander Zee has said.

"For the most part, yes, but they'll ask about your relationship with Roman, and being honest is better than being evasive. I know where Vander Zee wants the focus, mostly because he's been the front line on this. But you're back in the game, so the questions will come. The team has been backing you the whole time. Everyone has said the same thing, Lexi—that they miss you on the ice, and you're an asset to the team."

"I'm just nervous. It's one thing to be on the sidelines. It's another to be in the line of fire."

"I know. But we're all behind you. The team is motivated to win this game for *you*."

I stop and take a breath. I'm so emotional. "I need to have my shit together so Roman isn't worried."

"Roman is fine. He's got this, and we've got you." She settles her palms on my shoulders. "All we're waiting on is paperwork to be filed. You wouldn't be back at the game if they were seriously concerned about your competency or your agenda."

"You're right. I know you're right. Thank you."

She pulls me in for a hug. "I was in your shoes last year. It sucked, but I got a great guy out of the deal and so have you."

"Roman is amazing." And I can handle the backlash that comes with marrying him because he's my person.

"Just remember that when the assholes are assholes."

"Everything okay here?" Vander Zee asks.

"Everything is awesome. We're ready to kick some ass," Hemi says.

Thank God for these women and this team. I wouldn't have made it through this without them.

The game is tight. Roman's focus is singular. After a goal scored by Bowman in the first few minutes of the first period, Roman has deflected every shot, and the enforcers are defending the net. But Bowman is on fire. His stick-handling skills keep improving. It's mind-blowing to watch him snag the puck out of midair.

But in the end, it's this maneuver that's essentially New York's downfall. Bowman gets a penalty in the third period for high sticking, and Madden scores the tie-breaking goal during the power play, giving us the lead with only four minutes left in the game. We manage to hold on. It's a rough loss for New York, but a solid win for us.

My anxiety is at an all-time high as we enter the press box a few minutes later. And I'm unprepared for the number of microphones suddenly in my face. "Coach Forrester, this is your first game back in three weeks. Rumor has it that you're married to Roman Hammerstein? Are these two things connected?"

"I've already answered that. Coach Forrester was on leave and has returned to her role as coach," Vander Zee states, brow furrowed in irritation.

"Were you involved with Hammerstein before you joined the team?"

I go with honesty, because lying seems pointless and will only create more issues down the line. "I met Roman a few years ago, but I hadn't seen or spoken to him again until after I joined the team as an assistant coach."

A woman thrusts her microphone into my face. "You made history this year as the first female assistant coach in the league. How do you think marrying the team goalie will impact the opportunity for other women to progress in the league?"

I knew this question was coming. But it's still a knife to the chest. "How many men have married their subordinates and faced the same public ire?" I throw the question back at her. "Look, love doesn't always have convenient timing. Sometimes it shows up when you least expect it and knocks your whole world, or in this case, your whole team off balance." I roll my shoulders back, thinking about how proud my husband already is of me. "And let's be real, I was under a microscope prior to marrying Roman. I have been since I stepped into this role. It doesn't matter that Roman is retiring. I will always be the assistant coach who married the goalie during the season. But he is the love of my life, and I'm the love of his. And I will take whatever is thrown at me because he is worth it. My being married to Roman might not be convenient or palatable for the masses, but it doesn't change the fact that I'm good at my job. I was the most qualified candidate for the position. And I believe my track record this year indicates that I am still the most qualified person for the job."

"Why did you want the job? Was it so you could get closer to Hammerstein?" she asks.

I level her with an unimpressed glare. "I have lived and breathed hockey since I was three years old. It is my life and my very first love. It's second now only to my husband and my sisters. I wanted this job because it gave me the opportunity to work with one of the top teams in the league."

"You work primarily with the defensive line," she states.

"For this team I do. I was a defensive player during my hockey career. It's where my strengths lie." I pause a moment. "We're talking in a circle here. Our team stats speak for themselves. My being married to the goalie can't skew the numbers."

Vander Zee steps in. "Coach Forrester is an asset to this team and we're grateful to have her back. She's been instrumental in helping bolster our enforcers and working with Hammerstein and Coach Boxer to prepare Ryker to take over next season. And she's done a damn good job, which everyone on the team has already stated over the past few weeks. Several times. If you're looking for a scandal, try another team. Can we please focus on the game and the on-ice performance of the players, rather than our assistant coach's personal life?"

"I do understand the fixation, though. Our goalie is a pretty great guy," I add.

Vander Zee cracks a rare smile and that gets a round of chuckles from the media.

The questions shift to Roman's retirement and the fact that Hendrix is in a contract year. Vander Zee vague-talks around it. In house, we all know how Hendrix feels. He's expressed interest in coaching with Roman at the Hockey Academy next year. I can't blame him. Life is short, and Peggy is his priority. He wants her to have a career and pursue her own aspirations, just like Roman's wants for me.

Vander Zee answers a few more questions before we leave the press behind. "You handled that well, Forrester. They'll keep pushing this angle for a while because it's juicy gossip as my daughter likes to say." He rubs the back of his neck. "But they'll move on when they realize there's no dissension on the team over it."

"I know."

"I'll keep Hemi and her team on top of social media, but once Roman retires, things will settle down," he assures me.

I'm the biggest target out there now. "I had to have thick skin to get where I am. That won't change. I'm sorry for the headache it causes you and management."

"Honestly, it would have been a battle regardless. If you'd waited until off-season, we would have heard about it in the fall. At least he gets to finish his last season happy." He clasps me on the shoulder. "I'll check on the guys and make sure you're not getting an eyeful."

I wait outside the locker room until I get the all clear from Vander Zee. When it's safe, I join the rest of the coaching staff and the team.

"You did well," Boxer says as I take my place beside him.

"Thanks, I appreciate that." It's nice to know that despite the headaches I've caused the team this season, I still have his support.

Fielding steps up and gives a short good-work-and-excellent-playing speech before we leave the arena and return to the hotel.

"I have plans for us tonight." Roman guides me in the opposite direction of the team.

"We have a flight in the morning," I remind him.

"I'm aware, but it's the first time we've been together in New York since the weekend we met, and I want the night with you." He kisses the back of my hand and guides me to a waiting car. "Don't worry. We'll make it back to the hotel tomorrow morning before anyone notices we're gone."

My stomach is full of excited butterflies as Roman helps me into the back of the waiting car and slides in next to me.

"What about all our stuff?"

"It's already taken care of." His expression makes my

stomach tighten as he stretches his arm across the back of the seat.

My phone chimes with a message from the girls, asking if we can chat. Roman pulls me close so both of us are visible in the dimly lit car as I video call them.

"Hi, Lexi! Hi, Roman! Great game tonight!" Callie exclaims. She plops down on the couch between Dred and Fee.

"Nice win," Dred adds.

"I only caught the third period because I had to finish an English essay that's due tomorrow," Fee admits.

"I proofed it. It's an excellent essay." Dred smirks. "Very passionate."

"Thank you." Fee rests her chin on her hands and bats her lashes. "I loathed the book, but it's good to know I can still write something compelling."

"Exceptionally compelling." Dred bumps her shoulder.

We chat for a few more minutes before we wave goodbye and end the call.

"Dred is the best," I tell Roman as I put my phone away.

"I agree. She's been good for them." Roman kisses my temple. I'm glad we can help her a little as well. The extra money we're paying her—which she tried to refuse—can't hurt. I don't imagine the rent in her building is cheap.

I lace my fingers with his. "You know, when I took this job I wanted it to be a good move for all of us, and I feel like we've given my sisters the family they always deserved."

"And you, you deserve it, too." He lifts my fingers to his lips and kisses each one.

The car stops, and the driver lets us out in front of the hotel we stayed at the weekend we met in New York. "We won't get much sleep tonight, will we?"

"I hope not." He chuckles and brushes his lips over mine. "I thought a trip down memory lane would be welcome, especially with how challenging the past few weeks have been."

"This is exactly what I needed."

"Good. I'm glad I got it right."

That same giddy anticipation I felt when Roman invited me back to his hotel all those years ago overwhelms me as we step into the lobby. My stomach tightens at memories of that weekend—how voracious Roman was, the way he owned my body and brought me limitless pleasure. How dedicated he was to uncovering every way to wring an orgasm out of me.

"How long have you been planning this?" We pass through the lobby to the elevators.

"Since our wedding. I know we'll have time for a proper ceremony and honeymoon once the season ends, but I wanted to steal a little time with you and pay homage to the weekend that changed my life." He ushers me into the elevator. The doors slide closed, and he waves the key in front of the sensor, hitting the button to the penthouse floor. "I was crushed when I woke up alone. I want to replace that memory with a new, better one where I wake with you in my arms instead."

I run my hands up his chest and link my fingers behind his neck. "I'm sorry I left the way I did. I didn't want you to think I'd slept with you just to advance my career."

He settles his hands on my hips. "I wasn't ready back then—any more than you were—for what was ahead of us. But we're here now."

When the elevator doors slide open, he links our hands and guides me down the hall to the same room we stayed in three years ago. Pink rose petals litter the floor and the bed. Champagne chills in a bucket, and green apple slices with caramel dip adorn the dining table. It's exactly what we came back to after we went for a private dinner at an exclusive restaurant all those years ago.

Knowing Roman the way I do now, I'm aware that this level of extravagance is reserved for only the most treasured people in his life. Even then he made me feel special. Wanted. Protected.

I turn to face him. "I love you."

"And I love you." He kisses me. "And I'm going to show you exactly how much I appreciate and love you, as my wife and partner."

"No one loves me better than you."

"Come." He laces our fingers and guides me to the bathroom where the massive tub waits, filled with steaming water, rose petals floating on the surface. The scent of orange blossom brings with it a deluge of fond memories.

"We had so much fun in that tub last time."

"You soapy, covered in bubbles is a delight." He pushes my hair over my shoulders. "I loved how soft you were. And I appreciate it even more now that I know all the sides of you." He takes my face in his hands. "You're going to be my sweet angel and let me take care of you exactly how I want, aren't you?"

My knees go weak and a shiver skitters down my spine. "Yes, Roman."

His smile grows wicked. "Good girl."

Heat floods my center as his fingers trail down my arms and he slowly, carefully undresses me, pausing to kiss and nibble exposed skin as each article falls to the floor. But he avoids all my most sensitive places. We both know I'll be putty in his hands by the time he finally touches me where I want him to.

He traces my collarbones as he circles me, lips ghosting my shoulder as he adjusts my position so I can see our reflections in the mirror. "Look at how beautiful you are." He cups my breasts and kisses a path up my neck. "And you're all mine, wife."

"Only yours, husband."

He's still fully dressed, wearing his post-game suit as he runs his fingers through my hair and carefully braids it. I'm in such awe as I watch him work. This huge, imposing man can be so wonderfully gentle—and such a demon between the sheets when his careful control snaps—belongs to me.

When my hair is secured, he moves it to hang over my shoulder, his chest pressed against my back. One hand skims my hip, and he circles my navel with a single finger before dipping lower. At the same time, his other hand slides over my collarbones and up my neck, caressing the edge of my jaw as he turns my head and presses his lips to the corner of my mouth. He grazes my clit and growls the same phrase that made me melt all those years ago. "I'm going to make this pretty pussy weep for me tonight, Alexandria."

"Yes, please." I arch into the touch, pressing my ass against his still covered erection.

"My beautiful wife, always so polite when I get you naked," he murmurs.

He steps back, and I whimper my displeasure. His answering smile tells me tonight will be the most delicious torture. "Undress me, wife."

I eagerly loosen his tie as his fingers trail down my side and over my hip. I already know what's coming as I rush to unbutton his shirt, and I moan as his hand slips between my legs. He cups me in his palm, and I falter.

"The sooner I'm naked, the sooner I'll give you what we both want."

He drags his fingers back and forth, barely grazing my clit. My pussy clenches in anticipation. I'm already on the edge. It won't take much for him to make come, not with all the memories of our time together here overwhelming me.

"So wet already. Would you come if I filled you with my fingers? Cream all over them before I even get you in the tub?"

He reads me so well, knows exactly what to say and do to make me hot and needy.

I manage to slide the final button through the hole as I lift my gaze to his, bite my lip and nod. He releases me so I can rid him of his jacket and shirt, but as soon as they're gone his hands are on me again. Fingers exploring between my thighs, making it impossible to concentrate.

I struggle with his belt, and the fly of his pants as he

dips a single finger inside me, then withdraws and circles my clit. My knees nearly give out, but I manage to get them undone.

His hands leave my body again. "You don't come until I'm naked."

I groan, the ache between my thighs almost unbearable now. I sink to my knees and tug his pants and boxers down his thighs. His cock juts out, thick and hard and weeping.

I tip my head up and lick my lips.

A salacious grin tugs the corner of his mouth. "We'll put the caramel dip to good use a little later." He crooks his finger. "Come here, angel."

I rise and he wraps his hands around my waist, spinning me around, he sets me on the edge of the tub and angles me so I can see our reflections in the mirror.

I part my thighs before he can even issue the command.

His lip curls deliciously and he glides a single finger through my slit. "Should I get you ready for my cock?"

"Yes, please." I'm shaking with anticipation as he eases a single finger inside, pumping once before he adds a second and then a third, stretching me. I give myself over to the sensation, pussy contracting as the orgasm rolls through me.

"Fuck, you're coming already." Roman's fingers disappear and I clench around nothing as he spins me around. "Grab the edge of the tub," he commands. Excitement makes my blood hot. We did this the first time we were here, but in the living room, me holding on to the couch as he fucked me from behind and held my braid.

I do as I'm told, and he wraps my hair around his fist and gives his cock a rough stroke, coating himself with my juices.

"Ass out." He smacks the right cheek.

I arch my back and he twists my head toward the mirror. He rubs the head of his erection over my pussy. "Ask nicely for what you want," he demands.

I love that he knows exactly what I need. What I crave. And

that I understand his desires the same way. I arch further and wiggle my ass. "Please, Roman."

He cocks a brow and taps my aching clit. Waiting for the filthy words he loves so much.

"Please fuck my greedy pussy."

"Good girl." He fills me in one rough thrust.

His praise satisfies a deep, carnal need to please him. And those two sweet words send the orgasm rushing through me. I shudder as Roman starts a punishing rhythm, hips slapping my ass on every stroke.

He uses my braid to pull my head back, leaning in, eyes on our reflections as he slides in and out of me. "Look at you, my perfect doll, taking every inch of my cock."

I can't stop coming, or moaning his name as he hammers into me, fucking me, claiming me, owning me. His teeth sink into my shoulder, and he fills me one last time, cock pulsing as I clench around him.

When we've both come down from the high, he slowly eases out, wearing a satisfied smile as his cum drips down the inside of my thighs. "Now we can use the tub for its intended purpose."

I laugh and his eyes crinkle at the corners. He lifts me easily over the edge, which I appreciate since my knees are overcooked spaghetti noodles. Roman climbs in after and moves me to straddle his lap. I settle over his erection as we kiss and touch, fingers and lips exploring.

When we're both desperate for more of each other, and I'm once again begging him to fill me, he dries us off and carries me to bed. Still in no rush, he pulls the sheets back and stretches out over me, fitting himself between my legs. I wrap them around his waist, unable to pry my gaze from his. So much about this night is the same, but the emotions are different. He's the one person I can give all of myself to.

This time he's slow and tender, filling me in one smooth stroke, he stays deep, eyes on mine as he makes love to me. In one night, we reframe that weekend, create new memories to go with the old, replacing the hurt of ending our time without a goodbye with the promise of our forever.

"I love you," he whispers against my lips.

"I love you, too. Endlessly."

I come in waves, pleasure sweeping over me as he rolls his hips. I moan his name and cling to his shoulders, as we tip over the edge together. I'm lost in him, drowning in his love.

We lie there for long minutes, just kissing and touching before he leaves to get a damp washcloth so he can clean me up. "Should we enjoy the caramel and apple slices the way they were meant to be?"

"You mean actually dip the apples in them and not your dick?" I ask.

"Exactly." He kisses me softly. "Let me get you a robe."

He helps me into the soft plush terry, and we snuggle on the couch and feed each other while we talk.

"I wish my mom could have met you." My throat tightens with emotion.

"I wish I could have met her, too."

"Our relationship wasn't easy or perfect, but she would have liked you. She would have been happy that I found someone who loves me the way you do."

"My dad would have felt the same way about you," he says softly.

"Does the hurting stop eventually?" I ask.

Roman's smile turns soft. "The edges aren't so sharp after a few years. I still miss my dad, but the way it hurts is different, if that makes sense."

"I think so. It helps a lot that I have these new women in my life. I've never had that before." I had teammates, and friends, but these women are special. I feel blessed to know them.

"They are wonderful people, and I'm so glad they've become a support system for you. When we get back to Toronto, we can start planning our summer wedding, if you want one," Roman says.

"I do. Just something small and intimate, though, with the people we love the most."

"Exactly. And then we'll go somewhere private, where I can love you all day long."

That I get to spend my life with this man is a joy and an honor. "That sounds beyond perfect."

CHAPTER 45

ROMAN

ROMAN

How's the game going tonight?

FEE

Second period just started, but so far she's shutting out the other team!

ROMAN

That's amazing. Keep us updated!

FEE

I will!

A short video of the on-ice action follows, as well as a photo of Fee and Dred sitting together in the stands. Dred has become like a pseudo-sister-aunt to those girls over the past few months. Lexi and I are extraordinarily lucky to have her in our lives. On nights like this, when the Terror has a game and so does Callie, Dred accompanies Fee to watch Callie.

"How's the game going for Callie?" Hollis asks as we make our way to the arena.

"The second period just started, but it's a shutout so far." I slide my phone into my pocket.

"Wishing you were there?"

Always so fucking perceptive. "Yup. Soon enough I will be."

"Soon neither of us will have the same travel schedule."

Hollis is still on the retirement train with me, and that gives me something else to be excited about when I step into coaching shoes at the Hockey Academy.

"I know. As sad as I am to be hanging up my skates, I'm ready for it. I want time with the girls. I want to be present for Callie." The elevator doors open, and we step inside.

The past month has had its fair share of ups and downs. The annual gala was last weekend, and it was nice to watch the date with a hockey player auction and not be part of it this year. It was also fantastic to have my wife on my arm. Sophia, who won the date with me last year attended with the Waters. She was introduced to Tristan's dad, who came to show support, and the two of them spent the night talking.

The media coverage of the gala touched on my relationship with Lexi, but for the most part the focus stayed on the auction, which is a good sign for next season.

In addition to raising a huge amount of money for charity through the gala, the Terror is slated to make the playoffs. But we're not at the top this time. I'd love to be in the same space we were last season, but a short off-season has an impact. While other teams had an extra month to recuperate, we were fighting for the Cup. Not to mention all the other changes.

"You're enjoying being a pseudo stepdad, eh?" Hollis rubs his bottom lip.

"It's nice to parent with someone," I agree.

"Do you think you'd want to start again?"

"If that's what Lexi wants, then yeah. I'd take time off, be the primary parent so she can focus on her career."

Hollis laughs.

"Why is that funny?"

"You didn't even hesitate. You're already planning for this, aren't you?"

"I mean, I've thought about it. Callie's only nine. I'm forty. If Lexi gets pregnant in the next couple of years, I'll still have lots of energy. I'd love to do it again, but *with* someone this time, you know?"

"Oh, I get it." He hides a smile behind his hand.

I arch a brow. "You can't be ready for that. You haven't even proposed yet."

"I will. Soon."

"Do not get my daughter pregnant."

He claps me on the shoulder. "I'd like her to have some time in her career, and I'd like to be married for a couple of years before we start that discussion. But it's good to know where you stand."

"I just want her to live a little."

"I know. Me too, Roman."

Hemi and Peggy are waiting at the end of the hall for us.

Peggy's eyes narrow. "You two look serious."

"You look beautiful," Hollis says smoothly and gives her a quick kiss on the cheek.

"You good?" Hemi asks.

"I'm good."

Dallas pushes through the doors to our right. "Honey? There you are. You were there one second, and then you were gone." Dallas adjusts his tie. He's dressed in his typical plaid-suit uniform.

"You were too busy looking at your pretty face in the mirror." Hemi wears a smirk.

"Hemi really owns your ass, doesn't she?" I chuckle.

"One hundred percent yes. All day every day." He stops in front of her. "Permission to put my lips briefly on your lips because I won't survive until after the game if you say no."

"You can kiss me. But don't try to slip me the tongue or I won't be nice later."

"Oh, honey, that was the wrong thing to say." He winds his arm around her waist and pulls her against him.

She laughs and tries to turn her head, but his other hand is in her hair. "I was kidding." He kisses the end of her nose, then gives her a peck on the lips before he releases her.

"Where's Ash?" Hemi asks.

"Heading down with Flip and the rest of the crew."

The elevator doors open, and the four of them step out, along with Tally, Essie, Shilpa, and Nate, whose face is the color of a beet. Makes me wonder what kind of conversation the girls were having on the way down.

There are hugs and back pats before we make the short trip to the arena, where the girls and Nate split off, heading up to the box. Lexi's already with the other coaches, and I'll see her shortly in the locker room for the pre-game strategy talk.

We're closing in on the end of the season, and tonight will be a tough game. The last time we played Boston, they handed us our ass. Every point counts when we're this close to playoffs.

We suit up, and the mood in the locker room is tense but hopeful.

"I know this season hasn't been an easy one," Vander Zee begins. "We've seen a lot of change, and there's more coming. But last year we took home the Cup. We're still that team, and we can win against Boston. We did it last year, and we can do it again this year. The skill is there; the will is there. Dig deep and ignore the noise, because I know there's been a lot of it this season. Focus on the goal, which is bringing Boston to their knees and securing the best possible spot in the playoffs again."

"We'll do you proud, Coach," Madden says.

There's a chorus of "yeahs" and "we got this" and a bunch of back pats before we leave the locker room and take the ice.

But the first period is rough. Grace ends up with a penalty in the first five minutes, and Boston scores a goal.

Madden makes up for it in the second half of the first period by tying the score, but we're working hard to keep Boston away from the net, and the puck always seems to be floating around our net instead of theirs.

At the end of the first period, I'm feeling the pressure, just like everyone else. We head to the locker room and plan strategy for period two.

"We should front load the first line to give us the advantage." Lexi crosses her arms. "And Grace, we need you to stay out of the penalty box. We can't afford to give them another power play."

Grace rubs the back of his neck.

"You're in the same league as Bowman with your stick-handling skills. Forget about everything else and be that guy tonight." Lexi points at Madden. "You're not idiot teenagers anymore. You're teammates. Put everything else aside like you have been and keep showing up for each other."

Madden nods. "I hear you, Coach."

"For the welfare of your team. For the legacy of the guys who are not coming back next year, play like nothing else matters but winning this game."

Madden starts clapping. "Beautiful speech, Coach Forrester."

Lexi rolls her eyes. "Fuck off, Madden."

"I'm serious."

Everyone starts clapping, and then they start whooping, and I'm halfway to a hard-on because that's my fucking wife bolstering the team.

Vander Zee stands back, wearing a smile, all proud peacock. "Let's get our asses out there and score some goals."

Within the first two minutes of the second period, Madden scores with Grace as the assist, giving us a one-point lead. Boston comes back at us, trying to even it up again. But the shift is exactly what we need. Madden and Grace are playing like a unit, and it's fucking magic.

Boston ties it up at the end of the second period, but Stiles scores another goal at the top of the third, and with the help of defense, we manage to keep the lead, win the game, and secure the position we want in the playoffs. It wasn't easy, but we're one step closer to where we want to be as a team—and not just for the playoffs. Hopefully the progress Madden and Grace made in recent months will follow them into next season.

Before I take off my gear, I check my messages. Callie had a shutout tonight, which is a huge deal. I wish Lexi or I could have been there to witness it, but I know that time isn't far off. Lexi has already sent a huge congratulations, and I follow suit, with promises of dinner out tomorrow night to celebrate her win.

"We need to go out tonight," Flip says as he strips out of his gear. "We fought too hard not to enjoy it."

"Everyone up for the Watering Hole?" Hollis asks.

"Yeah. Not many more opportunities like this," I agree.

"I'll text Aurora." Hollis types a quick message.

Half an hour later, we arrive at the Watering Hole. With Shilpa pregnant and showing, the club is not her scene. It isn't really mine at this point either, but I'm all about going with the flow. Peggy throws her arms around me. "You were awesome tonight, Dad. The whole team was."

"Thanks, kiddo." I give her a squeeze.

She smiles up at me. "I'll be sad not to have you in the office all the time next year, but I'm excited for you to be at the Hockey Academy."

"I feel the same way." It'll be a transition, like all the others. It feels easier this time, though. Having Lexi and the girls has shifted my focus. "But at least you still live across the hall from me."

"Hollis and I aren't going anywhere." She gives me a squeeze and kisses my cheek.

She joins the girls, including Dred, who left a sleeping Callie in Fee's care. They're all sitting at their favorite table, laughing and chatting.

Lexi tucks herself under my arm. "You feeling nostalgic, Goalie?"

"Yeah, Coach, I am."

"They're still your family. That won't change."

I kiss her temple. "I know. It's been a great run, but it's time to move forward. Who knows, we might be raising the first female goalie the league has seen."

She looks up, eyes alight with the possibility. "Wouldn't that be incredible?"

"It would." I can see Callie rising through the ranks, see my wife doing the same while I train the next generation. The future is taking shape, and I'm in love with the way it looks.

I'm ready to slow down. To give Lexi time to build her career. To be a dad to Callie and Fee. To change gears. To have a family of my own to love and grow with.

Lexi joins the girls, who are deep in conversation about Rix and Tristan's upcoming wedding, and I join the guys.

Tristan hands me a beer. "We'll miss you next year."

"I won't be far. And who knows, I might get a chance to coach your brother." Brody's at Tilton University, just like Tally. He's on a hockey scholarship and has had a great first season with the team.

"Yeah, it'll be a busy summer for us. That's for sure." He claps Nate on the shoulder. "Good thing we've got Essie to help with all the planning, eh?"

He sips his beer. "She's definitely highly invested in all things wedding related."

"Only a few more months and you'll be a married man." Dallas sighs. "I have to wait a whole year." Dallas and Hemi are planning a summer wedding at his parents' place up in Huntsville next year.

Tristan smirks. "I'm pretty sure you'll survive. Besides, you don't want to share the spotlight with me and Rix."

"That's the damn truth." Dallas clinks his bottle against Tristan's, then turns to Hollis. "When are you joining the club?"

"Soon. Just waiting for the right time."

"I'm perfectly happy over here in the single club." Nate taps his bottle against Flip's.

"One day that'll change." Flip takes a swig from his bottle.

"We'll see." Nate's gaze shifts.

I follow it as Essie passes on the other side of the bar, heading for the bathroom.

I keep my mouth shut. But I'd bet it's only a matter of time before those two stop dancing around each other.

We stay for one beer, then head down the street to the condo. Fee can certainly stay with Callie on her own, but I feel best when all my girls are safe with me. I wait until we're alone in the elevator before I curve my palm around the back of Lexi's neck and pull her close.

She tips her head up, expression quizzical. "What's this look?"

"I want a family with you."

"You have a family with me. It's blended and atypical, but it's a family. You and all your girls." She smooths the lapels of my suit jacket.

"I want a baby with you."

Her eyes flare. "You want to knock me up?"

"Yeah." I can see it already—Lexi's rounded belly. "I want you to be the mother of our child. I want to do this with you. I want middle-of-the-night feedings, and first steps, and first words with you. I want all the experiences I never had. And I want to watch you be an inspiring, badass mom to our baby."

"Honestly?" Her expression softens, and she links her fingers behind my neck. "I want that, too."

"Yeah?" A smile spreads across my face.

Her eyes heat. "The image I have of you holding a baby, our baby, is..." She practically purrs. "Yes, please."

The elevator doors slide open, and I let us into the penthouse. Both girls are already asleep, but Lexi and I kiss Callie good night anyway before we disappear into our bedroom. As soon as I lock the door, we're frantic hands and hungry mouths, peeling each other out of our clothes and kissing exposed skin.

We barely make it to the bed before she's pulling me on top of her. My cock slides over her clit, and she moans wantonly. "You're already wet and ready for me."

"I wasn't lying when I said the idea of you holding our baby does it for me."

I reach between us and drag the head past her clit, nudging her entrance, eyes on hers.

"I need you in me," she whispers.

I push inside and we both make matching, relieved sounds. I'll never get enough of her, of her softness, of the way we fit together. Of how good it feels to be connected to her like this, surrounded, submerged, complete.

I frame her face in my palms and slow things down now that I'm exactly where I want to be. Lexi wraps herself around me and we move together, making love. The orgasm rolls in, slow and gentle, dragging us both under at the same time. Perfectly in sync.

She's my heart and my home. My wife.

My future.

CHAPTER 46

LEXI

"Do you have a minute?" Shilpa pokes her head in my office.

"Yeah, of course. What's up?" In the weeks since Roman and I have been married, the tension between Shilpa and me has dissipated—at least outside the office. She's careful to keep things professional here. Which means in this moment I can't read her at all.

She raises a hand. "It's good news."

My shoulders come down from my ears. "I like good news."

"The internal review paperwork has officially been filed and you are completely cleared."

"That is such a relief." The rock that's been in my stomach all these weeks finally dissolves.

"I know it's been rough and the media will still have their feelings about you being married to Roman, but in the eyes of the league and management, none of the allegations had any merit. Every member of the team believes in you and values your role as their coach." There's genuine pride in her voice and on her face.

"That's really good to hear." I look away, working to keep my emotions in check.

While it's been business as usual, knowing that the review is finally filed, and I've been cleared of all allegations makes everything feel that much better. Vander Zee and Boxer have been great, but Thomas has been frosty. He's friends with Donnie, and I'm sure he's conflicted, but all of Donnie's allegations just made him look like a chauvinist asshole.

The relief is overwhelming. "The stress has been something else."

"I imagine it has." Shilpa rubs her rounded belly. She's just started to show. She's due in early fall.

"For both of us." I motion between us.

She laughs. "You aren't the first woman to fall for a player, and Roman is a special guy."

"He really is," I agree.

"It'll be easier when he's not playing next year." She sighs and leans her shoulder against the jamb, fiddling with the end of her braid. "I know I was harsh—"

I raise a hand. "You've already apologized, and you don't need to explain."

She looks at me a moment. "Well, then I'll just say I'm so glad you're as strong as you are and that you and Roman found a partner in each other. He has a huge heart, and he needed someone to share it with." Her phone chimes in her pocket, and she glances at the clock. "I have a meeting offsite, but I'll be at the game tonight."

"I'll see you there."

She leaves me feeling a whole lot lighter. I would text Roman the good news, but I feel like this is better said in person.

Vander Zee knocks on my door twenty minutes later. "Shilpa gave you the news?"

"She did."

"It came out as I expected." He drops into the chair across from mine.

"It's a weight lifted," I tell him.

"I have some other news," he adds.

"Oh?"

"Donnie has been relieved of his duties as equipment manager. We felt it best for the team climate that he no longer work with the Terror."

"He's been fired?" I might not like him, or the things he put me through, but he has a family.

"He was given a severance package and offered transfer opportunities, but not in the professional league and not in management."

"I see. Thank you for letting me know." I would have managed, but it will make the end of this season less stressful for all of us. "I think Roman will probably be relieved to hear that."

"Agreed. Hopefully, it will ease any worries."

"I'm sure it will." As much as he tries to roll with things, this has been just as hard for him because he didn't have control over the outcome.

"The team will miss him." Vander Zee taps on the arm of the chair, pensive.

"They will, but Ryker is up for the job. He has the skill set and a good head on his shoulders to go with it."

"You're right about that, and Grace and Madden seem to have settled down." He raps on my desk. "Knock on wood that trend continues."

"As long as those two can stay away from each other's shirts and sandwiches, we should be okay."

Vander Zee snorts a laugh. "Seriously. I still don't know what to think about that."

"I don't think any of us do."

His phone buzzes in his pocket.

"Get that, if you need to."

He pulls it out and frowns as he reads the message. "Well, this isn't ideal."

"What's wrong?"

"It's not team related," he assures me.

"Still, anything I can help with?"

"Tally and the boyfriend had a fight. She was out with friends last night, and apparently, someone saw her talking to some guy, and now the boyfriend is tossing out accusations." He runs a hand through his hair.

"What kind of accusations?" I ask.

"He thinks she's cheating on him." He blows out a breath. "My wife is relaying this through text message, so I'm only getting part of the story. I wish Tally would break up with this kid. I don't like him. And I definitely don't like that he's pulling this shit. Final exams are coming up, and she doesn't need the added stress."

This guy sounds like a whole lot of red flags, but I don't want to overstep. "Sometimes when people are insecure, it's because they've had that experience before," I hedge.

"I know. But we can't tell Tallulah that. I don't get why she's with this guy. Eline is trying to get her to come to the game tonight. Will Fee be there? It could be a good distraction."

"I'll ask." I send Fee a quick message.

It only takes her a minute to respond. She says she's in if Tally's coming, and she's already messaged her. Within two minutes, the whole thing is arranged.

"She's always been such an easy kid, and that hasn't changed, but this boyfriend of hers…" He drums his fingers in agitation. "If this is anything to go by, I'm not sure how I'll handle it with her younger sister."

"I feel this in my soul," I tell him.

"I can't imagine what it must have been like for Roman last season." He shakes his head. "I have a lot of respect for that man."

I only saw what was covered on the hockey sites, but knowing Roman the way I do now, it definitely wasn't easy for him to see his daughter with his best friend. "He loves them both very much. It helps that Hollis adores Aurora, but it was tough for all of them."

"Yeah. I just want Tallulah to find someone worthy of her."

"She will. Sometimes you have to learn what doesn't work for you before you find what does," I say.

His phone buzzes, with a call this time. "That's my wife. I really hope I don't have to bury this guy for hurting my daughter." He brings the phone to his ear. "Hi, darling, is our little girl okay? If I take care of him, he won't be a problem anymore." He gives me a chin tip and leaves my office.

Poor Tally. It can't be easy trying to date with a dad as protective as Vander Zee.

I message Roman.

LEXI

Walk to the arena together?

ROMAN

Absolutely.

He shows up at my office fifteen minutes later.

"I have news."

"I-need-to-call-Sam kind of news, or get-out-the-balloons kind of news?" he asks.

I laugh. Hemi's brother Sam is intense. I don't know what his job is, but Dallas jokes that he's a fixer. "The paperwork has been filed. I'm fully cleared."

"That's fantastic."

"And Donnie isn't with the Terror anymore."

"That's even better news, because I had some plans for him that might have made my retirement a challenge. We're celebrating the hell out of this later." He closes my office door, turns the lock, and strides across the room. Taking my hand, he pulls me out of the chair. Roman's arms circle my waist and his eyes spark with desire.

"You shouldn't look at me like that when we're in the office." I lace my fingers behind his neck.

"Stop looking so tempting, then, beautiful wife." He strokes my cheek. "Thank you for weathering this storm with me. I know this hasn't been easy."

"Loving you is worth it."

He drops his head, and the kiss is soft, a tender promise of what's to come later.

EPILOGUE

ROMAN

"Fee, can you test this for me?" I hold out the spoon.

"Can I test it too?" Callie moves to stand beside her sister.

"Absolutely. Grab me another spoon."

Callie opens the drawer, picks up another one, and passes it to me. Fee waits while I dip it into the marinara.

"It'll be hot, so blow on it before you taste it," I warn.

"You tell us this every time." Fee blows on her spoon.

"I know. I'm a dad. It's engrained in my dad DNA to protect you from even the smallest of potentially harmful situations. Like a burned tongue."

Callie giggles and blows on hers too. Then they test the sauce at the same time. It's a regular ritual in our house. Whenever we can, we make dinner together, and the girls always perform a taste test before we plate the meals.

"What do we think?" I ask.

"Maybe a touch more salt," Callie suggests.

"Just a pinch and it's perfect," Fee agrees.

"Who wants to do the honors?" I ask.

"It's Callie's turn." Fee passes her sister the salt.

Fee has settled in over the past couple of months. It helps that it's off-season and that I've retired from the league. She had to deal with a lot of speculation from her peers during her final months of high school, but she still graduated with honors. She was also accepted to Tilton, the same university as Tally, and they're both excited to have a friend on campus.

Callie adds a pinch of salt, and Fee stirs it in. We perform taste test number two and deem it fit for consumption.

I send a message to Peggy, letting her know dinner is ready. We have a family dinner at least twice a week. Our table is always full of life and laughter, but especially when I'm surrounded by my girls and my best friend.

Peggy and Hollis come over with a salad to add to the table. She hugs me and does the same with Fee and Callie. They've grown close over the past several months, and so have Peggy and Lexi. My daughter regularly reminds me that my wife is a decade younger than me and closer to her age than mine.

Life couldn't be better.

"Where's Lexi?" Peggy asks.

"She was tackling a few emails in the home office. I'll go get her."

"It's okay. I can do it." Fee rushes down the hall.

"Thanks, kiddo," I call after her.

Fee reappears in time to help us bring everything to the dining room, but she's alone. "Lexi's coming. She fell asleep."

"Is she feeling okay?"

"Yup! She's fine," her voice pitches up.

I narrow my eyes. "Are you sure?"

"Super-duper sure. She's in the bathroom. She said she'll just be a minute." She grabs the Caesar salad and heads for the dining room.

We put dinner on the table, and Lexi appears a minute later, hair pulled up on top of her head in a messy bun. Her eyes are still heavy with sleep, and she has pillow lines on her face.

"You okay, angel?"

"I'm fine. I just passed out hard, I guess. Sorry to keep you all waiting." She rounds the table and gives Peggy a hug before she takes her seat next to mine, leaning in to kiss my cheek.

"You've been tired lately." I kiss her forehead. She's sleep warm, but not fever warm.

"I promise I'm fine." She squeezes my hand, then addresses the table. "Dig in, everyone. This looks great!"

Fee bites her lips together, and the two of them exchange a look.

"Okay." I set the serving spoon down. "What's going on?"

"What?" Lexi blinks up at me, but her voice is pitchy.

I motion between her and Fee. "As Fee would say, there's a vibe."

"Oh!" Peggy grabs Hollis's hand. "Oh! I think I know." Her face lights up with excitement.

"Know what?" Hollis is obviously as confused as me.

Lexi takes my hand and rolls her shoulders back. "I'm pregnant."

Everything slows as I turn to face my wife. She looks serious, and expectant, as she smiles up at me.

I settle my hand on her low belly. "Pregnant?"

She nods. "Pregnant."

Time moves again, the air suddenly electric with emotion.

"This is so exciting!" Peggy hugs Hollis's arm.

Callie's mouth drops open.

Fee claps gleefully.

"When did you find out?"

"Like ten minutes ago," Fee offers helpfully.

"I've been feeling…not myself. Tired. And I've had an upset stomach, so I took a test and fell asleep waiting for the results. Fee woke me up and surprise!" She does jazz hands.

I push my chair back and pull her to her feet. I take her face in my hands, my smile so wide it feels like it could split my cheeks. "We're having a baby." I kiss her, then hug her, then run my palms up and down her arms. I don't know what to do with myself. "We need to get you to the doctor. How far along are you? We're having a baby!"

She laughs. "We are having a baby."

"Are you ready for a baby?" I ask, although that question is rather pointless since it's already happening.

Her eyes shine with happiness. "We've got this."

I press my lips to hers again, then skim her cheek until I reach her ear. "We're having a private celebration tonight after everyone else goes to bed."

"Of course we are. If I can stay awake."

There's a flurry of hugs and laughter and tears, all happy ones. I'm over the fucking moon. Dinner is full of buoyant chatter. Callie's already excited about being a big sister. Peggy is all smiles, and Fee is clearly thrilled because she found out before anyone else. She needs that closeness with Lexi.

After dinner, we gather in the living room. "I feel like we need a family meeting," Fee declares.

"I think that's a great idea." I stretch my arm across the back of the couch, and Lexi snuggles into my side.

Peggy makes a move to stand, but Fee grabs her hand. "I want you to stay. We're all family."

"You're sure?"

"We want you to be part of this." Fee rubs her hands up and down her thighs. "So, Callie and I have been talking—"

"—about our last name!" Callie finishes.

"Ours is different than Lexi's and yours, and now that we're a family and we're going to have a little sister or brother, we thought maybe we could all have a last name that matches."

"I love this." Peggy rests her cheek against Hollis's arm.

"You can have the same last name too!" Callie says.

"Thank you, Callie, but eventually I'll be a Hendrix. Although, I'm all for designing a family crest to unite us."

"That would be so cool! Fee can draw it!"

Lexi kisses the back of my hand. "I love all of this."

"Should we make a list of last names we like? I can grab a pen and piece of paper from the kitchen," I suggest.

"Or we can use my iPad." Fee gets it from the table, along with the art pen. "Seriously, Roman, sometimes it's like you're already in your grandpa era."

"He likes paper lists."

"I like paper lists," Peggy and I say at the same time.

Everyone laughs. And I love it. I love that I'm surrounded by my favorite people and we're having a family summit about our last name. And that I get to be a dad all over again in just a handful of months.

"The trees thank me for intervening." Fee grins cheekily, then offers, "So we could do a mash-up, like Forrest-Stein."

"What about Forehammer?" Callie asks.

Hollis hides his face in Peggy's hair.

Fee purses her lips and writes it down. "Forehammer, got it."

"Forrest-Hammer? Or Hammer-Forrest? What about including part of your last names as well?" Lexi asks.

"I'd like to add that as another middle name since Rose can work as a first name, too," Fee says.

"Can I do that, too?" Callie asks.

"Of course." We lob names back and forth, writing them all down, then narrowing the list to our top two favorites before we vote and settle on Forrest-Hammer.

"We can get started on the paperwork right away so it's in place for school in the fall." I want these girls to feel like this family is truly theirs, not a replacement for what they lost, but something new they can grow with.

That sparks a conversation about university for Fee and how excited she is about being on campus with Tally, especially since they're in the same program, and Tally has all her notes from first-year classes.

Eventually Peggy and Hollis excuse themselves, and I walk them to the door.

I turn to Hollis. "Can I have a minute with Peggy?"

"Of course." He gives me a back-pat man hug. "Congratulations. You deserve this."

"Thanks. I appreciate it."

He kisses Peggy on the cheek and crosses the hall, disappearing into their penthouse.

"Are you really okay with me changing my last name?" I ask.

She takes my hands and smiles up at me. "Absolutely, Dado. One hundred percent yes. Hollis is going to propose soon enough, and then I'll be a Hendrix. Callie and Fee need this, they need *you*, and to feel like they're part of this family. I think it's a beautiful thing to do, for all of you. And I'm so, so thrilled that you get to have a baby with Lexi." She squeezes my hands, and her eyes well. "I've waited a long time to see you happy like this. You have the biggest heart. I have felt so loved and cared for and protected, and now they get to have that, too. You deserve to be a dad with someone, and Lexi is the perfect person for you. You balance each other, just like Hollis and I balance each other."

"No one will ever replace you. You know that, right?"

"Oh, Dad." A tear leaks out of the corner of her eye. She doesn't try to hide it or wipe it away. She hugs me tightly before she steps back. "We have the most special relationship. But now you get to be my friend, and not just a parent. And I get to watch you be the most amazing dad to these girls. To see you this happy fills my heart with so much joy."

I pull her against my chest. "I love you, kiddo."

"I love you, too, Dado. Now go dote on your girls." She backs up and winks. "I've had the pleasure for twenty-two years. It's about time someone else gets the experience."

I give her one last squeeze and wave her across the hall, then go in search of my wife. I find her in the spare room. Someone has already taped two pictures to the wall with nursery ideas. I wrap my arms around her waist from behind and settle a palm on her stomach. "Was this you?"

She shakes her head. "Fee."

"She feels good about finding out first."

"I was holding the test in my hand when she woke me up." She turns in my arms and runs her hands up my chest. "How's Peggy?"

"Happy. Supportive. Excited to have another sibling." I skim her cheek. "How did I get so lucky?"

"I keep asking myself the same thing," she whispers.

"However you want this to look, Lexi, we'll make it work. If you want to take time off, if you want to go back so you can stay focused on your career, I'll support you, no matter what. We're in this together. We're a team, you and me and the girls and this baby. We've got each other."

"I love you so much. I love how safe you make me feel. Protected, cared for." Her fingers brush along the edge of my jaw. "I didn't know this kind of love was possible, and now that I have it, now that I have you, I can't believe I let you go in the first place."

"We found our way back to each other." I kiss her hand. "When the girls are in bed, I'd like to show you exactly how much I love you."

A coy smile quirks the side of her mouth. "Let me check on Callie."

It's another half an hour before I close and lock the bedroom door. I take my time with Lexi, teasing her, tasting her, kissing every inch of her before I settle between her thighs.

"Everything is so sensitive." She moans as my cock slides over her clit.

I stroke her cheek with my thumb. "I look forward to the third-trimester hormones and your insatiable appetite for my cock."

"I'm already insatiable." She rolls her hips and whispers against my lips, "Please, fuck me."

"How can I say no to you, angel?" I line myself up. "Especially when you're being so polite."

She bites my shoulder to muffle her moan, and I shudder at the sensation of being sheathed in her softness. Slipping my fingers into the hair at the nape of her neck, I grip gently. "My beautiful wife, I'm going to fuck you sweetly as often as you like." I pull out to the ridge and push back in, slowly, gently.

"Please, yes." Lexi pulls my mouth to hers, muffling her soft mewls and needy moans. After a little while, she comes in waves, body quaking with her release, and I follow, sated in a way I've never been before.

After I clean her up, I gather her in my arms.

She lifts her head, brow furrowed. "Oh crap."

"What's wrong?"

"I have to get a new dress for Rix and Tristan's wedding. I've already gained five pounds. There's no way I'll fit into that slinky number a month from now."

"As if I need a reason to spoil you. We'll take you and the girls shopping tomorrow and get you something you'll feel comfortable in." I kiss her temple.

"They'll love that." She laces our fingers. "It's wild that Connor is coming."

"Tristan invited the whole team. He's not the kind of guy to leave one person out."

"Hmm… We should place bets on who we think is most likely to engage in the dreaded wedding hookup."

"Flip's been on his best behavior lately, so he might have a slipup," I note.

"It could happen. It is his sister's wedding, after all." Lexi makes circles around my nipple.

"What about Dred?" I muse.

"Oh! That's possible. Who would she hook up with, though? None of the guys from the team would go there." Lexi traces the outline of my pecs.

"You don't think Flip would?" He's been pretty adamant that they're just friends, but who knows.

"Oh no." Lexi grimaces. "They're like brother and sister. But the most drama would come from a Connor and Dred hookup."

"Oh. That's vicious, but I can see it. They got along surprisingly well when we planned the whole Christmas surprise."

"And he drove her home," Lexi adds.

"That's true. I just don't know if Dred would be willing to go there with the guy who fucked her best friend's sandwich."

"I still have a hard time believing that happened." Lexi snorts as she rolls over and rests her chin on my chest.

"What about Tristan's middle brother and Rix's bestie? Those two are hella awkward around each other." She's forever putting on lip gloss when he's around and he's forever trying not to stare at her.

Lexi's eyes light up. "Oooh, do you think there's history there?"

I shrug. "Dunno, but as Peggy would say, there's a vibe."

"Okay, so my money is on Dred and Connor and yours is on Nate and Essie?" she confirms.

"Sounds good."

"If I win, I get to pick the position for an entire week," Lexi declares.

"And if I win, I get to go down on you for as long as I want."

Her grin turns impish. "I almost hope you win."

I roll her over and fit myself between her thighs again. "Oh, angel, I already have."

Join my Newsletter for even more Roman and Lexi:

Preorder I COULD BE YOURS, Nate and Essie's standalone second chance romance:

I COULD
BE
YOURS

NEW YORK TIMES BESTSELLING AUTHOR
HELENA HUNTING

ABOUT THE AUTHOR HELENA HUNTING

NYT and USA Today bestselling author, Helena Hunting lives on the outskirts of Toronto with her amazing family and her adorable kitty, who thinks the best place to sleep is her keyboard. Helena writes everything from emotional contemporary romance to romantic comedies that will have you laughing until you cry. If you're looking for a tearjerker, you can find her angsty side under H. Hunting.

OTHER TITLES BY HELENA HUNTING

THE TORONTO TERROR SERIES

If You Hate Me

If You Want Me

If You Need Me

If You Love Me

If You Play Me (coming Fall 2025)

I Could Be Yours (coming Summer 2025)

TILTON UNIVERSITY SERIES

Chase Lovett Wants Me

THE PUCKED SERIES

Pucked (Pucked #1)

Pucked Up (Pucked #2)

Pucked Over (Pucked #3)

Forever Pucked (Pucked #4)

Pucked Under (Pucked #5)

Pucked Off (Pucked #6)

Pucked Love (Pucked #7)

AREA 51: Deleted Scenes & Outtakes

Get Inked

Pucks & Penalties

Where it Begins

ALL IN SERIES

A Lie for a Lie

A Favor for a Favor

A Secret for a Secret

A Kiss for a Kiss

LIES, HEARTS & TRUTHS SERIES

Little Lies

Bitter Sweet Heart

Shattered Truths

SHACKING UP SERIES

Shacking Up

Getting Down (Novella)

Hooking Up

I Flipping Love You

Making Up

Handle with Care

SPARK SISTERS SERIES

When Sparks Fly

Starry-Eyed Love

Make A Wish

LAKESIDE SERIES

Love Next Door

Love on the Lake

THE CLIPPED WINGS SERIES

Cupcakes and Ink

Clipped Wings

Between the Cracks

Inked Armor

Cracks in the Armor

Fractures in Ink

STANDALONE NOVELS

The Librarian Principle

Felony Ever After

Before You Ghost (with Debra Anastasia)

FOREVER ROMANCE STANDALONES

The Good Luck Charm

Meet Cute

Kiss my Cupcake

A Love Catastrophe

www.ingramcontent.com/pod-product-compliance
Lightning Source LLC
Chambersburg PA
CBHW011922270225
22672CB00002B/2

9781989185964